Gabriel Marchant

Gabriel Marchant

Only connect the prose and the passion, and both will be exalted, and human love will be seen at its height. Live in fragments no longer. Only connect, and the beast and the monk, robbed of the isolation that is life to either, will die.

E.M.Forster: *Howard's End (1910)*

Also by Wendy Robertson

Journey to Moscow:
Cruelty Games
A Woman Scorned
The Real Life of Studs McGuire
Lizza
Flight: Twenty Seven Short Stories
The Romancer: A Practical Guide To Writing Fiction

Gabriel Marchant

A Painter's Tale

WENDY ROBERTSON

Room to Write

Published in Great Britain

by Room to Write

Copyright © 2014 Wendy Robertson

ISBN-13: 978-1496179470 (Trade Paperback)

ISBN-10: 1496179471

Cover image is the author's own drawing inspired by a Tom McGuinness print in her possession.

Published by Room to Write

http://roomtowritepublishing.wordpress.com/

Dedication

This novel is dedicated to all those whose lives impelled them to dig in the darkness, who still found the grace there to create beauty. In particular I honour the inspiration of the art of Tom McGuinness. Ted Holloway and Norman Cornish in addition to the literary inspiration of the writer Sid Chaplin. All of them, in their unique fashion, flourished as young people through the magic of the Spennymoor Settlement

Acknowledgments
Thank you to my friends on the innovative *Room to Write* team, for their editorial skills, their literary inspiration and their support. Thank you to Avril Joy and Gillian Wales who have always sustained my faith in good writing.

Gabriel Marchant

About The Story

In 1963, paying public tribute to his late mentor Archie Todhunter, the eminent painter Gabriel Marchant, reflects on his early days when, as an out of work miner in 1936, he met Archie, the charismatic warden of The Settlement, an arts centre in his home town.

At that time, unemployed and feeling very low, Gabriel is rescued by the encouragement he finds at The Settlement, where people out of work are inspired by Archie Todhunter and the enigmatic German Rosel Vonn, a sculptor and artist who teaches there. Travelling with him on his journey are his best friend Tegger, who will become a writer, and the clever, witty schoolgirl Greta who will change lives in her own way.

Later, both haunted and inspired by images of life and work underground, Gabriel's paintings finds first local, then national fame and his life is changed forever.

As he tells the whole tale of how he became a painter Gabriel Marchant celebrates the liberating nature of art in hard-pressed lives and the role of people like Archie Todhunter, those magical change-makers in lives like his own.

Contents

Dedication
About the Story
Acknowledgements

Gabriel Marchant

1.November 1963: Only Connect

Gabriel Marchant - not normally nervous - coughed nervously. His wife was always his sharpest critic. This morning, trying out his Archie Todhunter eulogy on her was more nerve-wracking than the real thing would be, with hundreds of eyes on him and hundreds of ears listening to his every word.

Now she looked into his eyes. 'You should definitely mention the assassination of Jack Kennedy, Gabe!' she urged. 'It's quite coincidence. Great men passing and all that.'

'Archie was hardly a world figure, love,' he said. '*He* was not like Kennedy stopped short in his mission to change the world.'

She was a great fan of Jack Kennedy and, like many of her generation, had taken the President's recent assassination very personally. He has seemed to them the hope of the world. Now she shrugged. 'Archie changed your world, Gabe. He changed mine.' She was sitting stretched out on a chair beside the window, the light of morning glinting on her hair.

Gabriel watched his wife closely thinking that even now she glowed with the sparkling earnestness of the girl he first knew. He coughed again and continued in 'I might say something about that…and about Archie coming all the way down here to Torquay to retire.' He scribbled away. 'OK I'll say all that about Kennedy and Torquay and then I'll say … "strangely enough, Archie Todhunter – the magician who has just gone from us - had his finest hour so many miles from this sunny place in the West with its wide bright skies and long golden sands."'

She nodded. 'Good start, that…'

Gabriel put on his glasses and peered again at his pad. 'And then I'll say, "In those days when Archie turned up in Brack's Hill, my own home town had an iron necklace of colliery wheels and ironworks, threaded with rows of crude houses built close enough to the pit and the ironworks so a worker could roll out of bed and get to work in a matter of minutes."'

She shook her head. 'Say something good about Brack's Hill, for God's sake, Gabe,' she instructed. 'Don't labour that dark satanic mills bit.'

He scribbled again on his pad and went on, '"I have to tell you that on the best days of full employment and good pay, this network of streets hummed with affluence. It had its Saturday market, its shops and travellers, pubs and chapels, its chip-van and its football field, its racing tracks for horses, dogs and running men. It had its thriving Salvation Army Citadel, its five chapels and three churches with spires…"'

He broke off. 'But I can't deny the hard times, can I, love? That was why Archie was there at all. Here, listen! "Brack's Hill itself was a very working-class town. Even there, though, fine levels of hierarchy and the genteel aspects of snobbery still flourished. So inevitably there was conflict: skilled against unskilled; in-work as opposed to out-of-work; physically strong as opposed to the physically weak; pigeon men against others; football men against others; garden men against others; respectable women as opposed to women for sale; people with bay windows opposed to those with common straight windows; people with clout, such as councillors and shopkeepers, doctors and clerics, as opposed to those without clout which was more or less the rest of the population…" '

She was smiling across at him. 'You do have this way with words, Gabe. Archie would have loved your rhetoric.'

He coughed again, adjusted his glasses and held his notebook up to the light. ' "Archie Hunter was an outsider. He belonged to none of these groups. But later on it was he who made it possible for some of us later to desert Brack's Hill, to flee its confining darkness and move into the more fluid social systems of the Midlands and the South of England. In the process we had to iron out the dark edges of our speech to avoid being called *Geordie* all of our lives. Archie was our change-maker. He made possible our entry to orchestras and theatres and choral groups where some time in the future we would complain of the philistinism of the poor little town whence we came." '

She interrupted his rush of words. 'You've never done that,' she said fiercely. 'You've never whined or blamed our people. You love them…'

He took a breath and ploughed on. ' "So when the demand for coal and iron faded in the wider country our little town was just about left for dead. By 1936 many Brack's Hill people had no work, little food, less dignity. Those with savings had to raid them to survive. When the savings were drained and the insurances had run out, humiliation and isolating boredom stared them in the face. In some cases formerly proud and self-sufficient individuals became the walking wounded. In less fortunate cases they were the living dead.

One of the first to lose his job after the General Strike of 1926 was my own father. He was one of these living dead. In doing what he eventually did to himself he was merely confirming that for years he had lived, day by day, as a dead man..." ' His voice faded away.

Gabriel's wife sighed but said nothing at this. He looked down at her and scribbled that line out. Then he wrote it in again.

His voice rolled out again. "'Into this dark and difficult place came a magician whose name was Archie Todhunter. And this, ladies and gentlemen, is the man we honour today. Archie was a strange, ambiguous man, whose creative energy redeemed not only the pride and the self-esteem of the lucky group of individuals with whom he was in daily contact, but the nature of the town itself. Archie changed these people. He certainly changed me, forever,"

Gabriel paused and smiled slightly as his wife nodded vigourosuly in agreement. ' " There was much talk amongst us in those dark days about the power of the many and collective responsibility. Such ideas kept us going. But Archie was unique in that he saw the awesome significance of a person as an individual. His was a kind of secular religion. His place - his temple, you might say – was The Settlement in Queen Street in Brack's Hill – this modest place now so very well known. Yes, Archie was interested in you as an individual and how you might connect with the world at large. He was interested in what made you tick and was keen that you should make a creative thing of your life and inspire others to transform their own. Archie Todhunter's magic worked for me so well that my dark places, in the end, were transformed into my raw material, my avenue to the light...'

His wife clapped her hands, beaming up at him. '*Avenue into the light.* Lovely! That'll be fine, Gabe. They'll love it. Archie himself would have loved it wouldn't he? Even when he was pushing his people into the limelight he liked a bit of it himself. Remember that time with the prince?' She came across, took his note-pad from him and kissed him on the mouth.

She frowned. 'The pity is that there'll not be time down there in that great hall to tell the whole story of Archie and you yourself, where you sit together in the history of Brack's Hill? Someone, some time, should tell that story don't you think?'

2. Back to 1935: The Petrified Forest

When I was seven, my father brought these stones for me home from work. 'Why Gabriel hinny,' he said, tipping them out of his pocket. 'See here what I got for you in the dark.'

He'd brought them home in the pocket of the work-suit in which, seven years before, he'd married my mother. He'd worn the suit for chapel on alternate Sundays. Then on Mondays, like thousands – even millions - of other wives, my mother folded the suit into a brown paper parcel and took it to the pawn-brokers. Then, on alternate Saturdays she would take it out of pawn. Pitmen, then. were paid on alternate Saturdays.

According to the unique legend this suit was finally returned in a tattered state because, according to 'Uncle Joe', who kept the pawn shop, some scallywag had sneaked it out of pawn to wear and to ruin. 'Uncle Joe' did not charge my mother the redeeming fee that day and on the Sunday my father didn't go to chapel. That was when my mother demoted the suit and my father wore it for the pit. It took her months to scrape together some money to buy a decent second-hand suit from the widow of a man who had died,

But that old work suit did have usefully capacious pockets. In those pockets were the stones he brought home for my seventh birthday. He emptied them, tipping the stones out onto the table, throwing up a cloud of coal dust that shimmered in the light of the fire.

I settled down at the table, placed the stones in lines and peered at them. One by one fingers my touched their gritty surfaces. My nose wrinkled at their watery, rank smell. One by one I brought them right up to my eye so I could see more clearly the leaves, the fish and the lizards so perfectly impressed there. One stone was so very small that I had to put my eye really close to make out on the fragment of blue-grey slate the shape of a sea urchin. A magic creature.

'Why?' I asked my father. 'How?'

He was answering me in those days.

'Why Gabriel hinny, these stones are from the petrified forest,' he said, unlacing his big boots and shaking them over the hearth so hard that they spat out grains of coal, igniting fireflies in the air.

In the many years since then, etched onto the back of my mind, I've had this recurring image of my mother picking up his boots and cradling them in her arms like a baby: an image of her looking down at him, her eyes sparkling with love. I've tried to paint that scene since, and never succeeded.

My father went on then. 'The coal we win, like, and the deep seams we win it from, were once great forests. That's millions of years ago, Gabriel! Millions of years. More years than there are stars in the sky. Believe me, hinny, I've seen whole trees down there! And the sea is down there too. Because in those seams are great stone fish. One time those fish swam in rivers and across the great sea that covered the face of the earth. The trees and the fish were all there before the Lord even thought of man. The leaves from those trees fluttered in the bright sun of Heaven.'

I tip-fingered the hard stone feeling that ancient world now alive in my hand, buzzing in my head. In my mind the pit where my father worked began to grow into a magic place: a place of wonder. Young as I was, I already knew it as a place of pain. I'd seen the sealed-up blue scars - they called them 'medals' - earned when my father's back scraped the roof of the low seams. I had felt the scabs on his knuckles caused by mistimed blows from his pick or an inconvenient fall of coal.

But on that day, the day he brought me the stones, my father showed me a different world: a place of endless time and natural splendour.

Even in those early days I liked to draw. I copied the stones - the leaves, the seahorses and the antique lizards - into the hard backed lined notebook   bought for me by my mother at the corner shop. My father, one Sunday morning when his hands were clean, showed me once how to place these stones on plain butchers' paper and rub my stubby pencil over it. This gave me a shadow form of the leaf or fish, perfect in every detail, which I would stick into my notebook with flour paste.

Magic.

These times of unemphatic joy came to an end, of course, in the year 1926. By November in that year the miners, the last workers to stay out after National Strike, had just been forced back to work. My mother, exhausted by her own fight for survival, gave birth too early that winter and died, taking my baby brother with her into the night.

My father, a clever man, active in the union, was never allowed to work again in any pit. He was not alone.

3. Getting to Know Colour

I have wondered from time to time whether I got my profound love of drawing and painting from my Aunt Susanah, wife to the Priorton schoolteacher Jonty Clelland.

Susanah's own story is interesting. She was related to me because she'd been first married to an uncle of mine who died in Wormwood Scrubs at the time of the Great War. They said he'd been beaten to death. He had once been a great footballer: a hero in the district. But after his death no-one spoke of him because he refused to take up arms and was what they called a *conchie,* snarling the word. Another, surviving *conchie* was my Aunt Susanah's second husband a schoolteacher whom she married after my uncle died. This one, called Jonty, still dabbled in politics twenty years later. He'd got into bother a while back over some Blackshirts and went to prison. It was in the papers.

Aunt Susanah herself drew and painted pictures. She was known for it. On the wall of the house I shared with my father there was this picture of hers. *Kingfishers by Glittering Water* by Susanah Clelland. She gave the picture to me for my fifth birthday. But she lived in Priorton, some miles away, so I didn't see much of her.

So you might say there *was* a chance that I got my delight in drawing from Aunt Susanah. But, although she would never have called herself an *artist*, I think it was much more likely that it was my grandmother who set me away She knew nothing about the arts. But she knew enough of politics to feel a deep chilly anger at having to feed her family on strike wages, or later on no money at all. This anger was distilled into fury at seeing her daughter–in-law die of hunger, forcing her grown son home again trailing his motherless child.

This child was me.

So me and my Dad came to live with my grandma in nineteen twenty seven. She fed us and took care of us for three years. Then, after five years she fell ill herself. And then she died. They said it was pleurisy but I've no real way of knowing, as she was never attended by the doctor before he came to give us her death certificate. When she died she was still wearing her usual crossover apron. In her coffin she looked like a silver haired doll.

We were actually called *lucky* because by then I was in the pit so we could keep the pit house

But in those early years when my father and I lived with Grandma, her narrow house seemed to me to be flooded with colour and distinctive shape. It was Grandma who - when she made hooked mats on Hessian canvas - showed me it was possible to recreate the sun and the moon with plates and tin lids for templates. She showed me how to create balance in a square and order in a rectangle; how you could make explosive red stand out against dense black; how yellow lives bright when set against green.

Her choice of colour was bold and uncompromising: for her there was no settling for the safe blacks and greys of a mining life. Such a freight of colour burned in her head that neither wall nor picture frame could hold it. She was indeed an artist. Her canvasses were the circles, squares and rectangles of Hessian canvas - you couldn't call them carpets – that she made to cover the floors in this meagre house. These mats survived for many years, eventually faded but still doing service as a barrier to the damp coming up from stone laid straight onto soil.

When I was very small I would sit underneath this stretched Hessian, peering up at the shadow of her prodding hands and watching the stubby back of the mat grow and grow. From there I could see the sun and the moon in negative: the underside of outrageous sunflowers and plump sprawling geraniums. Later, when my hands were bigger she would let me wield her big scissors and cut useable strips from old clothes and discarded furnishing cloth. She would let me poke and prod the cloth through the stretched canvas and make my own world of colour.

One day my grandmother smiled with quiet glee when a neighbour brought her the end-pieces of green velvet curtains that had been cut down in a house where she worked. She hoarded this treasure and when Easter came she made a small stepping mat with a design of trailing ivy set against pale grey flannel. A graceful present for the narrow house.

Grandma didn't always confine herself to the colours that came to her second-hand; she did not just cut up into strips the discarded coats and dresses she bought for pennies from the junk stall on Priorton market. She had her own ways of making her palette of colour. For months she'd be haunted by an image of the next mat in her mind and would save to buy penny dyes to colour some plain unpicked cloth. In even harder times she would strip berries from bushes and floral lichen from stone walls and squeeze them to a coloured juice. Then she would infuse the dull cloth with startling brilliance so she could punch purple suns and blue trees into the Hessian.

I would help her to mix and stir the dye, dipping my fingers and holding them up to see how the light made my flesh glow through these vivid colours. One day I swirled my dripping fingers across my father's' newspaper, and made an image of a coiled red snake. This was before he had read is precious newspaper, so I got a beating with his thick leather belt for my troubles.

My grandmother kept the paper image of that red curling snake and later that year copied my snake design for a stepping mat that she made secretly in the dark hours of the night. When it was done she parcelled it up for my Christmas present. That mat is on my wall now, alongside my own early painting of the White Leas colliery wheel.

She also charred larch wood in a firepit pit on the green at the back of the house and made charcoal for me. I used these stubs to draw on more sheets from the butcher. Those first pictures were messy but it felt very good, making that hard black mark. She bought stubby pencils for me, using her eternal 'tick' – her credit - from the corner shop.

On one birthday she persuaded my father to buy me my first tin of paints. Sacked from the pit, he'd obtained a month's work with a company that moved furniture for families who were going to the Midlands and the south of England to find work. They would pack two or three households to a wagon. 'In my wagon,' he'd say, 'are packed the lives of twenty people. You don't have to live inside a stone tent like we do if you can pack your life in a van.'

He enjoyed this work. 'You're your own boss out on the road. You see a bit of the other bright world away from the North,' he said, a rare smile flitting across his face. 'I wish I'd known that before. I'd not have spent those years underground.'

Then this moving company went bankrupt and he lost that job as well. That was the last time he worked and probably the last time I saw him smile.

As for me, at least I had my paints and now I began to make my mark on things. I would paint on old newspapers and broken-down cardboard boxes. The woman at the Co-op kept back big sugar bags and flattened them for me. They were poor things, those first daubs: scrappy copies of my grandmother's mats; pictures of things around the house; pots and pans, my father's old bent boots; my grandma's Singer sewing machine.

On my first day at school my mother took one of my drawings to show the teacher. I won a prize for a painting in my first week there. And I was always a good scholar. Every teacher encouraged me and told me I had a great future with this talent to draw. At the grammar school, where I'd won a free place, more than one teacher took me to one side and told me that with this talent I was really too good for the pit. My talent would be my salvation.

All this made not one jot of difference, of course, to my future. When I turned fourteen my father got wind of a job at White Leas Colliery, the second largest pit after Brack's Hill.. So I left school and went to the pit. I had to go. I'd no great confidence in my teachers' judgment. My father called what they said flattery: people looking after their own jobs. My Grandmother was dead by then and I had no one to fight own my corner.

So it happens that on the first pay-Saturday after I start the pit I turn up at home to see my Aunt Susannah standing four-square on my grandmother's sunflower rug. My father stands, arms folded, in front of my Aunt, whose first love had been my conchie uncle. The crackle of a recent quarrel zings in the air.

In her arms she's clutching a large flat parcel. She smiles when she sees me. 'I have this for you Gabriel,' she says, placing the parcel carefully on the table.

My father lifts a stoneware milk jug and a cup from the table and brushes past me as he takes them through to the scullery. I stand uneasily on the hearthrug. She looks at me. 'You still have smell of the pit about you, Gabriel' she frowns. 'Sad in one so young.'

I curse myself for blushing. I glance up and catch sight of myself in the mirror above the mantelpiece: this stranger, this pit boy. The black pit-dirt is in the pores of my skin, on the inside of my reddened eyes.

'So how was the pit, Gabriel?' she says.

I shake my head, wary. 'It's the pit,' I mumble. 'You know.'

I can hear my father in the scullery clashing about and avoiding coming into the kitchen because my aunt is here.

She shrugs. 'Sad, I was, to learn that you'd had to go down there. My own brother Davey changed forever the day he went down the pit.' *Dewi*. She says his name in the Welsh way. There are a lot of Welsh folks around here. Come up for the work.

'Davey?' I say. I've heard of no Davey.

'Killed in the Great War. He liked the army better than the pit.' There's this dark look on her face. 'Much better than the pit. Davey turned down the pit for the army, just like your uncle, who they killed in prison, turned down the war to fight for peace.'

I rub my chin. It's itchy. Bristles are poking through these days. 'I can see what he meant.' I say.

She turns to the parcel. 'I was sad, hearing you'd left school, you being such a good scholar at the grammar school. My Jonty's friend teaches there. Mr Jackson, his name is. He says you are a good artist. And clever it is, too,'

I sniff and cough, holding down the dusty air of the pit screens. 'I needed to work. I need the work. My dad can't get work. They won't let him back.'

'I know that Gabriel. Your father is a man of principle.' Now she pulls a great flat book out of its brown paper nest. The book's slate coloured cover is scrawled across with the name *Rembrandt*. 'This man is a genius. This is a book of his picture plates. I bought it at an auction of the property of a schoolmaster in Priorton. I thought it might just do for you.' She opens a page and tips the book towards the window. 'Look!' she says, turning the pages.

Many of the plates are black and white but have shades and depths that make them glow. Others are coloured. Such colour! Such harmony of flesh and light. I feel drenched in sweetness, as though I've drunk a cup of Golden Syrup all at once. The colours lambast me from the page: the glow of the glistening flesh, the subtleties of the folds in the garments; the mysterious life in the eyes of the subjects. 'Crikey!' I say.

'As you say. Crikey!' There's a small smile on her face.

I don't know what to say. 'Thank you,' I say loudly. 'Is this really for me? I've never had nothing like this before, like.'

She looks around. 'Is there anybody else in this house who is an artist? Of course it's for you.' She's staring at me with odd concentration.

I shake my head. 'Me, I'm no artist.'

'Oh yes you are. You're an artist and a good scholar, and if that… if your father wants to forget that then *you* must not.' She pulls on her gloves. 'Well, my Jonty's waiting for me at the station. We're off to Durham. We have a Labour meeting there.'

'Don't go, I... Something to drink? Some tea?'

She laughs a contented, confident laugh. 'Indeed I think your father'll only settle when I get out of this house, dear Gabriel.' Her Welsh voice sings in the air in the narrow cluttered room. She puts her clean glove on my dirty pit jacket. 'Promise me you'll draw still, and paint still, Gabriel. In spite of the pit? In spite of those men there who'll think it's - well - a *cissy* kind of thing?'

'Well, I...'

'Promise!'

'To be honest Aunt Susanah, I don't think I can stop myself. The drawing and painting thing.'

Her laughter rings out and she reaches up and kisses me on my blackened cheek. For minutes after she's gone I can feel the soft imprint of her lips on my cheek. My heart aches now for my mother, even though I don't know if I really loved her and am not sure that I remember her properly.

If my father sees the tears in my eyes when he comes in with the clean pots, he doesn't say. He puts the pots in the press, and with his back still to me he says gruffly. 'What was that about then?'

'She brought me this book of paintings.'

'That Susanah wants to mind her own business.' His tone is more growl than voice.

I wrap the book in the brown paper, and - holding it gingerly in my coal-black fingers - I take it upstairs and put it on the windowsill of my bedroom where it may catch the light.

4. The Nature of the Goaf

It might be an obvious thing to say that the pit - when you first enter it - as I did at fourteen - is black-dark. And this is no ordinary kind of black-dark. It's not the darkness of night which you know will be followed by dawn, nor is it the dark of the Northern Hemisphere when you know the South is bathed in light. Even in a thickly curtained bedroom you know there will light out there behind the curtains the next day. Extraordinarily, down there in the pit there is simply no light at all. What you find down there is another dark behind the dark. There is no next-day-dawn.

The flickers of our pathetic firefly helmet lamps barely pierce this unrelieved darkness. Any pitman knows that beyond this darkness stand ancient rooted walls and ramparts of rock that were born in darkness and will remain in darkness until the death of the world.

And - having experienced such dark - when you come up in the cage and step out into the dusty world of the pit yard, you feel you've never known such light. You've never seen such blues, such distinctive ochres, such sultry and vibrant greens. The very faces of the boys coming from the screens are baby pink, their eyes are blue sapphires, the inside of their lips, their slipping tongues, are carmine.

This very dark underground consumes you; this is what eats into you at first. But I my father's birthday gift redeemed me... Eventually I found that I could change my dense reaction to this dark by bringing into my mind my father's petrified forest where the leaves once fluttered in the light of day, where fish once swam on sunlit seashore and seahorses bobbed in the ebb and flow of primeval tides.

That saving vision was my father's gift to me and has stayed with me for the whole of my life.

When I'm feeling low, this blackness, this absence of colour is the worst of the pit. In my lowest times it seems that this black is the blackest of blackness, the essence of absence. The pitmen have a word for that darkness down there. They called it *the Goaf*.

But as I work on down the pit my eyes become attuned to a peculiarly dense co-existence of light and colour. I begin to relish the dark rainbow of the mining seam: the intense blues and purples, the odd prickle-pinpoint of red which - when you get to it - turns out to be the stray beam of a miner's lamp as he walks a curve returning from the coal-face.

So in time the pit, this great dark warren, begins to disclose to me the colours of the old forest infused with the sunlight of ancient times. Down here the rainbow has darkened, become dense, imploded. Yet nonetheless it surely survives threaded cunningly through the stone. I spend a lot of time pondering on the impossibility of showing this colour: will it ever be possible to convey to the unknowing world how such vibrancy takes possession of my eyes down here in the dark.

Of course, among my fellow pitmen I have to keep all these weird reflections to myself. They value more direct and masculine talents. It is strue, though, that these hard men appreciate the cartoons and likenesses that I chalk on the gallery walls and the ends of coal tubs. In this same access to gentleness the pitmen appreciate other men who can spout poetry or sing the songs that echo through the dark galleries.

However they find the wilder aspects of colour and any flights of verbal fancy embarrassing, and can dismiss them as *womanish* – great insult. So I keep my own council about my inner reflections on light and colour and consequently am known to be *close* and silent.

But Tegger, my *marra*, the poet and fabulist given to flights of verbal fancy from time to time, is never driven to silence down here.

Tegger, and me went to school together from when we were five. He's always been the bright, noisy one; I'm always the quiet one. Tegger has broad cheeks and a smile that flickers across his face like sunshine. He has heavy, almost fat shoulders. His hands, chunky as a span of butchers' sausages, beat the air as he tries to make a point. His nature is easy-going, but it's a mistake to be deceived by his simple manner. He's no simpleton. I never knew a wiser man. He'll pat you on the shoulder, almost hug you when he is really excited about something. This hugging is uncommon around here, but the men shrug it off genially enough. 'Only Tegger's way,' they say. 'Daft as a brush, that bugger.'

Like I say, Tegger and me have been together right since our first day at infant school. At first I grew tall while he stayed small. We started the grammar school together and left together on the same day, both starting the pit on the same day. After three months down the pit he began to grow taller and to broaden out, putting the meat on even in the leanest times. His mother said he showed every ounce of his keep. His father said he grew in the dark, like a bloody great mushroom.

We always work the same shifts, Tegger and me. He knocks me up at three thirty in the morning and our feet crunch side by side on the mixture of slag cinder and dirt that make the black path to the pit. Our feet know the way themselves: the yellow lights strung on drooping wires every thousand yards ensure that we don't stray and boot our way South or North, out away from this place of deep fissures and dark caverns.

Tegger hunches his shoulders against the morning cold and keeps his head down all the way. But me, after a while, I'll look up, my eyes skimming the shades of black, grey and purple that define the very early morning. The sky at now is the densest black but sometimes the morning star rises poking through the blanket of night. And I will dwell on the thought that beyond this well of darkness there exists a world of light, a rainbow universe where the whiteness shatters into ribbons of colour.

One of my grammar-school teachers gave me this book of science with wonderful colour plates. It has a whole section on *The Rainbow* and how it's made: how white is the presence of all colour and black is its absence.

The fact is, as I say, I am lucky. In the end I get to see great colours down the pit. Just a flicker, just a touch of light from your lamp liberates colour from the *Goaf,* that intense blackness behind blackness that is the eternal night of the pit. I begin to feast my eyes on the purple sheen on the coal seam and the glitter of fool's gold; the soft plum red of a man's inner mouth, the gleam of his eye; the flutter of the silver grey moth still surviving down there, and the skittering swirl of the blind mice moving along the rails.

In the hierarchy of the pit, physical strength and critical judgement of the fall of a seam are considered of the greatest value. *Strength –* well, I and Tegger have that in abundance. We are young and fit. In the matter of *judgemen*t we are probably suspect. Tegger has his own kind of manic wisdom but like I say, they often call him a fool. My judgement, I'd claim, is mostly sound. But I have this habit of daydreaming - of light-dreaming – that sometimes gets in the way of concentrating on serious work.

There was this one time in the pit when I had this extraordinary dream of light that set away something that is still resounding like a struck bell through my life. It happened like this.

****

This day in the crush of men in the cage Tegger and me stand shoulder to shoulder. The men's faces are already filming with that first crust of coal-dust; mouths are tightening with grim anticipation, weary acceptance. The talk fades as the cage fills and we crush together. Tegger turns his bulk sideways to make room for two more men at the other end of the creaking cage.

By the time we get in-bye - nearly a mile's walk – the hewer has done his work and we take over from the putters, who have a tub full, ready for us to push on its way. When you start work the shift yawns before you like an un-leapable chasm. But, in truth, time is broken up into pieces; we have full tubs to move, empty ones to return: there is the dicey pull of the turns on the road; there is the low roof that leave only a breadth of space between your fingers and the stone.

Time passes.

There are the occasional calls of the hewers; there is the roar of song from Tegger who is the master of songs from the theatre and the picture-houses. The men shout at him for being a daft bugger but they still encourage him to sing.

Tegger's voice echoes in the galleries and a distant voice joins him in a chorus. Then someone shouts at them to shut their noise. Me, I wonder how he finds the spit to sing. My mouth and throat are silted up like a river mouth and I have to pace myself with my water bottle or it won't last a shift.

Such things as this pace your work time: they break it up; they rescue you from the yawning cavern of the shift.

We always stop for bait time, to eat our mid-shift meal. These days we stop for this. I've heard my father say how in his early days they used to work straight through the shift, eating as they worked.

At bait-time the pit changes its nature. You can hear and see different things in the space around you. The beat and the grind of the winning of coal comes to a halt. The wandering firefly illumination of lamps is dimmed to rest the pitmen's' straining eyes. A moment of peace pervades the galleries: we sit in a quietness undercut by the drum and thrum of the pumps as the men, in their holes and corners, enjoy a bit crack with their marras.

Tegger and me usually go to a familiar nick in an old bit of face, well out of the way of the stinking place where men squeeze through to relieve themselves and evacuate their personal waste. We crouch on a long off-cut from a prop placed across two pieces of stone, and get out our bait tins. We flick off our lights and feel for our dinner. It's simple enough fare: jam sandwiches cut thick as bibles fill my bait tin. In the dark I can't see my black fingers staining the white bread. If the jam's a bit gritty I put that down to the pips in Mrs McVay's blackberry jam.

Tegger and me talk a bit in the dark. Then he sings a new song for me, one he's made up, about four pit lads and a dog that lost a crucial race. His rendition gets applause from further along the gallery.

'Give us another one, son!' One of the men shouts.

'Yer should be on the stage, you, lad,' shouts another.

Tegger gives them one more song: this one is about a pigeon man who had a winning pigeon which survived an epic storm on its way back from Whitehaven. After that there are no new requests and the murmur of voices tells us that other more important discussions are afoot: about the state of the country and arguments for and against going to Spain to help the working lads there to win their war with the grandees and the priests. A lot of the men are for that.

I close my eyes against the dark and listen, letting the murmuring in the gallery flow over me. Tegger's shoulder lies heavy against mine and I realise he's having a five minute nap that will keep him going for the rest of his shift. I close my own eyes. Around me the gallery stills. Tegger's breathing drifts to a sustained puppy dog snuffle.

Now I open my eyes, blinking. The pit face before me suddenly blazes with light, the dark behind it glowing through threads of silver. I lean across to feel my lamp but it's still in the 'off' position. I look back at the old coal face and the gleam is still there. Phosphorous I think. I've read about it; heard about it in old pitmen's tales. I screw my eyes tight then open them. It is still there. This gleam is too great for phosphorous. The hair on the back of my head prickles and I scramble with my lamp to click it on again.

And now the gob of light from my lamp throws itself into the black chasm, chasing away the luminescent gleams and streaks of light. The chasm is no longer gleaming, no longer a place of magic; beyond the pit-lamp's beam the darkness sulks its way, swamping into the space.

But now, now! I can see a figure. I screw up my eyes, and then lift up my lamp to make it out. Is it another man, moved into the dark to relieve himself? A pony on the wander? Worse has been known.

This is neither man nor pony. I can see now that it's a woman. She has a shadowy face; her dark clothes are relieved by a glittering red patch on her shoulder: a brooch maybe, or a flower? I squeeze my eyes tightly together. A strand of light from my lamp touches her hands and they reach out to me: long slender fingers. I pull back hard against the wall. The stone cuts into my shoulder blade.

Women are not allowed in the pit. The common superstition is that the presence of a woman brings bad luck. Like any great ship at sea, the pit is a place of *men*. Here, men are free to be themselves: to work and fart and talk and swear among their own absolute kind. I've heard the most saintly of men swear down here, using the old words that echo back from the lacerated wall of the chasm and resound down through a thousand years.

And now this woman is moving towards me. I push my back even further into the wall. I don't want to see her face. I don't want to know whether it's my mother or my grandmother, who are both dead. Or whether what I am seeing is the face of all the mothers of all the lads killed in these galleries. It strikes me that perhaps the intensity of the pit-gate mourning vigil of women has created a disembodied presence down here: the absolute woman who searches for their lost ones.

My head spines, runs with questions.

Answers flow into my head, through my veins. This … *thing* … is more than any of that. Perhaps the earth herself is enfolding us all in work and sleep. Is she forgiving us our gouging, our cutting and harvesting and reclaiming us for her own? In our blind wander, our sparkle of imagined colour, our helpless charging and working of the depths, are we her unborn children? Are we born back into the bright world at the end of each shift? And then at the beginning of the next shift are we sucked back into her overwhelming void as the cage drops yet again and spews us out into the galleries, the wounds we cut in her side?

A thrill of fear chases through me as my lamp calls forth an answering glint in her hidden eyes. I grab Tegger's meaty arm. 'Tegger! Tegger! D'you see her? D'you see the woman?'

'Gabriel! Gabe, what is it, man?' Now it's Tegger who's shaking me. My head's groggy and full of shadows.

'What is it, man? Y'are dreaming, man.' He punches my shoulder, hard.

I am shaking and sweating. 'Tegger! Did you see the woman?'

'Mistake to go to sleep, marra. Never go to sleep down here.' He turns up his lamp and our end of the gallery blossoms into dark shadowy normality. 'Come on, lad. Tony Soames'll have a tub near ready for us.'

I'm mad at him for his disbelief. 'I didn't sleep, Tegger. *You* went to sleep, not me.'

'Nah! Me? I've never gone to sleep down here in my life. Dangerous that. *She* takes hold of you when you've gone to sleep. Ask the old lads. Never gan to sleep down below.'

I shake my head to get the woman - and the sleep - out of it. I know better than to discuss this woman with the other men. But I wonder how many of *them* have this dream, this dream of the earth as a woman, in a place where no woman must enter.

Now on this shift, after this experience, I feel the need for the heavy work of pulling the tubs. In this hard, grinding work all these fantasies of engulfment and possession fade away. And I'm the better for it.

5. Cast Off

Like I say, my father hasn't been down the pit since the big Strike. Still, he's faithful to his mates. He attends Lodge meetings. He walks behind the Bracks Hill banner at the Big Meeting in Durham in July. But he himself no longer inhabits the deep earth. He no longer pushes himself on his side, shoulder-first, to traverse a narrow seam. He no longer gathers at the Deputy's Kist to get his orders from the Deputy. He no longer sweats in the dark, pushing tubs up inclines and holding them back on the down ways. He no longer sits in the dark having a crack with his marras while he eats his bait. He no longer looks into the dark with his eyes wide open.

Sometimes I think he misses the pit more that he misses my mother. Pits of one kind or another have mothered him, swallowed him whole since he was ten. But now he's been spat out and prevented by the mean machinations of men from returning to those depths. His spirited activity in the Strike led to his banishment. Now in these ten years he's learned to be quiet. His spark is quite extinguished.

He always loved the pit but he loved the surface too. On Sundays when he was still working when before my mother died, , he'd take me on long leg-aching walks out of the town, beyond the clanking iron wheel. We'd tramp to the woods and ancient coppices that thickened in the crevices of this hilly land like hair on the human body. We'd gather bluebells and yellow aconites and, on two or three days a year, we'd fill the raised hem of my jersey with mushrooms which glowed grey-white against the late spring grass.

In the woods we'd watch the water voles and the hatching drone flies. We'd turn over stones from Roman buildings carved with letters of legionary tribute. We'd climb the old trees, scrape off lichen and roll it in our fingers till it stained our skin green red and purple. And we'd fill our pockets again for my grandmother to make her dyes.

One time, high in a tree, I disturbed a ball-like bundle of sticks and sent it flying. My father told me how I had destroyed the squirrel's nest. He said that now the squirrel would have to make a new home and would blame me to his friends.

In these much bleaker days my father's one consolation is his allotment, away from the narrow rows of houses but still within the shadow of the great wheel. He has this strip of land that he farms like any small farmer did in feudal times. In these days I suppose fealty is paid to the pit head and the wheel rather that any visible lord of the manor. I suppose the feudal lords still do exist, in Bishop's palaces, in mock castles in the southern counties, or in counting houses in the City. They draw their dues from our blood and sweat but we don't see them face to face. Their power and energy was once visible in their wheels grinding long and slow. Now even they are still. The Brack's Hill seam has closed.

I have just two years down below to participate in this visual feast, this primal battle with the woman, before, like my father I am cast out of this darkness into the light of unemployment. Up to now my 'lad's wages' has kept my father and me afloat in bare poverty. My father, banned now from the pit, has lived his days in dark dreams but up to now he has still managed to conjure up food from his allotment for my dinner when I came back from the pit.

But now I am cast out.

Unemployed, bereft of the black inspiration of the pit and with too much time on my hands I draw with some fanaticism. I use remembered images of the galleries and the men in my drawings. I make my own charcoal in the way my grandma showed me and beg sugar-bag paper from Mr McVay at the corner shop. I iron the paper with my mother's flat iron and use the sheets to draw my pictures. My father makes no comment on this activity: merely sucks on his empty pipe and stares at the guttering fire.

Every day I take a shoulder sack onto the pit heaps and pick up pieces of scrap coal to keep our fire going. This irony is not lost on us; here we are, pitmen scratching for coal on the waste heap of a mine where we have previously won millions of pounds' worth of coal for the owners.

But I'm not just collecting coal like the others. The heaps have other appeals for me. This town is pockmarked with these man-made hills. They rise like pyramids from the green valley floor. My favourite slag-heap is the one by the dog track. This slagheap is the highest of them all. The railway that used to pull the trucks full of spoil up to the top of this particular heap is rusted now. No engine has steamed up here since the twenty sixth of May when the big strike started. The spoil heap hasn't grown, but with every winter's frost and every spring's rain the slag settles and moves and throws up its treasure. I never come here without finding a fish or an elaborate flower, a seahorse or a finely scaled animal. My collection in our front room cupboard grows apace.

These days I confine myself to three fine specimens a trip. First I collect a whole lot of them in my canvas sack. Then I sit on a high rock and lay them out, examining them minutely, before I make my final selection.

I sense the perverse satisfaction in my father when the main seam a White Leas closes and I lose my job. I sense his prickly disapproval when after some weeks I come in to say me and Tegger have got jobs in a drift mine out by Killock Quarry. This means a good four-mile walk each way. Still, it was not bad through the summer, as the road leads across Killock Common and along a narrow path through Killock woods. The drift mine itself is in the middle of the wood on the edge of a stand of stunted pollarded oaks.

In summer this walk has its own delights in terms of flora and fauna. But this last winter it has proved to be a cold and weary trudge. Many days I wish I could stay at home with my father even in his present misery. But I have to do this work for the money. These days turning down work is like uttering blasphemy in a church: a sin against God. This is worse, though, in that turning down work would demonstrate contempt of your fellow man.

My father's allotment is a long narrow strip alongside five other strips which edge, side-on, to the last row of houses built by Lord Chase for the first opening of Bracks Hill Pit. The houses are small and narrow and overshadowed by the long pit wall. The allotments, however, look out over open land towards Priorton, the much older town which clusters round an ancient Priory. The allotment is not a unpleasant place to spend a fine Sunday afternoon.

Years ago my father built himself a little shed here, made out of the packing cases that brought the new winding gear up to the pit in nineteen twenty, after the Great War, before the first big Strike. My father's shed is orderly, his tools and implements, (most of them made by hand by his own father) each tool has its own special hook. In the very worst days these spades and forks, like my father's suit, have travelled backward and forth to the pawnbrokers. My father resented even the temporary loss of his tools more than the pawning of his own best Sunday suit.

He grows vegetables in neat rows, He breeds rabbits. He collects eggs from his clucking chickens: these are all we had to keep us going from nineteen twenty six to nineteen thirty when I left school to go down the pit. Some of this produce he would sell to pay the rent for my grandma's house after he was sacked and had no right to it. After I went down the pit my father and I paid no rent to Lord Chase's agent for the house and my wage, small as it was, made a difference.

Like I say, my father didn't like this - me earning a wage when he didn't. On paydays he'd be missing all day down the garden, way past the coming of evening darkness. He didn't like to see me come in with meat bought from the butcher's. He didn't like to acknowledge that he couldn't provide for both of us.

He has cast me off. These days he rarely speaks to me in the house. He ignores the scribbles and drawings on scraps of paper that I leave on the table for him to see. I leave them out for a day or so, then pile them up and put them in the drawer of the press in the dark parlour.

Saturday afternoons and Sundays I still walk the lanes and climb the slagheaps for new specimens. Then there is this one Saturday that I see a woman moving between the whin bushes that are growing deep roots into the foot of the heap. This woman is tall and slender. She wears a long wool coat and a close hat which covers her hair and shades her face. Even from a distance I can see that the woman is not from round here. The coat is too well cut. The face is too rounded. No sharp angles from staved off hunger.

The following Monday, me and Tegger are laid off at the drift mine. We tramp round other places looking for work with no result. My father grunts when I tell him, but I know there's some perverse satisfaction in him.

On Saturday again I go up on the slag heap and I see the woman again. I go up again on the Sunday. And I wait for her by a sprouting lime tree that hooks improbably over the path leading to the heap. Amd she is there again.

I move beside her and take her arm. 'So what is it?' I say. 'Here again is it?'

She twists away from my grasp. She's older than I thought. Perhaps as much as thirty-five. 'Stop that!' she says. 'Will you stop it?' Her accent tells me she is not from around here.

'You've been watching me.' I say. 'I've felt your eyes on me.'

Her face is a long oval and her eyes a clear grey. Her hair, the colour of clean putty, is swept across her brow and away under her hat. No one, though, would call her pretty. More one of your plain Janes, if you ask me. There's many a bonnier girl here in Bracks Hill turning up at the chapel dance or clustering at the entrance to the Priorton Odeon.

She frowns. 'I simply walk here. This is what I do. I walk.' She talks in a very strange way.

'You were spying on me.' I'm beginning to feel like a fool. 'I saw you!'

She smiles. Her teeth are small and even and very white. 'So why would I spy on you? Whoever you are?'

'Why do you come to this place? This slag heap. It's not for the likes of you.'

Her head goes up. 'So! What *is* the likes of me, sir? I walk where I will. Now let me pass.' She walks past me and I watch her narrow back as it recedes down the lane back towards Bracks Hill. Her feet, clad in boots, (fine stitched in green leather), crunch on the cinder gravel of the pathway. She leaves behind her a faint smell of lilies, a smell I last encountered at my mother's funeral in the chapel the other side of Bracks Hill pit yard.

By the time I get back to the house I'm in a fine stew. I clash the pans about while I put together some kind of dinner. I survey the low dark scullery with loathing. I sit on a stool to clean my best boots but no matter how much I spit and polish they look what they are: worn down patched boots which have seen much better days.

But still the woman is on my mind.

6. Good Advice

Tegger threw open the door to find a man speaking to a crowd of people, a book in his heand. Twenty-one faces turned towards him.

'Sorry, I thought....' He drew back, red-faced.

The speaker stopped speaking. The room faltered into silence.

'No. No. Come in!' The speaker – a man with smooth film-star hair -gestured towards him with the book in his hand. 'No. No. Come on in sir. We're nearly finished here.'

Clearly this man was Archie Todhunter. Tegger had heard talk of him in The Lord Raglan. The talk was that he'd been a doctor once. They said he was Scottish, a bit of a 'Red' and a bit of a wizard and had acted with the great Tyrone Guthrie. Here at the Brack's Hill Settlement he'd got people to play-act. And apparently he obtained wood and leather so the lads on the dole could make boxes and mend shoes and bags for themselves and their families. The word in the Raglan was that they weren't allowed to sell the stuff they made.

The word was also that this Archie Todhunter was an agitator and gave talks on the Russian writer Lenin and said people should take things into their own hands. None of this bothered Tegger. Speak as you find was one of his many mottoes.

The men and women clustered around two long trestle tables turned back to look intently at the man at the front.

Archie Todhunter continued. 'So, friends, perhaps the great Anton Chekhov is our man. He talks sense and he talks deep. His people wait for the future as we do. He, like ourselves, is caught in the web of the past. I have here only four copies of the play, so you'll have to pass them amongst you. You'll need to hand write your part when you get it. I'll be interested to hear what you think of this play. If you don't care for it, I do have a play of my own…' He paused. 'Read it, and see what you think about this one,' he repeated.

Some of the people were getting to their feet when Archie stopped them with a raised hand. 'Oh yes. An announcement! We have a new volunteer, courtesy of Artists Intenational, at the Settlement. She is a very accomplished artist who will work with the painters and drawers among you, on Tuesdays and Saturdays. And she will help us with our designs for the plays. If you know any artists among you, let them know.'

Tegger noted that this man assumed that there would be artists and drawers among them.

Archie Todhunter went on. 'This is good news for our people here. She will be an inspiration to us all.'

Tegger watched as the people shared the books between them, made arrangements to read together or to pass on, then drifted away. A striking, rather ugly woman dressed in bright colours stayed behind and helped Archie collapse the trestle and put the folding chairs up against the wall.

'Now then son,' Archie came to shake him by the hand. 'Who are you?'

'Tegger McNamara,' said Tegger, taking off his cap. ' I've come about...'

'And this lady here is Cora Miles, the actress.'

The woman's hand slipped into his, warm and firm.

He thought it was a long time since he'd shaken hands with anyone and here was a second time in minutes. Shaking hands was a fussy habit, unwelcome among pitmen. 'Dinna be soft, man!' the men would say.)

Cora Miles slipped into her jacket: a graceful, tidy movement. 'I'll go up now, Archie,' she said to Todhunter. 'Brew some coffee?'

That was another thing. The word at the Raglan was that Archie Todhunter lived tally with an ugly woman. No one did anything about that, of course. Dour comment was possible, but interference was not the style of the people of Bracks Hill.

Tegger had made it his business to study his own intricate people. He even wrote stories about them when the spirit moved him. He knew that underneath the bible-thumping of chapel people and the gossip of the rest there still existed a philosophy of live and let live. Tegger knew the history of the town. This was not an ancient community. Most families had been incomers. The uneven flux of work at the pits and the ironworks meant that people were always moving in and out of Brack's Hill.

A hundred years before Bracks Hill had been just that: a hill with junipers on its foot and scrub and whinny bushes on its higher reaches. A necklace of coal pits had built up around the town, exploiting cruelly low seams of fine quality coal. The availability of coal led to the establishment of an iron works: These ad been serviced by the new railway that led the coal and iron to the coast, to be shipped to London and places further afield. The railway imported workers into the town from all over England and Scotland, and when the time came exported some of them to places where the work was more plentiful.

Tegger observed that many of these men and women, though virtuous themselves, had seen and known enough to realise that conditions for virtue were not written on tablets of stone: that bad individuals did good things, that good people had bad edges. Every family had its grey sheep. 'There but for the grace of God go I,' was not an uncommon saying in Bracks Hill. As was 'leave well alone.'

Tegger surmised that the pragmatism of moving and settling, moving and settling, meant that it was a wise thing to keep your own counsel and not interfere with others. This was especially so in the case of this Archie Todhunter who had imported such benefits to the town with his workshops, his playmaking and what was grandly termed his Poor Man's Law centre. It was the Law Centre that had enticed Tegger McNamara into this alien territory on a cold evening in May.

Todhunter settled in a hard wooden chair by the open fire and pulled up another for Tegger. 'Now then young feller. What can I do for you Mr ...McNamara, was it?'

'My name is Edgar. People call me Tegger. They say you give advice, sir. About the Means Test and that? They tell us that you're a poor man's lawyer.'

Todhunter fitted a cigarette into a short amber holder and held a newspaper spill to the fire to light his cigarette. He took a deep, grateful draw. 'Well,' he said, the smoke trailing from his lips with the words. 'We've a few books, some government pamphlets, and a lot of goodwill. So we can give advice. What advice would you need, Mr McNamara? Tegger? May I call you Tegger?'

Tegger liked the man's graceful manners. 'It's just ... well, I've got me Ma and Da there at home with three little'ns. Seems they won't get the dole with me in the house. The Means Test people are hot on that. Working age and all that. I have this bit of a job leading night-soil out to the farms. Pays pennies. They can pay you what they like these days. Well, it seems with my bit, me ma and Da canna get anything. The Means Test lads have it all wrapped up. If I bring in a wage we're worse off than if I didn't work at all. Can't we make a case, like...?'

Todhunter shook his head. 'That is the case. And as you say, Tegger, it's a mistake to cross the Means Test man. Only ever worth fighting a winnable cause. Remember that.' He drew again on his cigarette.

'If that's the case I'll have to go away. Leave Brack's Hill. Go down London or Coventry like some marras of mine,' said Tegger. 'But my Ma'd sure miss us she needs me help with the little'ns. Me Da's in his chair day and night, coughing. She really does need my help with the bairns. For their sakes I couldn't afford to move.'

Todhunter stared into the fire. 'Some of the men deal with this problem by going up on that land behind Trent Street to live in the vans.'

Tegger was shocked. 'What? Up there, living like tinkers?' There was a huddle of round-topped vans behind Trent Street on a bit of waste land where men gathered who had no other place to go. He had walked past Trent Street, coming home after early shift, and seen the men gathered round a flickering bonfire in the dark afternoon. The place seemed impregnable, as though it were a glimpse of another time, another place. 'They are shiftless, those lads. Layabouts,' he said now.

'Ha!' Todhunter barked into the air. 'Is it up to you to judge men you've never met? The pit they work in may have closed; their families moved on or even died. They have no roof over their heads except that stretched canvas. Some of them come here to the Settlement for classes. They are good people. I know that one of them is moving out to join the Navy. His van will be free. If you move in there then the Means Test man must allow your family their fair money.

'Well...' said Tegger.

Todhunter sighed. 'Is there no other person you could move in with?' he said patiently.

Tegger shook his head. 'I've this friend who'd welcome me I know. He lives with his Da. But he's just been laid off from the drift mine and if I moved in they'd be in the same boat as my mam and dad.'

'Right!' said Todhunter briskly. 'Shall I walk up to Trent Street with you tomorrow to talk to this fellow? The one I know?'

Tegger stared at him. 'I could go and see my family during the day?'

'Yes. But you should be careful not to be there in a routine daily fashion. And not at night. Or it will be noted.'

'Well, I suppose I'll have to do that, then.' said Tegger sorrowfully. 'Live in the van?'

Todhunter smoked on in silence and Tegger wriggled in his seat, wondering how he could escape. 'Well, Mr Todhunter....' he began.

'What job did you do in the pit?' said Todhunter abruptly.

'I was a putter, pushing and pulling the tubs underground.'

'It must take some strength, a job like that.'

'You either get strong or give up, I can tell you.'

'Have you done anything else down there?'

'A bit of joinery. I was 'prenticed to the pit joiner first off but I gave up because the pay was poor. Strength pays, in the pit.'

'Were you any good? At joinery?'

'Yeah. Close enough for pit-work, like they say.'

'Ah. Good,' said Todhunter. 'Good. Well, there's no pay here at the Settlement but we do need a joiner to help with repairs on the hut that we're going to use as an art workshop. And we'll need help to build sets for our new play, whatever it turns out to be. As you would see, that's not quite decided yet.'

Tegger shook his head. 'I canna do that, man. I wouldn't know where ter start. Making stage stuff.'

'We've got a time-served joiner here already, out of work of course. He could do with a hand. He'll teach you,' said Archie patiently.

'I don't know...'

'Well,' said Todhunter briskly. 'Just think! You'll be stuck down in the van at Trent Street. You can't spend all your day at home. What else have you to do?'

'If you think....'

Todhunter stood up. 'Well that's fixed, Tegger. Meet me here at two tomorrow and I'll take you up to Trent Street to meet this fellow with the van.'

Tegger made for the door, then looked back. 'That drawing class?' he said. 'Can anyone come?'

'Well then,' said Todhunter. 'Are you a painter as well as a joiner?'

Tegger laughed and shook his head. 'No fear of that. Happier with a pen than a paintbrush! Words and songs, that's me. No. Paint brushes is me marra, a lad called Gabriel. He draws, even paints sometimes. And he's good. And he has time on his hands just now, like the rest of us.

'Tell him to come here to the Settlement, then. He'll be more than welcome.'

'Ah don't know. He's a close bird, is Gabriel. Quiet, like. Stubborn. I doubt you won't get him in here.'

'We'll see, Tegger,' said Archie. 'We'll see.'

7. The Magician.

Archie Todhunter, who didn't mind using clichés, always said that supping with the devil was a small price to pay if you got your wicked way in the end. The *end* for him, as he preached many times, was the Holy Grail of personal enhancement and enrichment of the common individual.

This zeal for the *common good* was not unique to him in his family. He'd inherited it from far-off ancestors, those bog- and hedge-ranters who had roared their conviction to the heather and the bewildered locals since the Reformation. Then came his great-great-grandfather who had been, more recognisably, a church minister: and his great-grandfather who had been a missionary in Africa; and from his grandfather, a missionary in China; and from his father, a medical missionary born and bred in China, who came home once on leave and (to the genteel despair of his Edinburgh cronies) had fallen for a very simple woman who worked in a manual trade in the Glasgow shipyards. He married this common woman when she was pregnant and sailed away to China with her after she'd given birth to Archie, whom she left to her Glasgow sisters to bring up.

Then when Archie was twelve his father died in China and, instead of coming home, his mother became a missionary in her own right. She was, by all accounts, famous for her bravery, her piety, her absolute gentility and her powers of persuasion.

Despite this pious inheritance, somewhere in his young life Archie had lost God. Perhaps his loss was engendered by his common Glasgow aunts, to whom God was an amusement rather than an edifice. Perhaps he had lost it at the boarding school to which his Edinburgh grandfather had sent him when he realised what heathen doings were afoot in Glasgow with the aunts. At this boarding school the teachers, all men of the cloth, frightened young Archie so much that the only thing he could do was go to sleep in their lessons and dream of his mother and father in China.

Whatever the cause, Archie survived his childhood with the cadences of the King James Bible off by heart and no place left in that pulsing organ for God himself, or for any true belief.

His short time at university was godless enough to save him backsliding from his unbelief. At this place, though, he did find himself exercising his inherited missionary muscles with involvement in the university charities: soup kitchens, literacy missions and clothes collections for the poor.

His real debt to his university - the real inklings of his fate – came through his involvement with the student drama group: the student orations, the rehearsed readings, the plays, the impromptus staging of a wide range of dramas. The plays, for him, had the fascination of dreams made fact. They revived for him the wildest fantasies of his drab schoolroom, when he would force himself into a living dream of greeting his parents, (strangely dressed as coolies), as he came off the slow boat which had taken him to China. Or there was the waking fantsy of his parents - still dressed as coolies - arriving at school in a tall motor car, ready to take him away, to take him home. He'd generated these dreams many times but they remained mere rehearsals: they were never transformed to fact. Archie never met his parents in real life.

At university he strode the stage in minor roles in an hysteria of wild belief which, he thought, imbued his performances with power. So powerful were they that more than one director told him to calm down, to stop corpsing Romeo, or Shylock, or Hamlet, or whichever hero being played by his acquaintance, the luminously talented Jack Tarrant.

That same Jack Tarrant, of course, had gone on to play the leading light on the London stage. Archie later read in *The Stage* that Jack was being tempted to go to America to play Doctor Watson to Claude Rains' Sherlock Holmes in a new talking picture.

The truth was that Archie proved to be of greatest value backstage. He picked up lighting and stage production very quickly and, on taking up a hammer and saw, found he had inherited his Glasgow grandfather's carpentry skills, rather than his Edinburgh grandfather's belief in God. He also, through reading the drama text books of the day and contemporary criticism, kept his amateur group up on theatre trends. He was always urging the group to take more risks, to embrace the *avant-garde*

This obsession, of course, robbed precious time from his study of Gray's Anatomy and his explorations of the mystery of the oesophagus amongst other organs. Rehearsals took his attention away from practicals where one morning his professor, pausing in his demonstration, held forth in a pea-whistle voice on the fact that intellectual enlightenment would only ever dawn on the alert and the observant. The trilling of his professor's voice brought to Archie's mind the mendacious chaplain at his school. Even so fell into a doze and dreamt of his mother rowing up the Yangtze in a narrow boat. The fellow beside him dug him in the ribs and he woke to the fierce glare of the professor who'd obviously just asked him a question.

He struggled to sit upright. 'Beg pardon, sir…? Beg pardon?'

'Pardon? Pardon?' The bird-man's face was magenta. 'I must ask you sir, to think of the hundreds, nay, thousands of young men who would give their eye-teeth to sit in that seat and who would attend closely, learn his profession with respect. Shame on you, sir!'

Of course, Archie failed his exams and was advised by his old and not unfriendly tutor not to re-sit them.

'To be honest, Todhunter, as far as I can see, you've no real aptitude for the combination of drudgery and delight which is at the core of general practice,' the old man told him gently, surveying his sweetly curving meerschaum pipe with great care. 'No doubt you have abilities, my boy. A brain, even! You are said to be hardworking. 'He glanced at a paper on top of a pile on his desk. 'I understand you played a vital part in the last performance of a certain drama group? Worked day and night, it says here.' He raised his watery eyes and looked into the deceptively innocent orbs of young Todhunter. 'Be careful, my boy, of where you choose to work day and night. For in that you forecast your fate.'

The old professor was right. It was Archie's fate to replace the drudgery and delight of general practice with the drudgery and delight of provincial repertory theatre: to play hundreds of small towns at the end of endless freezing train journeys. Still, he took delight in the warm reception they might get in the smallest dingy place and relished the task of acting in everything from the plays of Demosthenes to those of Mr J.B Priestly.

The highlight of Archie's theatrical career was a year with the great actor manager Tyrone Guthrie, that lanky giant in slippers, that natural Irish aristocrat, that genius of the mundane and everyday.

In Guthrie's company Archie, albeit in very small parts, played alongside Robert Donat, whose physical beauty melted the hearts of both men and women and who was later to grace the silver screen. Years later Archie and Cora saw his film *The Count of Monte Christo* at the Priorton Hippodrome. Archie applauded long and loud and ignited the auditorium, rang with long applause for a man who, in reality, was sipping new-fangled cocktails thousands of miles away in California.

In Guthrie's company, as in others, it was Archie's technical expertise that was in demand. He could now turn his hand to

62

anything: lighting, carpentry, accounts. For this he was rewarded occasionally with a second- or third-lead, usually detective inspectors or horny-handed labourers. The reviews of his performances - there were always reviews - tended to condemn him with faint praise. Guthrie certainly spotted in Archie the coarser, down-to-earth qualities of his common Glasgow mother and saw it as a lode to mine, especially in these days of more realistic theatre.

When the company stayed in one place for a whole season Archie always sought an opportunity in the local community to make a social contribution. He ran theatre -workshops, put on modest plays (which he wrote himself) with local youngsters. These had to be staged in the afternoons or early evenings so he could get back to the theatre. Guthrie was loud in his praise of Archie for this work and in the end went with him to attend a final rehearsal.

That day as they walked back to the theatre the sharp fen wind licked towards them through the side-streets, treating them to the stench of garbage, old food and barely transformed human waste.

Tyrone Guthrie wound his long scarf more tightly round his neck and pulled down the wide brim of his hat. 'Teaching, Todhunter! I can see that that's your true bent. What wonders you worked with those benighted people! Any eye could see it. You have indeed brought a shine to their lives! We, mere players...' He paused, allowing the power and admiration rise into his voice from his elongated body. '... *mere players* are weaklings by comparison. Can't think why you don't go for it hell for leather, Todhunter. Go for the full thing, old boy. Give up this precarious, silly, illusory existence. Turn aside from this bumpy road on which we walk. Give it up! Go! Do the thing you were born to. Help those poor people. Teach them! Show them!'

The muscles in Archie's neck stiffened with the effort not to cry. For nearly a year he'd waited, watched and learned from this great man. He had treated him with an attention close to idolatry. He had learned so much and offered every fibre of himself in return. Now his idol was casting him to one side like the discarded peel of an orange. 'Give it up?' he said hoarsely.

'More to the world than the theatre, dear boy...' Tyrone began.

Liar! said Archie to himself. Bloody liar! *He* lives for the theatre. *He* would die without it. *He* knows it's the only thing. The only thing. Inside the long sleeves of his coat Archie's hands knuckled up into fists. He coughed. 'You might just be right, Tony,' he said brightly, using the intimacy of that name for the first time. 'You might just be right. I do like working with those youngsters. Bringing light to their eyes. Giving them hope for the future.'

This speech, thrown off so very lightly, was the finest piece of acting he had ever achieved. He'd been graceful. He had been modest. He had to retrieve what he could.

Tony Guthrie slapped him on the back. 'Good man, Archie.'

Archie noted that he returned the compliment of the friendly Christian name. 'Play to your strengths, play to your strengths dear boy.'

So, Archie noted, my acting is my weakness. Thank you very much.

At that moment their roads divided and Guthrie went loping off. Archie looked after the hurrying figure and contemplated his future bereft of the urgent glamour, the tarnished dreaming of the theatre.

The thought came to him that here he was, at thirty, embarking on a career not unlike his father's. There would be no God or gospel of course, no wise Chinese eyes. But for him, like his father, the greatest satisfaction would be to bring light where there had been darkness; to bring The Word where there had been silence.

8. Cora

Cora Miles had turned up at The Settlement two days after Archie took possession of the building: a large place, originally a pair of houses on Queen Street in Brack's Hill, donated by a charitable tobacconist who had moved to Durham City.

Archie had been working at the house on his own, unloading several vans of theatrical kit that he'd begged, borrowed and stolen from people of goodwill up and down the country. Inside the house two men were converting two smaller front rooms to one larger room. Men out the back were converting outhouses to workshops. Painters and plasterers sloshed away upstairs. All this industry gave Archie cause to smile: for the time being at least he counted as a one-man revival of the dire employment statistics in this town.

In a smaller room downstairs he moved three boxes to get at the table which would be his desk and sat there surveying the bustle and the boxes from which he would conjure his kingdom here in Brack's Hill. There was no denying it. He was pleased with himself. Two short stints in Wales doing youth workshops; a hard working year at Toynbee Hall in London before this project had fallen into his lap. A philanthropic trust had commissioned him to survey of the Northern Coal Field to find the place that would most benefit from their considerable investment. His two months survey had led him to choose this place. As he told the man from the Trust, he relished a challenge.

There was a hard knock on the door, before a confident hand immediately pushed it open. Archie stood up.

A tall, elegant, faintly ugly woman came to stand before him. She shook him by the hand. 'Cora Miles,' she said. 'I'm staying here in Brack's Hill and the woman I'm staying with told me what you were doing here and I thought I'd come to help.'

He cocked and eyebrow.

She went on. 'I've done ten years in Rep and have a good Socialist conscience. And I have lots of energy.' She looked around. 'Which you seem to need around here. 'She paused. 'You don't recognise me do you?'

Archie held up a protesting hand. 'Stop! Stop! Sit down will you, and get back your breath?' He surveyed the Amazon figure; the over-defined face with its carmined lips. He shook his head. Then to his alarm she stood straight, closed her eyes and opened them and at once seemed taller, narrower. Her eyes glittered. *The quality of mercy is not strained/It droppeth as the gentle rain from heaven/Upon the place beneath…*'

She was a statuesque Portia to be sure. And there was authority in her tone, implicit power in her stance. She had an old-fashioned theatrical delivery but Archie thought she was not bad, not bad at all.

'Brighton,' he said, smiling slightly. '1928. The Goodwill Players."

She stopped declaiming and her red mouth split into a wide smile. 'Right!' she said. 'Tony Guthrie lent you to us to do the lights when our electrician did a bunk with the juvenile lead. A boy at that! Guthrie said you were a wizard.'

That 'lending' had been the first time Guthrie had made an excuse to get rid of Archie, but not the last. Now he stared at her, his heart sinking. So there was to be no such thing as a fresh start. How could he come here to be the big impresario when this woman knew of his humiliation? 'I don't know...' he said.

'Saved our bacon, you did. We couldn't have gone on without you. You were the quiet angel. We all talked about you afterwards.'

He breathed more easily. 'Sit down Miss... er...'

'Miss Cora Miles. Née Wilkinson. But I thought that wouldn't look so good on a poster.'

'So what makes you want to work in this...?'

'Dark place? It's very dark isn't it? Stones nearly black. At least that's true of those you see from the bus.'

'Well, what makes you want to work here?'

'Let's see. I broke my arm, went to hospital, and when I looked up the Goodwill Players had got a second female lead and left me behind.'

'A bit extreme.'

'Well I did break my arm when I threw a left hook at the manager. He bounced off the stage.'

'Have you got a very bad temper Miss Miles?'

'Me? Gentle as a lamb, Archie. But that heel was trying to get into my …er… favours and wouldn't take no for an answer. So I socked him.' She surveyed her red enamelled fingers. 'Good riddance to bad rubbish, I say.'

'So they left you behind. A bit short of goodwill, eh?'

She laughed. 'That's it.'

'Still, how have you ended up here?'

'Well. I was out of cash as well as goodwill, so I came to visit an old friend who's a teacher up here. Fancied a free bed and a bit of a think to be truthful. My friend lives with a brother who's a Labour councillor. He told me what you were up to and said it was just up my street.' She looked round. 'You have a lot on your plate here.'

'So I have.' He'd no idea what to do with this woman. It was like being in the same room as a kitten the size of a leopard.

'I can help you,' she said. 'I want to help you.

'We're working here on an absolute shoestring.'

'Doesn't this Trust thing pay a housekeeping allowance? A place this size. Do you pay teachers?'

'Well, there *is* an allowance…'

'Right then. I'll do that for you. Work for a pittance. And I can help out with some English and Drama. Started out doing that in a school. Teaching! Deadly dull.'

He gave in. Here was a decision made for him. There were a hundred more important decisions he'd have to make. He leaned forward and offered her a cigarette. She picked it up with delicate carmined fingers and held while he fiddled with his lighter. He lit the cigarette; she inhaled and spoke as the smoke drifted from her mouth. 'So. I don't cost much and you will save me from the living death of the classroom.'

'There is an allowance,' he repeated.

'Good,' she said. 'Now, would there be somewhere to stay, here? My friend would keep me but her brother is dropping hints like bricks. Jealous, if you ask me. Thinks he's the bee's knees and she adores him. Funny if you ask me.'

'Cora!' he said.

'Just saying,' she said.

He sat down at last, leaned back in his chair and looked at the ceiling. 'There are a whole lot of rooms above, on the next three floors. The place rambles around over two original houses. The rooms one the first floor'll be for Settlement things. I'll have the rooms above them. There are two rooms above that.' Doubt crept back into his voice. 'I thought a housekeeper…'

'Done!' she leaned over and shook the hand which had no cigarette. 'The room then, and how much did you say you will pay me?'

In his peripatetic life Archie had been friendly and occasionally functionally intimate with women but he'd never hit it off seriously with just one woman. The truth was that for him the most glamorous people had been the men: actors like Jack Tarrant and Robert Donat; managers like Tyrone Guthrie. To him the women had seemed much lesser players. Even Flora Robson who'd had this thing with Guthrie and was said to be a great actress, was unbearably plain and demure out of role. It was the men, still with the fragments of makeup, their lashes still black with kohl, who seemed to Archie to be the peacocks. Of course this added to the power in the roles these men played; for Archie it made them overwhelmingly glamorous.

And when he looked into a cracked dressing room mirror and surveyed his own browned skin and his own kohled eyes Archie even found himself glamorous. This was so, even if he were playing some boring manservant or agricultural worker who came on in the third act. His fellow students, when he funked Edinburgh, had clubbed together and bought him a box of stage make up. The very best quality. He still had it. He still loved any excuse to use it.

The truth was he could not quite work this man-woman thing out. Perhaps it was because women, especially actresses, wore makeup all the time; they lacked the glamour of the men who only made up for the drama. He liked women well enough for conversation and the occasional pillow fight but, for him, they were never as attractive as the men were, at that moment when they were poised, ready to tread the boards.

'Mr Todhunter?' The woman in front of him dragged him

back from his reverie. 'Is that it then?'

He smiled slightly. 'That's it! You can go and get your luggage.'

Her curls bounced as she shook her head. 'No need. They're outside your kitchen door.'

So this was how Cora Miles came to be part of the Settlement. She had stayed by his side since those early days. She'd done everything, from moving and sorting boxes, dragging furniture, teaching classes, building sets, sewing costumes, making dinners and finally, ultimately, warming Archie's bed at night.

In his most frustrated moments Archie was irritated by Cora's assurance, her possessiveness and - it had to be faced - her highly studied vulgarity. But he was too shrewd to pursue his frustration. In his most lucid moment he knew he couldn't have made the Settlement a success without Cora Miles, although it was he who received the accolades and the growing fame for this trail-blazing project.

The Settlement was his fate, his mission, as surely as his mother's mission was in that village up the Yangtze. Was it the Yangtze? He couldn't quite remember now. His dreams of his mother in her coolie hat were fading. They were not even revived when he read, in *The Times*, of her murder by anti-Christian Chinese. The Times made her out to be quite the heroine. He was happy about that.

9. Father and Son

It seems that I've spent much of my life being angry with my father. Or, more properly, it seems that I've spent much of my life with him being angry with me. And today I'm spitting mad at him. I am white-hot-angry with him; angrier that he ever was with me. How dare he? How dare he do this to me? I'll burn in hell before I forgive him for this: what he has done to me today.

No work on so I've been out of doors all day. I took a bottle of water and walked through the woods towards the heap by Whote Leas Pit, now closed and sealed. Poking around as I go, I find a nest of a long-tailed tit (all camouflaged with lichen) and some starling and blackbird nests with eggs. I don't bother to take one. My egg collection was complete by the time I was fourteen and I wouldn't take eggs for the sake of taking them.

The farmer whose field edges onto the wood is cutting hay and leaving it on the field in swathes like sleeping green snakes. The air is full of the scent of cut hay. In the woods the bluebells and yellow aconites line up in ragged regiments among the juniper and the ash trees. I wish now I had my paint box in my pocket. I draw outside but I've never yet dared to paint in the open, where you can be seen.

Nudging around my mind is the familiar feeling of guilt at the fact that I'm out here in the light of day. Although these days me and my father have to live on garden stuff and our fire is made from pit heap gleanings, I still feel good. Here I am out in the daytime light, my eyes drowning in the colours of late spring.

Foreshift time. I should be down there in the dark.

I circle around and pause close the pit heap where I scavenge a few more lumps of coal and a near-perfect fossil of a dragonfly. I realise that the woman is around again but I ignore her and move on. She's leaning with her back to a tree, drawing in a small book. I know now from talking to Tegger just who this woman is: she is the foreign artist from the Settlement.

I've not bothered with her after that first challenge. I can't be fashed with the disturbance she brings to my world on the slag-heap. So I've avoided her by going further on from the heap, around behind the pit buildings.

I'm a long time away from my house. This hardly matters, as there's little to return to there, except for my father's sullen looks. It's dusk when I finally make my way home, through the back gate and down the yard. The back door is open but the house is empty. In the kitchen although the ashes are warm the fire is dead. I stir the ashes, get a scrap of kindling and relight the fire with the coals I've brought from the tip. Like most pitmen I cannot bear a house without a fire, summer or winter.

By the time I've got the fire raked and set it's dark outside. My father's still not home. This never happens. He gets home with coming of dark every day, as there's no light down the allotments, not in his little clapboard hutch nor those of any of the men. You can't garden by candlelight, after all.

Stewing more with resentment towards him than worry about him I go into the cupboard by the fire and rake out his old pit lamp. It takes a bit of a fiddle to light it but I manage to get it alight. Once it's lit it exudes a scent that is all pit: coal dust, sweat, human waste. For a second my brain fills with dark fear. I shake it off and set off up to the allotments.

As I pass the windows of the houses I catch the silver gleam of gaslight. Here and there light streams through an open door as well and I hear the lively rustle of laughter and talk: a sound that always calls up a kind of envy in me.

Soon I'm past the rows and the darkness moves in. The pit lamp lights my feet on their way, just as it must have lit my father's feet on his many walks in-bye in those far off days when he did work, like any normal man.

The allotments are deserted. The darkness distils the smell of chickweed and the air is filled with the uneasy rustle of stock not quite bedded down for the night.

I know something is wrong before I reach my father's patch. His hens are outside clucking and his cockerel is strutting around squawking and grumbling. They fly at me as I kick open the gate and I knee them aside. The door of his hutch is slightly ajar. I put my palm flat on it and it scrapes open across the earth floor.

Inside there's a cup on the rough table beside some broken-out plants. Scraps of white paper litter his potting table and sit on the clean earth floor like confetti.

I look around. The broken-backed chair on which he normally sits is missing. I know! Now I know. I lift my lamp to illuminate the hooks where he keeps the rope and his tools in a row against the rough wall. Like the chair, the rope is missing from the hooks.

Now I turn and run, my lamp swinging high then low to light my way. There's an oak tree at the edge of the allotment, on the far side, away from the pit wheel. This tree is old, older than Bracks Hill itself. They say it's nearly as old as Durham Cathedral. My father told me this when I was young but now, though I don't challenge him, I don't quite believe it.

I make straight for the oak tree. The light from my lamp clickers over the old chair. It has been has been kicked away and lies awkwardly on its side. I reach out to lift it and put it straight. Then I look upwards. I can barely make out the figure which hangs there still and very lumpish, hanging from a stout branch.

'You bugger! Your bugger! You fucking stupid old man!' Underground words bubble from my mouth. My eyes are blind with angry tears. I drag the chair across, climb onto it and try to hold him up, to take the tension off the rope. The rope jerks. His face swings towards me and I fall back. This is the face of a dead man staring and swollen, his tongue thick in his mouth. Relief flashes through me. This doesn't look in the least like my father.

But the stuff beneath my hands is my father's jacket. The swinging boots, with their pattern of segs and studs, are his old boots. I place his feet back up on the chair and he slumps over, not swinging any more, just wedged between the chair and the tree: some inanimate thing.

Then I climb into the branches of the tree and cut him down with the knife I always keep in my pocket to cut the kindling. I kneel beside him and loosen the cruel knot. Somehow I hold him in my arms and whisper my hatred of him for this betrayal. How dare he do this thing to me? But I hold him close as any mother and rock him as though he really is my exhausted child.

Now my brain stops racing and allows the thought to occur that if I'd come back out straightaway to look for him, instead of fussing over the fire, I might have stopped him from doing this terrible thing.

I have to leave him. Forgetting the lamp I stumble in the dark until I find my way to Trent Street to find Tegger. He's in a van now, dossing with the other men. They live like tinkers just to get their families the dole. He gets dressed straight off, cocking an ear to my babble. 'Dead? You're sure? Naw Gabriel, it canna be true. Dead?'

'As mutton. As a doornail. I'm tellin yer!' I shout the words, scream them. I don't recognise my own voice.

He buttons his jacket and puts a soft hand on my shoulder. 'I'm sorry, old lad. Really I am.'

I shake off the hand. 'Don't know what to do,' I mutter. 'I don't know what the hell to do.'

Tegger, ever practical, takes me literally. 'We'll gan for the doctor right off, marra. And we'll take him down to the doctor's. Then....'

'No,' I say, at the door already. 'We'll get him home first. Then you can get the doctor.' I look round the bleak tent like space. 'I'll stay with him.'

My father is not so heavy in my arms: a mere bundle of frail flesh and dense bone. He's eaten like a sparrow for years, begrudging the food that passes his mouth. Tegger walks ahead of me, swinging my father's lamp, turning round occasionally to flash the light high, to illuminate a lump of wood or stone which might be in the way.

But for the weight of my dead father we might be walking in-bye on night shift.

At the house Tegger stops me from taking the cut rope properly from my father's neck. 'Naw, bonny lad. Leave it there.' His voice is tender as a mother's. 'The doctor'll need to see it.' He places a blanket right up, over my father's gaping face. 'Yer dinnet want to be seeing that, marra. Not at all.' Then he pulls me back down the stairs and sits me in chair. 'Now, bonny lad, you sit there an' I'll go and get this feller. This doctor. Now stay!' He might have been gentling a wild dog.

He puts coals on the fire that I relit nearly two hours ago and leaves me. The door clicks behind him. By the time I've watched the fire burn in and flare up again Tegger is back with the little bald doctor with the thick accent. This fellow takes a look at my father, prods his face and his neck, and makes a note in his book. 'He is dead.'

'I know that.'

'From the rope.'

'I know that too.'

'Where did this happen?'

'In the wood, just beyond the colliery.'

'You should leave him there so I can see.'

'Aye. And you'd think I'd leave my father hanging from a tree like a common felon? Naw. I cut him down and brought him home.'

'Well. Well.' He sucks his very fat lips. I notice he has pyjamas under his long tweed coat. 'I will need to see the site tomorrow in the light. The tree.'

'I'll tek yer there' says Tegger. 'I'll tek yer.'

'No. The son must come. He found his father. I will need him to tell how that was. Now we will go to the police station to report this.' He turns to me. 'You should have gone straight to the police,' he says. 'They will not like this.'

The next day, along with the doctor and the policeman, we tramp back down to the allotments. All the fellows from the allotment are there. They're about their business with the spade and the fork, sure enough, but as we pass they take off their caps and greet me without looking into my eyes.

'Now, Gabriel, bad business.'

'Aye it is.'

'Now Gabriel. A bad day, this!'

'Aye, it is.'

Some greetings are no more than grunts, but there is sympathy and fellow-feeling even in that sound. My father's old marra Stevie is my father's' place his putting water and grain out for the banty hens. 'Now, Gabriel,' he grunts. 'I hear about thee father.'

'Aye, Stevie. Thanks for seeing to the stock.'

He shakes his head and vanishes, the gate creaking gently behind him.

I show the policeman the hut: how neat it is. The scraps of white paper are like random flakes of snow sprinkled on all that neatness. The sergeant gathers these bits carefully and puts them into a used envelope that he places in his pocket. We make a weary procession, threading our way through the allotment paths, past the colliery and up towards the oak tree. At the clearing the sergeant examines the cut rope very carefully and writes things in his notebook with a licked pencil. Just beyond the line of trees a band of hawk-eyed children like birds in a row watch us carefully.

'We'd better have this down,' says the sergeant. 'Or that lot'll be playing hangman....' he coughed. 'Sorry lad. Not too delicate, that.'

Back at the house he makes his way up the narrow stairs with the doctor. Tegger and I, drinking thick sweet tea below, hear the rumble of their voices above. The fire burns merrily in the black grate.

When the doctor and the sergeant come downstairs they refuse Tegger's offer of a cup of tea and stand uncomfortably on my grandma's clip-mat whose rising golden sun is slightly dusty now. The doctor has replaced his pyjamas with a much-creased three-piece suit. I bet when he takes if off at night it stands up with the shadow of his shape inside it. Even his shoes are creased, standing there on my grandma's clip mat.

He looks at me through thick glasses. 'No doubt, I very much fear, that your father is hanged.'

'I know that,' I mutter.

The sergeant says. 'We need to be sure that your father did it to himself, Gabriel.' He takes the envelope from his pocket and tips out the scraps of paper on the table. 'Bit of a jigsaw, this.'

I move beside him and we spread the pieces out. It takes us thirty minutes to get the pieces in some kind of order. Then the words jump out at me, scrawled across the paper is my father's immaculate hand. '*God I ask thee is this all I am to have? If so then it is not sufficien*t.'

'This writing?' says the sergeant, gently enough. 'Is it his?'

'Aye,' I say. 'Look in the Bible on the shelf. He used to copy bits, when he was still bothering with life.' I leaf through the Bible and find the policeman a marked passage: some miserable stuff from the Book of Job.

The doctor and the policeman compare the writing and nod their heads. The policeman returns the paper scraps to his creased brown envelope. 'There'll be an inquest,' he says. 'But I think....'

The doctor nods and the two of them leave. We can hear their voices still rumbling as they walk down the yard: rough against smooth; rough against smooth.

'Why, you bugger!' says Tegger.

I look up at him wearily. 'What's that?'

'That pair thowt somebody'd done that to your old feller. Done him in. Mebbe even you. That you'd done it!'

'Well they was wrong, wasn't they? He did it to himself. Anyone can see that. Wanted a get out. Stupid bugger.'

Tegger comes and puts an arm round my shoulder. 'Come on, Gabe. Sit down here. I'll sit with you.' Then he goes across and draws the curtains.

I hear him moving round the house closing curtains in all the rooms. It's our custom to close curtains when we have the dead in the house. I remember we did this when my mother and my baby brother died. And then, when my grandma died.

Now Tegger comes and sits beside me, shoulder to shoulder in the darkness. Only the flicker of fire tells me we're not fifty fathoms below the earth, sitting on a block of wood waiting to go out-bye, back into the light.

10. Under Siege

In the days after his father's funeral Tegger couldn't get Gabriel to come out of the house at all. He called three times and each time Gabriel shouted through the locked door for him to go away. The fourth time Gabriel let him in. His hair was rough and he blinked like a pit pony coming into the light.

The house was awash with Gabriel's drawings and paintings. These were pinned on chairs and cabinets, on walls and curtains. Every painting and drawing that Gabriel had done since he was eight or nine was on display in the narrow house. Tegger realised that his friend was saying 'This is me!' in defiance of his father who'd never been comfortable about his son's soft habit of drawing all the things he saw. *What good were such things? The workings of a marshmallow mind.* The old man's thoughts trembled all around them in the room, in defiance of the rough papers and boards pinned around the room.

'Hey Gabe, these really all yours?' said Tegger, almost too heartily. 'They're bloody good.'

Gabriel shrugged.

Tegger blinked hard for a second to shut out the misery he saw in the other boy's eyes. 'I've told you before haven't I? You need to go to this drawing group the German woman runs at the Settlement, Gabe. They like her, the lads down there. She's got some of them framing their pictures. They're hung up about the place. Like real pictures they are. But none of them is as good as yours here. Some are not even as good as those you did when you were a kid. But this one...And this one. Great, man! You should get yoursel' down the Settlement. Fool if you don't. They have paints there. Easels. The whole kit. There's this artist woman, like I say, working there. And there's plays with actors to teach you. And there's this queer feller that's running it. He ralks about the famous playwrights like they were his best marras. George Bernard Shaw he calls GBS. Can yer credit it? Bliddy Communist, shouldn't wonder. But he is really a very canny feller. Get yerself down there, man! Better that than going crazy in this hole.'

Gabriel rubbed his hands over his tired eyed. 'Will yeh go now, Tegger? Leave it will yeh? Leave us alone.'

That knocking on the door is too loud. Too loud altogether Tegger again. I wish he'd leave it. I shake the sleep from my eyes, push my fingers through my hair and open the door. But it's not Tegger. It's my Aunt Susannah, clutching a brown paper parcel, and her husband, Jonty Clelland.

'Gabriel?' she says. 'We've been away in Glasgow but we heard about Matthew and are come to say we are sorry for your sadness.' The Welsh lilt of her childhood is still in her voice. 'A terrible thing it is… We were away, and when we came back… '

I stand there, sleep ridden, unshaven and stare at her. I must smell like a stoat. She peers past my shoulder into the dark kitchen behind me. 'Perhaps we could come in?'

I stand back and feel a flutter of shame as they stand helplessly on the fireside mat, unable to find a place to sit. My aunt shivers. 'No fire, Gabriel? Cold day, it is…'

I stare helplessly at the dead fire. 'It went out.'

Jonty Clelland takes off his jacket. 'Now then,' he says. 'I'll light the fire while you two... well… talk.'

She opens the brown paper parcel and places a book on the table. It is smaller than the Rembrandt book and has etchings rather than colourplates. She opens it at two prints: one of ship foundering in a storm at sea, one on landscape, called *The Deluge*.

'Turner!' she says. 'The master of light!'

I peer closer to see dark prints in shades of black and white. They could be drab but the pure white light at the centre of the deluge on one and the edge of the sinking boat lit by the beam of an spproaching rescue vessel – these flash out at me reminding me of the impact of light in the Goaf. 'Turner!' I say. 'Never heard of him.'

'But now I see you know Mr Rembrandt.' Susanah looks around the room at the rough drawings that I've pinned to the walls, on the front of the press and above the fireplace. 'I didn't realise you'd done so much, Gabriel. You kept it up, I see.'

'You gave me that book, remember? Rembrandt.' I nod at the battered, fingered book propped up on the press. 'I've used that. Looked at it, and thought about how he did things. He's a clever man."

Despite the Rembrandt book we're not close, Aunt Susannah and I. And I know little of Jonty Clelland, now kneeling by my fireplace. This second husband is carefully raking out the fire ashes that have been there since the day my father hanged himself, was a conchie: some say beneath contempt. But he doesn't lack courage. There was a do, a year back where he took on the local Blackshirts. It was in the papers.

'Gabriel? Gabriel,' her sharp voice brings me back to myself. 'I said how were you doing for work?'

'Work? Are you having me on? There is no work round here,' I say. 'I was one of the last to lose work when the drift mine closed. And there's no work for anyone in Bracks Hill or White Leas.'

She peers at a drawing pinned to the back wall; this is a picture that I drew from memory, of a miner crawling in a narrow seam. 'You're very good,' she sighs. 'I wish I'd kept up my drawing.' She glances at Jonty Clelland's back. 'But there is so much to do.'

He looks up at her. 'You can draw, Susanah. You know you can draw as much as you like.' He stands up, balancing a bucketful of ash in his hand. He's staring at her, frowning.

She smiles at him. 'I know Jonty, love. I know that. It's all right, Jonty. Get that fire done now, will you?' She turns to me. 'Jonty was saying there's a really good art class at the Settlement. There's a German artist there. She's very good. Archie Todhunter sings her praises.' She looks round at the drawings and rough paintings hanging in the room. 'You'll get more inspiration,' she said. 'You'll develop into the artist you can be.'

I look again at work which now seems dark and tawdry. Picture after picture of men underground. Some of the images are almost facsimiles of each other. I can see that I am saying the same thing time and again. 'These are rubbish,' I say. 'A lot of rubbish. Me father called them *rubbish*. He hanged himself to be rid of the sight of them. And me.'

She puts her hand on my arm. 'Now, Gabriel, sorry for yourself, is it? We'll have none of that. I tell you what. Let's you and me go in the scullery and clear that mess up. By that time Jonty'll have the fire well away and we can have a cup of tea....'

'I....' I say. I put a hand up, almost fending her off. 'There's no tea.'

She burrows in her bag. 'You've no tea? Well lucky it is I've brought some. And scones from the Co-op.' She laughs. 'Bought cakes. Aren't I shameless?'

It's nearly an hour before we manage to sit down and eat the scones and drink the tea. By now I am soothed by the calm presence of these two. I look across at my Aunt. 'You yourself should go and learn off this woman.' I say. 'Take it up again yourself.'

She shakes her head. 'No. That'd not do, Gabriel. Jonty and I have other fish to fry.'

I look across at the man closely for the first time. He looks quite a bit older than her, his eyes are netted with fine wrinkles, his curly hair is thinning. 'I heard they put you in prison over that do with the Mosley men,' I say to him.

'So they did, son, but I survived.' His voice is modulated like the schoolteacher he used to be.

'D'you still teach in school, like?'

He shakes his head. 'They don't want jailbird-schoolteachers,' he says cheerfully. 'Been sacked more than once.'

'Jonty himself puts in a bit of teaching for free at the Settlement here. Where the German woman does the art.'

'What do you teach there?' I say it for something to say.

Jonty shrugs. 'I teach some folk to read, who never could. They have time now. A bit of history, decent stuff about the Chartists and Cromwell.'

I remember now that years ago he was sacked for all that conchie stuff, even before the Great War. And here he is, sacked again from a job that was a thousand times easier than hewing coal. He doesn't look like a revolutionary. Mild faced and lightly boned in his shiny black suit, you'd have taken him for a down-at-heel-preacher, or indeed a poor schoolteacher.

Later, I see the two of them out of the house and watch them make their way down the narrow back street. Within six steps she has put her arm through his and is looking up at him, smiling and talking away twenty to the dozen.

I pass slowly through my tidied scullery into the tidier kitchen with its bright fire and sit in my father's seat by that fire.

Now I'm floored reflecting on that linking of arms, that intimacy. I suddenly remember my mother quite clearly. She comes to me again out of the mists. I remember how she tucked my hand in hers on the way to the chapel. How she spit on her hankie to scrub my face outside the school gates on that first day of school.

But still I cannot remember her enjoying any tender moment with my father. In none of my young years did I see a gesture between them as tender as my Aunt Susannah putting her arm through Jonty Clellands's as they walked down in our back street.

11. The Good Teacher

'You see?' The teacher Rosel Vonn leans forward; her pencil moving swiftly across the paper. 'Dark to light dark to light. We represent the forms of objects on the flat surface of this paper.'

I recognise again the woman from the White Leas slag heap. Her putty coloured hair hangs down in a loose plait down her back and she's wearing a course linen smock daubed with flecks and spots of colour.

Trying not to make it obvious I lean back half-sideways so I can see the still life, a tall water jug and the small kettle taking shape on the paper beneath her hand. The background recedes. The objects bloom into three dimensions on the page. For me this is familiar magic. I am quietly pleased that I already know how to do this without her instruction.

She sits cross the wooden school chair as if it were a horse. Beneath her smock I can see the fine serge of her skirt pulled taut across her knee. 'There you see?' she is saying to the man beside her. 'You lift them out of the darkness.' She unpins her own drawing from the easel to expose again the stiff, honest effort of the middle-aged pitman beside her. 'You see?' she says. 'The truth is that nothing has an outline. The outline grows from the depths that you dig out with your shading. You make the shape with the transition from light to dark. Do you see? You may think you see the outline but really it doesn't exist. Not truly. Do you see? No outlines.' Her tone was quite severe.

'Aye. I see, missis.' He says meekly and moves to unpin his own sheet from the easel. She puts a slender hand on his. 'No. No! You do not need to start again.'

'Aye, missis. I do. This is like a bairn's drawing. Just look at it,' he says. I can see what he means. He turns the paper over and re-pins it on the other side. 'If what you say's right that thing's beyond retrieval. Beyond retrieval. It's all outlines.' Then he turns away from her and peers closely at the jug and kettle, narrowing his eyes. His heavy jaw is set like granite.

Now the teacher drags her chair to the next man who is painting, at her suggestion, from a limited palette: Flake White, Raw Umber, Black and Yellow ochre. From the other side of the room I hear her tentative suggestions to this man. I see the section of the man's painting grow under this new instruction; I watch his as his frowning concentration increases a hundred-fold.

She has circled the room twice and had still not approached me at all. I don't know whether I want her to or nor. I try to forget about her, stretch right back in my chair and half close my eyes to increase the perspective in my drawing.

****

It was really my Aunt Susanah who got me here to the Settlement. Tegger thinks it's him, so I haven't disabused him. Tonight when he finally pushed me through the door I took one look at the set piece, the tall jug with the kettle beside it standing before a drape of rough cloth, and almost walked straight back out again. I had such object lessons at school and just loathed them. Still, my mind was changed by the fine smell of linseed and the sight of the seductive pile of high quality paper on the side table, which also held a thick pot jar full of sharpened pencils. I've never drawn on such fine paper, I've had never handled pencils like that. So I followed the actions of some of the other men; pinned the paper to a board and selected three pencils: an H, an HB, and a 3B.

The drawing that grows under my hand is not a delicate in-depth study of the jug and the kettle so carefully arranged before us on the stool. It's the inside of a garden shed, lit by a stream of light through the window: every detail is there. The spade and fork stand against the wall; a pile of jam-jars, broken plants and a bucket are scattered on a rough bench. From the hook on the wall hangs an old coat with gaping pockets and creases at the elbow where the wearer's arm bent a hundred times to dig the earth and plant leeks or seed potatoes. Its pockets bulge with stones, ancient unplanted seeds and the hairy string that he used to tie up last year's runner beans. From a hook beside the door a heavy rope snakes against the wall, its end fashioned into a noose.

The teacher circles the room again, watching the drawers and painters, talking to them briefly or sitting beside them, drawing swiftly as she talks. Twice she circles behind me and twice I tense up, waiting for her comment. Each time she passes me without a single word.

Then she settles by her own board and draws swiftly, building a wall of concentration around her. And I forget her and become absorbed again, relishing the fine paper, the dense impact of pure graphite on its flawless surface. After so many years drawing on waste cardboard and flattened sugar bags this is heaven.

So between them Tegger and my Aunt Susanah have got me here into to this dingy room with half a dozen other fellows who have a bit of skill in drawing. I know I'm good. Better than any of these fellows here. But you wouldn't think that for the attention I'm getting. The German woman's taken no more notice of me than if I were a block of wood. If it weren't for the decent paper and the new pencils, I wouldn't have stayed. Even they aren't worth being treated like a block of wood. This is the last time I'll come here. Paper or no paper.

She's off her chair now, on the other side of the room, talking to a fellow about warm tones and dark tones. I unpin my own picture, roll it up and put it inside my coat. Her head goes up.

She knows what I'm doing. But still she goes on demonstrating the need for a warm highlight on the edge of the kettle.

The man sitting beside the teacher peered across the room. 'What's up with young Gabe?' he said. 'Marchin' off like that?'

The man who had been sitting next to Gabriel said. 'The young feller? Rolled up his drawing and went off.'

'Mebbe he thinks he's not any use,' said the other man.

'Good enough but he weren't drawing the right thing, was he?' said the man who had watched young Gabriel Marchant at his easel. 'Some jumble from down his old man's shed. I bought eggs from the old feller one time. But you should have seen his drawing. Gabe had that shed there to the last nail, the last knothole, the last sunbeam.'

Rosel Vonn went back to put the finishing touches to her own drawing.

'Gabriel Marchant!' said the first man. 'Queer business, that, about his father.'

'What was that?' said Rosel Vonn suddenly. 'His father?'

They looked across at the art teacher in surprise.

'Why, hinny, the old man hanged himself, didn't he?' said the first man. 'Out of his mind, they reckon. More'n one feller done that, with there being no work and bairns going hungry. No wonder he was down. I'm tellen yer.'

Rosel closed her eyes for a second. 'How terrible,' she said. She thought of herself and her own bad times in Germany after the Great War when she had cut herself and made her blood run to relieve her own pain. She busied herself gathering pencils inot an old OXO tin.

'Aye, terrible enough,' said the first man. Then the two men turned away from the topic, following an old habit of pitmen not dwelling on death: it was such a certainty in their lives that to focus on it us seen as an unholy waste of time.

Archie Todhunter, who was packing up his own things after a pleasant time daubing at a very passable image of the still life, looked up at Rosel Smidt. 'I thought the boy's drawing was quite fine,' he said. 'It seems to me that the boy needs a bit of encouragement. Don't you think so, Rosel? You said nothing to him.'

'I have worked to do,' she said stiffly. 'He is ill-mannered. I meet him outside and he is very ill mannered.'

Archie caught up with Gabriel by Trent Street. 'In a bit of a hurry to get off, my lad?' he said breathlessly. He'd had top run to catch up. 'One minute you were there, the next you weren't.'

'Nowt in it for me, sir,' said Gabriel looking down at him. 'I'm not going back.' With the light behind him all Archie could see was his face was in shadow inside a halo of curly hair.

'You're a good hand at drawing, son,' said Archie. 'I said so to Fraulein Vonn.' They had decided on shortening her name to Vonn, thinking that Brack's Hill people would have trouble getting their tongues round her full German name.

'Well, *she* didn't think so.' Gabriel said, wondering just who this man was, this busy body with the slicked back hair, round glasses and plummy voice.

'Others needed her more than you do, obviously. And she knows them. She's been working with them for weeks. She needs time to get to know you.'

Gabriel shrugged.

'Come one more time, Gabriel,' said Archie. 'Just try it one more time.'

Gabriel shrugged again. 'If it bothers yeh, sir. One more time.' And he turned on his heel and walked away.

My next time in the class is all too short. The single bulb is not enough to compensate for the fading external light which is barely making it through the dusty skylight. Someone has taken off the shade off to make the light better.

People in the room grumble, then the teacher takes off her glasses and glances around at everyone except me. 'Well, if you wish, next week we can meet at two instead of four. That will give us in more hours of daylight.'

I am frustrated by this. The light in here even now is better than at home where the gas throws off a bluish shade and drowns the colour so that it's not true.

Obediently we collapse our easels and stack them in the corner cupboard. They are crude things, joiner-made, but they certainly do the job. I go to the pegs to get my coat, pull it on, roll up my picture and put it in my inside pocket. When I turn round the teacher has gone. The bile within me rises so high I can taste it.

The man who stopped me in the street is locking the cupboard. I realise now he must be the boss. This Archie Todhunter that they talk about. 'Go and talk to Miss Vonn, son. Go after her,' he says. 'If you feel like that about her, go and tell her.'

By the time I get to the outside door she's many yards away. My boots spark as I crash along the pavement. I nearly trip over the sprawling legs of two men who are on their haunches outside the tobacconists.

'Watch it, man, will yeh?' One of them looks at me angrily.

I catch up with the teacher on the corner. 'Hey!' I grab her arm, which she wrenches away.

She looks me in the eye. 'Do you always attack people?'

This stops me. I look down, not able to meet her eyes. 'I was not attacking anybody. Just trying to see what you're about, that's all. Why you think you're too good to talk to … to … people.'

'Well Mr.. .'

'Marchant. Gabriel Marchant.'

'Well Mr Marchant, what I am about is what you saw in there, in the room. Painting. Drawing.'

'I saw you drawing on the slag heap. I saw you there in the room. You certainly know what you're about. You're good.'

'Yes, I do.' She doesn't deny it.

'But....' But I don't want to whine about her not giving me any attention. I gag up.

'You're a very good draftsman yourself Mr Marchant.' Her tinkling accent sits in the air between us.

I'm hot with embarrassment now. 'I thought yer.... you had no time for my stuff. In there, like. You never bothered to look at my... You never said nothing.' Now she'll think I'm whining and fishing for compliments at the same time.

'You seemed to be getting on fine in there on your own. You've had lessons, surely? You have style. A sense of perspective. Light. You know *light.*'

'Yeah. I did have lessons. At school, like. Not since then, though.'

'You've not drawn since you left school?'

'I didn't say that. I draw all the time, like.'

In the silence that follows I feel her withdrawing, going away from me. Then she speaks. 'Well Mr Marchant. Perhaps you'll come next Saturday? I look forward to that.' And she's away clicking along the pavement in those bobbin-heeled shoes of hers.

I stand for a second, feeling lost. I don't want to go home again, to sit in my father's chair and feel him all around me. A hand on my shoulder spins me round. 'What cheer, Gabriel? In the land of dreams, are yeh?' Tegger, slaps me on the back, makes me jump. 'I seen you talk to the German woman? I bet she thought you're some kinda genius, eh?'

'Nivver said a word. Not till just now.'

'Jealous, man, that's what she'd be. Ready to help the ignorant. Not so ready for the not-so-ignorant.' He sets off back on the way I have just come.

I feel the vacuum, the space he has left behind. 'So where you off then, marra?' I shout after him.

'I'm goin' just where you came from. I told you before. Got myself involved in the play! The feller Todhunter said I could help with his play. Hey!' He comes back and punches my shoulder. 'You come along Gabe. All hands to the plough. You can carry my nail box. You can even carry my pencil.'

'Don't be daft, man.'

'Come on! What else have you to do? What have you to lose? Come on!'

So now it seems I've got mixed up in the play. That fellow Todhunter has more tentacles than an octopus.

12. The Players

The room where they do the play is not the scruffy painting shed, but is the long space that is two rooms knocked into one. When Tegger and me get there it's crowded with twenty or so bodies sitting on hard wooden chairs set in a circle.

I know some of these people. There's Nathan Smith who was a putter once at White Leas pit; there are a couple of other pitmen whose faces I recognise but whose names I don't know. I saw them in the cage ,many a time. There's Mr Conroy, the pit joiner and McVay, brother-in-law of Mrs McVay who has the corner shop. He used to work in the hardware shop where my father got his nails. That's now closed so he must be out of work.

A couple of older women, dressed neatly in their Sunday coats and hats sit head to head, talking. The three seats under the old house window are taken up by two younger women and a girl with plaits wound round her head who's wearing a navy blue school Grammar school tunic.

In the corner near the inner door is the slender man with the round glasses who painted the clumsy still life; the one who came after me in the street. Archie Todhunter who runs this whole show. Beside him sits a heavy featured woman, wearing make up.

I've made sure Tegger and me sit by the outside door, in case I want to run.

Tegger's mouth is to my ear. 'That's Archie Todhunter, who's in charge of this whole shebang.' 'Feller with the glasses.'

'I know that. He was at the painting class, wasn't he? He's nothing of a painter. Paints like he's doing poker-work.'

'Well, mebbe that's what he does for relaxation. *This* is his thing. This play. We can't be good at everything. I'm a proper dunce at darts, but I'm a dab hand with my hammer and saw. And with my pen and my bit of paper.'

Todhunter shuffles his papers on the table and looked up over his glasses. An instant silence settles in the room. He sits as still as a foot runner at the start of a paying race. The level of concentration in the room is powerful. The people on the chairs forget about whether there's food on their table at home; whether the bairn would have to miss school on Monday; about the baby being off his food. Clearly they know their man. They focus on Archie Todhunter's face and wait.

'Well!' he says, examining our faces in the circle one by one. When he reaches us he nods at Tegger. 'Nice to see you, Tegger.' His gaze turns to me. 'Another newcomer. Are you a joiner as well as a painter? If so we are twice blessed. We'll certainly need you in this new play.'

My face is red now. Faces turn towards me. A murmur of interest flutters round the room.

'Nah,' says Tegger. 'Gabriel here's a putter. He's no joiner. But he could paint you a scene, mebbe. Dab hand with a paintbrush is Gabriel.'

'So I have observed. All the better for our play,' says Todhunter nodding.

'I didn't ....' I glance behind me towards the door, wondering how long I should stay.

But Todhunter has moved on. 'Now then.' he said. 'Our Richard III last month was very well received.'

'Except for the Priorton Chronicle,' says a small bird like man at the back. 'What does *bowdlerised* mean? It said bowdlerised.'

There are one or two lewd suggestions *sotto voce* but Todhunter waves his hand.

'It means we ... well, I ..... plucked the heart out of the play and adapted it for the little stage in the Methodist Hall. Herbert Grossmith was criticising my writing. We don't worry about Herbert Grossmith of The Chronicle, ladies and gentlemen, because he's an overwhelming ass, a big fish in a small bowl, a cockroach among ants.'

There are shouts of appreciative laughter at this.

He goes on. 'No, friends, our play was a success because in all, over the Friday and Saturday, from Bracks Hill, we had a total of a hundred and thirty people who saw our play. They appreciated the irony, wept at the tragedy and applauded you to the roof at the end. Beside this the sainted Herbert Grossmith is as a feather in the wind.'

The painted woman sitting beside Archie joins in the laughter. 'Mr Grossmith was very cross that he did not have a front row seat,' she says. 'He asked me whether I knew who he was.'

An inner door opens and we watch as the painting teacher woman comes into the room. She's changed herself now to a jersey and trousers and her hair is brushed and tied with a green ribbon close at her neck. She looks younger. Todhunter waits till she settles down and turns back to his eager audience.

'Well ladies and gentlemen I thought we might do with a change. We did the Shaw to some effect. Some of us tried out the Chekhov, which, though a wonderful play, seemed a little to much of a tangle on our tongue.

There was a murmur of rueful agreement at this.

He goes on. 'So I thought we'd try something different.'

A buzz of interest.

'It'll give Herbert Grossmith something to blather about. He'll have a field day on this,' said Archie with some satisfaction. From a battered black folder he pulls out a wadge of papers. He puts his palms underneath it and holds it towards us, like some kind of offering. 'It is called *Coal and Blood*.'

Nathan Smith calls from the back. 'So who's this one by? Mister Shaw again? Zola? You talked of the man Zola once. It was him wrote about coal. I read that. You'd think the man had spent his life underground. A writer, but...'

Archie shook his head. 'No, Mr Smith. This play is ... well ... by an unknown writer.'

'Archie won't tell you,' says the woman beside him. 'But ...'

'I wrote it myself,' says Archie gruffly. 'No doubt you'll do me the kindness of telling me where I've gone wrong. You usually do. I'm quite sure that Herbert Grossmith will be only too eager to tell me.'

'You can be sure that we'll be pretty eager ourselves,' says Nathan. The rest of them laugh loud at this.

'So what's it about? ' says Tegger, ever practical.

'It's about Coal and Blood.'

'Gan on,' says Tegger, wriggling bavck in his seat. 'Tell us the story, Mr Todhunter!'

Archie puts down his sheaf of papers and stares at us. 'Well,' he says, 'first I want you to see our stage. Stage left, a tunnel in the trenches in the Great War. A group of four men, miners-turned-soldiers, are trapped. They huddle under muddy tarpaulin. The roof of the trench bears down on their heads. The time is nineteen sixteen, bang in the middle of the Great War. Stage right, a coroner's court. Here they're investigating an explosion where nine men have been killed in a pit on the home front. On a half-height platform, stage centre, are a group of women. At some points in the play they mourn the deaths of their sons and brothers down the pit or at the Front. At some points they read the letters from their loved ones in France. They talk about the War. Some of them carry white feathers.'

'Flipping heck,' says Mr Conroy, the pit joiner. 'Three sets on one stage?'

'Stage right, sits a coroner on a dais. Before him, five chairs. It is, in miniature, a coroner's court.'

'What happens? What happens in the story?' asks the young girl with plaits.

'A very good question Greta. It is not, after all, a mere tableau.'

'Something's gotta happen,' said Tegger. 'Yeah.'

'Well what happens is, in the course of the inquest, we find out about the blast that killed these nine men underground and how the managers tried to blame it on the men, though really it's their own negligence that caused it. And the wives act as a chorus singing the praises of their menfolk and, second by second, undergo the agony of their loss.'

'What about the lads in the trench?' says McVay.

Archie Todhunter shuffles his papers. 'Now these men, from the same families, are also, by the magic of theatre, trapped by a fall in this tunnel they've been building under the German lines. They spend their time talking about the war and how it will be so much better afterwards.'

'Little did they know,' said McVay to a jeering ripple of laughter. 'A land fit for heroes! What?'

'Well, just as we learn bit by bit about the extinction of the lads in the pit, the soldiers are finally rescued by other miners, soldiers who are tunnelling towards them. They survive, for the time being at least, but the miners at home do not.'

'Cheerful sort of feller ain't yer Mr Todhunter?' says McVay.

'So, what's it really about, then?' says Nathan. 'This play.'

He's shrewd, is Nathan.

Archie Todhunter glances around us all. 'It's about sacrifice and whether it's truly worth it.'

Jonty Clelland, the *conchie*, pops into my mind.

'And we all know the answer to that,' says McVay.

'Well?' says Archie. His face is strained. I can see that he's worried as to whether they like it. The silence goes on too long.

'I think it's bloody brilliant.' The words burst out of me. 'I never heard anything like it.'

They all turn round to look at me.

'Me too,' says Tegger. I can feel his excitement. 'Ah think it's bloody brilliant. Real people. Real lives. I never knew you could write about such things.'

'Folks want cheering up, not making miserable,' said McVay gloomily. 'Misery enough out there.'

'There are jokes in it. Some of them are very funny,' says the made-up woman sitting beside Archie Todhunter.

The painting teacher speaks up. 'The set will be very interesting to make. The darkness of the trench. The polished wood of the court. The village, the pit-wheel in the background. I see it.'

'How d'yer get three stages on one, then ?' says Mr Conroy the joiner.

'Well,' says Todhunter. 'That's where you and young MacNamara come in. I thought we could have some rollers or tracks. Something like that.'

'A turntable!' says Tegger suddenly. 'Like the ones they turn the trains on, in Priorton station. Turn it round, you get the new scene.'

Mr. Todhunter's glance glitters round the circle, from one of us to the next, and to the next. He relaxes, satisfaction gleaming from his every pore. He knows he has won. 'Well?' he says. 'Is that possible? There is scaffolding to be had. I saw a set done in London which was just scaffolding. A different scene on each platform.'

Mr. Conroy nods. 'No reason why not,' he says slowly. 'Use rollers. Make a special ...'

'So we can do it?' said Todhunter.

'Don't see why not.' the man repeats.

Todhunter lets the silence sit in the room. 'Well then, shall we do it or shall we not?' he says, surveying us all again. 'Do you all want to do this?'

'Aye. Gan on,' says Nathan Smith, 'wuh'll give it a try.'

'Good,' says Todhunter. 'We'll give it a try.'

'No point in wasting all that work you've done,' says Conroy. 'Yeh must've burned the midnight oil over that, Mr Todhunter.' He nods towards the battered black folder,

'You're sure there are some jokes in it?' says Tegger.

Todhunter nods towards the made up woman who is now handing out wadges of paper to each person. I look down at my sheets and try to hand them on to Tegger. 'I'm not ....' I say.

The woman puts a hand on mine. Her nails have polish on them. 'Keep it,' she says. 'You never know. It's all hands on deck here.'

Todhunter glances at a sheet in his hand. 'Nathan! I thought you could be the coroner. Mr McVay, I thought you could be the corporal in the trench ....' He goes on, giving out the parts with assurance. Seems like he's written the parts with many of these people in mind. He'll know their turn of phrase, the idiosyncrasies in their voices. Nathan Smith, as a lay preacher, knows how to impose his tones on the air, is the obvious choice for the coroner.

Todhunter turns to the schoolgirl. 'Now, Greta? You did such a good job last time that I've written this especially for you. You'll be Dorothy, whose father was killed in the explosion and whose sweetheart Arthur is in the trench, afraid for his life but putting a brave face on it.' His eye moves round the circle and finally settles on me. My collar is suddenly too tight. 'Perhaps you could take the part of Arthur, Gabriel? You're the only one here young enough as far as I can see. Apart from Tegger and he's going to very busy building the set.'

I shake my head so hard my cap comes off, and I have to scrabble on the floor to get it back. 'No. No. I'm just here..... I said I'd help Tegger with the joinery, the painting.'

Even that was more than I'd thought when I came in. Why on earth did I agree? What am I doing?

Todhunter rubs his head with his hand. 'Oh. What a pity. Perhaps you would just read the lines today? Till we get someone else?'

Tegger nudges me. 'Gan on, Gabe' he says. 'Nowt to lose.'

I blow a very long sigh and keep my head down.

'Very well.' Todhunter is obviously satisfied. He turns to the painted woman. 'Now, Cora here will read Mrs Olliphant, who is the most ....er.....opinionated of the women and I will read Mr Jerry Molloy who, as the mouthpiece of the coal company, is the villain of the piece.' He turns to the painter 'Fraŭlein Vonn …......' he said.

The painting teacher shakes her head firmly. I wish I had her resolve. 'Absolutely not Mr Todhunter. I will help you in every other way, but no, I will not climb on the stage and be an English woman. Is impossible. *Unmöglich.*'

People shuffle in their seats as the German world echoed hollowly in the room.

'Well there were Belgian refugees here in England the War I thought ….' Archie Todhunter stares at her for a moment. You can see his tactlessness dawning on him. 'Well perhaps you will listen hard and tell us of anything you think might make it better.'

Then, with a few false starts, we embark on the reading. It's hard to read and have to concentrate to bring to mind the movement between the coroner's court, the trench, and the cluster of women. This is hard to do just as we are sitting here in our circle. But as the reading becomes more assured, the characters so cunningly dreamed up by Todhunter start to rise up in the room between us. The sense of the arguments which lie there like bombs underneath the lines begin to infect us.

Nathan Smith becomes measured and magisterial, Todhunter combative, McVay quick, choleric and soldierly. Cora Miles is strident, bitter, euphoric and mournful in turn as her lines demand. Even I find my voice breaking with Arthur's terror then becoming stronger again as Arthur thinks of his father's courage down the pit. This tragedy in the trenches is no worse than his father's plight in the pit. He sees that.

I see it.

When the reading has finished, we all sit back, somehow drained. Funny that, as it's only been words. No action at all.

'So,' said Todhunter. 'Is it a play?'

'Aye. It is a play all right, Mr Todhunter' says Nathan heavily. 'But it'll make folk angry, about the war and the pits, both. They'll go out sparking into the street.'

'But that's what it's about, isn't it?' I can't resist saying this. 'We've cause to be angry, all of us. This is important.'

Todhunter takes off his glasses, breathes on them one by one and polishes them on his shirtsleeve. 'So you'll do the role of Arthur then, Mr Marchant?'

'Well, ah ....'

'Gan on, Gabe, ' said Tegger.

'Yes,' I say, knowing already that I'll regret it. 'Yes, I suppose I will.'

13. Greta

I leave Tegger behind talking to Mr Conroy about the logistics of a turntable on which they may set the scenes and walk slowly out and along the street, contemplating my own folly. How have I got myself into this mess?

There is a clatter of feet in the street behind me. 'Wasn't that wonderful?' It's breathless female voice. 'Isn't Mr Todhunter wonderful?'

It's the girl who read Dorothy's part, the one they called Greta.

'What?' I'm mad at this girl. I don't know why.

'That play! Isn't Mr Todhunter clever?' She has a plain narrow face and bright snapping eyes behind round glasses. Her school Burberry is tightly belted. I can see she's no child, even if she is a schoolgirl. 'I thought you read Arthur very well, Gabriel.'

I'm nonplussed. Do you say thank you when somebody says something like that to you? 'Thanks,' I feel awkward. 'You too.'

She falls into step beside me. 'Where do you live?' she demands.

'Past Sinker's Row.'

'I'll walk with you as far as Inkerman Street,' she says firmly. 'That's where I live.'

'Well,' I say. 'I ....'

'Well what?'

'Just *well*.'

She talks on about the Settlement, about how wonderful the Richard III had been, how clever was Mr Todhunter. 'And Cora! You wouldn't believe, looking at her, but she's such a fine actress. She can be an old crone or a young girl in a blink. Makes you really believe in who she is, there on the stage.'

I wish this kid who isn't a kid would shut up. I want to think of some of the things Archie Todhunter has put into the mouth of young Arthur in the play. How glad Arthur was, to get out of the pit into the army. Like Aunt Susanah's brother, Davey. *At least way above the trenches*, Arthur says in the play, *you can see the deep blue sky.* But then he goes on about how here at the Front the digging and the tunnelling makes him think of the pit. Of course he doesn't know that their present dilemma in the caved in trench exactly parallels that situation back home with the men trapped, and killed, in the pit.

'And both our fathers die.' The voice chirrups beside me.

My father hanging from the oak tree.

'What?'

'In the play. Arthur's and Dorothy's fathers die together in the explosion. Their names are read out at the court.'

'Yes. Yes.' I wish this kid would go away. 'Which school did you say you went to?'

'Alderman Harrington. I'm in the Fifth. Top of my class in English, History, Maths. I do extra lessons in Latin and Greek and I'm doing extra lessons in German with Fraülein Vonn now. My French is not really so good.'

'That's a pity. Not speaking French must be a real problem in Bracks Hill.'

My sarcasm flows over her.

'I would be good at it. I can do anything you know. Dozy French teacher. Monsieur Mercat. He's asleep half the time. The other half he throws blackboard rubbers at you. Look at this!' She stops and I have to stop too. She puts her head up to the gaslight and lifts the heavy plait from the side of her face. There is a healed cut, still livid. 'See! Monsieur Mercat did that.'

I'm angry at this Monsieur Mercat, even though it's not my business. 'What did you do about that?'

'Two hundred lines. He gave me two hundred lines and called me an *imbecile*. That's imbecile in French.'

'Sounds nasty, him. Never met that feller. He wasn't there when I was there.'

'You were at the Alderman Harrington?'

'Aye.'

'But....'

'But what?'

'But you .... you're a .....'

115

'Pitman?'

'She flushes a very bright red. 'I'm sorry that was....'

'Stupid. Aye it was.' I say. Then I let her off the hook. 'Mebbe you're wondering why I'm not an unemployed clerk or an unemployed shop assistant, rather than an unemployed pitman?'

'Well...' she sighs. 'Yes, if you want to know.'

'I left school when I was fourteen and went down the pit. Easy as that.'

'Oh. I'm sorry.'

'Why should you be sorry?'

'Well, the pit...'

'The pit's a very special place those fathoms down in the earth. You'd never know, of course.' This finally shuts her up and we walk the rest of the way to Inkerman Street in blessed silence.

This Greta has made me think of girls. And women. The only women I've really known were my mother, my grandmother and my Aunt Susanah. And now except in flashes I cannot remember whether I actually loved my mother. But memories now have started to crowd in on me. I've close memories of her presence in the house. A certain softness and lightness. The smell of food cooking. The sight of the crown of her head with a long white parting as she bent to fasten my shoes. Sometimes I think I can feel her hand on my head, her palm so large that it covers it easily. Once this memory flashed across me, of a time when we walked along the back street to the dairy farm which butted onto the end of the pit row. The farmer sold milk from the cows that he led down a quarter of a mile of Bracks Hill roads to graze on a far field.

My mother and I walked to the farm hand in hand and I smelled the curd like bitter flowers as the farmer's wife ladled it from her cauldron into our can. Then my mother allowed me to help her carry it along the backyard, my small hand clutching the wire handle. There was only the two of us, so I must have been quite small. I imagine my mother would be pregnant but I how would I know?

The baby joined our family like a stranger in the night. The next day my mother was up at her baking and my brother was lying there swaddled so only her face showed, in a shopping basket by the fire. My mother was very thin and her pale face was nearly blue.

I think these elements of my mother and the soon-to-die baby that shoot into my memory now are an abstraction, like the pigments which go in a colour but are invisible to all except the painter.

Like I say, now I don't know whether I ever loved her, or whether she loved me. I know that with her death the icy chill of bitterness came to sit in the air of the house. And, of course, there were never any touches of love, no talk of love between me and my father. It's true that I was comfortable enough with him at first as we lived our men's life together. My Aunt Susannah came to the house but he didn't make her welcome and the visits stopped. He did not care for the woman's touch.

The girls in the school were a different species from my mother or my Aunt Susanah. In the primary school they had different classrooms and there was a great stone wall between their part of the playground and ours. At the grammar school we sat on different sides of the classroom. Even with the other boys I was known to be silent, though they never knocked me about which was quite surprising. They stood at a distance, or I stood at a distance: which way round I do not know.

Then I went to the pit and even that contact with women was all over and I lived quite comfortably in a world of men. They would tease me about being the quiet man, or make fun at the drawing but there was no harm in that.

I liked being with the pitmen underground. There was enough variety among them to keep you entertained. There were the silent strong men who won respect through their work, there were the religious ones who spoke the Bible like daily doses of honey; there were the singers who sang and the poets like Tegger who spouted; there were the drinkers and the cursers, the gamblers who worked out their odds, the clever and the simple, the sly and the transparent.

Underground in the dark there was always enough variety for me without the complication of women.

But Tegger, even at school, was one for the girls, lying in wait, teasing, throwing pebbles at them from high places, attacking them with snowballs in the winter. The first poem he ever spouted was about a girl who passed us on the way home from school. I know he's been with women but he doesn't brag about it. To my certain knowledge married women are Tegger's weakness. It's unspoken between us, of course. He wouldn't brag about that, not to me.

It's not that I haven't had those feelings:the knowledge that my own body has intrusive powers and sometimes reacts of its own volition. I pore over the portraits in my Rembrandt book. Those sensuous Dutch Burgher's wives and winsome boys with smooth faces: I'm drawn to their beauty with more than a painter's inclination. The very hairs on my body respond to the round arms and the artfully displayed full necks, white as winter stoats.

These were the feelings that pervaded my impotent body when I saw, or dreamed I saw, the woman down in that pit seam, in the Goaf. But no real woman has ever aroused these feelings in me. Housewives with aprons tied onto thickening bodies, coy teachers, giggling schoolgirls: females live in a world that was nothing to do with me.

But these days things are changing. There's that irritating German painting woman, old enough probably to be my mother. When she ignored me in the class the rage I felt prickled my skin and made everything about me erect. I read something somewhere. Probably the Bible. *A body is an unruly servant.*

Now here is this schoolgirl with snapping black eyes who must, if only in that play, by my sweetheart. The world creaks as it turns.

The women are clustered centre stage, coats supplemented by shawls against the cold. A child grasps her mother's skirt, her fine-bloomed skin crawling with a sense of disaster that she doesn't understand. Two elegant white whippets sit on the edge of the crowd, ears up, at the back of the crowd. Behind them is the columnated gateway of the court, beyond that we know the coroner sits, a black cat beside the coroner's chair.

A messenger enters stage left, his white beard shining in the left spotlight. The natural balance of his fine face is warped by a purple cloth binding a lump over his left ear. The lump is a roasted onion which was his grandmother's sure remedy for earache. He's been suffering from earache all afternoon but cannot resist taking part in these dramas of village life. His role is important. It is he who, from time to time comes out to tell the waiting women of the deliberations of the court. It is he who, on his first entrance, tells them about the black cat who sits curled at the feet of the coroner.

This is his sixth announcement.

'And now they're reading out the names of the dead,' he says. 'One by one. Injury by injury.'

'Have they mentioned our John-Joe?' says one woman.

'Aye. So they have.'

'Have they mentioned our Walter and young Sidney?' says another.

'They got a whole list,' he says. 'Such injuries.'

Maggie Olliphant a large woman, whose head seems laid on her shoulders with no neck, comes close enough to the messenger to smell the onion on his ear. 'And what are they saying in there, about why it happened?'

'Lord Chase's agent has been on the stand,' he says. 'He's saying it's the men's fault. Their negligence caused this!' Behind them the crowd of women drew closer together. A child cries. A dog howls.

Maggie Olliphant puts a hand on his arm. Under her palm she can feel the whipcord tension of old muscles. 'That can't be,' she says. 'That can't be, old man.'

He shakes his head. His ear is hurting like twisting knives. 'It's not over yet, Missis. That judge, or coroner, or whatever is no fool. He has a hungry look. He'd not be swayed by prince or potentate when he knows he's in the right.'

'Not bad,' says Todhunter, now. 'Well done, friends. It's coming along, this play of ours.'

There's this big news all round Brack's Hill. The Prince of Wales is to make a visit. To this town. To Brack's Hill. He'll visit the town on one of his tours to comfort the afflicted. He'll see go to the Club, to the Miner's Welfare. He'll hear the brass band. And the word is, he'll see the play we're putting on at the Settlement.

In the front row the equerry will cough and the prince will cross one immaculately clad leg over the other. He will take a snowy handkerchief from his pocket and half-pat the film of sweat from his face and discretely manages to give his nose a rest from what he experiences as the earthy half-human scents in the room.

14. Dev Pallister

Archie Todhunter's brief from the Trust was to maintain relationships with the agencies that had helped with the original survey. This had pinpointed Brack's Hill as a suitable location for the project. The Brack's Hill council, the local doctor-clergy group, the social service department, the Miner's Union, the schools and the University all supported and - to some extent - took responsibility for the Settlement project and made appropriate contributions in cash, kind and in flesh.

It could be argued that having a man like Archie Todhunter in their midst assuaged consciences of these men. As men of liberal persuasion they'd endured a decade of post war helplessness in the face of the juggernaut of the Depression. To have Archie Todhunter and his progressive, enlightened project on their doorstep gave these men a little faith that something might be done for the people of Brack's Hill. It also gave them something to talk about in conversation with liberal-minded friends from other hopeless environments.

Archie Todhunter did not have an easy run with the Brack's Hill people. Many of them had fought in the Great War for a better England. Even in these hard times such men and women tried to keep things together. They were shrewd people used to bargaining and focusing on survival and were often suspicious of the offerings by outsiders of Art and Literature. Sometimes they were more comfortable with the obvious patronage of the food and clothes parcels from other parts of the country and even from as far afield as America. The Trust itself was the initiative of an American patron.

The prickly Brack's Hill people could be quick to criticise if Archie made what they saw as an unsuitable choice of play or class. They would pay close attention to Archie's offerings playing the role of solid hard critics unfazed by the greatest poets of this or any other day.

In the abstract, Archie Todhunter admired their qualities. But face to face it was, as he would say, 'a different kettle of fish.' These people often seemed so preoccupied with the practical issues of unemployment that they could not raise their heads to the higher aims Archie had for his own flock.

One man whom Archie both admired and treated with caution was Dev Pallister, both a 'big' union man and a town Councillor who was on his way to being a county Councillor. It was Dev who, after the war in the teeth of opposition, had fought for Brack's Hill citizens to have their Public Jubilee Park. He'd been in the van when they'd converted the Higher Elementary School to a Grammar School, to put Brack's Hill schooling on a par with that of there towns.

Dev Pallister was a man you needed on your side. He was also the father of Greta, the young hopeful in the drama group. One day Archie found himself sitting in his little office defending to Dev Pallister the practicality of the Settlement provision. 'We offer classes here in basic literacy, Councillor Pallister, and in literature and higher economics. In the French and German language. Basic Physics. You must agree with me that all these might allow some people at some time to hoist themselves out of this morass.'

'Aye, Mr. Todhunter.' Dev took a half-smoked cigarette from his top pocket and lit it, flicking the match away with his nail. 'But we have plenty basic classes already. Down at the Club. Wednesday, Thursday mornings. We tek care of our own.'

Archie wriggled a bit in his office chair. Although he liked to sustain and atmosphere of informality with his clients and students he made sure he was at his desk when he talked to Dev Pallister. 'Mr. Pallister, there are seventeen thousand people in this town. How many of these do you have in your classes? Ten? Twenty individuals? Surely there's more need than this. The men who don't get into the Club for one reason or another. Young people, for instance. Women.'

'Women?' Pallister blew on the end of his cigarette and made it glow. 'Young people?'

'Your own daughter benefits from classes here. She is a clever girl, Greta.'

'If you want to bring ... personalities into it Mr. Todhunter, that young woman's in no need of extra classes. She has a full week of lessons at the Grammar School. Homework too. Your … drama is just the icing on an over-egged cake.'

'Six of the men involved in that play are unemployed miners from your own union.'

'I'll give yer that,' said Pallister.

He left a silence hang the air that Archie had to break. 'But it's not the drama we're on about just now Mr. Pallister. I've got a new application in with the council for a year's support for these new classes in literacy and economics.'

Pallister leaned over and stubbed out his cigarette in Archie's half full ashtray, intensifying the acrid smell of burned tobacco that sat in the air. 'The Council's sympathetic with the aims of the Settlement, you know that Mr. Todhunter. They can see what you and what this place is doing in the town. All credit to you, I say. But, like, our first priority is food, clothes and boots for men whose boots have worn out and no wherewithal to replace them. Some of the children canna go out in bad weather, canna go to school because of no shoes. And there's some old'ns has to drink tea instead of taking a meal. And it's money plays a role in all that. These people have done their practical in economics, Mr. Todhunter.'

Archie bit back the retort about not living by bread alone and stood up. 'Well, Mr. Pallister,' he said evenly. 'I just thought it might be useful to have a word with you,'

Pallister stood up and brushed the flakes of ash from his

shiny jacket. Archie didn't reach to shake his hand, as he would have if it had been Dr Gilliphray. He knew these miners saw touching as affected and over-fond; he'd learned to stick by that unspoken rule.

At the door Pallister turned. 'Far as I can, Mr. Todhunter,' he said. 'I'll support your application in the committee.'

'I'm obliged,' said Archie.

Pallister paused. 'Our Greta. She's doing all right at the drama, then?'

Archie nodded. 'She's very keen. She has a remarkable memory.'

'Aye. Saying whole nursery rhymes when she was two, she was. Read the nursery rhyme book properly when she was three.' And he was gone.

Archie put his head down on his hands and closed his eyes. Five minutes later Cora came in to find him like this. 'Now what's up with you, you poor old boy?'

'Just had Dev Pallister in.'

'Seems too old to be father to Greta, that one,' said Cora thoughtfully.'

'Tried to warm him up about those funds for the new classes.'

'And did you manage to do that?'

'Perhaps, I did. To be honest I've no idea. He's harder to read than an orang- utan.'

'What did he say?'

'He did say he'd support our bid. But who's to say he will? Usually feller can't see beyond his nose. All wrapped up in cries for food and clothes. Like the rest of them he can't lift his eyes to the horizon,'

'Listen to yourself Archie. It's you who don't see past your nose. Some of the men and women who come here do worry because of the state of their clothes, their shoes. They're down to their last jacket and where will the next one come from? Yet they still come.'

He shook his head. 'They have no culture, these people, not a shred. Nothing to build on. We're in the land of the barbarians, Cora. Our offerings are as nothing.'

She came close to him where sat and put her arm around his shoulder and pulled him to her. 'You talk such rubbish sometimes, Archie. Two hundred people came through our doors last month. They're hungry for culture, this lot. Eagerly seeking what we have to offer.' She put him from her and he stood up and went to stand by the fireplace.

'Anyway,' she said, 'they do have their own culture. The football, the bowls, the pigeons, the club. The singing. One man told me they have all the newspapers in their Club. And they read. You said so yourself.'

'The Club's about beer! About men comforting each other into oblivion. Low culture, where poetry is anathema.'

Cora sat down in the seat which Pallister had just vacated. 'You're getting to be an old grouch, Archie. And you're not seeing things properly. This football, these bowls, these pigeons, maybe that's a kind of poetry to them.'

Archie smiled, suddenly cheered up. 'Really Cora, you are a joker. You do get strange ideas. Just you concentrate on keeping this place straight and the classes organised. When I want your advice about culture I'll ask for it. Aren't I the expert after all?' He lit a cigarette from his own, and leaned over to hand it to her. 'Smoke?' He went to sit in the padded chair by the fire.

As they sat for a while in companionable silence Archie thought that Cora was the easiest woman he had ever known. 'Remember the day you turned up on my doorstep? What a day that was!'

'I thought you were a bit of an old grouch then,' she said, surveying the glowing tip of her cigarette. 'But now I think you're not a bad old stick, all things considered.'

15. Staging a Play

We're familiar enough with the play now. Tegger has read it and Archie Todhunter had taken his advice on some of its elements. We've had more meetings in the big room to read the play in sections. That girl Greta Pallister has her words off already. Archie Todhunter stops and starts the action, growling, coaching and cajoling us like a benevolent Sergeant Major. He makes me read Arthur's lines from one end of the room to the other, to Greta Pallister, whose voice in return sounds like a chirruping bird spiralling in the space between us.

'Project your voice! *Project*, don't bellow!' Todhunter says. 'These are intimacies you must share with strangers.'

As he makes us read the lines again and again. I battle to become Arthur, desolate at the impossibility of trying to communicate from this muddy trench (which doesn't exist) to a place back home (which *really* doesn't exist; it is after all, make-believe). Arthur's voice begins to tremble as he covers up the foulness of his situation with his hopes for tomorrow, when the war will be won and he will return and the he and Dorothy will live happy ever after - he working at the pit and she in the little house they would share. As we *project* our voices down the long Settlement room you can almost smell the roses round the door.

In the end I, (Gabriel, not 'Arthur') am in revolt. I glance at Tegger, knowing he has had a hand in all this. 'This is rubbish,' I say. 'How could he say that? Happiness? Safety? Look what really happened. Poverty. The dole. Crippled soldiers begging in the street. Look outside this very door.'

'Rubbish?' says Todhunter evenly. He's leaning back, with his bottom hooked onto the table they use for the books on library days. 'Rubbish, you say, Gabriel?'

'Well,' I calm down a bit. 'It's all very nice to hear but it's not the truth, is it?'

'We know that now, laddie,' says Todhunter. 'But they didn't know it then, did they? They hoped they'd win the war and return to a land fit for heroes.'

Tegger shuffles his feet; I can feel his eyes on me, then moving on to Todhunter as we take each other on.

'That's just what I mean.' I say. I'm wary of this man. He's like a fisherman playing us wall with his line. 'It's false, making our characters say things we know are a lie.'

Todhunter draws on his cigarette through his fancy holder. 'Irony, my boy! You're talking about the irony of the situation. You'll not be alone in your perceptions.'

'Irony?' I do know the word.

'Irony's not confined to Shakespeare, laddie, nor the lives of the long dead. Irony infuses our lives today. That flare of anger that you just described. *A land fit for heroes.* That's the irony. That sense of hypocrisy, of wasted lives. That's what the play's about, is it not? Lives wasted by bad management underground or by cod generals in the trenches. Don't we want people to recognise this? To join it to their own experiences? To reflect on what happens when they put their fate in the hands of incompetents? Colliery managers, generals, princes and kings.' His voice becomes grim, losing its usual jocular tone. 'All those who see unique human beings as fodder for their cannons or their grinding mills.'

Cora, lounging in a corner waves her cigarette in Archie's direction 'Go lightly Archie. These are young creatures. Tender birds.'

'It's their lives. Their country,' says Todhunter gruffly.

My brain hums with his words, buzzing like a hive of bees 'Sounds like treason to me,' I say. 'Scoring off against generals and kings.'

'Now you're getting it!' he says. 'Now, can we get on with this rehearsal? Then I'll give you my notes and then the redoubtable Fraŭlein Vonn needs this space at six for her stage design meeting. We need our set.'

The painting teacher's surname has been reduced to *Vonn* because it's really Von something-or-other, an unpronounceable German name that does not sit comfortably on the tongues of people around here,

The room empties just on six o'clock, apart from Tegger and me and Mr Conroy, the joiner, who have been volunteered by Todhunter to build and paint the set designed by the "redoubtable Fraülein Vonn".

At one minute past six she comes in with a big, black folder in her arms which she places carefully on the long table. She shakes hands with each of us in turn. Her handshake is firm, her glance as direct as any man's. 'Mr MacNamara? You have helped Mr Todhunter with the writing, I hear?'

'Me name's Tegger, er, Miss…er.'

'That is a strange name,' she says.

'It's for Edgar, miss. But I'm always known as Tegger. You can call me Tegger.'

'And you can call me Rosel.' she smiles at him with her small white teeth and glances across at me. She might not be young and is no beauty but there's something about her. Tegger's eyes go glassy. He's smitten all right.

'And this is my mate Gabriel Marchant, Rosel. You can call him Gabriel,' he smirks.

She shakes my hand. 'I know Mr Marchant … er … Gabriel from the art class.' She has been civil to me lately, although she leaves me strictly to get on with my own stuff.

'And from the slag heap, she walks by the pit heap, Tegger. ' I say, watching her closely.

Her grasp is really strong. I look directly into her eyes which are the colour of the grey-blue glass in the side window of the old chapel. 'I'm called Gabriel, like he says.'

'What is it there, at this tip that you search for with such care?' Her voice is soft, careful, coming from somewhere deep in her throat. Now I wonder what it must be like to think in one language and speak in another. I can smell her perfume. Sweet and light. I imagine some neat German flower. Tight. Symmetrical.

'The petrified forest,' I say. 'I look for the fossils of fish and birds. Insects. From the forests and rivers that were her before man. That's what I look for.'

Her fair brows rise almost to her hair line. 'I see.' She pulls her hand from mine with difficulty and turns to the joiner, Mr Conroy. 'And Mr Conroy,' she says. 'We know each other do we not? We meet at Mr Todhunter's I think.'

'Aye so we do. Mr Conroy, you can call me. Mr Conroy,' says the old man. He's having none of this first name rubbish.

Her nod sweeps across us all. She avoids my direct glance. Then she takes her papers out of the black folder and spreads them out on the table. 'This is Mr Todhunter's rough sketch.' she smoothes out a crumpled sheer of paper. On top of it she places another smooth crisp sheet. 'I have sketched his idea the stage in this way. Like so.'

This is Todhunter's rough scene sketched in much greater detail. The three settings are drawn in deftly: the army trench, the coroner's court, the podium with its cluster of women. She has added figures of the actors in role. She has portrayed us exactly in simple direct strokes. Nathan, masterfully authoritative as the coroner. Jake McVay squat and scant-haired as the corporal, Archie sharp-suited as the pit manager, me in uniform with an improbable halo of curls, Greta Pallister, with her circle of plaits, narrow and earnest among the more shadowy women. Behind it all is the massive circle of the colliery wheel, the cluster of dark colliery buildings. Above it all, washed in bright colour is a blood red sunrise.

Tegger whistles.

'That's good,' says Mr Conroy. 'Clever, like.'

'So how are we supposed to get all that on the stage in the church hall?' I say, 'it's very elaborate.'

She looks at me sharply. 'Ha! So you think I am proud, Gabriel, that I show off?'

'I never said that. I'm just wondering how that might be a stage set, like. It'll be hard to get it right.'

She shrugs. That movement is so foreign, so unlike any movement my mother or Greta Pallister would make. Her narrow shoulders move with an elegance that whispers of grand parties and fine rooms. Don't ask how I know this. I just do.

I do not know whether it will work,' she says. 'I am an artist, not a stage designer. I draw from Mr Todhunter's sketch and from watching the rehearsals. It is for you to make a stage from it.'

Mr Conroy's peering at the paper. 'Need to break it down into parts,' he says. 'It's not impossible.'

Tegger frowns at him, and then counts the 'parts' off on his fingers. 'One. Painted backdrop of the sky with colliery wheel where the women stand. Could we build one? Two. Coroner's court. Furniture. Three. Trench dugout. Wooden framework, *papier-mâché?* We made models at school like that didn't we Gabe? And what about some kind of big gun looming over it all?'

'Not enough room,' I say. 'It would take up too much space. Remember the stage in the chapel hall. That's the space we'll have.'

'The greatest problem is that we need to see one part only at a time,' said Rosel Vonn, frowning. 'I know you have thought of a turntable. But we must make the audience look at that part only, when the action takes place there.'

I'm peering at the paper myself now, as interested as any of them now, forgetting about Rosel Vonn and the way she ran away from me at the tip and has been ignoring me in the art class. 'Light,' I say finally. 'Lanterns.'

'How's that, marra?' says Tegger.

'Well, when the coroner speaks he turns up this elaborate lamp on his desk so you see him and all around him. Like a halo. When we need to watch the lads in the trench they can have lanterns, like Tilley lamps. Same with the women. There could be a kind of street lamp by them which goes on when they talk.'

'Yes,' says Rosel Vonn. 'This is good, Gabriel.'

I squeeze my eyes half shut, staring at the drawing, imagining the dark stage where the light leads the action. 'And you don't really need a colliery wheel or a gun, do you? What you need are models, like shadow puppets, see? A kind of outline model of a pit wheel which you shine a light through, so the black shadow shows up against that sunrise. And a machine-gun. You could do the same with a machine gun for the trench scenes. A silhouette.'

In the silence that follows I'm embarrassed at my enthusiasm. Then Tegger whistles. 'Why Gabe, man, yer clever devil.'

'Could work,' said Mr Conroy slowly. 'Idea's simple enough.'

'Is a good idea,' said Rosel Vonn. 'Have you seen such a thing Gabriel, on the stage before?'

I shake my head. 'I've never even seen any play before, never mind a stage.' I imagine Rosel Vonn on the staircase of great theatres in Berlin: all chandeliers and sweeping dresses.

I suppose you might say that this is how Rosel Vonn and I have come to something of a truce. We work on the set together, our proximity mediated by the energetic enthusiasm of Tegger and the measured pipe-smoking wisdom of Mr Conroy.

It's still more or less the same in the art class. In there I get used to drawing and eventually painting without much comment or guidance from Rosel Vonn. I've been preoccupied with Rembrandt lately. I try to make some kind of sense of his way with light, to come to grips with his sheer sorcery in bringing white exterior light into his interiors. In the class I make crude attempts at mimicking him, which go unremarked. What with all that and two nights play rehearsal a week I seemed to spend little time at all in my father's house. That, of course, is to my liking.

16. Apollo and Zeus

Greta Pallister stayed for every minute of every rehearsal, even those that did not involve her. She sat in a corner, sometimes reading a book, sometimes doing her homework, sometimes writing in a small notebook which she always carried with her.

Greta knew very well that she was clever. She was the only member of her family to take up her place at the grammar school. Her parents had won places in their time. But they couldn't take them up because, even with scholarships, the grammar school took money. Her father Dev, although he was a Councillor, like other miners who had been active in the Union, was still out of work.

Greta's eldest brother Robert, who had emigrated to Canada in 1927, sent home money earmarked for Greta's schooling. The second eldest, Joss had moved to London where, after a false start as a dishwasher in an hotel in the Strand, he found a steady job as a servant to an elderly man who enjoyed being read to. In that job, with 'all found', there was still money left to send back home to help out.

Money from these two brothers kept their parents on their feet and Greta at grammar school. It also freed their father Dev to get on with his jobs as union man and Councillor without excessive worry.

At the grammar school, Greta's slightly dusty appearance and pitmatic talk came to be overlooked as, test by test, examination by examination, she won all the prizes. In the end she not only learned her Geography and History, her French and her Maths, she also learned to round up her vowels and put on her *ings* and *aitches*. Greta was an adaptive organism in the body politic of Brack's Hill.

All this, added to her success in Archie's plays, did her no harm at all at school, where her teachers had started to talk of scholarships to Oxford and Cambridge. They urged her to round out her vowels and sound the endings of her words.

Such verbal sophistication, of course, was not called for in the case of this new play *Blood and Coal*. Tegger's laughing and mockery made sure that she dropped the rolling imperatives of Shakespearean speech and revisited the talk of her early childhood. She kept her clarity but she had to flatten her vowels and now drop her *ings* and *aitches* to sound authentic.

Archie, with more than a few insightful; suggestions from Tegger MacNamara, had written a play which had rhythms of its own. The speeches of the soldiers, the women, the miners and the lawyers followed each other like spoken anthems. Greta did not miss the glance which passed between Tegger and Archie when sT he compared the rhythms to those of Chaucer's Canterbury Tales. Well, she thought, they could think what they liked.

She wondered what her mother, who rather wallowed in her daughter's evolved ability to 'talk posh', would think when she saw the performance. She'll have a fit, thought Greta. A proper dickey-fit. Mrs. Pallister saw herself a bit above her less fortunate penurious neighbours. Wasn't her husband Dev a big man in the union, which seemed even more important now there was no work? And he was a Councillor as well. Hadn't her sons taken their chances, made their way in the world and hadn't the whole family benefited? Didn't they have an end-house with a bay window?

But now, with the performance, thought Greta, she would see her daughter, talking pitmatic again!

But Greta reveled in all the business of the play. In her rather myopic eyes the ever-silent Gabriel Marchant was as beautiful as Apollo. She copied some school notes into the notebook that she always carried with her. *'Apollo's beauty had as its essence strength, reserve and emotions in full control.'*

She somehow squeezed in some time to join the Saturday painting group to see more of her Apollo. She witnessed his battle with light and colour in the context of the deep dark of the pit; she watched him poring over the prints by Turner and Rembrandt. She noted in her book:

He is the god of light and of inspiration which itself is the soul's light. Gabriel moves like a panther and, though he says very little. When he does his voice is deep and distinct: it make profound music. As he reads his lines (it's taken him ages to get them off by heart), his voice penetrates the very corners of the long church hall. He doesn't need to raise it and project like the others. It has timbre.

Greta looked up the *timbre* in her little dictionary to see she'd got it right.

Except in the actual process of the rehearsal Gabriel would not really meet her gaze. No matter how long she hung around it was never long enough to catch his gaze in the natural run of things,

Greta was not so surprised at his rejection. The young men of her acquaintance, even cousins, found her looks un-entrancing, her lack of flirtatious skills confusing, her bookishness next door to repellent. She didn't seem to know how to tease and flirt and, if you got off the wrong foot with her, she'd bore you with some facts about the discovery of Australia or the significance of the Magna Carta. On top of that Greta was clumsy. She had large hands which didn't work too well and tended to knock things (like glasses and cups) over.

Gabriel said so little that it was hard, sometimes, to tell who he really was. *'And thereby,'* wrote Greta in her diary, *'hangs the problem. The German woman fills his eye. She's always head to head with him. There are sparks between them. They say she's a proper artist. Half the time he looks like he hates her. But other times they are over at his board scribbling away like they are joined at the hip. Siamese twins. There was s picture of some of those in the News Chronicle. Weird.'*

If Gabriel was the new Apollo in Greta's life, Archie Todhunter was the Zeus. She drank in every word he said, noting the most outstanding of them in her diary. She thought of Archie as clever, even learned; funny, full of life and a fount of wisdom and anecdote. She compared him very favourably with the male teachers at school whom she was supposed to admire.

'*Putrid, fossilised, timeservers!*' She wrote this in her diary with a flourish. '*If they're not gibbering with shell shock they're inventing stories of saving the Empire. And they pinch your arm to make a point and pat your bottom when no one is looking.*'

But even they were livelier than the schoolmistresses. These venerable women retreated to their lair – the female common room – and only emerged to deliver their lessons in parrot voices or to give you a hundred lines for saying pass instead of *parse*.

'*Thank God for text books,*' wrote Greta in her diary. '*There at least you come across some light, some scholarship.*'

After she joined the Settlement she wrote down '*Thank God for Archie Todhunter! At least he has some fire and believes in what he's saying and thinks he can change the future. He might be wrong but this is still a good thing.*'

Greta was very wary of Cora Miles. The woman was kind enough. She would take Greta into a corner to show her how your body can reflect the words that are coming out of you mouth. Or the way you use your body can give meaning without even speaking. '*More.*' Greta wrote in her diary. *She showed me how your body can add to the meaning, help the audience to know what the play's really about.*

This had been invaluable when they put on *Loves Labours'*

Lost when Greta despaired of her clumsy body. She was certain that her clumsiness would bleach out the delicacy of Shakespeare's poetry and make it poor fare for the audience. Cora had helped her to avoid that. Greta began to understand that on stage she could be another person, even a not-ugly other person.

But kind as Cora always was, Greta felt that somewhere underneath the kindness, the firm touch there lay a distinct mockery. Occasionally, when other people were present she would call Greta *'Archie's acolyte'.* This would make Greta blush and the others would laugh, not always kindly.

Archie himself was reassuringly bland with Greta. He spoke to her evenly, with neither the talking-down of the others or the mocking kindness of Cora. If she made an intelligent remark in his company she would be rewarded with his close attention and a further request for her opinion. The others might exchange glances. Even roll their eyes.

'What's that you're writing?' It was Tegger MacNamara, peering over her shoulder.

She jumped, putting her hand right across the page. 'Nothing. Just some notes. A notebook.'

'Nowt wrong with writing, kidder. I'm a bit like that meself, nowadays. Writing things down,' He looked up and past her, then set off across the room. 'Hey Gabe! You off, marra? Hold on.' It seemed they had some business with Rosel Vonn.

Something about scenery

Greta watched the two boys   go off, heads together, one dark and one fair. Then she put her books in her satchel and her coat. She would follow them as far as Inkerman Street. At a safe distance, of course.

She closed her book and tucked it in her satchel.

17. A Man-Made Place

Rosel Vonn had settled in quite well at the Settlement, which was part dwelling place, part meeting place, part office, part school. Rosel had lived in many households in her life: her parents' intricately gorgeous apartment in Berlin; her father's sprawling studio in Paris; her uncle's tall house by the sea at Sunderland; various accommodations and lodging houses in London, then in Paris. But she'd never lived in such a strange place as this Settlement House in Brack's Hill.

Todhunter and Cora were kind enough to Rosel. but surprisingly not curious about her. Apart from the lunchtime meal that Cora made for them all at noon each day, they left Rosel to her own devices. She made her own breakfast and supper in the Settlement kitchen; she worked with her artists, painted her own paintings, helped with the scenery and drew in her own notebook. She was feeling felt good about the fact that she was drawing and painting freely now for the first time for years.

She watched with admiration as Archie Todhunter managed this place where so much happened. Every day except Sunday, after ten o clock in the morning, the Settlement buzzed with activities: daytime classes in cobbling watchmaking, French and embroidery; daily visitors to read the newspapers from cover to cover; in the evenings there were weekly discussions of news and current affairs led by Todhunter, the poetry circle led by Cora, some Economic History with a Mr Jonty Clelland; the twice weekly library; the cornet lessons given by Mr Poppel from the grammar school; the play rehearsals. And now her own fine art classes.

All these activities seemed to give the building an intense inner light. Despite being very shabby and only half painted, it outshone the rest of the houses in the drab road. It probably outshone every other house in the town.

The activities often went on into the night. This meant Archie and Cora kept theatrical hours, not rising till nine or nine thirty some mornings. Rosel, an early riser herself, got into the habit or going out for a walk before they were out of bed.

On one of these mornings she cut herself a slice of bread, put that in one pocket, her drawing pad in another, and let herself out of the back door. She walked the length of the High Street, past two yawning young men who were opening up shops and sweeping pavements. A ginger-haired man with a high forehead was unloading a wagon of beef and heaving the carcases into the Coop butcher's shop.

The men peered at this smartly dressed woman with interest. This was no skivvy going to scrub for someone on High Row, no shop-girl going to stand behind a counter all day. She was too well dressed. It was true that the women who worked in the shops on the High Street were well scrubbed, respectable. They even wore a flash of colour now and then. But this woman had the look of something more than that. She wore a striking red scarf around her neck; another gauzy scarf with silver stars on as a bandeau, instead of a hat. She was no chicken, but she was slender and shapely like the mannequins you saw in the Co-op window. But why was she out so early? The way she was dawdling she had no work to go to. You could bet on that.

Many of the shops which Rosel passed were boarded up. Those that were open were putting on a brave show, even if the colour of some of the items on display was bleaching down, showing signs of age. The stock was not moving, not moving at all.

Rosel cut through a narrow alley behind the High Street onto a row of low houses with small square windows. These were much lower that the other houses she had passed: perhaps just one storey. Smoke surged from the chimneys to weld itself to the general pall of smoke above the town. Each house in the row differed from its neighbour in fine degrees of visible poverty.

She walked on and made her way around the silent colliery buildings out towards the White Leas pit heap and the patch of woodland and the river beyond. Up there above the low hills that lapped towards the horizon, the sky looked brighter, the air looked clearer. Her lungs ached for clear air.

Looking across towards the pit heap she could make out the now familiar figure of Gabriel Merchant. Feeling her gaze he raised his head and saw her. He stared for a minute then put up his hand and started to scramble towards her. 'Hey!' he called. 'Miss.....er Rosel.'

She waited. He came level with her and put out his hand, palm flat. 'This is what I look for. Thought you'd like to see one.' he said. 'Up here on the heap.' Lying in the palm of his hand was a piece of slate lined with the delicate tracery of an oak leaf. 'From the petrified forest,' he said. 'Fathoms deep.'

She touched the veins of the leaf with a finger. 'A miracle,' she said. 'All those thousands of years.'

He pushed his hand forward, against hers. 'Here, you can have it,' he said.

She shook her head. 'No. It is your collection.'

'Have it!' he said. 'Me I've got hundreds.'

She took it from him. It was warm from his hand. After thousands of years in the cold earth, now, today it was warm. 'Thank you. I shall treasure it.'

He looked at her sharply, to check for mockery.

'Really,' she said. 'It *is* a treasure. You know that.'

He looked along the pathway she had come. 'So, are you off somewhere, like?'

'I thought I'd make my way there, towards that woodland,' she said. 'It looks brighter there. I feel the need for fresh air.'

'You can see Roman stones over there, your know. Not as old as this one, but quite old.'

'How do you know they are Roman?'

'Everybody knows. They have Roman markings.'

She hesitated.

'I'll show you.' He set off, quickly into his swinging stride. She followed, skipping now and then to keep up with him. They walked in silence. Once into the wood he headed down a narrow pathway through blackthorn bushes, some gorse and a stand of beech trees. Their feet slapped on wet grass. Then they crunched down to a clearing with a kind of gravel beach. Here the river swirled round into a wide basin formed by a cliff of sandstone, before moving on to wend its way towards the distant sea. The sun pierced the cloud for a second and lit the edge of the water where it escaped the shadow of a cliff.

Gabriel used his broad forearm to sweep leaves and twigs from a sandstone ledge. 'You sit here a minute. I need to look around. I think they were somewhere near the edge. It's a while since I saw them.'

She sat down and watched as he made his way along the edge of the river, pulling away at brambles and low branches. Suddenly hungry, she took out her paper-wrapped bread and butter and started to eat. She'd just finished and was brushing crumbs from her dress when she heard him shout. She followed his voice and, careful of her shoes and the encroaching water, she edged her way round the corner.

He'd pulled away a thicket of bramble and was brushing the surface of a narrow stone with the sleeve of his coat. 'Look,' he said. The surface of the stone had some kind of indented design with letters underneath.

'What does it say?' she touched the lines with her finger.

He shook his head. 'Gravestone or altar I should think. There's a number there. *One. Ex. IX.* That means nine, doesn't it?'

She looked round. The clustered streets of Bracks Hill lay to their right, rolling countryside on the left with the railway viaduct of Priorton in the distance. She looked around. 'Where does this stone come from? Is it a Roman place? It looks wild, untouched around here.'

He shrugged. 'It's a place. A man-made place. See there! Five flat stones in a row. A landing spot or something. Upstream though, there was a camp, a military camp. There are stones from that camp in some of the farmhouses round here. When the Romans went people shipped the stones down on the river, so mebbe this one rolled overboard.'

She looked up across the turbulent basin of water, to the cliff on the other side, then back to Gabriel's face. 'This is a magical place,' she said. 'As well as a man-made place.'

He nodded. 'It's all right, isn't it?' he said. 'My father showed me it once when I was very little. I used to come here with Tegger before we started work. We used to play soldier games. Huns and British.' He blushed. 'I'd almost forgotten about that,' he said. 'Who you are. You coming here from Germany...'

'Can we sit down?' she said. She led the way back to her stone seat. He sat further along, his booted feet dangling over the water. She waited until he was settled. 'Do you live with your family?' she said.

He shook his head. 'I live on me own. My father's dead. Mother too.'

She flushed, remembering the men in the class: what they had said about Gabriel's father. 'Goodness,' she said. 'I am so sorry.'

He stared away from her towards the swirling water. The silence seemed to go on too long.

She reached into her pocket. 'Do you mind if I draw?' she said. 'I would like to draw.'

He looked up, frowning.

'That's why I come out to walk away from the town, Gabriel. To breathe clear air. To draw. And this is such a beautiful place.'

'Suit yourself,' he said.

With a speed that surprised herself she executed two drawings: one of his drooping figure staring into the water, one of the whole scene, with the rearing cliff and the circle of trees and the stones at awkward angle.

In the end he hauled himself to his feet and came to stand beside her. 'What's it you're doing?'

She turned her book towards him. He looked from it back towards the river, then handed it back. 'You're very good,' he said. 'A good artist. I see that in the class.'

'So are you,' she said.

'You never say so,' he said. 'You never say so, in the class.'

'You know it. You know that very well,' she said. 'You don't need me to tell you.'

He stared at her. 'Mebbe I do,' he said.

She jumped down. 'I will have to be back to The Settlement. I promised Cora I would call at the baker's to get some fresh bread for Mr Todhunter's breakfast toast.'

Now she shoves her notebook in her bag and sets off walking very quickly away from me, away from this *man-made place*. I watch her swinging stride until she's out of sight and then sit down where she sat before and breathe in the last of her scent. I look and look at this scene again, through her eyes. Her drawing here has made it strange, this place where I played Huns and British with Tegger, this place where I used to tramp with my father when he was still a reasonable man.

I wish now I had my own notebook with me. Perhaps I should draw this scene myself. Perhaps that will make her begin to talk to me about my painting and help me to understand what I'm really trying to do

18. Being German

When Rosel got back Cora was waiting for Archie's bread, toasting fork in hand. She nodded at a letter on the mantelpiece. 'A letter came. It has a German post mark.'

Rosel peered at the writing. 'My father,' she said.

'Archie says he was an artist too. Famous.'

'I would not say this. There was an important set of drawings from the war. Archie has the book.'

'I would like to see that.'

'It might make you very sad, Cora. War. It does not glorify those things. For this reason his work is not admired in Germany now. According to my brother they have burned many copies of it in the last few years. It seems it is now decadent to show the true face of war,'

Cora nodded. 'I can see such things can be a threat. Like Archie's play. They want glory and sacrifice, not the true face of pain,'

Rosel looked sharply at Cora. 'This is true. What you say is true.' She made her way to the stairs,

'You must be very proud of your father,' said Cora behind her.

'Proud?' Rosel turned. 'I had not thought of it like that. At present I am very worried. He is a very outspoken man and has no care for his own safety.'

Cora nodded. 'I can see that might be the case.' She waved the fresh loaf at Rosel. 'Now I'd better see the old boy up there gets his toast. I count it as a favour to everyone these days if he gets out of bed the right side. Nice hot toast can do the trick.'

In her room Rosel tore open the envelope. The letter, in his flowing hand, was full of the terrible things which were happening to him. But even so he still showed an unusual interest in her life in Brack's Hill. *Why do you live in such a far place? London I know has its attractions even with these days. Your work with artists there seemed appropriate. But, liebling, to bury yourself so far away* …He was suddenly there fussing over her here in her small upstairs room. She could almost smell his cigar and the pomade he wore on his hair. To keep the feeling of him with her, she sat down and wrote back by return.

Settlement House
Queen Street
Brack's Hill
June 1st 1936

My Dearest Papa,

You ask of the people with whom I find myself? They are kind, these people of Brack's Hill. But you have to dig deep to get under their hard, sometimes blank looks. If they are curious, it is in a sidelong way. There is a kind of courtesy, a discretion about this, which I like. Their humour is equally sidelong. Often I have to get Cora or Archie, with whom I live, to explain. Sometimes I miss the humour altogether. I only know it has been a joke when the people around me splutter into laughter, half of it at my own ignorance of their allusions. Even after my years in England I find it so different from our German way which is more direct, perhaps more intellectual and distinctly more cruel. You write to me in some embarrassment about the current jokes against the Jews and how you are jeered at for not laughing with the jokers.

But this issue of prejudice is not one-sided. Twice when have I walked into a place here - once a house, another time a shop - someone has spat on the floor. Three times have I heard 'Hun' hissed behind me in the High Street here, and when I looked there were only blank stares. I have had one letter which called me a 'fucking' prostitute and informed me the only good German was a dead one. That is a very rude word. I went with the letter to Archie - Mr Todhunter and he took it from me and rolled it into a spill which he lit from the fire and used to light his cigarette.

He is a cool person.

Did I tell you they call me Miss <u>Vonn</u>? I hope this does not disturb you. I thought it a good idea, as people here can't seem to say our second name.

I asked Archie Todhunter if he had fought in the war and he said that, for good or ill, he was in China looking for his mother at the time and only came back to start his medical studies in 1918.

'Your mother was in China?' I said.

'Aye. She was a missionary' His face was carved from stone.

It was hard to know what to say. I worship form and the intoxication of creation but you know that I recognise no God. 'She must have been a good woman,' I said to him.

'I suppose so. I barely knew her. And when I went to China I couldn't find her. It was true that to some people she was an icon of virtue and sacrifice. But she seemed to have nothing to do with me. Other English people there were kind to me.' He sounds brisk, as though this does not matter.

'You didn't help her in her work?' I ask him.

'She would know that God was long lost to me.' He smiled a cool smile. 'I set up childish playacting with the few English that were there. And some Chinese taught me how to gamble. They are great gamblers."

I like this man, Papa, although he is hard to know. But in general here in this town I have met a certain tolerance. I feel comfortable with the people here. You used to say that the English and the Germans had so much in common: a steadiness in the face of difficulty; an ability to organise others; a natural patriotism and an appreciation of good leadership; a sense of responsibility to their world wide empires. I feel that this is so.

So, dear Papa, I am well, and this is an interesting time in my life. But I worry about you.. Perhaps you would be safer here? Write, write, and keep writing so that I know you are well.

Your devoted Rosel.

She sealed the envelope, her mind still dwelling on her father. In the years of his youth his view of this special relationship between the Germans and the English was not uncommon, intensified in people like her father by a sense of kinship. Was not the King of England cousin to the Kaiser? As a young man her father had been to parties and soirées with young Englishmen. And he had skied with them in Switzerland and the Italian Alps. In 1899 he was engaged briefly to an Englishwoman whose family had a house in London and a sprawling estate in Leicestershire.

His brother, Rosel's Uncle Berti who now lived in Sunderland, studied architecture and design in London as well as Paris, even though London was not so fashionable then for such studies. This unfashionability suited her uncle, as he liked to be different. Sausage-and-mash and eels, for which he'd acquired a taste in his Limehouse lodgings, were regularly on order in his Berlin house. In London he had met a widow from South Shields and had settled down with her in Sunderland, where his portraiture was much appreciated by shipbuilders looking to their own posterity.

Then there was her father's housekeeper's cousin, a woman from Dusseldorf, who had once been a maid attending the English royal children. At the beginning of the Great War she'd had to leave the Palace to come back to Germany. According to Rosel's father there had been tears all round. Apparently German was commonly spoken in the Royal Household and the Royal children spoke it well.

As with all patriotic Germans Rosel's father and brother had fought in that war, as did her cousin Humbert. After his first sojourn as a stretcher bearer in the trenches, which provided the inspiration for his famous paintings and book of drawings, Rosel's father had seen no action. He got himself involved with the development of vehicles for bad terrain and made some modifications to tank design. Her Uncle Berti had been assigned a kind of errand boy to a General who avoided the front like the plague, so he was quite safe.

Her father had seem the Great War as an unfortunate, wasteful but basically honourable fight between equals. He considered the final punitive Treaty he disgustingly dishonourable. But, Anglophile that he was, he blamed it on the rapacious vengeance of the French who had, after all suffered more than one defeat at the hands of the Germans.

In the years after the war her father welcomed the crude directness of the National Socialists. He supported their resolve to end the reparation payments; he welcomed their frontal attack on the downward spiral of the German nation. But these days everything had changed. These days he was increasingly worried about the rapacious campaign against Jewish people. He'd had to stand by while his friends were attacked and robbed of their livelihood and their homes; he'd had to dismiss his Jewish servants, some of whom have been with him for decades. He could not even consult his Jewish doctor who was a long term expert on the vagaries of his wayward colon. In one letter he wrote to Rosel. *Things are not as they should be, liebling. They make tyrants of us despite our inclinations.*

Rosel put down her father's letter. At least, she thought, here in Brack's Hill I've not been confronted with such hard decisions of conscience. But sometimes I feel uneasy at escaping from it all. Sometimes, working with Archie and Cora, with the painters and the set builders, I don't think of father or of Germany for days, even weeks on end. My greatest problem is not to get too excited about the talent of these people here. Especially that remarkable talent, that one boy who feels his way into his art by some kind of instinct. He does not say much. But he did give me a fossil of an oak leaf and showed me that magical man-made place. Perhaps that was saying something.

She took the fossil from her coat pocket and held it up to the mirror. Such a very ancient thing. Her gaze lifted to her own reflection. 'And you, Rosel Von Steinigen. You are a very old thing too. This is a boy. You must be very careful. Very careful.' Her breath steamed the mirror as she whispered the words to herself. 'Be careful indeed.'

19. The Matter of Shoes

'It's an idea,' Archie stroked his non-existent beard,

'The artists, this will give them a purpose. Something to aim for.' Rosel had proposed that some of the artists should draw, perhaps even paint, the players in their roles. 'They will need some disciplined work on figures. Some of them draw people as though they are sticks of plasticine. There is no sense of bone, muscle. And the clothes of course, they are a problem. At the Slade we drew the classical statues. Forms in the round.'

'Naked figures?' said Cora. She whistled, 'Now that could be embarrassing.'

Rosel shook her head. 'Only women artists in the room. And only statuary. My great regret is that only the men drew from life.' She sniffed. 'Ridiculous.'

'And did you never draw from life?' persisted Cora.

'Of course I did,' said Rosel. 'It is impossible otherwise to learn. I made private arrangements.'

'Men. You drew men?'

'Cora!' said Archie. 'Leave it alone.' But he was smiling

slightly.

Rosel threw up her hands. 'They were no more than limbs, the arms, the legs branches of trees. We are artists, not whores.'

Cora whistled again. 'One or two curious knots, I'll warrant,' she said.

'Cora!' Archie's mild reproof had as much impact as a feather on a rhinoceros.

'Well!' she said. '*In the buff.* Art's as good an excuse as any.'

'We'd have problems if you'd want to strip off my miners, Rosel.' Archie coughed. 'They're a prudish lot above the ground. It would be round Brack's Hill like fire that we're running a brothel here. We'd lose our funding in a day.'

'Yes,' said Cora. 'They stretch a point with Archie and me, even if they disapprove. They go along with the pretence. Hypocrisy is an unkind word for it.'

Rosel shook her head. 'It would be very good if they did take off clothes. If any of the more talented artists here manage to go on with their art and go to a proper art school they will have to draw from life however prudish they may be. They will have to learn about muscles and bone, the beating heart within.' She sighed. 'But for now I thought we would draw the players in the parts they have in the play. In those clothes. That child - Greta is it? - in her apron, the miners in their pit gear, you as the agent, and the coroner, in your waistcoat suits and...' she paused.

'Gabriel Marchant in his muddy army uniform,' put in Cora, her painted mouth in a wide smile. 'Now that boy would be beautiful in anything don't you think Rosel? Root and branch. Root and branch.'

Rosel ignored her. 'We could mount an exhibition for the days of the performance. Perhaps use the images for playbills and the programme. Is there a printer's where we could make some plates?'

'Woah! Woah!' said Archie. 'This may be too much. It's only a play, after all.'

Cora scowled at Archie. '*Only* a play? So what're you up to Archie Todhunter? The play's important, you know it. It's not some end of the pier farce for child miners. It's more than that...'

Archie shrugged. 'I don't want it getting attention for the wrong reason. The play's the thing. The paintings are individual works, my dear. Individual works in the field of art, not drama.'

There was a silence as all three of them contemplated Archie's jealousy of Rosel's burgeoning achievements, as though it were a small animal on the floor between them. Finally Rosel said slowly, 'Perhaps, Archie, my miners drawing pictures will give them something to say for themselves. Something unique. Some message that will come purely from themas indviduals and connect with the wider world. Not through.... Not through the medium of words and contrived scenes.' She paused. 'You do not like this I think, Archie?'

Archie laughed suddenly. 'You've caught me there Rosel. Fair and square with the wee green gremlin tugging at my heels. Yes, yes. Of course. Paint your pictures, print your posters. We can apprehend their message with our eyes as well as know the play.'

The feeling of rigour and purpose in the Saturday painting group is so strong that I have to keep as my own secret my obsessive copying at home, segment by segment, of the Rembrandt paintings in the book given to me by my Aunt Susanah.

I do this in secret because both Rosel Vonn and Todhunter are beginning to frown on it. For her, copying is a taboo activity, 'That slavish, slavish habit,' she calls it. Todhunter, who - although a genius at the drama - I know to be less a painter even than me – well, he goes on about being 'true to yourself', and how you can 'invent your own way of seeing - your own way of painting.'

So it seems now that copying Rembrandt has become my secret vice. But how else am I supposed to tackle this problem of light as it inhabits flesh, clothes, sky, the very stone walls of this grey town, the very depths of the pit? It's very frustrating. The more I pursue this delicacy, this luminosity, the more fugitive these qualities of light seem. At least in this slavish process of copying I can explore, however crudely, inch by inch, the way that an assiduous master captured light like a butterfly hunter catches his fluttering prey. In this I know I'm training my eye, not necessarily learning how to paint.

In this I'm no slave, whatever Rosel Vonn or Archie Todhunter might say.

****

Archie was in his element working intensively on the monologues and dialogues, putting individuals through their paces under hard pressure, in the style of the great actor managers. He listened when people strained with the dialogue, made changes and adjustments as he went. He kept Tegger by his side, notebook in hand. Tegger himself was vocal about just where Archie had gone wrong. 'Nah, he wouldn't say it like that, he's say…'

Archie encouraged Tegger to alter the texts, pasting and cutting the scripts until some pages were sheer patchwork. Archie talked to Tegger about the balance in a line, a phrase, in a speech, which could be achieved even when that speech stayed true to the way Brack's Hill people spoke.

It was Tegger who suggested using songs of the Great War as part of the chorus. When they tried this Nathan objected. 'Yer makin' gam, aren't yer? Makes a joke of the whole shebang. Songs! This is about the death of miners, man!'

'I don't know about that,' said Archie carefully. 'It adds a measure of counterpoint to the whole action.'

'Counterpoint be b…' Jake stopped himself. Women present.

Greta leaned forward. 'I think it gives a kind of… rest … from how serious are the other parts of the play.' she said. 'I like it. Some of the Shakespeare plays have dances and concerts in the middle of a play, you know.'

I watch and listen to all this, not, if I'm honest, caring one way or the other. Of course, I'd always support Tegger in this or any other deal. And the way he brings Todhunter's grandiloquent ideas into the genuine way of thinking and talking of this place – well he's a wonder. It's no less telling that way. In fact it's certainly more powerful.

At this moment I'm more concerned about a large hole in my left shoe and whether I'll get home with the shoe on. I put newspaper in for a sole but that had got wet on the way here and has broken down completely.

The rehearsal has finished. 'Comin' down to the workshop to help build the soldier's trench?' Tegger calls across. I shake my head and hurry out, moving too fast to be waylaid by Greta Pallister. Once outside on the wet pavement my feet squelch and I have to limp to stop my shoe dropping off altogether.

I let myself into the house and stir up the fire. Then, as I try to ease off the shoe it falls to pieces completely in my hand. It's hopeless. The shoes have been mended twenty times. The edges are totally broken down. They're un-mendable, even with the careful craft of the lads from the cobbler's workshop.

It's such a basic humiliation, no shoes. It stops children going to school; it stops adults going out to look for work. You can't even go for a walk to pass the time.

'Twelve bob even for a second hand pair! Where will that come from?' I ask the question of the empty room and no answer's forthcoming,

So now I am stuck in the house days on end. The weather has turned into a very un- Spring0like whirligig of sleet, snow, hail and rain which has set in for days. No shoes for me means no rehearsal, no painting class for me. I'm not glad of this. I'd go to both in my stockinged feet but would die at the attention this would bring me.

Even Tegger can't 'tice me out, though he's tried,

I've taken the time to finish off the Rembrandt *Night Watch* It's a bit of a rough and tumble of an effort but I think I've caught one or two of the figures right. I put it beside my copy of *The Old Woman Reading* and in front of that disastrous copy of *Susannah and the Elders* where I got the flesh all wrong.

Now I get out the larger of two boards, wooden off-cuts from the workshop. These, at Rosel Vonn's suggestion, I already primed two weeks ago with a mixture of Flake White and Raw Umber. I pull my grandmother's sewing machine out from under the window and drag the kitchen table into its place in the light. On the table I prop up the primed board, using my grandmother's flat irons. Here it will catch what light there is, even on the darkest day.

Now, on the table beside it I put the cigar box of paints - some curled up and half-used. These have been supplied by the teacher who talks to me now but not directly about my painting. Rosel said the tubes were old ones from her dead uncle - no use to him she says. And very high quality.

Now, loading my fine brush with thinned down Umber I

draw in the scene which has been hammering in my head. Shadowy figures of men slumped in the foreground. The roofline of the seam, the straining props. I am working round the space, back-centre, where the woman must go. The white space.

Even by the window the dark in the kitchen reminds me of the gloom of the pit bottom and I'm reminded of the weary heart with which you would set out into the dark for yet another shift. I hear a sigh behind me and whirl round, sure that my father is there. But of course the room is empty. The fire rustles again and a cinder slips down towards the hearth. I close my eyes tight, then open them and start to paint.

In the middle of the afternoon I'm just straightening my back and stretching upwards to rest my muscles when there's a knock on the door. When I open it my visitor is shaking down his umbrella. He smells of old tobacco and whisky. 'Mr Todhunter! ' I say.

'Hello Gabriel!' he says, looking past me.

I stand staring at him. My eyes blinking in the stronger outside light.

'Is it feasible that ye might ask me inside, laddie?' says Todhunter, shifting from foot to foot, umbrella in one hand, a bulky looking sack in the other.

'Yes, yes, come in.' I lead the way through the scullery and back into the kitchen. I hurry to pick up the new painting and lean it to face the wall in the corner. 'It's a bit of a mess… just me,' I say.

Archie stares at the opened paints on the table, now otherwise bare. 'Wouldn't say so,' he says. 'Seems very neat. Nice fire.' He places the closed umbrella in the corner beside it. He nods at my drawings, pinned up on every wall. 'Nice decoration.' He nods towards a study of the defunct winding gear at White Leas Pit. Then he walks across to peer at each of the drawings in turn. He peers at my Rembrandt copies one by one. I resent his cheek. As well as this I'm conscious of my bare feet and equally conscious of the wrecked shoes on the hearth. I can't put them on, or my feet will fall right through them.

Archie Todhunter comes back to the table, lifts up the bulky sack and tips its contents out onto the surface. Shoes tumble out, exhaling the beeswax smell of new polish. There are eight shoes, four pairs tied together in pairs by their laces. He stands them side by side in a line.

'What's this?' I say.

'Shoes,' drawls Archie. 'I'd have thought even you'd recognise shoes, Gabriel, artist that you are.'

The sarky bugger.

'Funny!' I say. 'Very funny. Musta been taking lessons from Tegger MacNamara.' I know Tegger must have told him about the shoes. Tegger's not blind, though he didn't actually mention shoes when he came.

'I want you to choose a pair. A pair that fit. For yourself.'

'I need no shoes.'

'Tegger MacNamara says...'

'Bugger Tegger MacNamara. Wants to mind his own business.'

'Your friend just wants you there at the Settlement. To help with the sets. He worries that you don't paint. There are these portraits…'

'I am painting.'

'So I see…' he puts a finger on one of the boards, still wet, leaning against the press. 'Rembrandt is it?'

'Aye, the *Night Watch*. Apprentice piece. No matter how many times I try I canna get the light right. And the figures…' I blurt out the confidence and wish I hadn't.

'Old Rembrandt had a bit more time to practise, and more light to practice in than you. He was older than you when…'

'Aye I know.' Now I have to say something. I blurt out the words. 'I know you don't think it's any good to copy stuff ….'

'You're right, I don't. It's false and, as you've found, it can be very disheartening.' It's a flat statement. Unequivocal.

'But that's how an electrician, a cabinetmaker learns, Mr. Todhunter. Copying the master. They see how he does it, then doing it in your own way.'

Archie strokes his cheek. 'It used to happen with painters, of course. Whole studios of apprentices copying the master.'

'Well. If it's good enough for them it's good enough for me.' He stares at me and I stare at him. Neither of us will give in.

Then he breathes hard down his nose and retreats. 'Well. Leave that for another day. These shoes…'

'I told you. I don't need no shoes.'

'Look Gabriel,' he says, his voice very hard. 'Those paints on the table, they're half-used, aren't they? They come from Rosel's uncle. Is that not so?'

'Aye.' I'm annoyed that he knows.

'And you don't object to using them?'

'No.'

'Then think of these shoes as paint.' He stands up. 'You need paint to paint. You need shoes to get you down the Settlement to work on your painting. Choose two pairs from this lot that fit well and bring the others back down to the Settlement in the bag.' He's already at the door. 'Get down there. They need you. You need them. I need you.'

I peer out to see that the rain has stopped at last but the afternoon has closed in even further. I shut the door and turn up the gaslight. There are two pairs of shoes that fit perfectly: my choice is a pair of black brogues with hand-stitched tops and barely worn soles. Also a pair of brown shoes in similar condition. Tucked into each is a pair of brand new woollen socks, I weigh the shoes, one pair in each hand. Who wore them last? A respectable man now ensconced in some cemetery? Or it might be a virtuous individual who has sacrificed his best shoes for the poor in the North?

I slip into the socks in the black pair and then into the shoes themselves. I tie the laces tight and walk up and down my grandmother's rug. It strikes me how much lighter they are than boots. But they're good and strongly made and will mend forever in the cobbler's workshop at the Settlement. These shoes will see me through a decade if need be.

Later that day, when I make my way back to The Settlement the members make no comment. I leave the bag of shoes in the empty office, just beside a big sack of clothes with a Herefordshire label on them. No one looks at my feet, clad in their shining shoes. Tegger, when I challenge him swears blind that he'd only said something to Archie when Archie tackled him hard about my absences. 'He was like a man off, Gabe, when you kept not coming. I thought telling him about the shoes would shut him up, marra, honest I did.'

I satisfy myself with giving him a good punch on the shoulder and then I squat down beside him to slop even more *papier-mâché* onto the side of the soldier's dugout.

I feel good to be out and about again. But them something niggles me. These shoes hang on to the end of my legs like foreign objects. I've sunk very low to have to accept charity like this. I dream of selling a picture and buying my own shoes and imagine the pleasure of handing these shoes on to some other beggar.

But later it's good to be here in the workroom at my own easel, to which I have pinned some new bark-surfaced paper obtained by Rosel Vonn. She comes up and watches me square it off. 'You're to paint Greta Pallister, Gabriel. Did you know this?' she announces. 'In her role as Dorothy. With her apron and her shawl. For the exhibition. This will be good, will it not? Greta is very happy about it.'

Greta? Well then. That'll be an experience won't it?

20. Talk of Princes

'The council are all for it Mr. Todhunter. An honour, the Deputy Chairman claims.'

Dev Pallister and Archie Todhunter were sharing a packet of prime Virginia tobacco which had been included, though Archie didn't disclose this, as a charitable parcel from the city of Chichester to the people of Brack's Hill.

Archie surveyed the bowl of his pipe, pleased that for this occasion he'd forsaken his beloved cigarettes. The tobacco was glowing nicely. Its scent sat nicely in his small office.

'So what's your view on this, Mr. Pallister? Cora says there's gossip about a royal visit. Is it true? What do you think of such a thing?' He kept his voice neutral.

Dev paused a moment to collect his thoughts. 'Well,' he said slowly. 'I suppose it shows we aren't forgotten. As far as the national scene goes, like.'

'Mmm,' Archie veiled his throat in the prickly balm of the Virginia.

'The newspapers'll be here. The newsreels. See the state of things.'

'Ye-es.'

'I don't know, but, that such a thing makes a ha'porth of difference in real terms,' said Dev gloomily.

'They say these things bring cheer to the people.' Archie, a republican at heart, was torn about what to think in real terms. He'd had a conversation with the Marxist Jonty Clelland about this idea and Jonty had talked about stolen heritage and royal romances being the opiate of the masses. Or something like that.

'Aye,' said Dev. 'The women like him right enough. My wife was real excited. Prince Charming *was* mentioned,' he said blackly. 'Worse than film stars. Pantomime stuff, if you ask me.'

'I suppose it will cheer people up,' Archie pointed towards the window with his pipe, to the wider world of Brack's Hill. 'Good for morale, according to the Times. The regions are grateful to the prince.'

'Grateful? Oh, well,' growled Dev. 'If *The Times* says so then it must be true.'

'Now, now, Mr. Pallister,' said Archie calmly. '*The Times* is the thermometer of the ruling classes. Even we *Manchester Guardian* readers have to take note sometimes, whether we like it or not.'

The two of them sat in silent for several long minutes, savouring the fine tobacco. Then, 'What I keep getting back to, though,' said Dev, 'is the zoo thing.'

'Zoo?'

'It might just cheer up a lot of people, and I credit that. I really do, Mr. Todhunter. But for all the world it's like we're in a bloody — excuse me — a bloody zoo. The world gawps at us with their newspapers and newsreels. We make pathetic backdrop to this Prince Charming, with our clogs and our blackened faces.'

'I don't see you in clogs, Mr. Pallister. And your face shines like a rosy apple as far I can see.'

Dev shrugged.

'Well do you think others — say those folks down in Wales who seem to have enjoyed a visitation, will think in that way? In the way you see it?'

'Mebbe others have more sense than me. Pragmatic. Is that the word? Take everything as it is, on the surface. Don't think deeper than that. Mebbe that's a good thing. Seeing the surface, going by the day.'

Archie pursued his idea. 'But won't our Settlement here make it different from one of those types of visits? And showing them the educational things you provide for the men at the Club? There's more to see here in Brack's Hill than clogs and blackened faces.'

Dev shrugged again. 'Mebbe they don't want to see the hope of individuals. Doesn't fit their picture. A more elaborate kind of zoo, mebbe. That's all. A zoo with a stage and with dressing up.'

'But it is different,' said Archie, leaning forward now. 'The play that makes its point about the exploitation of the working classes! Your Greta and the others showing their story? Making their point about just how they've been let down. And the crafts, the paintings – some of them are remarkable by any standards. People respect the product of the hand and eye like this in places all over the country, rich or poor. They look in pleasure, not in pity! Our performance, our products are not just on show here because the people who make them are poor and starving. The people of Brack's Hill show their talent. They show their deep humanity. They will show that it is *they* who have something to offer. Insight, pleasure. What you will.' He waved his pipe in the air.

'Mmm,' said Dev, admiring Archie's rhetoric. Not for the first time he thought the feller should try his hand at politics.'

'Mr. Pallister, you don't know who will catch sight of these events, or who it is will recognise the grace of the people of this town. Think of your daughter Greta, acting her heart out...'

Dev put down his pipe. 'I don't know that they'd actually see the play, like. When his Royal Highness was doing such a tour in Wales they say he averaged ten minutes a stop. Thousands of people at each stop. He'd not have time to see a single scene of your play.'

Archie sighed. 'Well I had thought...'

'Ten minutes, that's what I heard.'

'Well, then,' said Archie, 'we'd better make our ten minutes count, then. Or persuade the Prince to watch the lot!'

****

Later that night, after an affectionate if a rather unfulfilled wrestle in bed, Archie talked to Cora about the likelihood of a visit from the prince. 'It seems your gossip is correct, Cora.'

She sat up, clutching the eiderdown to her generous bosom. (The night was cold). 'Oh? HRH? Here?'

'*HRH?* Friend of yours, I suppose?'

She smacked him on the naked shoulder. 'Sarcasm doesn't become you Archie Todhunter,' she said. 'Of course I don't know him, but...'

'But ... what?'

'My last company but one we did that season in the West End. Mary Charteris who was married to the manager, she still writes to me. You've seen the letters.'

He groaned. 'That scrawl! Not worth reading. Gossip. God save me from stage gossip. Tittle tattle.'

'Well, her cousin sings in New York in a small way, operetta and stuff.'

'Cora!' He pulled the sheet over his head.

She pulled the sheet away. 'They say *HRH* – that's what they call him – goes about with this American woman. Very smart piece of goods...'

'Cora, will you...'

'You know what I mean. Well, seems he goes about with her – parties, cruises. Always on his arm. Hostess at his parties.'

'Nonsense. The Americans, how would they know this?'

'In the American papers, that's what. Photos and all.'

Her warm, slightly ripe smell suddenly made him want to choke. He shook his head. 'It can't be so. It would be news here. Just low American gossip. We would know it here first. *The Manchester Guardian* …' All at once he was very tired. He slid down the bed. 'Anyway, Mr. Dev Pallister wasn't too happy about the visit. Said it would be like the zoo.'

'That old sober-sides! Everyone here'll love it Archie! You watch. They'll give anything for a smile from the handsome prince. You just watch. It'll really cheer them up. Not much cheer around here, after all.'

Archie turned away heaving the eiderdown away from her. He spoke over his shoulder. 'I expect you not to say anything about that American gossip. Then nobody will be cheered.'

'Gossip? Me? Been on the wrong end of that too many times myself, to partake in gossip. I'll be as silent as the grave. You watch me.'

21. The Brooch

'Is it much further?' Rosel Vonn leans against a tree. She lifts first one foot and gives it a shake, then the other. The wet grass has stained the fine tan leather, changing it to black in some places. 'Look! My shoes are ruined.'

My shoes, the charity gift from a dead or a charitable man, are also wet with the combination of last night's rain, which has lashed the long grass almost to the ground, and this early morning's dew

'No more than five minutes! Honestly.' I hold out my hand. She takes it.

We've made our way through the trees and just passed the sandstone cliff where the river deepens and turns. The shoreline widens and we're crunching pebbles underfoot. We skirt another bend and ahead of us, framed by the trees, rises the fine tracery of the Priory walls and the church spires and bridges of town of Priorton. In the distance the winding gear of Priorton's two pits stand up against the light morning sky.

'This is all very fine,' said Rosel. 'If you take away the

mining wheels, it is like some fine towns on the Rhine.'

'But, me,' I protest, 'I'm fond of the pit wheel. Hasn't it got the black elegance of a bridge?' We clamber down onto the Priorton road. I drop her hand. 'The place might be prettier without it but what's any town without the signs it's prime work?'

I can feel the heat of the sun now on my back. Our shoes squelch on the drying road.

Rosel glanced towards the boy. His face was so clean that it looked burnished. He wore a white silky scarf round his full throat and his cap was jammed as usual on top of his overlong curls. She looked closely. For more than a week now she'd been making preparatory sketches of him, for her painting of him in his role of Arthur, the trapped soldier.

'Now up here!' I lead Rosel Vann away from the road again and set off up a steep path. We have to skirt round some farm buildings. 'Keep low!' I say. 'The last time I came by here the farmer threw stones at me, sent a dog after me. This big black and white sheepdog took me for a poacher. There's a lot of poaching these days. Who can blame a man for wanting a rabbit for the pot?'

I have never talked so much; I am almost babbling.

How did we get here? Well she has commented more than once about how silent I am. I've had to sit in the workroom for her to draw me, sometimes for more than an hour. So we've had to talk about something.

Then she started to ask me about the Roman Camp that I'd told her about that first morning. I found myself telling her, then, about the remnants of chambers and the stones scattered on the surface. Then somehow we were arranging to come and see it early the next morning when no-one would be about. It seemed essential to keep the visit s secret, though I can't think why.

I stop. The stones in the grass beneath my feet now are butted together in a neat row. 'Look! The road's coming to the surface here. '

She stops and scuffs some soil away from the stones beneath her foot.

'They say the camp stretched as far as you can see…' We cast our eye over the spread of farmland, the scatter of farms and hamlets, and the ever-present winding gear of pits in the distance.

'As far as the eye can see? How would they know?' she says.

I kick at the stone beneath my feet. 'This is one of the great Roman Roads. I forget its name.'

'Very famous? Then you must know it.'

'Watling Street! Dere Street! I've heard both said. It goes right down to Yorkshire. So they say.'

'I see. But would the camp like this really go for miles?'

'They've done excavations. Before the war.'

She shrugs: that elegant movement. 'Gabriel, I don't see…'

I pull her over into a clapboard doorway in the corner of the field. We enter a long dusty shed and close the door behind us. On the floor there are signs of excavations, though not recent. Someone has dug here, laid bare a long wall built of dressed stone. Dusty duck-boards lead safely over a muddy pit. Two discarded trowels stick out of the wall at odd angles. This makes me think of the soldier's trench in the play.

'I see.' Her fingers trail along the top of the wall. 'Would this be where the soldiers lived … slept?'

My turn to shrug, 'I don't know. Storeroom? Guardroom? It was certainly a room.' I jump down onto the mud, pick up a trowel and start to dig.

'Digging, Gabriel? It is like when you worked in the mine, is it not? Or the soldier's trench?'

She has caught my thought. I dig swiftly. 'I never did the digging when I in the mine. They call those men hewers. They are princes down the pit. I was never a hewer. I pulled and pushed coal tubs, full and empty. There is something here.' I start to dig round a lump in the soil as I speak, 'In the pit I just pushed and pulled tubs alongside Tegger. Ah!' I palm the thing up to her: a round piece of metal with a blackened pin attached. 'Here you are!'

She takes it. 'A brooch,' she says, peering at it. 'It's a

brooch.'

I jump up to stand beside her and take a look. My finger touches her palm as I turn it over. 'This is not part of the Petrified Forest. But mebbe it's even older than the Romans. The Romans left before the Dark Ages, so this must be pretty old.'

She offers it back to me. 'This is an amazing thing,' she says. 'Wonderful.'

I close her fingers around it and hold her whole hand tight in mine. 'It's yours.' I say. 'That's why I brought you here.'

Her hand comes up over mine. 'Thank you, Gabriel. You are kind,' she says. Her lips touch my lips, and the brooch in our joined hands is trapped between us. I push myself towards her and she backs until she is stopped by the rough lapboards of the shed.

She turns her head away. I raise my free hand and put it on her long neck, turning her face back towards me with my thumb. In her eyes I see the image of my own face. In my mind's eye I see the dream-woman, that day in the Goaf, crosshatched with this pale face before me. Now there are tears in her eyes and I want to jump the hurdles of time and space between us and press myself ever closer to her, into her, until we are one being. She stands still for a second then she starts to struggle.

The door to the shed rattles and a dog starts to bark.

I step back, put a finger to her lips and then lead her to a gap in the wall boards. 'Here!' The door behind us is being pushed open. 'Run!' I say. We don't stop until we reach the narrow path that leads back up through the woods to Brack's Hill. I wait for her, leaning on a tree trunk, gasping.

She plants herself before me and holds up the Roman brooch. 'So this is for me, Gabriel?'

I look her in the eye. 'That's what I said.' The brightening early sun turns her putty-coloured hair to gold.

She reaches up, now and kisses me on the lips. She tastes of blackberries and mint. My head is swimming. All parts of me are perking up. Even my toes in the new shoes curl up. I grab her hard and kiss her back, my tongue forcing its way against her teeth. Now her hands are on me and her fingers are through my hair and she pulls back to murmur in her own language.

'What d'you say? What d'you say?' My lips are thick against hers. I am mumbling almost into her mouth,

'I say you are a fine boy. A very fine boy.'

With the effort of Titans I pull myself away. 'Boy? Boy? Is that what you think?'

Her hands drop to her sides and the temperature drops several degrees. 'This is what you are,' she says. 'You are a boy Gabriel. Only a boy.'

I walk away from her then. I am ahead of her all the way home and she doesn't bother to run to catch me up. I am embarrassed. My heart is like a stone in my chest. My face feels taut as a sail against the sea air. At the edge of Brack's Hill we part without another word and go our separate ways.

22 Drawing People

Archie Todhunter has fixed it up for me to draw Greta Pallister by her own fireside. 'Authentic setting.' he said. 'The iron oven, the clothes on the overhead rail. Fitting.'

This job has turned out to be very difficult. I thought Greta would be pleased. The girl's been following me around for weeks with those sharp black eyes of hers. But she's awkward about the whole thing. 'Not so stiff,' I order her. 'Stand like you've just turned away from the oven.'

Mrs. Pallister watches us from her sentinel place by the window. 'That one has never done that - just turned away from any oven. Never even wore an apron, our Greta,' she sniffs. 'Never had to. She's a scholar.'

'It's just for the play, Mam,' says Greta wriggling her shoulders. She rolls her eyes at me. 'It's only a play.'

To be honest I can see what see what Mrs. Pallister means. Here's Greta, destined for better things, wearing her mother's old long dark skirt and blouse and a sacking apron covered by one in lighter blue cotton. On her feet are clogs which she's borrowed from her neighbour. Her fine hair is drawn into a long plait that snakes down her back and on her head is a knitted red beret with a pom-pom. This is not the image of a scholar.

As I draw her I note the fine bones of her face, and her long elegant fingers. This is an interesting paradox. Was there ever a pit-lass who looked like this? Fine long hands. Soft skin. The answer to that, as a matter of fact, is probably yes. The grammar school girl today was likely the pit lass of her grandmother's day. Intelligence is no bar in the pit. Look at Tegger. Look at me.

'Can I sit down a bit?' she says now. 'My legs ache?'

'No,' said her mother from the window. 'Stand yourself still. How can the lad draw you if you're wriggling round?'

'All right then,' I say. 'Sit down a bit.' I lift the sketch from the makeshift table-easel and put it beside the others: two quick close-up sketches of her head, her hands; a long full length study. I know I have caught the attitude of her figure and her pale blue-veined feet in their old-fashioned clogs.

Greta and her mother come to pore over the drawings on the table.

'You've got her to the very life!' Her mother's work-worn hand touches the surface of the paper, running a coarse fingernail down her daughter's profile. In that touch I can see unspoken pride and intense love. For a second in Mrs. Pallister's face I can see the young woman she was and the young woman her mother was, before her.

I look at Greta who – her spectacles back on her nose – is peering at these strange projections of herself on paper. 'You're as good as she says you are,' she says.

'She?'

'Rosel Vonn. I wasn't going to let you do this but she told me I'd regret it if I didn't let you do it. That you were a proper artist.'

I try not to think of Rosel Vonn and our last embarrassing encounter.

Mrs. Pallister took the full-length sketch across to the window to get a better look. I could see that she didn't want to part with it. 'You can have that one if you want,' I offered. 'Afterwards.'

She looked across at me hard. 'I thought these were for this exhibition thing'

I shake my head. 'No. These are my preliminary sketches. The first tries. The decent paints are down the Settlement. I'll have to work there. These sketches'll set it up and Greta'll pose down at the Settlement for a proper painting.'

I take the picture from her. Turn it over and write *'For Mrs. Pallister, drawn by Gabriel Marchant,'* in my best handwriting. 'I'll need it to set the big one away, but when I think that's all right I'll give this back to you?'

She smiles at me. 'Will you?' I wish I had a proper picture of our Neville or our David. All I have are those dead things.' She nods at the photographs of her sons which have pride of place on the mantelpiece. They are dead things: stiff photographer studio portraits, the same as a thousand others. 'I miss them' she says suddenly. 'And soon I'll miss our Greta here'

Greta put an arm around her. 'You won't miss me, Mam. I'll stay with you always'

Mrs. Pallister shook off her hand and sniffed. 'Oh no you won't, lady! Your brothers are away, out of this dead and alive hole and I'll get you away out of here if I die in the attempt.' She looks at me full in the eyes and I know exactly what she's on about. 'Aye. I'll have this one off you, son, if that's all right. An' I'll find a nice frame for it, or get a nice frame for it in Priorton. So, wherever this drawing is, our Greta will be living and breathing on my wall.'

It takes three long Saturday mornings in the painting hut at the Settlement for me to get Greta's portrait anything like. It was a bit uncomfortable there at first but Rosel and I have got over the embarrassing event at the Roman campy by pretending it didn't happen. She has completed a painting of Nathan but is not happy with it and will not show it. 'Why not?' I say. 'My picture of Greta is nothing like perfect but I let you see it'

She shrugs, 'Nathan was unhappy to sit. He is like these people here. A peculiar reserve. When he saw the finished article he said I must not show it to anyone. So I will not.'

'Well, that's a waste of work!' I say. 'You should tell him…'

She put up a hand to stop me saying anything further. 'A man owns his own image, Gabriel. If we take that away from him, he has nothing.'

'So what will you do with it?'

'I gave it to Nathan. I believe he has destroyed it. Archie did say he would talk to him.'

It seems that this thing we are doing, this making of images, has a kind of power. In a peculiar way I am comforted by this.

Rosel has urged me to hurry with Greta's portrait as there are others to do. So much for art as a long journey! Rembrandt took months over his paintings. Years! Now she is hassling me like a real schoolteacher.

I am now conscious that Rosel has the painting proper of me to do. Maybe she won't do that after the fiasco with Nathan. Or after the fiasco in the Roman camp with me. That'll be an ordeal, being painted by her. But whatever happens I won't destroy it. I would never do that.

I seem to have been with Greta Pallister all day. This morning I took her mother the sketch which I had marked for her alongside few more. Afterwards Greta and I walked across to the Settlement together. After these sittings I'm feeling feel easier with her. How can you feel awkward with someone you have drawn fifteen or twenty times?

As we walk she talks away about some teacher telling her something about the writer Ovid. I only half listen to her but I'm quite easy with her now. I wouldn't say I am as easy with her as I am with Tegger but you'd have to go a long way for that.

The thing is, although I've been looking at her on the

surface I feel now I've seen somewhere inside her, way below the surface. I feel that I know her and wherever we go in the future I'll always recognise her. I know now that she still watches out for me, even lies in wait for me, but this no longer makes me uneasy. She's young, just a kid, but quite a nice person.

I suppose I am beginning to understand what it is that she does. She watches for me in the way I watch for Rosel Vonn. Ever since that day at the Roman Camp, I have to admit I do watch out for her. Sometimes I lie in wait for her: I wait by the White Leas slag heap; at the end of Queen Street where the Settlement is. I wait and watch.

'He's waiting for you again.' Cora came to stand behind Rosel, peering past her through the sitting room window. She put a cup of tea on the table beside Rosel.

Rosel stirred. 'Who? Who waits?'

Cora laughed. 'The one that you watch. Standing by the lamp there. Young Gabriel with his golden halo'

Rosel backed away from the window into her room and sat down at the table to rescue the letter she was writing to her father. She was still worried about him. Now his friends – so called – were ostracising him because he had championed Goldstein the dentist and had actually warned him of a police visit. Now he had written letters to government officials about Goldstein.

He had rejected Rosel's suggestion that he should come here to England, or go to America. He'd dismissed that swiftly. *This is my country, Liebling. I will not abandon it. If the people of goodwill free who then would watch the fire? And I need to keep the watch for your brother Boris. In the army he's in their hands even more than I am. He stayed here last week-end. We drank French wine. It was like the old days. But he too is on edge about things.'*

'I've seen the boy watching you in the rehearsals.' Cora had settled down on the couch to stitch the hem of the apron that young Greta was to wear in the play.

Rosel's mind came back from the grand apartment in Berlin. 'Who?'

'Gabriel Marchant. Standing on the corner'

'This is not true, Cora. You imagine things. As you say he is merely a boy.'

Cora held up the apron and peered at her neat row of stitches.

'His portrait of young Greta it is very fine, I think he will work on one of you soon. As Maggie Olliphant.' said Rosel. 'That too will be a very fine picture!'

Cora would not be put off. 'Greta watches for him. And he watches for you,' she said.

Rosel shook her head. 'A very fine portrait of the girl,' she repeated. 'But in the style of Rembrandt, I fear, rather than Gabriel Marchant. The light from the window. The treatment of the clothes. Pure Rembrandt.'

Cora broke the thread with her teeth and rolled the end in a knot before beginning to sew again. 'Is there something wrong with that? Isn't Rembrandt what they call an old master? The boy could do worse.'

'Gabriel must have his own style.' Rosel shook her head. 'Or the old ones will possess him and he will not go forward. This is of great concern to me.'

Cora jabbed her needle into the fabric. 'So you're concerned about him, the angel-boy?'

There was a rustle of paper as Archie put down *The Manchester Guardian* with a vengeful swish. 'For goodness sake, Cora, will you leave Rosel in peace, with your jabbering? Of course she's concerned for the boy. He's a person of talent. He is her student. Of course he's interested in her, she's his teacher. But as for your sneaking insinuations, use your eyes, woman! You have a penny dreadful mind. The lad's young enough to be Rosel's son. Is that not so, Rosel?'

Rosel looked up from her letter. 'What was it, Archie?'

'I was just saying to nosy Cora here that young Gabriel Marchant is of an age to be your son.'

Rosel put her head back down over her letter so her face was in shadow. 'This is so. But I have no son, then or now.'

Archie raised his paper again, to read of the Italian leader Mussolini rejecting an offer of British land in Somaliland in return for keeping his hands off Ethiopia. 'I told you he'd never do that.' he announced.

'Who?' said Cora.

'Mussolini.'

'So you did.' Cora turned back to Rosel 'Did you hear about the prince, Rosel?'

'Prince?'

'The Prince of Wales. He's coming to Brack's Hill in November and the rumour is he'll come to see the play'

'Of course she knows. Everybody's talking about it. Even so it isn't certain,' grunted Archie from behind his paper.

'Well. I think he's coming and I think we'll meet him, that's for sure,' said Cora firmly.

Rosel looked at the empty sheet in front of her. That would be something to write about to her father. 'Why does he come here, the Prince?' she said, interest picking up in her voice at last.

Archie folded up his paper and put it on the table by his chair. 'He comes to show pity for the poor and dispossessed of this town. To draw the world's attention to it. To demonstrate his sympathy and that of his father the King. To reassure them he is on their side. He has done this in many parts of England. And the Empire, in fact. It's called the *common touch*. You have to have it if you're going to be king.'

'They say he's very handsome' said Cora. 'I've seen him on the newsreels'

'He's very short in height,' said Rosel.

'What?' said Archie.

She glanced across at him. 'My father says this.'

'Your father has met him?' said Cora, eyes wide. 'Actually met the prince? Where? How?'

'Before the War. Austria. Switzerland. Somewhere. Skiing. My father is older, but …'

'And he said he was short?'

'Barely up to my father's shoulder.'

'But he would be tall, your father, like you?' said Archie, interested in spite of himself.

'Yes. My father is more than one metre,' she nodded.

'But the prince is handsome. You can tell it on the newsreels,' persisted Cora.

'Perhaps they put only short people beside him.' said Archie thoughtfully. 'They do that in films.'

'Archie! You're such a misery!' said Cora.

Archie turned his shoulder to speak more exclusively to Rosel. 'You will have to speak with the Prince when he comes, you know.'

'I do not see this' said Rosel. 'There are many people for him to speak with in Brack's Hill. It is not my town.'

'Ah. But he will speak to you in German. He's fluent in that language, I hear.'

'I know this,' said Rosel. 'So are they all, in that family. My father tells me this.'

'Perhaps he should be careful not to speak in German,' said Cora, snapping off her last thread and folding up the apron. 'Not in Brack's Hill.'

****

My next portrait is Cora in her role as the stalwart leader of the women. I make sketches of her in the sitting room of the Settlement before I embark on the painting. Cora is very hard to draw. I screw up pages and pages of preliminary tries. From his seat in the corner, Archie looks on with amusement. I wish he would not stay in here while I do this.

Cora is more concerned. 'What is it?' she says. 'Am I that hard to draw?'

'To be honest, yes you are'

'So, why's that, then? Am I so ugly?' She looks me in the eyes.'

I shake my head. 'I look at you one minute and you seem this kind of a person, and another and you seem another . . . You've got me tearing my hair out.'

'Don't do that. Those curls are far too pretty to tear out'

'Cora!' warned Archie from his chair. 'Will you stop flirting, woman? He's young enough to be your..."

'Woah, Archie!' she says cheerfully. 'Can't I have a little flirt? Your friend Rosel Vonn can flirt away with all and sundry, and has all of her painters in love with her and half of our actors. So why not me?'

Despite my red face I pursue my immediate thought. 'Can't you just *be* Maggie Reynolds for me? Not Cora Miles dressed up as her. Or. . Lady Macbeth. Or . . . Titania. I want you to *be* Maggie Reynolds.' I feel suddenly quite desperate. I can't believe it but I have to turn away and blink the tears from my eyes. I don't know whether this is because this task is beyond me or the mention of the flirtatious Rosel Vonn.

Cora looks at me and is suddenly not frivolous at all. She closes her eyes then opens them. Her face is clouded with pain. Her shoulders hunch forward. The hands holding her shawl clench into knuckles. Then she peers towards me with pain-blanked eyes.

'That's more like it,' I say, flicking over another page of my drawing pad. 'That's much more like it, Cora'

23. Tegger

The morning after I've finished Cora's portrait I have a bit of a lie-in. I have been thinking and dreaming in paint for days. I smell of turpentine and linseed oil like a baker smells of yeast and the chips shop man smells of fish. I make myself a mug of tea and drink it slowly by the low fire. There is nothing to eat in the house and it's two days to dole day. I'll have something when I get to the Settlement. Cora always has bread there, and maybe some offcuts of ham from the butcher's. She expects it to be eaten. She makes sure there's no feeling of charity about this although that's what it truly is.

I tried one day to thank her for her thoughtfulness but she waved my thanks away. 'It's there for everyone,' she said briefly. 'Was it Napoleon who said an army marches on its stomach? Well to my mind all who come through these doors are Archie's shock troops.'

Cora's finished portrait is not bad, though I say it myself. She likes it and Archie growled that I 'had Maggie Olliphant to a T' but, he thought could be down to Cora's remarkable characterization. I don't object to this because I think it's true.

It feels too long since I've seen Tegger properly. There was the business of the shoes, then there was this thing – or this *no-*thing – with Rosel Vonn. And all the painting. Tegger himself hasn't been around. Archie Todhunter has asked me twice where is Tegger? Seems Tegger has some stuff for him. Some writing, some pages. What's he up to?

And now I'm missing Tegger myself, like you'd miss the wind in your hair.

So I set out to rout the devil out. I've never been to the encampment behind the High Street. The habit of avoiding it predates Tegger's living there. He usually - always -calls at my house for me, He has never wanted to see me there among that flotsam and jetsam of lost souls. I know this, even though he hasn't said so.

It's already ten o'clock when I get there. The thin drizzle sits in the air like a veil and the vans are a drab sight, pulled into a higgledy-piggledy half circle. Almost buried in long grass, they're a decrepit collection of wooden and metal wheeled contrivances, some solid topped, some with canvas drawn across them to keep out the weather. One man has dug over a patch ten feet square beside his van and set potatoes in it. At the centre of the circle are the still-smoking embers of what has been a big fire. Last night there must have been quite a blaze.

On the steps of a van painted dark green sits an old man He sucking hard on the stump of a cigarette and wearing a lumpy woollen muffler over his collarless shirt. His face is crevassed with the sucking pathways of a thousand cigarettes. I ask him about

Tegger. He has to stop coughing before he can try to answer. Then his eyes bulge as he coughs again and waves his hand towards a low narrow van painted dark blue. I rattle its battered wooden door and shout, 'Tegger!' I rattle it again. 'Tegger! Come on, man!'

A bear-like growl seeps through the wood and I push the creaking door open. I leave it wide open so that the smell of barely digested beer and cigarette smoke can force its way out. The space inside the van is the size of our back pantry. A narrow truckle bed. A metal stove of some kind. A cupboard. A chair with clothes thrown over it and battered boots standing unlaced beneath it. I pull back a curtain on a crude string to let in light through a roughly framed window.

The heap on the narrow truckle bed groans.

'Tegger!'

The heap groans again. I pull back the quilt to expose his curled up shape. He puts his arm up to shield his eyes from the light. 'Tegger! What is it, man? Get yourself up, will you?' I push at his elbow to expose his grinning face, his sleep-sticky eyes. 'What's on here?' I say. 'What's on here, man?'

One blue eye opens wider, 'Go away, man! Get away, will you!'

'All right then,' I turn and put my hand on the knotted rope that does for a doorknob.

His voice comes from behind me. 'Wait on, man! Sit yourself down out there and I'll be out in a minute.'

When, five minutes later, he comes to sit beside me on the caravan steps he has his clothes on, but that's the only difference between him and the dormant creature I saw minutes ago. His dark hair is still greasily awry, his feet are bare. His eyes are still squinting at the light. He stretches his dirty feet before him. 'Sorry, marra,' he says.

'What's all this?' I say. 'Living here like a stoat.'

'You know why. They won't let me live at home. The dole…'

'I know that, but look at the state of you!'

He offers me a cigarette from a battered five- packet of Craven As. I shake my head. 'What's happened here when I wasn't looking, Teg?'

He sucks hard on the cigarette and coughs briefly. 'Last Saturday I went to Sedgefield Races with a lad from here at the vans.'

'Races?'

'He'd heard of a brahma[i12] horse running here. *Ambrosia the Second*. What a runner!'

'You went to Sedgefield? How?'

'Walked.'

'What for? Why d'you go?'

'I told you. To put some money on this horse.'

But you haven't got any money.'

'Passed the hat round on the site. Remember the miracle of the loaves and the fishes? Everybody pitched in. We promised them a share.'

'And you lost?'

'Nah. Ambrosia the Second romped home. I told you he was a runner. We won. Twenty pound.'

'So you shared that out?'

'Nah. Not those winnings.'

'You spent it then? On…?'

'Well, yes. In a manner of speaking. We spent them on another horse. *Old Rascal.* He heard that was a brahma too. It won. Twenty to one.'

'It won?'

'Aye. Two hundred and twenty pounds.' He licks his lips as though the words are honey.

'What then?'

'We brought the money back here to the vans and shared it out, fair and square. Not a man on this site wasn't over the moon. Ten pounds apiece for just pennies outlay.'

'So what' d'you do with the money?'

'Well three of the lads went off to the station. Tickets to London. One said he was off to America but I have me doubts.'

'What about you. The rest?'

'Well we put money in the kitty for beer and saved the rest to take home, like. To the family.'

'And you did that?'

There was a long silence,

Then, 'Some did,' he said. 'Me and Tommy...'

'Tommy?'

'That lad that knew about *Ambrosia*...'

'What about him?'

'He knew this horse called *Old Licorice*, running on Wednesday. We were going to double our winning, see? For our families.'

'And you did this?'

'Well *Old Licorice* was away like a bat out of hell, so we though we were in for it.'

'But ...'

'The silly bugger jumped a shadow where there was no fence.'

'So you lost your money?'

'Not all of it. I had two pounds left.'

'So ...'

'So we brought it back, pooled it and went for a drink.'

I am weary for him. 'Yeh daft lad,' I say. 'Nothing for your Mam, the little'ns...'

'I know that, marra.' He throws his cigarette into the dirt and screws it down with his bare heel.

I stand up. 'Right,' I say. 'Get yer boots on.'

'Why should I do that? No-where to go.'

'Yer can't go anywhere smelling like a stoat, marra. First to my house and we'll get the tin bath out. Then breakfast. Only tea, but that's something. Then we'll go down the Settlement and get some grub. Todhunter's been asking for you for three days. Says you promised to show him something.'

'Some rubbish I've written,' he says. 'About the vans. There's this magazine he wants us the send it to…'

'Get that. Bring it.'

'I don't know where it is. I think we used those sheets to write the bets on. Tommy and me … '

'You can get yourself down our house and write it again, at my table. Come on, man! Come on, I say!'

24. Characterisation

Back at my house I make Tegger jump into a tin bath of tepid water from the fireside boiler. It takes the best part of an hour to get the smell of the alehouse and the stench of the racecourse off him. Then I set him down at my kitchen table with torn our pages from one of my old school books.

'I won't remember!' he warns,

'Write,' I say.

As I look at him sitting there, clutching the pencil in his big hand. I feel a sense of fit as close as a key turning in an oiled lock. Tegger rescued me when my father died. And now I've rescued him. Like changing positions in a dance.

So that's how I started calling for Tegger at the vans and bringing him home with me every morning. He wouldn't have come if I hadn't called for him. It's true that there's the risk that someone will lay him in with the dole for coming here but I can't leave him there in the dirt and the damp. And with Tommy the horse man.

It's through keeping guard on Tegger that I've managed become embroiled with this woman called Marguerite Molloy, who occasionally serves at the Lord Raglan and who's generous to a fault. If she likes you.

Days after rescuing Tegger I'd been painting all afternoon in the Settlement, trying to get to grips with the next portrait: Archie Todhunter in his role as the pit manager: the owners' man. He's there in the big workroom when I arrive. The finished portraits have been hanged here to make room to work in the painting shed. They are all there except that of Nathan. We are still not sure whether or not he destroyed his portrait.

Archie peers first at Greta's portrait and my just-about-finished picture of Cora in her role as Maggie Reynolds. The room smells of linseed. The surface paint, still soft and malleable, gleams like skin in the light of the overhead bulbs. I see now there's more work to do on both portraits. The light on Greta's face is not quite right. And Cora needs some aquamarine on the edges of her apron where the light catches it. We're out of aquamarine, the dearest of all the colours but Rosel Vonn says she has some on order. She's had a word with Archie.

'You've been putting a lot of time in here,' says Archie. 'These are not bad. Not bad at all.'

'Nothing else to do, have I? They'll take weeks to dry, the paint's so thick.' I say this just for something to say. I am never really very easy with Archie Todhunter.

Archie takes his glasses from his top pocket and looks at

Greta's portrait even more closely. 'This one's very ... believable, to the life,' he says. 'Stares at you out of history, out of time.'

The light falls on Greta from the left, it bleeds over her, turning her drab shawl to ochre, her heavy plait to pure gold. The thread of light on each hair was a bit of a challenge. I borrowed an especially fine brush from Rosel Vonn to tackle that. The light catches the generous pink curve of Greta's under lip and turns the earnest gleam in her left eye into gold. But her cheek ... her cheek! I have been clumsy there. It's not right. I'll have to do some more work on that.

'A very creditable piece of work.'

'It's not perfect. Needs more work on the cheek.'

'Rosel Vonn says you can work on something too long,' he says.

'She didn't say that to me.' It was Rosel who talked about the problem of light on full flesh, made me realise that Greta's cheek needs work. 'Anyway,' I turn away from the portraits on the wall. 'I'm here to make a start on your picture, now that I've got you standing still.'

He's a very hard man to get hold of. We had to sit a clear ten minutes looking at his diary for his to find spaces for these sessions.

'Ah yes!' says Todhunter, barely concealing a smile. 'Archie Todhunter as the pit manager? Where do you want me?'

'I thought I'd do some sketches of you in your office. Like the pit office, see?'

I work away at sketches of him at his desk; with a cigarette in its holder; with his pipe; without his pipe; with his fountain pen in his hand; without his fountain pen; standing up; sitting down. Then I sketch him in front of his desk, leaning back on it, hands in his pocket. The picture of confidence in his role as pit manager. I like this one. He chuckles when I ask him to push his trilby hat slightly further back on his head. 'Doing a bit of characterisation, I see, Gabriel!'

I shrug and pin another sheet to my board. 'It's gotta be right Mr. Todhunter.' I'm not happy about that smug smile of his. He thinks we're all children to be led with silken threads. I can't believe I'm the only one to see through him.

'So what....'

'Can you sit still, Mr. Todhunter? I need to concentrate.' He knows I mean for him to keep quiet. He raises his eyebrow and does as he's told.

As I sketch my mind goes back to Rosel Vonn. She's the one getting hold of all this paint for me. She'll give me curt advice, now and then when I'm painting. She worries too much about Rembrandt, I think. But sometimes I do wait for her, casual-like, so we can happen to walk along together. But that never happens.

And that very special thing has never happened again, after the time at the Roman camp. When I'm around she never appears. Either that or she's dodging down back streets to avoid me. So the fact is we're back where we started. Some kind of armed truce, I suppose. I feel like a little lad, stamping his foot and saying 'It's not fair! It's not fair! Look at me! Look at me!'

All the time I'm thinking this the drawings roll off my pad. Dozens of them.

'D'you think I could move?' Todhunter wriggles his trunk. 'Stiff as a board, old boy, with my knees braced like this.'

'That's all right Mr. Todhunter,' I say. 'I'm done here now.'

'Thank goodness for that.' He shakes one leg and then the other and then comes round to see my efforts. 'I must say, it's been like turning on a tap, setting you away with this art business.'

'I was away with drawing well before I got here to the Settlement,' I say through gritted teeth. 'My auntie can draw and my grandmother was great with the colours and textures.'

I put the drawings one on top of another, block them together, roll them and tie them with black tape. 'You've Wednesday afternoon clear in your diary. Is that right? I'll have the thing blocked in then and will start to paint. In the work room, that'll be.'

I can tell I've caught Archie out. I know that his fingers are itching to touch the drawings, to turn them over, to hold them up to the light. They're good. We both know that.

'No need to take them away Gabriel. I can keep them here.'

I almost give in. He has great authority.

I shake my head. 'I'll need them back at the house. I always pin them up around me. Take a look at them through the day.'

I would swear he's blushing. I really have caught him out. Archie Todhunter? Vain? Never. 'Fine, fine,' he says brusquely.

'Wednesday afternoon. Now then. Is it three o'clock already? I've the Reverend Coston Wells of Durham University coming to see me at three fifteen. He admires your work. Proposes sending some of his students here to...'

'The zoo.'

He frowns. 'Zoo? No. No Nothing likes that. Something about seeing what we do here and setting up a new...'

'Zoo.' I have to say it again.

'Have you been talking to Dev Pallister?' Archie manages a laugh. 'You're too thin-skinned, Gabriel. You'll get nowhere with such a thin skin, my boy. Your talent brings advantages to others in this place, they may be less talented but they're equally worthwhile. You have an advantage over them. To capitalise on this advantage you have to tolerate people like our visitors. Such encounters will get your work known.'

Capitalise! I scowl and button my jacket over my precious drawings. This watchful, managing side of Archie Todhunter harasses me. He can be too much in charge. Sometimes it's like I'm a pet dog or something: wheeled out every time he wants someone to be entertained by a few tricks.

'All I want to do is paint, Mr. Todhunter, nothing else.' I say. Then I sweep out like some *prima donna*. I'm only seven steps down the road when I regret my sharp tone with him. All he wants is for my own good: the good of all who come through the doors of the Settlement. I say this over and over to myself like a spell. It's just that his close watchfulness, his plain admiration does get under my skin. I can't think what to do about it.

Halfway down the road I realise that I meant to go and have a word with Tegger in the workshop but in my eagerness to get away from Archie Todhunter I've come away without doing that. From the street I look up at the windows on the upper floors of the Settlement, for any sign of Rosel Vonn. Of course there is no sign. I've made a proper fool of myself there all right. She's barely started on her picture of me. Fat chance that that will ever get done; now she can't even bear the sight of me.

All this is tumbling through my head when I turn into the yard to my house and see this strange woman sitting on the brick boiler in the corner of the yard. Beside her is a small enamel pan of fresh eggs. These appear once a week with no message. I know that they're from Steve, my father's old marra down at the allotments. The eggs come in very handy in these hungry days but I can't get the will to go down the allotment to thank him. I think I'm afraid I'll find my father there. Or something of him.

I pick up the eggs and survey my visitor.

The woman has bright hazel eyes and her skin is a deep golden brown: a change after the chalk-pale faces which are so familiar round here. Her great cloud of soft black hair is topped with a bright green beret with a feather fixed on it with what looks like a golden brooch. In my mind I start mixing the colours for her portrait.

The feather trembles as she nods and jumps down off the wall. 'Look at me, why don't you? Who're you?" she says jumping down from her perch. She's nearly as tall as I am.

'Who're you?'

'I asked first.'

'My name is Ga … Gabriel Marchant. This here is my house. That's my wall you were sitting on.'

'I'm looking for Tegger MacNamara. They said at the vans that he lived here now.'

I glance around suspiciously. 'He doesn't live here.'

'They said he did.' She laughs. 'Don't worry. I'm no official or anything.'

'He visits here,' I say. 'Most days.'

'Is he in?'

'How would I know? He just calls now and then. Here at the house,' I say carefully.

She stares at me, then her gaze sweeps down to my shiny brogues and back up to my face. Various parts of me prickle to attention. I turn away from her demanding gaze and put my hand on the door-sneck. I speak to her over my shoulder. 'You didn't tell me your name,' I say, leading the way into the house.

'Marguerite. Marguerite Molloy.' She follows close behind. I can smell her woman-sweat alongside a trickle of roses. *Attar of Roses.* My mother had a bottle with this on its label.. My father kept it by him long after she died.

We're standing in the kitchen, too close for comfort.

'Sit down,' I say. Then I squat by the fire and poke at it till it flames start to lick up the chimney.

She sits down, very tall on a kitchen chair.

'You don't sound like you come from round here,' I say.

She smiles. A chip on the left side is the only flaw in a perfect smile. Her lips are the colour of mulberries.

'You mean I don't *look* like I come from round here. So where do you think I come from?'

Anything I say will be wrong and she will laugh. 'How would I know?' I say.

'I come from South Shields.'

That's only on the coast twenty five miles away. I feel she must have come much further.

'My mother came from Brack's Hill but she lived there on the coast for a lot of years.'

'And your father?' Now I'll be in trouble.

'He came from Mauritius. He was a seaman.'

I have no idea where Mauritius may be. 'Did they come here with you?'

She shakes her head. 'He died in an accident at sea.'

'He drowned?'

She shakes her head again and the fine fibres of her hair are touched by the light of the fire. 'Not so lucky. He was a cook. The galley caught fire.' Her body moves with a faint shudder.

'Is that why you're here?'

'This is my mother's hometown. She was born here. I brought her here to be in her home place… truth is, she ended her days here.'

'I'm sorry.'

She shrugs. 'Well, are you going to sit down too, or will these questions go on for ever?'

I'm staring at her, drinking in the sight of her: the golden gleam of the flat planes of her cheeks, the way her night-black hair springs from her high brow. Half of me wants to touch that face, the other half wants to paint it. My fingers itch for my brushes.

I realise she's no spy. I know that now. 'What do you really want with him, with Tegger?'

'Well, I work at the Lord Raglan and he's there from time to time. He was missing for a few days. Then he came in a few days ago to treat the bar. Pile of money in his hand. Then he vanished again. I thought sommat might have happened to him.'

'So he … are you … courting?' What a daft word that is.'

'We're friends.' Her voice growls with annoyance. 'Apart from that, you mind your own business.'

Now there's a clatter in the yard and the subject of our speculations bowls into the room. His face lights up when he sees the girl. 'Why, Marguerite Molloy! What brings you here?'

'Well for one thing I thought you might be dead, as you were dead-drunk when last I saw you. The last thing I saw was you being carried out of the Raglan toes up. You looked like you'd heard the last trump.' Her tone is severe.

He laughs easily. 'Just a bit under the weather from the filthy brew you draw in your blessed pub, love. And also from other pubs further afield. You could fire cannons with that stuff. Charge of the Light Brigade, all right.' He looks at us, from one to the other. 'Now why are you two sitting there like two jars of jam? Let's get the kettle on and have a nice cup of tea.'

I'm aware of the sheaf of drawings stuck in my coat like a corset. I mumble something, and then make for the stairs. In my bedroom I take out my drawings a lay them carefully on the bed. Their laughter floats up the stairs and invades the narrow room like smoke. I'm reminded yet again of how easy Tegger is with women. His mother, his sisters, his various licit and illicit women friends - these are the ordinary taken-for-granted sentinels in his life. For me, in the main, women are intimidating strangers who may not be approached directly. They are the magical sirens of the deep seams.

When I get back downstairs I find another invasion of my privacy. She's peering closely, one by one, at my pictures, which still line the walls. Worse, she is singing their praises.

'Yeah,' says Tegger enthusiastically. 'He's all right, my marra. Yeh'll have to get him to paint your picture, flower.

I'm annoyed now, mostly because Tegger is expressing the very thing I was thinking only minutes ago. I charge back upstairs and shrug myself into my jacket and pick up the drawings of Greta Pallister.

When I get back downstairs she is still examining my pictures. 'I know this man has a gallery in Newcastle,' she says looking me in the eye. 'He would like these. I'll take you there, Gabriel,"

I ignore her. 'I've got a message to do,' I say.

'Yer off then Gabe?' says Tegger, not urging me to stay. The girl is surveying me with sharp-eyed amusement.

'Yeah. I'm off,' I say through gritted teeth. The door clicks behind me and I can breathe more easily. I make my way across the ten streets to the Pallister house which stands on a corner and has a bay window and demure net curtains.

Mrs. Pallister is pleased to see me and having looked at all the sketches is delighted with the worked up sketch that is her final choice. 'I've sorted this frame,' she says, pulling an ornate frame from the back of the press. 'A horrible picture of my grandmother, it was. I've given the frame a nice clean.' She proceeds to put my drawing into the frame, settling it behind the old Victorian mount, and then clipping the whole thing together. Then she hangs it on the wall where the other painting had hung and makes a great play of resettling it, making sure it is plumb-line straight. 'Sets it off, doesn't it? Our Greta to the life. Here, get a proper look, Gabriel.'

I stare at my work, somehow given new legitimacy by its heavy Victorian frame. It seems like someone else has drawn it. It exists outside of me. It is art. Is it art? I blush at these overblown thoughts and turn back to Mrs. Pallister, who's staring at me, beady-eyed. She's regarding me as though I'm some particularly delectable pudding which she is about to consume.

I become aware that she's actually speaking. 'What do you think?' she's saying. 'Could you do that?'

I frown. 'What?'

'A picture of my Dev. Greta's dad. He's a big man in the town and a portrait …'

I'm already shaking my head, unwilling to be consumed in one gulp. 'No question of that Mrs. Pallister. Sorry. I'm just learning, really. And I've all these to do for the Settlement. Too many really. But Archie Todhunter wants them all ready for the Prince's visit.'

Her round face lights up. 'November, Dev says. He'll be on the receiving line, of course. He'll shake the Prince by the hand. Did you see the Prince on the newsreel? Handsome as any film star, he is. Better. So concerned for everybody. Me, I read every single line about him in the newspaper…'

I wrest my gaze from her just to stop her going on. I look around. 'Is Greta about? Is she at home?'

She stops in mid-flow, disappointed at my lack of interest in the Prince. 'Well, she's upstairs doing homework or something. I have orders not to disturb her. She can be a madam sometimes.'

I can see why. This mother has a big presence and can be very disturbing in her own way.

She goes to the door and shouts. 'Greta!'

Greta comes very quickly. She must have heard the commotion and been waiting her cue. She has a red knitted cardigan on top of her uniform skirt and an ink mark on her cheek. Her plait is down her back and her glasses are firmly on her nose.

'The lad's brought the picture of you.' says Mrs. Pallister. 'Look. Doesn't the frame set it off?'

'I did say….' I say hurriedly. 'I thought you might like it. You weren't a bad model.'

Greta takes off her glasses to take a closer look, her finger on the glass. 'A strange thing, looking at a picture of yourself,' she says. 'Not like photos.' She has her nose two inches from the glass. 'A painting is you and not you. Photos can only be *you.*'

I'm backing towards the door. The desire to escape this house is overwhelming.

'Stay for a cup of tea, son,' says Mrs. Pallister. 'I've got Co-op cakes.'

'No …no. I…'

'We haven't time,' says Greta. She lifts her red knitted beret from the hook behind the door. 'We have to go to the Settlement. Special meeting of the cast. Five o'clock, wasn't it Gabriel?'

'But your father will be in!' said Mrs. Pallister. 'The tea!'

'Half an hour! I'll be back in half an hour.' Greta throws the words behind her like a ball to an eager dog. 'An hour, mebbe.'

We're out of the door before I can blurt the words out. 'What meeting? I just came away from there. Archie never said anything about…'

'Did we need to escape from her or not?'

I thought it was me who needed to escape. Not *we.* Here is Greta Pallister telling lies at my behest.

'We can easy walk across to the Settlement,' suggests Greta, her tone reassuring. 'That'll make it nearly the truth.'

We walk along awkwardly side by side, a foot apart. Around us a regular drift of people makes its way towards the High Street. The town buzzes on a Saturday night, even in these thin times. People gather to reminisce, to joke, and even sing in chorus. They talk of their gardens, their rabbits, of the horse that nearly won, of the lad that's really coming on in the foot-racing, of the new trumpet player in the club band. They do this even if they can only afford half a pint of beer in a whole evening. They do it even if they only stand outside the pub to talk. Talk costs nothing and truly seems to have great value. These gatherings are mostly men with a sprinkling of the more forward women. Perhaps the more respectable women have their own equally momentous gatherings, pondering their own and the world's affairs over cups of tea.

This thing about the women is a mere impression, a guess. My experience of women in their home life is the skeleton of a memory. For a second I wish it was my father who was striding down to the Saddler's Arms or the King's Head, and my mother who was staying home with her bosom buddies sorting the world.

I really am on my own on this planet.

25. The Promise

When Greta and I get there the Settlement rooms are open and empty. Like Church doors the doors to the Settlement are never locked. Archie Todhunter likes members to go in freely and work on their projects. In the early days there was a problem, Greta tells me, 'Some people just took it for a club where you could go and have a bit of a crack and a free read of the papers and a cup of tea. They saw it as a break from the house, like. Mr. Todhunter had to make it clear that you could only come if you had joined up, registered for a course or were changing your library books – proper members, you know.

'That seems a bit, well, mean, that,' I say.

'Yeah I always thought that. Just coming in here would be a break for some folks from the four walls of their house,' she says. 'We ourselves get a break don't we? We come and do our plays and our paintings and stuff. Sometimes I think that Mr. Todhunter has built a little empire of his own here, outside the world of the dole and the hunger marches and people being so miserable with no work.' She adds this as we come into the workroom. She goes to stand before her own portrait. She takes off her glasses and peers at it. Then she puts them back on and stands at a distance to take in the whole thing, scowling slightly as she concentrates.

I turn on more lights. The girl's close scrutiny of my paintings makes me feel uncomfortable. It's as though she's staring at me and I'm naked. I really want her approval. I really want Greta to like the painting, to like me. How can I want the approval of this child, this schoolgirl? I'm defensive. 'It's not finished,' I say at last. 'The cheeks are not quite dry yet. The tones will change, Darken, Eventually,'

She puts out a hand, palm outwards towards the painting. 'It is a dark picture isn't it? But there is so much light in there as well, isn't there? The light seems to come from inside the girl. From right inside her. Look at her, Gabriel. Did her mother love her? Did her father beat her? Did she play whips and tops in the spring? Did she take out her skipping ropes in the autumn?'

I stand behind Greta and try to see what she's seeing: the girl who is not really her. For me the whole exercise has been about representing Dorothy, Arthur's girl: the blocking in of the bulk of her body; the drawing forward of the points of light; the depths of colour in the shadows. I think now that this has worked because of my observation in the pit galleries, of the dense colour of the medium ground,

Greta turns towards me. The light from an overhead bulb glints on her glasses, making ellipses of light. 'Don't you see, Gabriel?' she says, her voice tense.

'Don't I see what?'

'This amazing thing that has happened. Mr. Todhunter – and now Tegger – have written about these people. The boy that you play. The woman that Cora plays. The girl I play. We have clothed them with our voices, words written by Mr. Todhunter and Tegger. And now here you are, you and Rosel Vonn. You have painted them. Brought those characters into their own life. You have made them real. Isn't that kind of magic?

I am so affected by what she says that I reach out to her and grasp her in an awkward hug that shows my delight in her delight. It truly is an awkward embrace. 'I'm glad you like it, Greta.'

She frees herself and pulls down the sleeves of her red cardigan. 'Gabriel?'

'What?'

'Did I do you a favour, sitting for you all those hours so you could paint this masterpiece?'

'It's no masterpiece, Greta.' She has me on the back foot here. 'But yes, it was a favour, if you like,'

'Well will you do me a favour? In return, like?'

She is a cunning one. I need to be careful here. 'All depends on what you mean by a favour.

'It's a very big thing Gabriel.'

'Like I say. It all depends. No matter how big it is.'

Her narrow chest heaves. She takes off her glasses, 'You'll know by now that I'm sort of very clever. It's common knowledge isn't it, around here?' This was a statement rather than a question,

'Pretty obvious, that.'

'And now they're all talking about me going to college, Even Cambridge. I'll probably get there.' She is so certain of herself.

Me, I can hardly think of tomorrow,'

She takes off her red beret and places it on the table beside her spectacles. 'It's very delicate, like.'

'Get on with it. Stop messing about.'

Her cheeks are pink She puts her hands flat on the table and looks down at them. I look too. They are fine, well-shaped. Her nails are perfect ovals. So perfect. I recall now how difficult they were to draw.

'Well,' she says, 'they tell me there's this college thing. Then I'll go on and get a decent job somewhere away from here. Maybe teaching in a school. Maybe I'll join the Civil Service. My dad says the Civil Service will run the country on its own before long, if we don't watch out.'

'So what are you doing here and now? Showing off how clever you are? I told you, I already know that.'

'No, no! There's no virtue in being able to mug things up is there? God-given, my Gran would say. It's nothing really to do with me.'

'So?'

'There's this one thing.'

I sigh deeply, 'Spit it out will you?'

'Well, whenever I look into the future all I see is a very dry life. All books and no...*passion*. I'm just reading this novel where it says we have only to connect the prose and passion or we'll remain beasts or monks. Or nuns like those women teachers in my school. There's this very clever one. Quite pretty too. But she's a spinster and lives on her own in a big house on Durham road and keeps two cats.'

I fumble with this idea. 'Suppose it's all right to be that teacher. Better than being some woman round here washing with a poss-stick on a Monday with four kids round her skirts and a husband who'll give her a clip if she steps out of line.,'

Greta leans forward and puts one perfect hand on my arm. 'But don't your see, Gabriel? In that picture that you've painted here Dorothy has a real life. What you've done is connect the painting with the passion. In those dark times Dorothy has a future with someone she loves. With Arthur.

I'm getting hot under the collar now,

She looks up at me, her eyes slightly unfocussed. 'Me, I'll be a very clever, dried up old spinster like some of those old trouts at grammar school.' She takes a very deep breath. 'I don't want to be like that, Gabriel,'

I'm even hotter under the collar now. And in other places too. First Marguerite Molloy. Now this, 'So, what are you saying?' I ask, keeping my voice off-hand.

'I'm saying that – just as a favour, a great big favour, I know.' She takes another deep breath. 'I want you to do *it* with me, Gabriel. That thing that men and women do. So I don't grow up to be a dried up old spinster, so I know what it's really like when I read about it in books. I've read it up. I know about it. You can be sure of that,'

Now I am beetroot red. 'Bloody hell!'

She laughs. A tinkling sound, 'Yes, It does sound weird when you say it out loud. You're blushing. Even *I* am blushing and I'm the brassent one round here.'

'Brassent fond!' I nod vigourously,

'Well?'

I stare across at the portrait then back at her.

'If you do this, Gabriel, I'll mention you in my memoirs when I'm an undried up old dame. Maybe spinster, but not dried up.'

I really can't think of what to say,

She puts on her glasses and stares at me. 'Don't tell me you don't know how to do it!'

'Dinnet be daft, Of course I do.' It's all hearsay of course. But I do have these urges that I've had to deal with myself: practice runs, you might say. It's certainly all in working order. And Tegger has told me all about the tongue kissing with lasses in back-street games. But I've never done the thing myself. Never.

'Go on, Gabriel!' Now there is a thread of desperation in her voice, 'Just think what you're saving the world from! Me as a miserable, frizzled up old trout raging at the world for vengeance for my virgin state,'

Now she's used the word virgin. I'm desperate. 'All right. All right! I'll do it.' Anything to stop her going on and on like this. 'But...'

She goes full steam ahead now. 'I've thought it all out Gabriel. You've to find out how we can do it so I don't have a baby. There are ways, I've read about that too. This is not one of those traps you know! I want to do it without getting caught. But I'm not really quite sure how that works,'

'Oh. So there's sommat you don't know!' I growl. 'I...'

'Don't you be so sarcastic,' she says fiercely. 'This is serious. Deadly serious,

'What I was going to say is that we shouldn't do this until after the play's over and done with.'

'Oh, I thought...' Her bottom lip comes out,

'Look Greta,' I say desperately. 'It'd be impossible to sort this now. Too much going on. All these rehearsals. The paintings, the sets. And all this fuss about the Prince.'

She shrugs. 'After that, then?'

'Yes'

'Promise?'

'Yes.'

'Say it!'

Girl games, I think. 'I promise,' I say.

She stands up and jams her red beret on her head ad pushes her glasses up her nose, 'That's that then,' she says brightly, 'I told Mam half an hour and I've got some homework to do.'

'I ... yes. Half an hour,' I say lamely. I watch the door as it clicks behind her. That girl has got me outranked, outflanked and quite defeated. And what's more she has me all worked up and I'll have to go to some private place to calm myself down before I can get on with anything, anything at all. I couldn't paint a bucket in this state.

My house feels deserted when I get home, although there is the faint cinnamon smell of a woman in the air. No sign if Tegger and the girl. Disappointed as well as relieved I take all my pictures, one by one, down from the walls of my house. I place each one in turn on the table and examine it.

Just as well, I think, that these pictures are not in the public eye, that they're not in public view. Those that are not mere apprentice-pieces are rough, ill-conceived things. My copies of Rembrandt's precious *Supper at Ammaus* and his *Night Watch* look as though they've been painted with pokers. I know that these new portraits that I'm working on at the Settlement are not great art but I also know that they are a world better than these daubs,

'So you really are a good drawer then?'

I spin around. Marguerite Molloy is looking at me through open stair rails. She's just as neat and finished as she was earlier, but her soft cloud of hair is now flowing free from her feathered cap. My gaze moves behind her and from the dark reaches of the staircase Tegger looms into the light and bustles her down the stairs. 'Gabriel, marra! You're back!' He's not embarrassed.

'I do live here, like.' I heap the pictures up into a neat pile, pick them up and make for the door to the front room. 'Your friend says she's just going,' I say over my shoulder. Then I slam the middle door behind me.

Two voices, man then woman, trickle to me through the closed door. Then I hear the back door bang. Then there is complete silence. I stack the pictures carefully in my grandmother's big press, and then return to the kitchen.

Tegger is sitting there alone, smoking a cigarette. 'What cheer, marra!' he says,

'You cheeky bugger!' I say. What can I say, really?

'Sorry about that, Gabe. Her turning up like that. She helps old Flaherty out at the Raglan. She's off there now. Starts at five, Finishes when they close

'And you...?'

'I was just there at closing time last week. We hit it off, me and her. She likes a laugh,' He pauses. 'She was dead interested on your pictures, you know.'

'None of her business.' I fill the kettle and press it so hard on the fire that the coal grinds and moves.

'She says she's seen pictures in a big gallery in Newcastle that're not as good as yours.'

'She can't have. These pictures in the house are daubs. Crude copies. Apprentice pieces. My private affair.' Still, I am curious, 'Which gallery was that?' I've never been in a proper gallery.'

'Just a big gallery. She didn't say.'

Now I can't resist my curiosity. 'Were you up there in my bedroom?'

'Nah,' he said, surveying the glowing tip of his cigarette. 'Not yours. The other one,'

Now thoughts of the gallery with rows and rows of proper paintings jumble up with thoughts of those two, upstairs on my father's bed, doing what they do. These days there's just a flock mattress on bare coiled springs in there. When Tegger was last in that bedroom he was with me, attending to may dead father's body,

I wanted to ask Tegger just what he and the woman did together. I mean, apart from the raw mechanics which any dog knows, I desperately wanted to know how you stopped the worst happening. The very worst thing. A baby can anchor a man as tight as any sea anchor. I know three men in this row alone anchored in such a way, with mouths to feed and no wage coming in. That will not be my story, nor will it be Greta Pallister's,

Tegger lights another cigarette from the last one. 'She wants you to paint her,' he says. 'Marguerite does.'

It's a great relief to laugh at such a stupid idea,

He grins up at me, 'She has money, you know,' he said, 'She can pay you to do it. You'll enjoy it. Be sure you will.'

To be paid to paint that woman! Now that *is* a thought,

26. Cutting Hair

Two weeks later I'm on my own in the painting shed, finishing the first stage of Archie Todhunter's portrait when the door opens and in comes Rosel Vonn. In my painting Archie is standing there by his desk. His blue fountain pen, his black bowled pipe and his amber cigarette holder are placed carefully on its polished surface. In his hand is his black cigarette-holder fitted with a glowing cigarette. The smoke is drifting upwards, partly veiling his face. For this portrait I've imagined Archie in his role as pit manager, 'the owner's man'. Looking at it now I see that this character retains something of Archie at his least creative and his most over bearing, overconfident and meticulous: fussy about small things.

But now Rosel is in the shed and is examining my paintings one by one. I have brought them here from the big room to work on the final stages. They all need some work and I've just acquired some bone black and aquamarine for the finishing touches.

Rosel stands there, focussing on the portraits quite casually. You wouldn't think she'd neglected me at all in these weeks. She has not offered to get on with painting me as Arthur. Now suddenly she's here, acting like the teacher, carefully appraising my work. I know I shouldn't react too strongly to this; she is my mentor after all. I should expect her careful appraisal,

But still she worries me. And, I have to admit it, she excites me.

Then she laughs and I nearly jump out of my skin.

'What?' I say. 'What is it? What's wrong, Are they so funny?'

'Your work has such *brio*, Gabriel. Such *élan*,'

'*Brio? Elan?* What're you on about?'

'Such energy. Such speed! Such style. You've gobbled up Rembrandt and Turner. You've ploughed your way right through my new paints, my new brushes…'

I wait, bewildered.

'And now,' she says, 'at last you make something good, something brave. Something of your own.'

'You're saying these are big clarty daubs aren't you?'

'Clarty? What's that?'

'Mucky. Sticky.'

She laughs up into my face and it's like light seeping over the horizon, 'No, Gabriel,' she says, 'it is as though, with all your energy you shake up all the rules in a bag, pull out any one that suits you and make up others of your own. But all these you make to work for you.' She steps back and the swinging bulb gleams on strands of her putty-coloured hair. 'Perhaps you are right. Perhaps it is a bit *clarty*. Still there is character here, even delicacy.'

Now I move behind her and try to look at my work with a

stranger's eye. I think of the day I stood behind Greta, wondering and worrying about what she thought of her own portrait.

'So what do you think about them?' Rosel says now. 'These paintings of yours?'

'We-ell. Cora, Archie and Greta were good people to paint,' I begin. 'They were all patient, waiting for me to do what I really can't. Or couldn't. I tried to paint them like they were showing me the dark and the light places not just in the people they play in the play, but in themselves. In their real selves. It seems now that those two things were happening as I painted them.' I pause. 'No, there were really many things happening.'

She nods, willing me to go on,

'All this time I am painting, having - as you say - gobbled up Rembrandt and Turner, I'm really thinking about the pit. How the dark works with the light. I'm thinking about my grandmother, who knew the magic of colour and the pattern of ordinary things. I'm thinking about my Aunt Susanah who gave me the Rembrandt book and painted kingfishers herself. I'm thinking how nothing comes from nothing...' My voice fades into the air of the dusty shed. I've never said so much in my life, about something that matters to me as dear as life.

'These paintings are good, Gabriel. Be sure of that,' she says slowly. She nods her head, her face turned slightly away. I will her to look at me but she resists. Now I want to her to pull me to her. I want to engulf her. I want to stroke her putty coloured hair and put my lips against hers, my cheek against her cheek. I want to be part of her. I want to be in her and to have her in me.

She knows this. I know that this is why she won't look me in the eye

She moves hurriedly to the door and looks somewhere to my left. 'Oh Gabriel! I have a terrible thing to ask you. It's for your portrait as Arthur. Could you get someone to cut that mane of hair of yours? Archie tells me that in the trenches they would never have allowed such abundance. *Short back and sides*, he said. *Arthur needs short back and sides*,'

I laugh at her now, my inner tension melting away. 'So you're not worried that I'll bring down the walls of the Temple?'

She frowns and at last looks me in the eye. 'The Temple? Ah yes, Samson !' She smiles. 'Even close-cropped, Gabriel you will keep your strength. A Roundhead, perhaps, though not a Cavalier. You see? I am well versed in your English history am I not?'

The door closes behind her and I set about my work again with – what was it? – *brio*.

It's Marguerite who cuts my hair in the end. She's in and out of my house regularly now, to see Tegger. I've given up worrying what my neighbours with think of this regular visitor trotting down the back street and letting herself into the house like she lives here,

I listen to their laughter up there in my father's room, and wonder whether there was ever laughter in that place. You would probably have to go back to the time of my grandmother and her husband to find laughter. And my grandfather was killed in the

South African war. When my father slept in that room it was a grim place to be sure.

One morning I came in with the milk from the corner shop to find Tegger sitting meekly on one of my kitchen chairs shouting and yelping as Marguerite cut his dark wiry locks with some very small scissors. She was making a very good hand of it, her brown fingers fluttering around his head like butterflies.

I watch for a second then ask, 'So,' I say 'would you cut my hair, then?'

'So,' she says, smiling across at me, 'would you paint my picture, then?'

She's quick, I'll say that for her. I shake my head, 'It doesn't work like that,' I say.

She puts her head in one side and carries on with her task. Tegger yelps as she nicks one of his ears. 'Hey, man! You've got me pouring with blood here!' He pulls his shirt cuff down over his hand and dabs at his bleeding ear.

'Well,' she says, cocking an eye at me. 'If I do cut your hair will you at least think about painting my picture?'

'I was thinking about it anyway,'

Her lips broaden into a smile as she ducks her head to concentrate on trimming Tegger's hair back to an inch all over. 'There you are, you baby. What do you think of that?'

He tucks away his bloody sleeve and stands up to examine himself in the over-mantel mirror. 'Not bad for an amateur, like,' he says. She flicks at him with the towel she's just removed from his shoulders, 'Bad boy!' she says, She turns to me. 'Next for shaving?' she says.

'Not as short as his, mind!' I warn as I settle down in the kitchen chair. Now I watch as my yellow curls mix with Tegger's dark hair on the stone floor. I wriggle a bit in the chair, then settle down. It's quite relaxing, having Marguerite move around me, snipping away. I have a lot of hair and it takes quite a time with her tiny scissors. Finally, 'There!' she says. She pats my shoulder just as she had patted Tegger's. 'See what you think.'

I peer in the mirror and for a second my father looks back at me. I blink and chase away the resemblance. My hair's not cut as close as Tegger's but still it's short and smooth as rabbit fur. She's certainly done a good job

Tegger sweeps up the hair with the floor-and tips the shovel full of it onto the back of the fire. For a second the air is filled with the sharp acrid smell of burning hair. My nose itches,

'Tell you what,' says Tegger, 'I gotta go down the Settlement to read some of my play to Archie.'

Tegger's the only one, apart from Cora and Rosel Von, to call Archie to his face by his first name. I don't know how that came about. Perhaps it's a writer-to-writer privilege. Archie has sent Tegger's story about the men in the vans to a magazine and they are going to publish it. And now Tegger, much encouraged, has written this play about the Hunger March. Believe it or not, it's supposed to be funny! Not much to laugh about there you would think.

There's certainly not much to laugh about here is there? Low dole. Now work, no money. Hardly enough food to keep body and soul together. The undertaker's having his best year for a decade. Without work people have to build a way of living that reminds them that they are human. Our way of doing this these days is all about The Settlement. Others find their way through their allotments where they grow flowers as well as food for the pot. For others it's their pigeons and the excitement of breeding and racing them. It's dawning on me that if you do something to the point of obsession you can stop the sheer pain and shame of having to live almost like a beast in these cruelly hard days.

'I tell you what,' says Tegger now. 'Why don't we all go down the Settlement and Marguerite can take a look at those big paintings you've already done. They's canny-grand, Marguerite. Canny grand. Just wait till you see them.'

In the street she walks between us, linking our arms as we march along. We draw quite a lot of glances. I'm not sure whether this is because of our saucy promenade or whether Tegger and me are shorn like sheep and look like a pair of book-ends.

At the Settlement Tegger vanishes into the office to see Archie and I lead the way to the big workroom and turn on the lights. My paintings have been brought out from the shed to finish their drying in this warmer atmosphere.

Marguerite stands in the centre of the room and whistles. *A whistling woman and a crowing hen brings the devil out of his den.* Where have I heard that? My Grandmother? Can't remember.

'Hey Gabriel!' Marguerite says, 'These are really good.' She walks along the line, stopping at each one. 'I tell you what,' she says, 'if I cut your hair for the rest of your life will you do one for me? Will you do one of these big pictures of me?'

I keep my face blank but my fingers are itching to do just that, Cadmium Red, Prussian Blue; Yellow Ochre, Veridian and Green Aquamarine. But just because it I want to do it so much I feel it's important, that I don't let her know all this. I cough. 'If I did paint one of these of you then it'd not be *for* you. You'd not own it. It would be mine. I need to keep the paintings together.' This thought has suddenly occurred to me: that I should start to keep them all together. I didn't know or why I think this, but I do. Maybe I should be more anxious to sell them: here I am, wearing charity shoes and without the price of another much needed jacket or the price of my next proper meal.

'Oh dear,' she says. 'I didn't think…'

I shake my head and say firmly, 'It's not possible. I need to keep them together.'

But she's so crestfallen that I feel I have to make her an offer. 'There'll be drawings and stuff.' I say. 'Maybe you can have one of those. I gave one for *her* mother.' I nod towards Greta's picture. 'She's put it in a frame.'

'Right you are! A drawing it is.' She's happy again. She moves closer to Greta's portrait. 'Is she your sweetheart then? Wonderful looking lass!

'Well, in the play she is. That's what these portraits are for. But in real life she's no beauty. She still goes to school.'

Marguerite laughs. 'Just see that look in her eye. She's no schoolchild.'

I sit down at the central table. It's stacked with books now, for the Wednesday afternoon library. The box where the library tickets sit is like a little wooden coffin. The tickets are filled in with Archie's immaculate script.

Marguerite comes to sit down opposite me. 'Tegger was tellin' me that you'd never seen proper paintings, hanging in a gallery, like. Up on a wall,'

'Tegger should keep his mouth shut if you ask me.'

'Looking at these portraits, it's hard to believe that you've never seen proper ones in a gallery. These look like proper paintings to me.'

'That's what they are,'

'Listen! I know this gallery in Newcastle.'

'Tegger told me that. I couldn't fathom how you could know about things like that. How could you be in a gallery in Newcastle.'

'Well, it was a rainy day and … don't you worry about why!'

'Is it very big, this gallery?'

'Yeah. Really big, Enormous. We could go there on the train to Newcastle one day and take a look at it.'

We? Now I'm tempted. 'Will Tegger come?'

'No reason why not. Anyway you're mistaken if you think he'd stay behind with us on a jaunt. We could take some of your paintings there and…'

The door clashes and Rosel Vonn comes towards us, her head

tilted in inquiry. 'Hello, Can I help you? Can I ... Gabriel, your hair! I did not recognise you. You look ...'

'Older?' says Marguerite cheerfully. 'Doesn't he? I made quite a man of him didn't I?'

'She cut it,' I say. 'Rosel, this is Marguerite. And this is Rosel Vonn. Marguerite..

Marguerite gets to her feet and shakes Rosel vigorously by the hand. 'Doesn't look quite the same without his golden locks, does he, our Gabriel?

Rosel frowns. 'You are his family?'

A peal of laughter from Marguerite. 'No! Me, I'm nobody's sister. More a friend you might say. Me cutting his hair was a bargain. And exchange of skills you might say. I cut his hair. He paints my picture.' She sits down again at the table,

Now I feel like an object – all hands and feet, I want to make all kinds of explanations to Rosel. That Marguerite is really Tegger's friend; that she has this wonderful face; this apricot glow on her skin; that my fingers itch to paint her.

But I can't say any of this,

Rosel nods, smiling with a chill politeness. 'I am sure that will be a great challenge for Gabriel.' She moves closer to me, putting Marguerite out of her eye line. 'Will you have time today to come down to the shed? Nathan and Mr. Conroy now have the dugout constructed. I need some preliminary sketches of you there. Archie tells me that Mr. Pallister has an army uniform that he will lend you. He says it will fit. I did not believe that at first but it seems that Mr.

Pallister has grown fatter as he had become older. But first you must collect it, the uniform. At Mr Pallister's house.'

I glance at Marguerite, Her black brows are raised and there is the shadow of a smile on her face. I feel that I am a ball, being patted gently between them. I look back at Rosel. 'So, then. What time?'

'Perhaps one o'clock this afternoon? While there is still light from the skylight?'

'Right. Right.' I clear my throat to stop myself from choking. I glance across at Marguerite. 'We need to get on now. I'll need that uniform from the Pallisters.'

Marguerite stands up, comes to full attention and gives a remarkably authentic military salute. 'Yes sir, captain. Anything you say, *mon Capitaine.*'

I bustle her out of the room. 'No need for that!' I burst out as we tumble into the street outside.

'No need for what?'

'That saluting business.'

'Hey, Gabriel, Where's your sense of humour? It's just a bit of fun. What an old grouch you are.'

We walk along the street, passing a woman who's pushing a cart with three bawling children in it. The woman glances across at us with dull eyes,

'I have to go to the Pallisters,' I say. I don't want Maguerite to come with me. What would Mrs. Pallister make of her?'

She shrugs. 'I have to get home anyway. This is my way.

Don't you worry your poor old shorn head.'

'Home?'

'I have two rooms at the Raglan. I've got my own outside staircase. That's something,'

'Is your mother with your there?'

The tumble of laughter drains away from her. I can feel the loss. 'I told you. I brought her home to spend her last days here,'

I remember this now. 'I'm sorry, I shouldn't have ...'

'Anyway she's not there at the Raglan. She might be hovering there above it but if she is she'll have very raggedy wings. But anyway you can still come for a visit. Any time you want. Like I say, I have an outside staircase. You could even come now.'

'Like I say,' I echo her. 'I have to get to the Pallisters.'

She shrugs. 'Suit yourself, honey. But you will come. I know it. Oops! Nearly past my corner. See you soon!' She gives another military salute and clicks away on her bobbin heels, the feather in her hat trembling as she walks,

I don't know whether this woman makes me mad or amused. I do know that I am looking forward to that train journey to Newcastle to take a look at this gallery. Of course I have no idea where I'll find the fare. I'm in debt to the corner shop for my milk and my daily bread. I've no spare money. None at all. Maybe I'll be forced to sell the painting to Marguerite after all.

27. A Triptych

So here I am at the Pallister house again. When I get here Greta is at school. Dev is out on council business and Mrs. P. is ironing at the kitchen table which is padded with blankets and covered with a singed sheet. A large clothes horse squares on to the fire and Mrs. Pallister has one flat iron on the hotplate and one on the table. There are piles of clothes ironed and un-ironed on every surface. The air smells of singed wool, lavender, and vapourised bleach. My Grandmother's house smelled like this on ironing day.

Mrs. Pallister laughs when she sees me. 'Why Gabriel Marchant! Where's your hair? I'd'a passed you in the street. You look a good ten years older.'

'Why thank you for that.'

'No, no. Still a bonny face. But where are those curls?'

'At the back of our fire, seeing as you ask. They made a good blaze.' Cutting and burning my hair had been like burning away the last of my childhood. No bad thing. 'I've come for Mr. Pallister's uniform,' I say. 'His uniform is to be my costume for *Blood and Coal*.'

'Yes. Mr. Todhunter came and talked to Dev about it. It's all laid out in the front room. Our Dev says you'd better try it all on, to see if suits.' She bustles me through the middle door and bangs it shut behind me. I can hear the click of crockery. The dreaded cup of tea is on its way. I'll not get out of here very fast.

The uniform is immaculate, except for three neatly mended holes in the left leg. The buttons shine out of their bed of folded khaki; the trousers have knife edged creases; the boots gleam like new tar. On the table, in a neat line, are three medals.

I strip off and step into the uniform. It fits perfectly. Against the back wall is a black japanned press whose three mirrors are cobwebbed with wear and damp. For a second in their milky surfaces I see a stranger: someone who fought through many hard battles and came back unscathed. How hard it is to connect the heavily built, round-jowled Dev Pallister with that young man in the mirror. I mimic Marguerite Molloy's salute in the mirror. Then I drop my fraudulent hand and shake my head, thinking that this could be disrespectful of both Dev Pallister and of the imaginary Arthur.

The door clicks and in bustles Mrs. Pallister. Her eyes bulge. 'My life! It's a ghost here. You could be Dev standing there! He was always such a good-looking man, was Dev. Even coming home covered in mud with lice in the seams of his uniform he looked good. Always.' She pauses. 'So many lost friends!' Her voice trembles. 'My own two brothers…'

I am helpless 'But Mr. Pallister came home,' I say urgently, to relieve myself of some responsibility for her pain.

She sniffs. 'Aye. That's true.' She puts her hand over the medals. 'What about these? He said you should wear these.'

'I can't do that Mrs. Pallister. It'd be such a fraud wouldn't it?'

She frowns. 'But Dev says Mr. Todhunter told him the painting would be of a lad who's fought in the war. A brave lad. You can wear it for that brave lad, and for all the brave lads, Gabriel. You can wear it for my own brave lad, Dev Pallister. He was not much older than you are now, then. Go on. Wear the medals for all the lads that didn't get back who didn't collect their medals.'

Words like this have been said so many times that it's a wonder they have any meaning at all, in these twenty years since - these twenty years of hard use. But here I am, nearly crying myself now. 'It'll be an honour, Mrs. Pallister.'

'Now you can go off and get your picture done, Gabriel. The uniform suits you. At least you won't have to wear it to go to war.'

I look down at myself, more immaculate in these borrowed plumes than I've ever been before in my life. 'No. I cannot walk through the streets like this. I'll get arrested for false pretences.'

She stares at me, and then laughs uncertainly. 'Well … mebbe not.' She ducks down behind the horsehair sofa. 'Here's Dev's kit[ii] bag. But all my good pressing'll have come to naught.'

'I'll roll it up carefully and shake it out as soon as I get back to the Settlement. Archie Todhunter'll keep an eye on it in between times.

She nods and leaves me to it. When I go through to the kitchen she has tea and Co-op cakes on the little table under the window. I eat my cake standing up, pleading great urgency, that the 'painter woman' is waiting for me at this very minute. 'You go, son!' Her glance is dreamy; the image of young Dev, just returned from the war, printed for a little while on her retina.

When I reach the end of the yard and calls. 'Gabriel, son.'

I turn. 'Yes?'

'I'll tell our Greta you called.'

'Aye. You tell her.' Then I swing down the back street, borrowing a soldier's heel-down hard-won gait. Then back into my mind rolled the promise I made to Greta: how I was to do her this extraordinary favour. I start to run.

When Rosel sees me in the reassembled uniform she shakes her head. 'But aren't we in the trenches for this image, Gabriel? Arthur is down there in all the mud. Is that not so?'

I look down at the immaculately pressed uniform, the white puttees. I imagine how long it took Mrs. Pallister to get it this way. 'We can't mucky this,' I say. 'Mrs. Pallister'll be mortified.' I shut my eyes tight. My head is tumbling with notions and images. Then I suggest, 'What about ... say, an image of Arthur as an immaculate soldier and then him in the trenches and mebbe as a miner before the war. Like, in shadows behind.'

'That's three paintings, Gabriel!'

'But that's the message of the play isn't it? A land fit for heroes? A fight worth fighting? I'll wear my old pit hoggers and my old pit vest for the trenches. And you can make it look like khaki under the mud...'

'Stop! Stop!' She holds her brow and shakes her head. Then she walks around to stand close to me and I get hot under the collar and in other places too. 'So we will have one in full uniform. One in the trenches. One in the pit. A *triptych*. I will have to work very quickly. It is illustration rather than art, but...'

'A what?'

'A *triptych*. A painting in three parts. Sometimes joined, sometimes not. Often used in religious paintings.'

'Triptych! Well I keep learning these new words from you, Miss Teacher.' I'm grinning like a fool now, pleased to get my own way and pleased that, for once, she'll have to pay me full attention while she paints me. At the very least I'll be able to watch and learn.

I had thought these sessions with Rosel drawing me would be personal, close. But I'm wrong. As the days go by she's very focussed on this task of the triptych. And all about the shed she pins drawings she's already made, of colliery wheels and Durham skies. There are odd ones of me (with my curls) looking sideways and straight on.

One day she brings in a wonderful sketchbook – her father's I think – that has pages and pages of scenes from the trenches. It's only when you look closer you can see that its German soldiers, not British, who are pictured there. I don't mention this. It seems too rude, somehow.

Rosel tells me exactly how to kneel, how to handle the

shovel, how to hold the gun. She looks and looks at me, but this time it's not personal. I might be a tree in the forest, or one of her marble statues. Still, I relish these times. I feel I know her better by her very actions, by the very furrow on her brow as she does a tricky bit of shading. At least after this we can never be strangers.

I'm in a bit of a muddle these days. I look at Rosel and I think of Marguerite Molloy. When I see Marguerite messing on with Tegger I think about Rosel. Then I even think about Greta Pallister and imagine myself with each of them in turn being close to them, like Tegger is with Marguerite.

Some kind of triptych, that.

Apart from Sundays, when things are a bit quieter, the weeks now for both me and Tegger are very full. I've little time to be angry at my father or bemoan the empty house. Tegger only manages to get away with the horse lads to the races once in a while. He's preoccupied with Archie Todhunter these days, and involved with him in the writing of a new play.

Then there are the long play rehearsals for *Blood and Coal*. The problem is that just when us actors are getting more confident that what we're doing is right Archie Todhunter is getting more and more dissatisfied with everyone's performance,. The players are getting restless.

Archie insists on going, line by line, breath by breath, through everyone's part, making the rest of us sit and listen when all we want is some time out for a smoke or a gossip. Tegger is usually there by Todhunter's side changing words and phrases, still tightening the whole thing up so it almost pings in the air.

Archie's concentration and passion make it impossible to complain out loud but there are mutterings behind his back. Nathan Smith has said more than once that it is worse than the bloody pit, with the Deputies bossing your every move. Greta frowned at Nathan once when he said this, telling him that Mr. Todhunter was only trying to get it right for all of our sakes, 'We'll all look like fools on the day, if it's not right, Mr. Smith. Think of the Prince!'

Nathan turned away and she didn't quite catch him saying 'Bugger the prince.'

'What d'you say, Mr. Smith?'

'Nothing. I say nothing to you, miss clever Greta.'

My scenes with Greta are not so uncomfortable now. They are becoming more natural I suppose. I wish I could be as objective about this as Rosel is about painting me. But I'm not as pure as that. Each time I find myself looking forward a little bit more to being Arthur and laying my lips on Greta's soft mouth. It makes me tingle. And I it brings the promise to my mind.

Archie is still raging on about *continuity*. He has it written down in his book and one day makes a show of reading it to us, enunciating every word clearly.

1. The connection (through the girl-and-boy-romance) between the trenches and the women seems to be working.

2. The connection between the trenches and the goings on in the coroner's court is working. The description of the miners in jeopardy and the soldiers' dilemma has strict parallels.
3. However, the connection between the coroner's court and the chorus of women – lead by Cora – is lacking.

Cora comes in for some stick from him regarding this, even though it's not her fault. Maybe because she, like Archie, is professional.

Tegger pipes up. 'I know what to do, Archie,' he says. 'Baffer Bray!'

'What?' says Archie, scowling at him. 'Who?'

'We could make more of the news comng from other parts of the action. There's Baffer Bray. He's this funny old gadgie. A bit … well … a shilling short. You know. He must be seventy-five. Always with the women, he is. Chatting, gossiping, like he's one of them. Should've been a woman, so they say down at the Raglan.'

'Well,' Archie glowers at him through a veil of cigarette smoke. 'Well? What would you have him do?"

'He could be like … that herald in Shakespeare. You know. Bringing news back to the village. Every time a new thing happens in the court he can run to the women and tell them.'

'Sounds a bit of a clart to me,' Nathan's voice bells out from the back.

'Not a bad idea,' says Archie. 'Write it!'

'What?' says Tegger, blinking.

'Take the blasted play away and write into it this herald of yours. What shall we call the old man?'

'Baffer Bray!' calls Nathan.

'Canna do that,' says Tegger. 'Not right. Taking from life.'

'Call him Granda Pew,' says Greta.

'Where d'that come from?'

'Search me,' says Greta.

Tegger turns to Archie. 'When d'you want we should do this then?'

Todhunter shrugs. 'Bring it here tomorrow night at seven and you and I'll go through it. If it works we can rehearse it on Friday. It will touch everyone, so we'll need a full rehearsal.'

'New material! At this stage!' groaned Cora. 'Oh Archie, really!' Only Cora could object to Archie's face and she's quite willing to do it.

This time Cora doesn't get away with it. Archie is furious. 'Let me do my business, Cora, will you?' His voice is icy.

I've never heard Todhunter speak to her like this. She goes bright red.

He goes on grimly. 'You mind your business and I'll mind mine.' Cora glares at him, her full lips trembling and she turns on her heel and marches out of the room.

Archie shrugs and turns back to Tegger, who glances at me. He knows this means him working tonight night and all tomorrow. He nods at me. 'You gan on, Gabe. Marguerite'll be waiting for us at the Raglan. Will you get down there for us and say I won't get down myself? Tell her Archie has me on a leash.

28. At The Lord Raglan

When I get to the Lord Raglan it's still early in the evening but even so the public house is buzzing with men drinking their single pints very slowly. The main bar resounds with the rhythmic clicks and calls from the two domino tables, the bustle and number calls of a darts game and the quieter hum of groups of men playing cards with piles of spent matches taking the place of non-existent money. I join the few stragglers and sit up behind the bar.

Marguerite is serving at the other end of the bar, her hair an iridescent purplish black in the light of the gas mantel. She's pulling pints and laughing, showing the cracked tooth which is her only imperfection. I feel tender now about this flaw, which makes her somehow accessible, less like a goddess. She laughs and talks with an old man as she serves him. It must take patience to humour people like that. Perhaps that's what she does with me when she praises my paintings and promises me a visit to this gallery at Newcastle.

There's no denying, though, that her face lights up when she sees me. 'Gabriel! You're sight for sore eyes.' Her gaze slips across my shoulder. 'No Tegger? Lost your twin?' As she speaks she pulls a pint of beer and puts it before me,

'That's why I'm here. Tegger's down the Settlement doing some extra work for Mr. Todhunter. Shouldn't think he'll get out tonight, or tomorrow night.'

She grins, unfazed. 'Well then, honey, I'll have to make do with you, won't I?' She pushes the glass towards me. 'Here.'

I shake my head, 'Can't buy that, Marguerite. I'm saving for new paints. Nowt to spare.' In fact, like a lot of the men in here, I've *nowt to spare* for food, if truth were told. The dole's swallowed up in the rent I have to pay Lord Chase now I'm not working in his pit. I get paints from Rosel Vonn but I dream of buying my own paints.

'Nah. Take it, Gabe. Mr. Flaherty over there includes two pints a night in my pay. Tegger gets them usually, so why not you, that's here in his place?' She pushes the heavy glass further towards me. It's almost touching my chest.

My father was never one for the public house and as a consequence I've never really bothered, except for the odd pint or two with Tegger when we were both in work. Tegger, though, he loves the pub: the gossip, the practical jokes and the storytelling are all meat and drink to him. Some of it - like Marguerite – he keeps to himself. Other bits resurface in these stories he's writing, with Archie's encouragement. It was at The Raglan that he heard the story about the two brothers and their journey to London and the Hunger March: that's the story that he's making into a new play, with Archie's help.

I sit back on my stool, take a sip of the smoky beer and watch Marguerite at her work. She's as neat as an egg: deft, smiling and efficient. A glow settles on her wherever she's in the room. In this sea of pasty underfed faces she is exotic: a flame of warmth in a cold place. No wonder old Flaherty gives her a bonus of two pints a night. She probably brings a hundred pints of business in some nights. Even in these days. There are plenty other pubs in Brack's Hill.

Around ten o'clock a surge of song bubbles up from a gang or Irish ironworkers in the corner. The ironworks has been closed for two years now so their beer money must, I imagine, come from more diverse sources. The Irish are very resourceful.

Marguerite drifts back in my direction.

'How long before you close?' I say.

She glances up at the mahogany wall clock behind me. 'Two hours, I'd say,' she says.

I tuck my pint behind a card advertising Players Cigarettes. 'Will you watch this?' I say. 'I'll be back soon.'

I hare through the streets and am back on my corner stool in eighteen minutes. I put my drawing pad and my pencils down on the stained bar. Taking a sip of my beer I square the room with my eye. The elaborate gaslights illuminate the bulky bodies, leaving the corners in smoky darkness. My pencil touches the paper. I draw Marguerite about her work: leaning over the bar, her head on one side, listening to some confidence from a very old man on the other side of the bar. I draw her narrow figure weaving its way through the tables, hands aloft clutching five empty beer mugs cleared off a vacated table. Then I move on to the men who are playing, talking, singing. The cameos grow under my hand and I become engrossed.

Someone whispers in the ear of Flaherty. At the edge of my eye I see him wending his way towards me. My sketching rate slows. Marguerite hovers behind the bar, watchful.

Now he's at my shoulder, 'Now, marra,' he says quite kindly, for he is a jovial man. 'What's it yer up to here?'

I put down my pencil. 'I'm drawing.' I keep my tone neutral. 'I like to draw, I draw every day. Everything and anything.'

He sits on the empty stool beside me. 'Gissa look, then,' he says comfortably, his fat hand with its sausage-like fingers flaps towards me.

I hold out the book and turn the pages myself. He peers first at the pages then out at the room. 'Bliddy hell, man,' he says. 'Yeh've got Joss Allenby to the life. And old Marshall Kidd. Yeh've got a good hand all right.' His eyes, sunk a little by the high pouch of his cheeks, bore into me. 'Tell yeh what, son. We need a new sign outside. That one's falling to bits. Musta been there fifty year. Mebbe…'

I interrupt him, 'I don't do that sort of thing, sir. Sorry, Mr.

Flaherty,' I can feel Marguerite's tension from behind the bar. Perhaps the fellow's not that jovial. 'I just draw and paint pictures of people.'

Clearly, he's not pleased. I flick through the book and carefully tear out the page that shows the scene by the dartboard, with Flaherty himself looking on, pipe in hand. 'Mebbe you'd like this one for yourself? Stick it up behind the bar? Put a frame on it mebbe?'

He holds it up to the light. 'Yeah. Yeah. I'll have that.' He nods at Marguerite. 'Hey Marguerite, lass! Give yer friend a whisky. I'm on this bit o'paper for posterity. Immortal, me. Nice frame and it'll sit behind the bar a treat.'

The men in the bar are all watching me now. I don't like this, so I close my book, put my pencils in my top pocket and slip away. I pass Marguerite who's clearing the table of the Irishmen who are also standing up ready to leave. One of the older men pinches her cheek as he passes her. Her eyes meet mine, full of patient endurance.

Much later I am sitting at my kitchen table when a loud knock rattles the back door. The sneck clicks and in comes Marguerite Molloy, her green coat caught at the waist with a big black belt, her hair tied back gypsy-wise with a red silk scarf.

I stand up from the table where yet again I've been poring over Aunt Susanah's book of Rembrandt plates. 'Marguerite!' I say.

'Gabriel!' Buried in her voice is a drawling echo of my own.

'What…?' I try not to think of the neighbours.

She sits down easily in the chair opposite mine. 'You asked what time did I finish? Well, I'm finished. Just five minutes ago. So-o. Maybe now it's for me to say, 'What…?'' '

I'm hot under the collar again. I sit down to face her, 'Just … I wanted to ask you about something. There was no need…' I glance round the room uneasily. The desire to escape from my own house does strike me, even in this tense moment, as ridiculous.

'Oh!'· One slender hand comes up to her forehead. 'What a disappointment!'

'It's just…' I am conscious of feeling my way towards something. So I start to feel my way further. 'I don't know…'

'Oh! What a disappointment.'

Why did I ask her, in the pub, about the time she finished? I didn't think it out. The words just came. I licked my lips. 'I wanted to talk to you, like.'

'What about?'

'Well, there's two things.'

'What two things?'

'Well, one, I wanted to fix up that Newcastle gallery. Visiting it. The gallery. I'll get the fare somehow.'

She nods. 'We'll go. Any time you want. Mr. Flaherty permitting, like.' She sits back in the chair. The collar of her coat slips back and her slender brown throat gleams like honey in the firelight. 'And the other thing. What was that?'

'Well,' I jump up, go into the front room and come back with a sheaf of papers. I put the big Rembrandt book on my mother's sewing machine under the window and spread the papers and sheets of cardboard across the table. One half of me can't believe I'm showing these things to someone who, to all intents and purposes, is a stranger. They're sketches and half-botched paintings representing that time underground when I saw the woman. They are fumbling, clumsy things. Clumsiest of all is my depiction of the woman who is somewhere between Christmas card pictures of the Virgin Mary and the faded print of Rembrandt's *Danae* in Aunt Susanah's book.

Marguerite peers closer. 'What on earth are these?'

I begin to talk to her about the woman I saw underground. I tell her how I saw the woman in the Goaf. How I may or may not have gone to sleep. I can hardly believe my own ears. I've never explained this properly, not even to Tegger. 'It's just like the whole of the earth is a woman. And, like, that time, somehow I saw this woman. This woman who *was* the earth. Since then this is something I really want to paint. More than anything else I want to do it. And I want to do it right.'

'Well!' Marguerite looks up at me, very direct now, not a trace of mockery in her bright eyes. 'Now, there's a story and a half. But what's all this to do with me, I'd like to know?'

I take a very deep breath. 'I've been thinking want you to be the woman. To …er… pose … for this woman in the Goaf.'

'Mmm. Well! I should'a known you didn't want me for my

bright blue eyes.' Her bright blue eyes pierce through me now and the heat under my collar has now spread across my skin, all over my face, right to my hairline.

I shuffle the papers together. 'Don't bother then, don't bother. Stupid idea anyway.'

She puts a hand on my arm, stops my manic gathering of paper. 'Woah, tiger! I didn't say it was a bad idea, did I? I never said I wouldn't do it, did I?'

I stand very still with her hand over mine, not daring to move. Now the heat has spread to every single part of my body and is having the worst pulsing effect. At last she releases me and with a swift movement unbuckles her coat and throws it across the back of the chair. 'How do you want me?' she says. 'Standing up? Sitting down? Lying down?'

Sweat is pouring out of me. 'What?' I say.

Then she laughs a wicked, wicked laugh. 'Gabriel Marchant! You little tinker!'

I close my eyes and wish to vanish into the rug into the very heart of my granny's sunflower. I close them even tighter, wishing that when I open them this woman will be gone. Bugger! A tear. Another. My eyes are filled with tears which begin to trickle through my squeezed lids onto my cheeks.

'Gabriel, Gabriel!' Marguerite's voice now is all tenderness. 'Come on, honey. I'm only having you on. Only teasing. You should know that.'

I open my swimming eyes and look into hers.

'Oh, baby,' she says, blinking. 'You'll have me bubbling next.' She moves away from me and sits on my father's chair by the fire. She leans forward, her hands slack in her lap. 'Now then, pet. We'll stop the teasing. What is it you really want?'

I sniff and knuckle my eyes to clear them. If I'm honest what I really want to do now is take her and kiss her. I want to pull her with me onto the rug beside the fire and do that thing I know how to do in theory but have never put into practice with any woman.

'I can't start here tonight but what I really want,' I say, sniffing and coughing at the same time. 'Is to make some drawings of you. I want to place you at the centre of this painting. I want you to give some life, some energy to my idea of this earth woman in the Goaf. Then I'll make those drawings into a painting. I want this one to be my very best painting, I want it to be the beginning of what I will be as a painter.. I'll need a really big piece of wood to paint it on.'

I'm embarrassed by the pretensions of the words coming out of my mouth but this is what I want to say. And I am saying it here, to a virtual stranger. I know for sure that now I've actually said the words my whole world has changed for good.

Two days later Tegger brings me a piece of solid oak, six foot by three, filched from the back areas of Mr Conroy's old joinery, now surplus to requirements.

He manhandles it into the scullery. 'Marguerite told me

you needed a big board to paint her picture. Back of an old wardrobe, this. Conroy said he had not need of it now. Bloke who had it went down to live in Coventry.'

I look at the board, run my fingers over it. 'It'll take some priming,' I say. 'But it'll do,'

29. A Truth Not Worth Knowing.

After the clash between Archie and Cora at the rehearsal Rosel Vonn noticed that Cora had stopped bouncing around the Settlement. She had stopped wearing her theatrical make up during the day and her curly hair was often grimy and unwashed. The house had stopped ringing with the broadcast banter between her and Archie. Doors were slammed. Grumbling voices penetrated even these stone walls.

One morning Cora brought a letter up to Rosel's room. She hovered in the doorway after she had handed it over. 'That will be a letter from your father, I suppose.' she said. 'German postmark.'

Rosel glanced down at the letter then up at Cora's strained face. She opened the door a little wider. 'Will you come in a moment?' she said. 'I have some lemonade here. I made it myself.'

Cora followed her in and sat on the bed. She glanced around. 'You have it very neat in here,' she said.

'Ah,' said Rosel. 'This is because all my mess of things are in the painting shed.' Rosel's rooms had always been neat. As a girl of fourteen she'd revolted against the Bohemian squalor of her father and her mother's apartments and decided to be neat. It suited her.

She handed Cora a glass of lemonade. 'So what is this, Cora? Is there something ... you seem so different. Down in the mouth. This wonderful English phrase.'

Cora stared at her with hard eyes. 'I *am* so different I ...' she hesitated. 'There has been a difficulty. Something difficult has turned up.'

'Difficulty? What is this difficulty?'

'I became pregnant. I am so old and I was pregnant.'

'A baby? Oh dear. You were...'

'No baby! Not now. I went to this woman.' Her voice was steely, neutral. 'She knew what to do.'

'And Archie? What does he...?'

'Archie doesn't know,' Cora said heavily. 'No-one knows except the woman who did it. And now you. It's a truth not worth knowing. It doesn't matter now.'

Rosel grasped Cora's hand in hers. 'And you? How do you feel?'

'It's left me low, my dear. I'm certainly too old for any of this.' Cora hesitated. 'It happened once before. Twenty years ago. I was fine afterwards. Fine. It was a relief.'

'You should have told Archie. He...'

'He is too busy with all these people, with this play, with all this talking, talking to the great and the good. He's too busy debating the Depression and his benevolent practical strategies to anyone who'll listen. Me? I'm just a carpet to be walked on. A nuisance. A fusspot. I am too stupid to criticise his play but still it makes him feel small.'

'He says these things to you? He shouldn't. Cruel words.'

'Perhaps he shouldn't. But I'm the only one in the world he can wail at, whom he can demean in private. Isn't he there for the public good? With everyone else he...' Now tears were falling unchecked from her eyes and dripping by her mouth. She licked her cheek and snuffled.

Rosel picked up a neatly folded handkerchief from her dresser and blotted Cora's eyes for her as if she were a child. 'Now then, Cora. Please do not cry. You have been ill. You are ill. You need to rest.' She pressed lightly on Cora's shoulder and the older woman collapsed back onto the bed, turned her head into the white pillow and cried her last tears into its downy surface. Rosel pulled the eiderdown up around her and patted her shoulder. 'You stay there, Cora. You must rest.'

Then Rosel went in search of Archie. She ran him to earth in the big room where the Wednesday library was in progress. He had perched himself on the edge of the smaller table talking to Mrs Stewart, who was doing sterling duty stamping to books. Mrs Stewart adored Archie. He stood up to greet her. 'Ah, Rosel. How are we today?'

'We are very well,' she said shortly. 'Archie. I need to speak with you.'

'Fire ahead! What can I do for you? The stage-set is

beginning to shape up. And the portraits - you and young Mr Marchant are going great guns… I only wish I could say the same for the play. So much still to iron out. These people think just learning the lines is sufficient.'

Drat the man, Rosel thought. He was in love with the sound of his own voice. She broke into his wordy flow. 'I wish to speak to you in private, Archie.'

He raised his eyebrows. 'Oh. Well. My office!' He looked down at the adoring Mrs Stewart. 'We'll talk about the new book order another time. Perhaps I'll catch you at the end of this session?'

He swept off without waiting for an answer and led the way to his office. He settled behind his desk, chose his amber holder and lit a cigarette. He drew on it, closed his eyes and opened them and spoke to Rosel with visible patience. 'So, Rosel. What is it?'

She was conscious of the theatricality of his actions. He was demonstrating his resentment at her sharp tone.

'It is about Cora, Archie.'

He wrinkled his nose. 'What is it about Cora?'

'She is upstairs at this minute on my bed. She is in great distress. She weeps.'

He put his cigarette into a convenient ashtray. 'I can't think why she's up there. What on earth is the matter with her?'

'You must go to her. Comfort her.'

He shrugged. 'She's a moody soul, our Cora,' he said comfortably. 'Artistic temperament, you know. Feelings first, brain comes after.'

'She is very, very distracted. I cannot calm her down.'

'She'll calm down soon. Been working up to something for a week or so now. Sulking, shouting, unreasonable. In front of the cast the other night, d'you know! It's not on, and I let her know it. How can this project be managed with...'

Rosel crashed her hand on the table. 'You ... you obtuse man! Is it only the mirror you see everywhere?'

He flushed and got to his feet. 'There's no need to be offensive, Fraŭlein. I think...'

'For goodness sake, Archie! I'm going out to the hut now to do some work. I will not be back for two hours. You *must* go up and see Cora. Go and see her, Archie.' She slammed the door on the way out.

Cora was still bundled up on Rosel's bed when Archie got up to the bedroom. She hauled herself up, rising like a seal from a sea of eiderdown. 'Rosel. I'm sorry ... Oh. It's you.'

He stood at the end of the bed, his hands loosely at his sides. 'Well now, old girl, what's this?'

She rolled back into the bedclothes. He could not see her face. Her voice when it came out was muffled. 'Go away.'

The bed creaked as he sat on the end of it. 'Of course I won't. You'll have to talk to me old girl.'

Muffled: 'What's she say? Rosel? What's she say to you?'

He sighed. 'All she said was that you were very upset and I

must talk to you. She's very bossy, is that young woman. German, of course.'

Cora emerged from the eiderdown. Her hair was half up and half down, her eyes were red with crying, and her face was creased. 'Do you really want to know? Why I feel like this?'

There was a pause. 'Yes, of course.'

'No you don't.'

'Cora. What kind of game are you playing?'

'It's not a game. Something very bad has happened. It has happened to you and it has happened to me.'

He threw up his hand. 'Happened? Happened? What are you talking about? How can anything have happened that I haven't seen? We live in the same house, for God's sake. We share a bed.'

'You never notice anything.'

'I have noticed lately that you're in training to play Catherine in The Shrew. Everything is wrong. The slightest criticism and you berate me. Despite the fact that we are behind with everything when there's so much to do.'

She brought her legs around so that she was sitting on the edge of the bed. Then she put her hands up to pin her hair back into place. There was a forced grace in her movement: a theatricality. 'It is about you, Archie. It is always about *you*.'

He went to stand beside the window, peering out into the afternoon gloom. 'Not me Cora,' he said patiently, reasonably. 'It's about the Settlement. If this place doesn't survive we will have let these good people down. This town! You, me, everyone. This place is the only thing that matters.'

She sighed. 'In one way you're right…'

'That's the ticket!' he interrupted her. He looked down at his watch, a present from his father on his majority, imported to China from Switzerland, and then posted, carefully wrapped, to Scotland. 'Look. It's nearly four o'clock. Your literature class will be waiting. Very successful, your literature class. Several people have told me how lively it is. How you encourage everyone. What is it you're reading now?'

'Mark Twain. *Tom Sawyer.*'

'Ah yes. Accessible stuff. That'll cheer them up. It'll cheer you up.'

She began to remake Rosel's bed, pulling and patting it to make sure that no wrinkle or dent showed her recent presence there.

Archie paused by the door. 'Oh, and Cora…'

She looked at him blankly.

'How about a bit of war paint, old duck? You don't look the same without war paint.'

The door slammed before she had chance to answer.

She leaned against Rosel's neat dressing table. 'Bugger, bugger,' she said. 'And bugger again.'

30. A Proper State of Light,

I have to wait for Rosel longer than I expected in the painting shed. I'm all togged up in my pit shorts vest and jacket; on my feet are my father's scarred and patched boots with the metal bands and segs on the soles. Around my neck is his pit scarf – now really mine. I am here looking at the nearly-completed portrait of me in the character of Arthur in Dev's smart uniform. The painting is lightly done, with washes of ochre and yellow for the khaki cloth and a splash of red on the cap badge and the row of medals. I think of the splash of red on the shoulder of the woman in the Goaf.

The face I see is surely mine but this man is not me. His eyes are straight and steady under the close helmet of golden hair. There is fear and tension in the set of the shoulders, the way the hands clasp the cap in front of him. Somehow the light touch of paint on the canvas allows a tremulous, uncertain light to sing through the portrait.

'Do you like it?' Rosel is directly behind me.

'Yes. Yes.' I struggle to say something sensible. 'It's very light. To get that much effect without using too much…'

'Paint?'

I look across at the other side of the room, at my efforts which now seem like heavy daubs: a consequence of me trying to work up a depth of shadow, a proper state of light. My paintings, to be honest, crude as they are, have more in common with Rembrandt than Rosel Vonn. Perhaps Rembrandt would not agree.

'Your work makes mine look like a right daubs,' I say.

Her denial is slow, but quite definite. 'That is not the case, Gabriel. You will find your own way. You use the old painters as your tutors and it is their image that you strive for, not you own. One day you will find your own way. These paintings of yours are wonderful. But you are on a journey, my dear boy, and this is not your destination. Even so, you are truly on your way.'

Then she is all busyness, pulling on her smock and dragging across the easel on which sits a draped canvas. She drags away a cloth to reveal that she's already blocked in the picture of 'Arthur' pushing a tub on the rail-tracks underground. His hair is long and tangled, very different from his military crop.

'You started without me. I say. 'And with my hair.'

'You had hair when I drew the sketches, Gabriel.' She opens her black folder and shuffles through drawing after drawing. They are all images of me. Down at the pit heap. By the river. In the rehearsal room. 'And the difference in the hair can make another difference between the Front and the pit.'

Leaving the drawings where they are she turns to me. 'Now, then! Will you brace yourself and push the edge of that table as though it were a tub full of coal? Your arms like so…' The touch of her hand, cool and dry, makes me shiver. 'Fine. Now if you will just stay there?'

She works on for twenty minutes, and then throws down her brush. I stand upright and ease my shoulders, wriggling them this way and that.

She perches on a stool and lights a cigarette. 'Is this how you'd be Gabriel? Down below?'

'No. Too hot. In the middle of the shift you have to strip down to the buff. I'd end up just in my pit-hoggers with a scarf round my neck to mop up the sweat.'

'Pit hoggers?'

'These short trousers. We wear them in the pit cos it can be hot as hell down there. And the scarf is for the sweat.

She breathes out. 'Well then, could you take off your things? Be like you really are down there? No jacket, no vest. Only the scarf. And the pit hoggers.'

I obey. She arranges my arms, the tilt of my head and we are in silence - thirty or forty minutes until my straining muscles can stand it no longer. I ease myself upright and wriggle my shoulders.

'Gabriel!' she says.

'You can't paint me if I fall over, now, can you?'

She stands back from her easel. 'Would you like to see?' she says. 'To see the picture?'

I don't know whether I want to do this, but I go to stand behind her and look over her shoulders. The head is just about complete. She has caught the closed, intent, intense effort. She has somehow enlarged the muscles of my shoulders, making them bulge. She has caught this more in lines than dense painting. The power in the painting is simply in the line of the brush. You can see it is a brush mark. There is no attempt to disguise this. Though I regret having to admit this, it is somehow the better for its lack of paint. 'You are very good,' I say.

Her narrow shoulders move in a shrug. 'I do not think so.' She leans forward and looks more closely at my painted head as it presses against the metal surface of the tub.

My eyes are focused on the nape of her neck which gleams like mother-of-pearl under her thick, plaited hair. Without even thinking I lean down and kiss it. She smells of lemon and musk, linseed oil and turpentine. She tastes of delight. My hands go to her shoulders and turn her round. She reaches up and puts her lips on mine. All these movements happen in the blink of an eye. Then her slender, paint-stained hand comes up to cup the back of my head. Her body fits itself against mine and we kiss properly. Oh, how we meet each other in this touching of lips. She twists somehow and seems to bury herself nearer to me. Her lips move against mine. Her tongue flickers and my mouth opens and a sense of her, of who she is, the sheer woman-ness of her threads through me like a wire. It reaches my penis then down to my toes and right inside my father's old boots.

Now I'm pressing her to me. To my chest, to my groin. I can feel her small breasts, her long legs. I am all heat. I want to be further into her. I have never done this before but my body is showing me the way. I want her.

Suddenly she breaks away and it's as though the world has broken in half, making me as cold as the worst winter. She looks at me, then puts the back of her hand against her mouth. 'Do you want this?'

'I want you.' My voice is reduced to a growl. 'Oh yes.'

She comes near again and puts her hands on my shoulders. 'We can have this once, but only this. No past. No future.'

'But Rosel…'

Her finger is on my lips. 'No past. No future. Just this. Remember?'

'Well…'

'Or nothing!'

I pull her closer. 'This, then,' I say. 'I will have this. Bloody hell. I do want this.'

,

31. News from Germany

Rosel crept up the narrow staircase, past Archie and Cora's silent room. Even in the buzzing aftermath of making love to the boy Gabriel, concern for Cora flittered through Rosel's mind like a persistent moth. She should go to Cora. Talk to her. There was truly a desolate woman.

But once in her own room she stripped off and crept along the corridor to the bathroom basin with its single cold tap and soaped and dried herself all over. She combed cold water through her hair, scraping it back off her forehead and tying it with a dark green ribbon. Only then did she look in the cracked mirror. For a second a much younger Rosel looked out: the Rosel who had laughed her way through life with her friends in Berlin, London and in Paris; the girl who'd painted into the night and had gone to spend time with much better painters to appreciate and learn from their fine skills.

That Rosel had been a quiet girl, a keen friend, a devoted lover to the two men whose lives, for brief spans of time, she had shared. She had shared her youth with these men and had made the non-returnable gift of her young years in return for the chance to learn from them. At each parting she sought the relief of cutting her arms, letting her blood run like thinned paint. And somehow once the cuts healed she was able to get on with her life.

And now tonight it had been her turn to receive the gift of someone's youth: someone who was as young to her as she had been to Phillipe and Viktor.

She made her way back to her bedroom and sat on her bed, knees drawn up under her chin. She could see herself clearly now in the dressing table mirror. She could see this woman who had made fumbling, ultimately exquisite love to a boy half her age, a boy who had clearly never done this before. For this boy she had been the first.

Now the face in the mirror looked all of its thirty-eight years. Yes, the forehead was fine and smooth, the chin taut. But lines round the mouth were deepening and the tender skin under the eyes was loose and faintly creased. What had she done today? How had she come to making such a mistake? She'd gone to the boy upset and concerned about Cora and somehow her defences had been down. While she painted him the tension in his shoulders, the earnestness in his eyes had made him much more than an object to be observed and painted. His cropped hair made him seem, for a moment, older, more like a man and therefore desirable and accessible.

She looked hard in the mirror to see if the woman reflected there had considered what she had done, had any shame in it. No shame. She saw now a woman whose skin was glowing with the residue of desire, whose eyes were sparkling with satisfaction and mischief. She groaned. 'Rosel, what have you done?'

But still she had no regrets. She dropped onto the bed and as she did so she noticed the letter underneath the intricate shelf of the dressing table. Her father's letter! She'd forgotten about the letter amidst Cora's drama and the need to rush down to the shed to paint Gabriel Marchant.

She padded across to take the letter down, tear it open and take it back across to the bedside lamp to read it.

The letter was not from her father. It was from her brother.

Meine liebe schwester,

I write to you in some despair in consequence of recent events. You will know that our father has angered the authorities in his vigorous protestations regarding the proscribing of his friends Herr Doktor Goldstein and Herr Bellig. He insists on consulting them and paying them. But he does not do it discreetly or quietly as some are supposed to do. He shouts it abroad. He makes his objections. Now finally we face the consequences. Two days ago our father was arrested and imprisoned. He was in a cell, stripped and humiliated for two nights. Yesterday I went for him and brought him back to the apartment. It caused me great embarrassment, but I alleviated this by not wearing my uniform. He was shouting and incoherent when I collected him. It seems they did not actually abuse him physically but he was very frightened. He is now at the apartment being cared for by old Frau Smidt. I stayed with him one night and he talked about you. Perhaps you should come? I do not know. I am not certain whether or how my position in the army is compromised. I do know that he our father is not safe, outspoken as he is.

Do you think he would be safer in England? That may be so, although having a sister and a father in England would probably compromise my own position further. I am not sure how much I care about this, if I am honest with you. Things are very difficult here. The virtuous way is turned up on its head. I cannot understand the arrest and the frightening of a harmless old man, nor the proscribing of harmless old doctors. You know how I have criticised the moneylenders and financiers who held the country to ransom in its hardest times. You know I have gloried in the reinstatement of Germany, in the rebuilding of her pride. Only now am I wondering whether the price is too much. Too much altogether.

There are men here who feel something should be done. But what possibly could be done without, well, great risk? So much is at risk. Even this letter to you is risk. It is perhaps the last time I may write to you in these terms, except by a messenger.

Our father has an old friend who lives in London. Sir Peter Hamilton Souness. He worked once at the Foreign and Commonwealth Office. Perhaps he could arrange for our father to come to England. Will you go to visit him, to tell him of all this? An invitation from him? Perhaps.

Greetings from your loving brother

Boris

32. The Woman in the Goaf

Tegger is intrigued by my idea of painting his friend Marguerite as the women in the Goaf. He tries to question me closely about it but I don't say much because I don't know what to say. I can't say what I think. I can only paint it.

'I was there when he saw her,' he asserts to Marguerite. 'I think it was a dream, me. But he said not.'

Last night I made love with Rosel Vonn. I think the whole of my life will be marked with this date. *Anno Domini. AD. Anno Rosel. AR.* I learned more about being alive and truly living in those hours in that rackety shed than I have ever known in the previous nineteen. I understood now about power and communion, about the two into one. I understood the weakness, the draining afterwards, followed by the almost instant hunger to experience it again. We did do it once more. It was impossible to resist.

I came home. And then after reflecting just a bit on what it was to be a man and my promise to Greta, I had the best sleep I've had in this house since my grandmother was alive.

The arrival on my doorstep this morning of both Tegger and

Marguerite made me blink. Then I remembered the arrangement I made with Marguerite. It was to be weekday mornings only, as the rest of her day right up to eleven at night really belonged to Mr Flaherty.

'Where d'you want this?' said Tegger. On his back he had a crude easel, sturdy enough. He eased it into the scullery space in front ot he primed board.

'Where y'gunna do it?' says Tegger, looking round the crowded kitchen. 'In here?'

I laugh. A bit uneasily, I admit. 'You sound like I'm gunna do a murder, marra!'

He frowns. 'Isn't there some primitive tribe somewhere who think that if you make their picture you take their souls? Watch out for Marguerite's soul, marra.'

He's no fool, is Tegger.

I am looking around the kitchen, seeing the orderly clutter through their eyes. 'You make me sound like a bloody vampire, Tegger.' This kitchen is no good. I can't paint her in here. Too much of my father in here.

'Hey, you! Language,' Tegger says idly. 'Lady present.'

I open the middle door. 'Right. Sorry, Marguerite,' I say absently. The front room is in darkness. The curtains have been shut since my father died. My grandmother's heavy parlour furniture sucks what light there's left out of the room. It's very dark in here. Yes. This will do.

'Hey, give us a hand!' I throw the words over my shoulder

and start to push the heavy table to the wall. They help me to pile the chairs on top of it. That space becomes a tangle of chair legs and leather-bound boxes.

I pull the one upholstered chair this way and that in the room until it occupies the darkest space. 'Right. That's it,' I say.

Tegger is red with all the effort. 'What a bloody jungle! Sorry, Marguerite.'

The girl is staring narrowly at me. 'What has happened, Gabriel? What's happened to you?'

'What're you talking about?' I say. But my cheeks burn.

'You're different. There's something different. You're more …' She pulls me around and stares at me. Her bright eyes bore into me. Reflected there I can see myself, sweating and plunging, making the double person with Rosel Vonn. Then Marguerite nods thoughtfully. ' … more certain.'

I drag myself away from her gaze and push the old press into the corner. Then I cover the looking-glass with my father's old black coat. There's still coal-dust in it, after all this time. It smells of the pit.

Tegger looks around claps his hands. 'I get it, marra. The seam! You're building the seam. Like a cave. Well, kind of…' His voice trails off.

'Where do you want me?' says Marguerite, still staring intently. She goes to stand beside the chair, the dark tangle of furniture behind her. 'Here?'

Her instinct is fine.

'Yes. Yes. But...' But how can I tell her that the earth woman was not wearing a neat jacket with frogged buttons on it, nor was she wearing lisle stockings and shoes with brass buckles. The woman in the Goaf had, in fact, been more or less naked.

She reads my mind and takes off her little hat and the jacket with the brass buttons. She bends down to unbuckle her shoes and looks up at me. 'How was she, this woman in the Goaf? Was she naked?'

'Hey Marguerite,' says Tegger. 'Steady on!'

'Well, I'm right, aren't I Gabe?' She stretches up to unbutton her blouse at the back. 'She'd have no clothes on down there would she?'

I look at her steadily. 'Yes,' I say. 'That's right. But there was something on her shoulder. Something with red. Like a flower.'

She continues with her unbuttoning.

'Hey Gabe, yeh canna do this.' Tegger is grim now. He means it.

She folds her blouse neatly and lays it across one of the inverted chair legs. Then she slips out of her skirt. 'It's only a picture, Tegger,' she says crossly. 'I've seen them in the gallery. It's art. Nothing else. Isn't that right, Gabe?'

'Yeah. Yeah.' I rummage in the kitchen cupboard for my father's old pit lamp and light it. When I return to the front room she is naked except for a cross-cut slip which reaches just above the knee. 'Is this all right?' she says, her eyes still burning into me.

Tegger is huffing and puffing beside me.

I place the pit lamp on the edge of the table. Already in my mind the table is a shelf in the seam, a natural consequence of the shot-fireman's blast. I look at Marguerite and I know it's not really 'all right.' Then she picks up the hem of her petticoat and pulls it over her head, and her full breasts settle slightly lower than they were before. She is larger than Rosel, more generously curved. But she is still beautiful.

She drapes the silk petticoat over her shoulder. 'Like this?' she says.

I nod.

Now she reaches up to take down her hair which must be very tightly wound because, once down, it falls around her like a rippling black ocean.

I root about in my grandmother's press and emerge with a tangle of red knitting wool. I pin it to the draped petticoat.

'Marguerite!' Tegger sounds desperate now, very young. 'That's not, it's not…'

'Oh Tegger!' says Marguerite. 'Go and make yourself some tea, will you? Gabriel and me have work to do here. It's work, that's all. Get that into your head.'

Of course this can only happen because Marguerite is so business-like. But for a second or two I'm clearly in severe danger of getting punched on the nose by my marra Tegger. As it is, he blunders past me and we can hear him clashing the pots in the kitchen. He's not pleased.

'Now,' she says, standing in exactly the right spot. 'Do you want me here?'

The last thing Tegger and I do is pull in the crude easel and place on it the heavy oak board nicely primed in glowing white.

It's hard to explain just what happened that morning and all of the mornings this week. Bit by bit my father's dark parlour becomes the pit: the area behind Marguerite darkens and condenses itself into the Goaf. The struggling beam of the pit lamp touches on the female form before me. The darker shadows in Marguerite's undulating figure and her cloud of black hair seem to join the darkness of the Goaf so that she floats within it, becoming insubstantial. Sometimes she is there. Sometimes she is not. Her blue eyes become passive receptacles of light, only existing because the rays of the lamp call forth some response.

For two whole mornings I achieve almost nothing. I just keep looking and thinking, feeling my way back to that time in the Goaf. A line here and there. A marker for distance but that's all. I am absorbing the fact of a woman's body. Of the woman before me. I am thinking about Rosel, who has made me know a woman's body.

Rosel is not around. According to Cora, who is a bit of a sourpuss these days, Rosel has gone down to London. In one way this is a relief, as I didn't know how I could see her again, after the other night. In another way it's bad because I long for us to be together again in just that way. But Rosel would definitely not permit that: she made that very clear. 'Only this time.' She said it as we parted that night. 'Only this time Gabriel!'.)

But without that time how could I now be looking at the body of Marguerite Molloy now, with such dispassion? Without that time with Rosel I would not be able to conceive in my heart, my brain and my busy fingers what the woman in the Goaf really means.

But I now I feel certain about her. I know. She is my grandmother who could pluck beauty from dross: she is my mother who barely mothered me: she is Rosel Vonn turning over and under me, unlocking delights in my soul: she is Marguerite Molloy shrugging herself out of her blouse, knowing me with her eyes: she is the pit, the earth herself opening to receive the miner's tribute, then spitting him out again, touched by a kind of magic even if in the process of his life she will breaks him down time and again.

It is not until the third morning that I start to work swiftly, blocking the body in, using my miner's-memory to bring to my eye the image of the seam with the rainbow gleam on the out-jutting coal in the foreground and the eternal density of dark behind the woman.

Tegger still keeps sentinel, making us cups of tea, keeping up the fire for Marguerite to warm herself when the standing still chills her. He goes out now and then to cadge coal and to pick up a sporting paper. He lays out his own notebook on the kitchen table and scribbles words and crosses out, scribbles and crosses out.

None of this is easy. The way the light works on Marguerite's beautiful brown skin has to be studied. I have scraped off and started again twice. But it is coming.

I will not let two of them see the picture until the sixth day. Even then I am unwilling, but Tegger has been very patient and wants his reward. So at dinnertime on Saturday and I drag the easel and the canvas through to the light in the kitchen. I pull off the flimsy green cloth I've been using as a cover. Then I turn the canvas towards the kitchen window.

'Oh!' Marguerite sounds a bit disappointed.

'Why,' says Tegger, growling. 'There's nothing there. It's all black.'

'Look!' I say. 'Look, will you?'

They move about the canvas, standing further and further back. Marguerite narrows her eyes. 'I see her! I see it!' she says, smiling at last. 'There's the red wool. Like a pinpoint of light. Just like the poppies on Armistice Day.'

'Why, you bugger!' says Tegger. 'One way you look, it's all black. The other it's all there. The woman. The seam. The Goaf. Aye. Yeh've got something here, marra.'

'It's not finished,' I say. 'Some of it's not right yet. Not at all.'

'But you don't need me no more, do you?' says Marguerite Molloy, who seems to know just about everything.

'No.' I shake my head. 'You've been just right Marguerite. Thank you for that.'

'So that's the picture for you,' she says. 'Now what about a picture for me? For my own?'

'No,' protests Tegger. 'No more! Let's go down the Raglan. I can't remember the last time I had a pint. All this art makes me very thirsty.'

I watch them go and then drag the easel back into the front room. The mocked up seam is still in there, and I need only to half-close my eyes and the woman is still there. There is so much to do to this painting yet, but for the moment I am satisfied.

Later, I sit at the table with my drawing pad and, from memory, make three sketches of Marguerite. In one of them she is pinning up her hair. In another she has one hand to her face, in that characteristic way she has. In the other she is perching on a chair leaning forward, listening, it seems, with her whole body.

I make a roll of these, tie it with string, and set out for the Lord Raglan.

33. A First Performance

Rosel has not been around for some time. Again, I feel two ways about this. One part of me is glad, as I feel too close to her now to be near her casually now. (I think she feels that too. The other part of me is dying to see her again, even if it is just to see, not to touch.

But there is plenty here take my mind off her. There is the painting of the woman in the Goaf. And the rehearsals are really coming on now. Tegger's alterations have now bedded themselves into the text and drummed themselves into our heads. Those words are as natural to us as breathing. It seems like we've moved onto some other plateau in the play; Archie Todhunter is now focussing on refinements of movement and demeanour; he is adjusting the pace of the whole thing, sometimes speeding it up, sometimes slowing it down.

He's a bit like a conductor. I've never seen a man conducting an orchestra but this I imagine is how it happens. A flick of the wrist, a hoisting of the eyebrow and the whole tone changes. In this it's like painting. In painting all these clamours and changes, tightenings and adjustments, happen within yourself, in the crackling flicker from the eye to the paintbrush in the hand almost without the brain intervening.

With a painting it emerges in the final integrated vision on the canvas. With the play as the players respond to the conductor the mood, the tone and the meaning of the play emerge as a whole thing.

I have to admit that all my reservations about Archie Todhunter have just about faded away. He is certainly obsessed. He is self-absorbed. He can be cruel. But I know now he can be very kind, even insightful in an oblique way. Think about the matter of my shoes. And on top of this he has these magical qualities that are tightening this play like a bowstring, so that when it takes flight, it will hit its mark.

This afternoon we run the play right through. Archie has invited some mate of his here, from his theatre days. And he's also invited the critic, Herbert Grossmith, who loves to criticise. I think Archie wants to show off his play and sharpen us up. Being obliged to perform our play before strangers certainly sharpens us up, puts an edge on our acting. Even Archie, normally so solid, so confident, so heels-to-the-ground, is on his toes.

He is all a-flutter.

It goes well. The moves are right, the timing is perfect. My main scene with Greta - halfway through the action - goes particularly well. Her lips part a little as we kiss and we cling together. I can feel her body (small and firm as a young branch) against mine. Her look of faint surprise and involuntary joy add to the impact. All goes well until near the end when Baffer Bray, acting the herald, puffs on to say that the Mining Tribunal looks like it's turning our way and – his voice roughens - that in France the Somme offensive has started.

Cora looks at him. Now's the time for her to embark on her big speech where, as Maggie Olliphant, she sums up the similarity of the situations here in the village and out there in the trenches on the Somme. Tegger has done some good writing for this scene, bringing life and energy into what had been rather a wooden lump of summary from Archie's pen.

Cora sets away, frowns at Baffer, and then stops. She starts again, frowning again. We can see the lines fading away from her. Mrs Gomersal, the prompt, has found the place is in the script and starts reading a hoarse whisper. The thing is, the text is altered (by Tegger), pasted over and she gets even that mixed up.

Archie's face is white with anger. 'Go back, all of you!' he growls. 'Back to the herald.'

So Baffer does his bit again. This time Cora makes her speech perfectly, stretching it out and slowing it down in just the way we have discussed in recent days. She is brilliant.

Finally the play comes to its poignant end, where the names of the dead are intoned on one side by Nathan, as the coroner, and the other side by Jake McVay, as the corporal in the trench. The final voice is mine, as Arthur writes his last letter to his sweetheart about his hopes for the future.

The visitors out front clap their hands. 'Well done!' says

Herbert Grossmith, glumly. 'I have to say it's a very fine play.'

'Well done everyone!' Archie's theatre crony smiles genially around the room. 'There is indeed talent here.'

The three men's heads go together and they begin to talk under their breaths, excluding all of us with the intimacy of their talk. Talking as they go they leave the dusty room, heading for the office where Archie has set up a bottle of single malt and three glasses on his desk.

Archie passes Cora without acknowledging her.

'Who is he? That other feller, not the journalist,' says Greta as we cluster around Cora, who pours tea for us from a large tin teapot.

'Corinthian Small,' says Cora. 'Actor-manager, leading light of the Corinthian Players. They're playing the Newcastle Theatre Royal next week. Chances are that old Corinthian might put on one of Archie's plays. Perhaps even this one! Archie reckons Small's a coming man. Pity that I spoiled his pudding.' Her voice grates dully, bereft of her usual actress's round tones.

'No!' protests Greta earnestly. 'It can happen to anyone...' Her voice trails off as Cora clashes down the teapot and storms out. '... what have I said?' she wails

Now it's Greta who's upset. Tears glitter in her short-sighted eyes. I jam my cap on my head. 'You off now?' I say. 'I'll walk you, if yer like.'

Cora was in their sitting room when Archie came in to retrieve his heavy coat and his trilby from the coat stand.

'Where are you off, then?' she said, fiddling with a small carving of a soldier on a side table. 'Off with your friends are you?'

He shrugged his way into his coat. 'Sarcasm doesn't become you, Cora.'

'It was just a simple question.'

'If it is so important, I'm going to the Three Tuns in Durham to have dinner with Corinthian and Herbert and the Dean and a few other fellows involved in the Settlement Project. Corinthian is very interested. And Herbert will write an article for the Echo.'

Cora kept her eyes on the soldier. 'You'll enjoy that, then, chattering away among your own kind.'

He jammed on his hat. 'Cora! What is it? You've been a proper sourpuss for days now. Not your usual self at all.'

'So you noticed?'

'And then there was this embarrassment today, just when ….'

'Of course you think I did that on purpose. I was mortified. I've never dried on stage. Never!'

He pulled down his shirt cuffs, pulled on his pigskin gloves and managed a grim smile. 'No. No, Cora. Don't worry. We've all dried in our time. And to be honest your recovery was the mark of a true professional. Corinthian said so himself. A true professional.. He said you'd be an ornament to any troupe.'

'Thank you Corinthian!' she said with a jabbing nod of her

head.

'So?' he said.

'So what?' she said.

'So what is the matter with you?'

She stared at him and wondered whether she should tell him the truth of just how she alone had made the decision to deny him his immortality.

He glanced at his watch. 'So, Cora?' he said.

She patted the head of the soldier statue and forced a laugh. 'Just put it down to woman's troubles, Archie. The bane of my life, woman's troubles.'

Archie relaxed. He transformed himself into what he saw as his really kind self. 'You have no idea, Cora, how many times I thank God that I'm not a woman. You have my every sympathy in these matters.' So saying, he swung out and the door clashed behind him.

She put out her tongue at the closed door. 'Thank you for that, Archie. That's all I need. Your sympathy.'

Something of the drama that occurred behind us in the big room has affected Greta and me. We're over-conscious of each other as we walk briskly through the bitter damp of the late afternoon. Our hands bump twice mid swing and the third time I grasp hers so our arms swing together. Her hand is smaller than I thought and soft in mine.

She starts to talk about Cora and her troubles, speaking

faster than usual. We reach her gate too quickly and she uses our joined hands to pull me round so I'm facing her. 'Have you thought about it, what you promised, Gabriel? The favour?'

I'll say one thing for her. She's forthright.

'I've been busy. These portraits, the play … anyway I said not till after the Prince has been.'

'But you have to find out. Have you found out?'

I have found out a lot of things since we last talked of my promise to Greta's but I can't say this to her. The words stay in my head, unspoken. 'No,' I say humbly. 'Not quite.'

'Well, don't forget!' she says very seriously. Then she reaches up and gives me a good, hard smacking kiss on the mouth. For a second we return to being Arthur and Dorothy: another kind of rehearsal I suppose.

Then I stand there and watch her swinging down her yard. Her mother has lifted the net curtain and is watching from the window. She certainly won't have missed our little extra rehearsal. It's a wonder she wasn't out with her fire-iron to give me a good clattering.

She's very protective over her Greta. I like her for that.

34. An Episode in London

'Dearest Rosel! It must be such a relief to be actually doing something up there in the dark North.' Vanessa leaned across to pour tea for Rosel. 'We do what we can here in London. Parcels for Spain. Money. Artists International had a very successful fundraising exhibition in Pamlico. Did you hear about that? And now we boast to everyone how one of our number is working up there among those unfortunate miners, bringing art to their lives.'

Rosel looked round at the comfortable room with its painted cupboards and its hand-printed curtains and back and Vanessa's beautiful, slightly worn face,

'There is no need for this, Vanessa. Your efforts with Duncan and the others are crucial. I wouldn't be there doing this work without your nomination and your support.'

Rosel had not planned to have tea with Vanessa. She had bumped into her in Bond Street and Vanessa had insisted on calling a taxi and bringing her home to tea.

Rosel had never been intimate with Vanessa or any of the other members of the Artists International group. Still, she'd spent time with them raising funds, going to meetings and agonising over the state of the poor and oppressed. In the end it had been quite a relief, with their support, to get on the train north and to do some real hands-on work.

'It must be too terrible up there, my dear. How can you bear it? I suppose it is far too depressing for you to get any work of your own done?' Vanessa seemed genuinely concerned.

'It is very hard, yes. But, no I am painting again for the first time for a long time. There are some very fine people there. People of talent. Of course, there is the poverty, so much illness.'

Vanessa nodded gravely. 'You are so brave dear. How you can work in a place like that ... well! The mere vagaries of family life perpetually stop me working.' She laughed briefly. 'Although my sister would have it that if I wanted to be an artist I should have resisted the desire to procreate. As *she* has.' She frowned. 'You, Rosel. Do you have children?'

Rosel laughed and stood up. 'I am afraid not. No, never before. And now it is rather late.' She looked at the fine clock on the mantelpiece. 'And now I will be too late. I have an appointment with Sir Peter Hamilton Souness.

Vanessa raised her brows. 'Peter? He's an old dear. You wouldn't believe it, he looks such a stuffy old thing, but he gave us a very generous donation for our Spain fund.' She stood up and shook Rosel heartily by the hand. 'So good of you to report back on your Durham adventure. The others will be fascinated to hear.'

Rosel was outside on the pavement before she realised that she had, in fact, told Vanessa nothing at all significant about her 'Durham adventure.'

Despite this little diversion Rosel was glad to be back in London again. What a relief it was to see the brighter, fuller faces, the more distinctive colours, the newer clothes in the streets and the shops. How restful to be among people unmarked by the stigmata of poverty and consequent starvation.

In her months in Brack's Hill, Rosel's understanding of the specifics of poverty had become more refined. She was beginning to distinguish between those who were out of work and active - even though dressed in battered clothes and ten times mended shoes – and others.

Somehow people like Gabriel and Tegger MacNamara seemed to draw luck to them: they manufactured the materials for their own salvation and remained optimistic.

Different from these were the unemployed and inactive people who occasionally flushed onto the street to stand on corners, lean on walls, to pass the long stretches of time before returning to cold, desolate houses. Then there were the very still people who sat in doorways or lurked down alleyways as though there was absolutely nowhere to go. Such stillness had the feeling of the cemetery about it.

Rosel knew very well that London had its own poor and its own hungry. She knew that the Depression bit at the heels of people even in this ancient, crowded and wealthy city. But perhaps the accidental pickings from this rich and affluent place might be greater. Perhaps the poor here were hidden in closed neighbourhoods. In the main, the places where Rosel strode in her quest for her father were peopled by the kind of people, sober suited and sometimes surreal, that you would find in any cosmopolitan city. She was used to this in Berlin. This meant of course that she felt more at home in London than she did in Brack's Hill.

On her first day in London she'd endured a cautious, even uncomfortable interview with a young secretary at the German Embassy. He had asked her sharply about her residence in England and her plans for returning to their homeland. When she told him about her artistic enterprises in the North he softened a little.

'The much-vaunted greatness of Britain is somewhat fugitive these days. The new Germany will not tolerate such poverty. It is being conquered now, despite the vengeful attitude of our neighbours.' He smiled slightly. 'We have policies and programmes, which will root out such problems forever. We are systematic, unlike the British, who bumble along with their *ad hoc* do-gooding.'

She let his words sink in, then took a breath and asked him about the possibility of her father coming to visit her here in England. He raised his eyebrows.

'My father has been ill. I thought he might come here to convalesce in my care.'

'Here?' A high-pitched laugh leapt from the narrow mouth like an escaping rabbit. 'In London with all these fogs? This rain?

'No,' she said. 'I'll take him to the North.' She took to

outright lies. 'The country air is clean and clear there. Not like these London fogs.'

To build up her courage for the next visit on her list Rosel had gone to a little shop in Bond Street and spent too much money on an elegant brown hat with a feather. She went to Marshall and Snelgroves and bought new lingerie and a simple black dress. Then she went on to a small boutique to buy a dark green jacket with silk frogged fastenings. It was here where she ran into Vanessa who had spirited her away for tea.

Later, in her comfortable hotel Rosel felt a pang of guilt as she sank into the luxurious bath before pulling on her new silk stockings and stepping into her new lingerie. This guilt was later enhanced as she sat in her fine green jacket and ate the substantial luncheon put before her by an attentive waiter. It was a long time since she'd thought the way that she looked was important.

Her appointment with Sir Peter Hamilton Souness was at three thirty. At three twenty nine precisely she rang the bell by his name at Frobisher Mansions, a high Edwardian block not far from her hotel in Bedford Square. There were four bells and four names. Would Sir Peter come pounding down the stairs?

The door opened and a long, very young face stared at her. 'Ye-es?' he said.

'I have an appointment with Sir Peter Hamilton Souness,' she said, her chin up. 'My name is Rosel Von Siegendorff'

The door opened wider and revealed the body that went

with the young face, which belonged to a young man of perhaps nineteen years. He wore the dark jacket of a servant and an incongruous green striped tie on his soft collared shirt. He nodded at her. 'Yes ma'am. Sir Peter is expecting you.' The words were chanted like a learned script. He opened the door wider and she stepped in. 'We're on the top floor, miss. But fortuitously there is a lift.' *Fortuitously!* The accent was high pitched, from the top of his throat. Gabriel Marchant came into Rosel's mind. *His* voice came from somewhere deep, near his immaculate second hand brogue shoes. This boy was somewhere near Gabriel's age. Rosel couldn't imagine Gabriel fetching and carrying for any gentleman. Even young Tegger would not do this menial stuff.

The lift was small, but ornately designed, the door representing a parade of cast iron pelicans. She noted the fine workmanship. The boy stood by her side. His eyes slid round to appraise her. 'I see you like green, miss.' His tone was cocky. Not so subservient after all.

'Yes. Yes, I do.'

'Me too. Green's my favourite colour.'

The lift whirred to a halt and he pulled upon the door. 'Here we are miss.' He opened a heavy mahogany door. Then he altered his demeanour and spoke out of the side of his mouth. 'I'd watch him this afternoon miss. Got up in a paddy and has got worse as the day's got on.'

They were in a square hall furnished with a fine Turkish carpet and a single table with a silver tray placed precisely at its centre. The boy knocked, then opened a door on his right. 'Miss Rosel Von … Von…'

'Siegendorff,' she supplied, moving forward into a room which, to compensate for the dingy afternoon light, was illuminated by two large standard lamps. each standing beside a winged armchair. On the long low table between the chairs was a large bound book.

Peter Hamilton Souness raised himself from one of these, moved towards her and took her hand. He was taller than she was, grey haired and slight. He had an old duelling scar on his left cheek. 'Miss Von Siegendorff! How good of you to call. Brownson!' he looked away from her towards the boy. 'Tea, I think.'

'Yes sir,' said the boy called Brownson. 'Thank you sir.'

Sir Peter drew Rosel into the circle of light cast by the taller lamp. 'Ah, Fraŭlein Von Siegendorff. I see in you traits of both your mother and your father.' He paused. 'Your mother was a great beauty.'

She laughed. 'In that I do not favour her.'

'Won't you sit down?'

She sat in the circle of one lamp and he settled down opposite her, the smaller lamp throwing light onto the side of his face, showing his delicate profile.

'Perhaps Miss Von Siegendorff,' he said, 'perhaps you inherit more of your father's elegant demeanour. Handsome rather than…'

She flushed. 'Well, Sir Peter, I don't think…'

He put up a hand. 'Ah, you're right, my dear. It is rude of me to be so personal. We have just met, after all.' He settled back in his chair and his face dropped into shadow.

'My father has told me you and he were good friends in your … when you were young.'

'So we were. We skied together, swam together, fenced together.' His narrow hand touched his cheek lightly. 'We also danced together and gambled together. In the summer before old King Edward breathed his last. To is they seemed to be seemed fine times. All was very right with the world in those days.'

'He always speaks of those days with great nostalgia, great affection.'

'Your father was fine company. And a fine artist.' He stood up. 'Anticipating your visit I look in some old papers and I found this.' He went to the desk and returned with a drawing mounted on card. It was unframed. The man depicted was clearly Sir Peter himself. But he was younger, fuller faced; his cheek was not scarred. The hair curled more fully and fell over his face a little. He was smiling a peculiarly sweet smile.

'You must have been very young, Sir Peter. It is a good likeness.'

He nodded. 'We thought of nothing but travelling about and sport and larks in those days. In retrospect it seems we were filling the cup which we knew would be spilt.' His voice fell away and he stared at the drawing as though he was seeing it for the first time. 'Of course, your father did not just sport and play. He drew and painted. He made the rest of us feel like lazy oiks.'

'It is his life,' she ventured. 'The drawing and painting.'

'Life!' He surveyed her under his beetling brows. She had the sense that he was put out by her interruption of his idyll. 'Yes. Yes. We parted when war was declared. Your father also made fine art during the war, you know.'

She didn't like to say that yes, she did know. This was her father, after all.

'I saw him in 1923 and he gave me that book.' He nodded at the familiar tome on the table, the twin of the one in Archie Todhunter's office. 'Their trenches. Ours. What's the difference? Fine drawings. It was a terrible war between old comrades.'

His monologue was interrupted by a rattle at the door, and Brownson bustled into the room. He was now dressed in a white jacket and white gloves and pushed a small trolley on which sat a silver teapot, two china cups and saucers and a plate of plain ginger biscuits.

'Ginger biscuits?' said Sir Peter. 'Can't we run to cakes, Brownson?'

'Sorry, Sir Peter. I would if I could. I could always nip out to Longton's for a few cakes … but…'

Sir Peter put up a hand. 'Cease! Cease! Ginger will do!' He looked at Rosel. 'Will ginger do, Miss Von Siegendorff?'

She nodded. 'I like ginger biscuits. I do like them.' Oh dear. She was being too emphatic in her anxiety for the boy.

'Then that *is* a relief. Leave the teapot Brownson. Miss Von Seigenendorff will pour.'

She sat forward on the seat to attend to the teapot as Brownson backed off and shut the door behind him. They could hear him whistling in the hall. Sir Peter raised his brows. 'I had hoped I would make something of that boy but I am now in doubt. Can't abide serving-women about the place, but these boys take some bringing on.'

Rosel laughed and handed him his cup. 'I think he is a fine young man. Such cheer. He seems very keen.'

'You think so? I am relieved to hear it.' He sat back again in his chair and sipped delicately at his tea. He looked at her over the rim of his cup. 'Now then, Miss Von Siegendorff. How do you find yourself here in England?'

Having put her at ease he now proved to be a good listener. His intent gaze and his occasional query made it very easy for Rosel to tell him about living at first with her uncle in Sunderland, of her studies in London, her attempts to make her living from painting and now her work at the Settlement sponsored by Artists International.

'Now that must be a thankless task for you,' he murmured. 'There is so much to do about this poverty and no will to tackle it head-on here in England. As always, we wait for it to fade away. Your own government has it all in hand, I hear.'

She stared at him for a moment. That had been the message of the man at embassy too. Some might claim they were right.

Roads were being built in Germany, guns were being made. There was a new prosperity in the land. 'It is about my father, Sir Peter. I came to talk with you about him.'

'Perhaps you would be kind enough... my name is Peter. You should call me by my name. How is he now, your father?'

'Well ... he is physically well.'

'And does he still paint?'

She shook her head. 'I can't think so. He's in some kind of trouble. He was arrested.'

He frowned. 'Arrested? Old Max? Now that is a surprise. What has he done? Robbed a bank? Acquired a work of art by nefarious means?'

'He was arrested,' she said, 'because he spoke out. About his friend Herr Doktor Goldstein whose house was taken.'

'And what had this man done? Had he robbed a bank?'

'No.' she said impatiently. 'It is to do with this prohibition on the Jews. Many of my father's friends have been affected by this.'

Sir Peter frowned. 'I read of new arrangements...'

'Well, my father was in prison for two nights. They humiliated him and he is not even a Jew. Goodness knows what is happening to the Jews.'

Peter took a sip of his tea and his glance strayed from her to the window. 'So, Fraülein Von Siegendorff – Rosel - what is it you wish me to do?'

'I wondered if ... somehow ... my Father could come here.

He would be safer here.'

'Would he come? He's a great patriot. He would not leave Germany, surely?'

'It is not the same for him. The country is not the same as it was.'

'No? We have good reports of it. We hear that the future is being forged.'

'*We?*'

'No matter. So you want your father here?'

"It's the only thing I can think of. To keep him safe.'

As she nibbled at a ginger biscuit she noted his teeth which were too large and slightly yellowing to be anything but his own. He looked at her under beetling brows. 'I'll see what I can do, my dear. A word in a few ears, perhaps. Works wonders, don't you know? I will give you my telephone number here in London. Telephone me one week from now and perhaps there'll be something to tell. Now then, your father's address in Berlin…?'

35. Nathan's Portrait

'Can you do something for us, kidder?'

I look up into Nathan Smith's lined face. I'm drinking a welcome cup of tea in the Settlement kitchen as I've run out of even tea at home. Tegger has just gone in to see Mr. Todhunter. It seems the news is that his story is to be in one of these magazines he's always talking about.

'Aye. What is it, Mr Smith?'

Nathan sits down opposite looks at me earnestly. 'D'you know that the German woman…'

'You mean Rosel Vonn?'

'Aye, her. Well she painted this picture of us, you know, like the ones you did of Todhunter and Greta Pallister.'

'Yes. But she says you had second thoughts about it.'

'Aye. Seemed like such a vanity like, sitting there and then this picture if me. And when I saw myself, why…'

'You were embarrassed?'

'Aye. Seemed like so much showing off to me.

'So you didn't want it shown?'

'No. And I told her that. And I think she's put out. Not too pleased.' He sits there staring into space a second.

I remember that they say Nathan burned the picture, 'Well, Mr Smith, I'd'a thought that was your right, if you didn't want it seen it, shouldn't be there to look at.'

'Aye, but the trouble is that I've seen the other paintings around the place and now see it's all about the play, not about the folks in the pictures. And I'm a bit … well… well I thought it wasn't right on her. The German woman.' He's still looking away from me, out of the narrow window.

'So…?'

'I went looking for her to say mebbe we should put it up with the others. But she's nowhere around. Cora Miles says she's gone to London and she doesn't know when she'll get back.'

'So…?'

'So I wondered if you could get it from the shed. I could have another look and mebbe we could put it up with the others.'

So he can't have burned it. Rosel must have it tucked away in the shed somewhere. 'Well, I don't know…'

'Look, I'm gunna have to tell the woman I'm sorry, isn't that enough? If she sees it up when she gets back that'll be half the battle.'

In the painting shed are the racks Tegger and Mr Conroy have built from old floorboards so we can leave our work there if we want. We find Nathan's portrait tucked in Rosel's space alongside a big battered folder with her name on it. I haul it out and put it on an empty easel underneath the skylight. It is really good: lightly painted in her style but Nathan is there to the life. She's done something very clever. He sits there, the respectable coroner to the tip of his polished boots. But also it is still, essentially Nathan, the big miner who has spent half his life scratting for coal underground and still retained his dignity and humanity.

'It's good, Mr. Smith,' I say. 'Very good.'

He stares at it, and nods. 'Aye, I thowt you'd say that,' he says quietly. 'Now, can we get it in the big room beside the others?'

We set it up in the big room and, after looking at it again and surveying the others, Nathan wanders off. I return to the Settlement kitchen and pour myself another cup of tea. It'll be nice for Rosel to see Nathan's portrait beside the others when she gets back. But maybe she won't bother to come back. Maybe London is a softer option than up here. Who could blame her?

I would blame her. I want her here. Then, refreshed by the tea and stirred by thinking of Rosel I suddenly want to go back home and get on with my painting of the woman in the Goaf. There are still things about it that are not right, not right at all. I have turned the bundle of red wool into an actual poppy and that was a big mistake. It'll have to go back to be a bundle of red wool.

36. The Treatment of Men of Honour

Rosel arrived back in Brack's Hill to what seemed like an empty Settlement and a letter that looked as though it had been dipped in seawater.

Liebchen

I understand Boris has recounted to you my rather difficult news. To explicate: it was not just the fact of the arrest. In that dark place they made me strip off my clothes. I was so much reminded of that first time as a boy when I came to England to school. They made me strip there as well, then, to my bare skin. In my cell here, at least they shouted at me in my own language. What language! What words! They talked about betrayal. I told them of my work in the war and my medals. I shouted to them that there was no greater patriot than I. That was when they struck me, with their fists and the butt of an old rifle. And they laughed and joked as they did it. Sie verlachten (It was so much worse than the laughter of those foreign boys in that English school.) Two nights of this and I was sure there would be worse to come. I slept in snatches and I dreamt of you and Boris and the time you visited us in Berlin. Do you remember? On the second night in prison I thought I saw your mother, ghostlike, before the bars. She was wearing that long, red scarf. Do you remember the red scarf?

Then the next morning they came into the cell and I looked at the wall, not wanting to look towards them. They threw my clothes on the floor and leaned on the wall and laughed and nudged each other as I dressed myself. This was hard, with the injuries to my right hand. It passed through my mind that at least at one's execution one was allowed the dignity of trousers.

Then the officer came in, clicked his heels and called me <u>Meinherr</u> and told me he knew quite well my book of war sketches and that his father had also fought in France. It seemed now that there was to be no execution. Boris was there and I think I babbled and moaned to him I know not what. He was not in his uniform but is still as beautiful as ever. (He is worried now with some justification, about his own position.)

The apartment was open when I returned. For a day I thought things were back to normal, except for the injury to my right hand which meant I could not execute my daily drawings. Then the next day when I went to the Institute the doorkeeper barred my way and told me that no man of my name worked in that august institution and Jew lovers like me should launch myself back into the gutter where belonged all traitorous scum.

So I am safe for the moment. I thought you might wish to know this even though our paths have diverged in recent years and your uncle, my much-mourned brother, became your father in my place.

Your affectionate *Papa*

****

Rosel stood in the passageway between Archie's office and the stairs and read the letter twice. She closed her eyes and leaned against the wall, clutching it to her. How strange that at this stage in her life she was being called on to take care of her father; that, having escaped his suffocating care as a child, it was now her turn to care for him, to feel protective love towards him, instead of the wary regard she had cultivated all her adult life to keep him at a distance.

When she was a girl she had been his obsession, his rapt attention to every detail of herself and her life had been oppressive. Now though, she felt affection, appreciation, even love for him. A victim himself, he no longer held any threat for her. Somewhere inside her she relished the change.

So she was glad that she'd done what she could. Sir Peter seemed confident that things could be taken hand despite being rather vague about the options. But now this letter meant there was only one option. Her father had to get out, to come to England. She would have to take care of him. She looked along the narrow hall cluttered with books and boxes, stage props and dumb bells. He could not stay here. She would have to make enquiries about renting a house. There were empty houses enough in this half derelict town. The rent would be cheap. Or perhaps he could go to her uncle in Sunderland.

On the second landing she bumped into Cora, who was reeling from the bathroom to the bedroom she shared with

Archie's. She was white as a ghost. Rosel shoved the letter into her pocket and took the other woman's arm. 'Cora! You're ill!'

Cora smiled wanly. 'Yes. Not quite ticketty boo. Bleeding again. Bit of reaction, perhaps. I thought it would be all right, like last time.'

Rosel helped her into the bedroom and onto the bed. 'I should get a doctor...'

Cora shook her head. 'I only need to rest. I will be all right. It only took a couple of days last time. It will take longer now as I'm such an ancient wretch. Rehearsal Wednesday night. So long as I am well by then.'

Roes; frowned. 'I thought you'd already had it done? That it was over?'

Cora smiled wearily. 'That's what I told you.'

Rosel took her arm and led her into the bedroom. Cora told her about the Settlement players performing for two of Archie's cronies. 'They seemed to like it,' she smiled wanly.' despite me drying in my big speech.'

Rosel tucked her into the bed and leaned across and plumped up her pillows. 'You should really tell Archie, Cora.'

Rosel felt rather than saw Cora's vehement rejection of her idea. 'Not his business, darling. Not his business.' She took a breath. 'So how was dear old London? Nice to get away from the dark satanic hills into the bright lights, eh?' She managed a chuckle. 'And did you get your business done, darling? Paramour, was it? A good looking woman like you is wasted among these poor dejected folk.'

Rosel shook her head. 'Even if, like you, I am a bit of an ancient wretch?' she laughed. 'No, it wasn't a paramour, you naughty woman. And as far as I can see the people here might be poor but they're not dejected. At least not those who come to the Settlement.' She thought of Gabriel and wanted to see him, to talk to him. She would see him tomorrow. Not for a repeat performance of the last event. Definitely not that. They had agreed. But she wanted to talk to him about her father and her brother. With Cora in this state and Archie so distracted there was no one else to tell. She would see him tomorrow, go to his house.

That night she sat in Archie's office and turned over the leaves of her father's war book. She looked into the faces of the men and boys there; she appraised the sensitive touch and the specialist skills of her father, the artist. She looked at the crumpled bodies, the strained faces, the weary eyes; at the images scattered by explosion: bodies dismembered, without centre: the sense of a civilisation in total breakdown. It was interesting that the Kaiser himself, now still in Holländisch exile, had survived all this. He possessed a copy of this volume and was said to be very fond of it. He had attended the ceremony in person to pin the medal on her father's chest, in recognition of his artistic valour.

Some of the faces drawn here were so young, embittered but lacking in guile. Surely there was some honour for them, even in these slimy sodden trenches.

But there was no honour in the way her father or his old

friends were being treated now. None at all. Were there still men of honour in Germany? There must be. Her brother Boris was surely not the only one. So what would they do now? And if they took action would they themselves be shot? Or worse. Her father was in danger but surely so too was Boris. How could they tolerate this? She sighed, closed the book and put it back in its canvas case. .

Perhaps Gabriel could have the book. It would go alongside his Rembrandt and Turner books and be another authority for his reference. So he would know that, in her country, there were still men of honour. Her father and her brother were among these. One could only pray it would not lead to their downfall.

37. The Gallery

You might think it strange that at my age I've never ever been further than the twenty-five miles I'm travelling this morning. Not even as far. I've travelled in trains of course - to Priorton, the nearest big town, and to Durham for miners' meetings when I still had faith in the Union. As well as that me and Tegger once went on the train to spend a day at the coast. That day we walked up and down in caps and mufflers, heads down against the cutting wind the sea rolling alongside us as dark as any of those prints of Mr Turner. But I gloried in the roaring sea which continually made and remade itself. And we met a man there, who showed us how to find certain stones, smash them on the rocks and open them up to find things he called *ammonites*: sea relics even more ancient than the fossils from the pit. I keep them now all in the same box.

Later on Tegger wrote this ragged rhyming poem about our time that day by the sea with the coal sludge tippling from the coal staithes into the seething foam. I keep a copy of in the same box as the ammonites and fossils.

But today coming the Newcastle is a different thing altogether from visiting the seaside. The train brought us to this city: a big black sprawling place, its wide river mouth spiked with ship-masts and cranes, its narrow streets threading the riverside and its warehouses rearing up from the reaches of this great greasy river which lifts and moves on, ultimately flowing out into that very sea that me and Tegger walked by three years ago, looking for ammonites.

The train puffs its way over the high bridge and a landscape of high buildings is laid out before you like it's this great canvas. Even the smoke and grime cannot disguise the grandeur and grace of the buildings, rising up behind the massive warehouses on the quayside. But parts of this quayside are ominously shadowy and quiet There is little work here too: the unemployment affects the dockers and shipbuilders, the same as coalminers.

Once out of the station - some kind of big cathedral in itself - the city grows around you. Marguerite Molloy knows her way here and leads us up a great busy street like it's her own front yard. She turns into a place called the Old Lion Café where we're served meat, potatoes and carrots by a woman in a crisp, white apron. I have to admit that I wolf it down. It's a good while since I've had a meal off a plate like this. Just 'getting by' on insufficient money does not involve meals on a whole plate, although it might be for some, whose wives weave wonders, but not so for me there in the house on my own.

Marguerite pays for our meal like she paid for the train. She's wearing a pale grey coat with cloth buttons and a grey cloche hat piped in red. She draws glances from both men and women here in the café. Me and Tegger can't object to her paying, as there's no money in our pockets. She's told me firmly that this is part payment against the sale of the sketches I am carrying in her music case and a reward for the amazing painting of her as the Woman in the Goaf sitting in my front room.

It was Marguerite who suggested I bring some drawings along with me, to show the people at the gallery. I told her they'd not be interested in some lad off the street. She called me an old sober-sides, bought the

 music case from the pawnshop and insisted I fill it with sketches. I did that to humour her but I know I'm right. They won't be interested.

Still, it's a day out and the company is all right. Tegger's on good form, spinning like a top across the wide pavements, peering into shop windows, swinging around stone columns like a street kid whirling around a lamp post. Now and then he grabs Marguerite's hand and she suffers it for a while before wriggling away.

All this liveliness fizzles out of us when we stop before the double doors of the gallery and look at them with awe, taken aback by their height and dignity. An old woman with severe hair and a black coat comes up the steps behind us and glares at us until we give way. The doors don't worry her. She opens them as though these great doors were the doors to her own house.

Tegger one of the doors as it swings back and pushes it open. 'Come on, marra,' he says. 'Haven't you and me been in scarier places than this.'

The big entrance hall smells of wax polish and mild chemicals and looks like the main hall at my grammar school. A woman at a desk on our right looks up. Her glance falters past our threadbare coats and down to our shoes and back again. Maybe she doesn't see lads in their dusty Sunday best each day. Maybe it's just the shine on my black brogue shoes that's getting to her.

'Yes?'

'We've come to see the pictures.' My voice echoes in the high room and trembles in the dust.

'We brought some pictures as well,' Tegger rushes in. 'My mate here, he's a painter.' He grabs the music case and pushes it towards her on the desk.

She takes off her glasses and peers at me. 'A painter, is he?'

'I told you,' he said. 'Look at them pictures. You'll have seen nowt like them.'

'It's not up to me,' she sniffs. 'I don't know whether the assistant curator is at the gallery today.'

'I bet you say that to all the artists,' grins Marguerite. 'You should look at them, Miss. I've seen some of your pictures here. These of his are as good as some of those, any day. I'm telling you.'

The woman's mild eyes sweep up to Marguerite's smart hat

and drop to the bobbin heels of her shoes. 'You *tell* me, do you?'
She sniffs again.

I reach out for the case. 'No need to bother,' I say.

The woman's hand comes on mine, preventing me from
taking it away again. It is a surprisingly smooth hand: small, white
and well kept. The nails are polished. The fingers are plump, like
little white sausages. I look back up at the woman's mild, lumpy
face in surprise.

'Leave it,' she says. 'I'll ask someone to take a look at it.'

'We have to get back for the three forty train. We can't
leave the drawings,' says Tegger firmly.

'Go and look at the exhibits!' She is equally firm. 'Come
back in an hour.'

We wander off, not quite knowing where or even how to
look. Gradually I begin to take it all in. The walls are heavy with
great, dark canvasses – portraits of men of importance with the
accoutrements of their high-level trades around them: shipmasters
and judges, aldermen and jewel-laden women with haughty looks.
On some of the works the paint has dried and is chipped with age
and the characters of the people portrayed are masked rather than
revealed by the painting. I think of the lightness, the sheer
transparency of the way Rosel paints and the jewel-like depths of
Rembrandt, even in book prints. And I know I've seen even
better than the work on these walls.

Then I come across smaller pieces with more recognisable
contexts. Moorland landscapes where the painters have captured

the peculiar qualities of the light. I think of a painting in my Rembrandt book, of a landscape in a thunderstorm. Of Turner's black and white landscape etching. I turn a corner and am confronted by a seascape where the turbulence of the sea is perfectly captured by the still magic of colour. This is a seascape by Turner, that tops any painting in this gallery. It is just sea and sky, but in truth it is sheer light. I know his fine treatment of light from his etchings. But here the breath is knocked out of me by the full blown brilliance of light in Turner's painting. I am winded by it.

'Gabe! Gabe! Come on, marra!' Tegger is tugging my sleeve. 'It's after three! Yer standing there in a daze.'

When we return to the entrance hall the woman at the table is smiling slightly. 'Did you enjoy the exhibits?' she says.

I nod. 'It's a great eye-opener,' I say. 'I liked the Turner. So much light charging at you from the canvas.'

She nods. 'He is not so fashionable these days, but that is a great painting. His handling of light...'

My turn to nod. 'It's real nmagic,' I say.

'Well, Mr...'

'Marchant.'

'... Mr Marchant. Our assistant curator has looked at your drawings. He has told me to inform you that we have a summer exhibition for amateur painters and would very much welcome a submission by you.'

'He's not an amateur,' says Tegger, jutting out his chin.

'Well,' I say, feeling warm inside. 'Mebbe aspiring rather than amateur.' I am properly humbled by what I've seen.

'Well, he did say this was promising work.' She hesitates. 'These two drawings…' They are at the top of the pile. One is a sketch of Marguerite bending to unbuckle her shoe, her long arm a graceful line down the side of the painting. The other is an old drawing of my father asleep in his chair, his head to one side, his mouth slightly open. One arm hangs over the side of the chair, the other hand, calloused and work-worn, is curled in his lap.

The woman looks me in the eye. 'I have this friend who works in a small commercial gallery in the town. Do you mind if I show her these? She could show them to her boss and he might sell them for you.'

I shake my head dumbly.

'Man!' says Tegger.

The woman is looking at me, her eyes hopeful. 'If you give me your address, I will write to you and tell you what she says.'

I scribble it down. It's probably the last I'll see of these drawings. But it has to be something, if somebody - especially somebody who works in an art gallery - thinks they're worth showing to someone else.

There was no answer when Rosel knocked at the door of the low house. She knocked four times, then, very tentatively, reached for the sneck and clicked the door open. She found herself in a narrow scullery with a row of empty jars on a shelf and an enamel bowl on a stool beneath a single tap. Dishes stood in line on another shelf and a single gas ring stood on the table under the window.

An archway led left to an open staircase and right into a square kitchen with the customary black range. The fire was dead ash, but when she touched it, the iron range still held residual warmth. At first the room seemed chaotic, with piles of papers and books scattered about and half-done drawings pinned up on the walls. But there was some order in the piles and some sequence in the drawings. The kitchen table was set up with rows of paints, two big white sinner plates for palettes and jam jars with, she presumed, turps and oil. Above them was a small volume of Turner's etchings. On the sewing machine under the window a hefty volume of Rembrandt prints lay open at his depiction of *The Ascension of Christ* with the foreground figures almost entirely in the dark and the background figure of Christ illuminated from above. She turned the pages to another image, marked by Gabriel, of Bathsheba, opulently, luxuriantly naked, a note clasped in her powerful hand.

Rosel turned her head this way and that to listen to the house. It was quiet; there was no noise from the street. Then she opened the door to the front room. The curtains were closed and it was in complete darkness. She had to squeeze past upturned furniture to turn up the gas lamp to illuminate the dark room. Here indeed was chaos. Chairs and tables were pushed back against the wall, heaped higgledy-piggledy on top of each other.

She turned to survey the room and blinked hard. In the middle of the room on a clumsy joiner-made easel was a very large painting. She peered at it, and then dragged it around to face the light from the kitchen door. Now she could make it out: dark foreground with a barely lit figure of a man; intent; rigid with fear or perhaps wonder. In the deep middle ground was the figure of a naked woman, more slender than Bathsheba but borrowing her glowing flesh tones. She had some kind of drape over her shoulder with a flower pinned to it. Her gaze was not Bathsheba's modest sideways glance but this woman looked directly, powerfully out at the crouching man and past him out of the picture at whoever might dare to look.

The way the woman was lit was strange. At one angle she was entirely in the dark. At another angle she was in the light. Unlike Rembrandt's Christ, with light streaming from above, this woman drew light from somewhere inside herself. Behind her, surrounding her, framing her, was the densest of black whose blackness was enhanced by graining of purple and red, green and aquamarine.

Rosel took a breath. What had the boy been up to? This was in a different class from his naively gifted paintings of Greta and Cora. Derivative as it was, this painting had something unique, something purely of himself in it. And obviously he was keeping this work to himself.

She frowned. Why had he not spoken to her about it? Perhaps he'd taken too much to heart what she and Archie had said about copying. How many hours had this taken? He must have burned midnight oil. Is that not what the English said?

She heard the click of the kitchen door and froze. Then she sighed. She'd been caught snooping and would have to pay the consequences. 'Gabriel?' she called.

'Gabriel?' came an echo.

She went through the middle door to face, not Gabriel but another woman, tall, a little stout, not much older than herself.

'Gabriel?' repeated the other woman, fine dark brows arching. 'Is Gabriel here?'

Rosel smiled. 'I was looking for him myself,' she shrugged, and put her hand out to shake the other woman's. 'I am Rosel <u>Vonn</u>, Gabriel's - art teacher. Or friend, perhaps. I teach him to paint.'

The woman shook her hand warmly. 'So you're responsible for all this?' She nodded at the walls. 'More like a studio than a kitchen, isn't it?' There was an attractive lilt to her voice.

'And you're..?'

'I am his auntie. Susanah Clelland. It is a while since I saw Gabriel and I wondered how he was doing. Seems like he's doing all right.' She moved to the window and peered at the Rembrandt book. 'Ah. Seems like he made some use of them.

'You gave him the books?'

Susanah smiled happily. 'Well, there's no college for him round here. I thought the books might help.'

'Well,' said Rosel, 'he is certainly inspired.'

Susanah peered at the sketches on the wall. 'Goodness, what progress he's made! Look at those figures. You must be pleased with your pupil. You must be a fine teacher.'

Rosel shrugged. 'He teaches himself. He finds his own way.' She hesitated. 'There is a big piece in the front room...' She led the way. 'Nothing to do with me. I believe it was something of a secret.'

Susanah let out a long, unladylike whistle. 'Well. What's he saying here? Look at that woman!'

'It's a very ... ambitious piece of work. This is the first time I have seen it.'

'So, what do you think of it? Do you think it is good, then?'

'Yes. I...' Rosel led the way back into the kitchen and turned the leaves of the Rembrandt book. 'It is full of references. Look - see those dark figures in this Rembrandt painting? And see how he's used Bathsheba as a reference for the woman figure?'

They returned to survey the painting again.

Susanah frowned. 'Yes. Yes. But this woman is entirely herself. Lit from within, see? See the way the black hair spangles up with the wall behind? Ah yes!' she said thoughtfully. 'Yes! It's in the pit, and this man here, scared nearly witless, is a pitman. This woman's a kind of ... a dark goddess. It is such an imagination the boy has.'

'I see now,' murmured Rosel. 'Before I was only seeing the references, but now…'

'So, you've had a proper eyeful, then?' The voice that came from behind them was hard, jeering. 'Poking in where nobody invited you?'

38. Other People's Affairs

The two women whirl around like a pair of thieves caught in the act. My Aunt Susannah is the first to break the silence. 'Well, Gabriel, we didn't hear you coming.'

'That seems likely, seeing as you're poking around...'

'We were just...' Here in my house, among my things Rosel takes on the aspect of a stranger: a woman nearer my aunt than me.

'Poking your nose in other people's affairs.' I push my way past them to turn down the gaslight. The front room and the painting sink into darkness. The women scurry into the kitchen. I follow them and shut the room door firmly behind me.

My Aunt Susanah is the least embarrassed. And to be honest it's really difficult to stay on your dignity with someone who has known you so long. She sits down in my father's chair and says, 'Well Gabriel, *bach*, no cup of tea for your old auntie or your teacher?' Her tongue is clearly in her cheek.

I'm still fuming as I fill the kettle, still angry as I put out my father's best cups and saucers. I have just parted from Marguerite and Tegger at the railway station. I want no talk. I only want to think: to see with my inner eye the magical light streaming from that canvas of Turner's in the gallery. All light: no surface: no outlines. Only light, only dark.

What I wanted most this evening was to sit and close my eyes and think of the Turner. And to imagine those pictures and those frames and those people walking by in the gallery, sharing with me the visions of the painters. What must it be like for people to see your work at its best like that? And to understand what you're trying to say without a word said? Brack's Hill now seems to me to be a small place, away from everything that means something. This makes me sad and I want to pursue the sadness on my own.

The two women are talking around and through me: about art and painting and Germany and the problems of German rearmament; about Berlin and the way things are the same there as here, only in some ways so very different. Rosel tells Susannah about her father and some problems he has, living there. And my brain is still hanging onto Turner's wonderful swirl of light.

I put cups and saucers into their hands and now it's like they are *both* my aunties, even though Rosel is more slender, more youthful.

'I'll leave you two to it,' I say. 'I've gotta do something.' I grab my cap and muffler and race out. At first this is just to escape them but I find myself making my way up through the town towards the pit heap and the reservoir pool. I walk the paths of my childhood, scramble the heap and pick up a fossil of what looks like half the body and the wings of a firefly. No head. After a while my breathing returns to normal and my vision of Turner's sky stops thumping away at the core of my brain.

I get to thinking about Rosel being there, in my house. Then I had this brainstorm. Rosel there, talking to my Aunt Susanah. My body quickens as it remembers making love with her in the work-shed and I wonder what tricks on myself my brain has played in seeing her as my auntie's mirror. This is Rosel. My friend: for a moment my lover.

When I get back to the house the door is open as usual but the house is empty. I've no idea how long I've been out. My father's old wall clock tells me two and a half hours. So I set out again. Rosel will be back at the Settlement. I have to talk to her about the Turner and that great building in Newcastle stuffed full of pictures with gold frames fit for a Rajah's palace.

As I go into the Settlement there is a kerfuffle in the small vestibule. My heart sinks. Jake McVay and Greta. I've missed the rehearsal.

Greta is beside me, her black eyes glittering fiercely behind her glasses. 'Where were you Gabriel? Tegger had to read your lines and do you know what? He really kissed me? I had to kiss Tegger! I slapped his face. Archie was mad.' The sides of that full mouth are pulled down. 'Archie was shouting at everyone. Ready to cut his throat as far as I could see.'

'Sorry, sorry. I forgot.'

'Forgot? Well!' She pouts, looking older now than her sixteen years. 'Better things to do, have we?'

I catch up with Archie in the office. 'Look Mr Todhunter, I'm sorry…'

He flicks a hand at me. 'Don't worry, dear boy. You didn't let me down; you just let down young Greta and Nathan. And you let down all the people who've been your friends and comrades all these months. We started half an hour late and not one of them turned in a performance worth a bucket of fish.'

'Look. I've been to Newcastle today, and this just slipped my mind…'

'Slip your mind, did it? Well it didn't slip Tegger's mind. But he was here on the dot was young Tegger. And he, I believe, accompanied you on your afternoon odyssey?'

The sarcasm of the man.

'Well, mebbe Tegger should be Arthur. Mebbe he's a better type, being on time and all that. He might as well. Seeing he wrote all the words, like.' I pause. Archie likes to keep up the fiction that the play is his alone. 'Well. All the words that count,' I finished.

My betrayal hangs in the air. Archie busies himself with inserting a new cigarette in his holder and lighting it with the butt of the old one. He grips the holder with his teeth and speaks through it. 'Get out,' he says. 'Get out of my office.'

Only Cora is left in the hallway. With a turban around her head and that white face she looks twenty years older. Seems like she's making a good fist of the role of Maggie. Lives it outside the play. 'I'm looking for Rosel,' I say. 'Is she here?'

She frowns at me as though she doesn't know me from Adam. 'Rosel? Oh, Gabriel! Where were you tonight? Archie was spitting coals. Big trouble. You mustn't cross with Archie, you know. It doesn't pay.'

'I got... I got delayed.'

She takes off her character-shawl and folds it carefully into a square. 'Well now. You should remember that to Archie Todhunter, what preoccupies him is the centre of the universe. And it has to be the centre of everybody's universe.'

'Seems like.'

She takes off her turban and her abundant toffee-coloured hair falls about her shoulders. This should make her look younger but today it doesn't. She looks haggard. 'But you got here?' she says. 'In the end?'

'I was looking for Rosel,' I say. 'Like I say.'

'Oh.' She stares at me very hard. Her eyes very wide, as though we are deep in water and she can't quite make me out. Then she glances back at the empty corridor. 'She's upstairs in her eyrie,' she says. 'Keep going till you can't stop. Yellow door.' She's acting my conspirator. I belt up the stairs three at a time but hesitate outside the yellow door. Push my hand through my hair; straighten up my necktie. Then I knock on the door. A strangled voice invites me in and I am inside.

Rosel is tying a green silk dressing gown with a yellow

tasselled tie. The room smells spicy and over-warm. The tall single lamp illuminates the side of her face.

'Gabriel!' she says. 'I thought you were Cora.'

'She sent me here. I was looking for you.'

She picks up a brush to smooth her already smooth hair. 'Archie was raging about you at the rehearsal.'

Back at my house she looked as old as my Aunt Susannah. Now she looks as young as Greta Pallister. 'I know! Everyone has said so. And you can see it on his face anyway. He told me to get out.'

'Why did you run away?' She sits down on the bed. 'From the house.'

'You were there, poking about my things. With my aunt.'

'I apologise. I apologised then. It was wrong. It was … a strange moment.' She looks up at me. 'I see Nathan's portrait is here now, beside the others. How did that get there?'

'He talked to me. Seems he changed his mind. It looks well beside the others.'

'I am pleased that you think so,' she says, staring at me with those light eyes of hers.

I sit down on a chair beside the door and stretch out my legs in front of me. My brogue shoes – still highly polished for the trip to Newcastle - shine in the lamplight.

'Your auntie seems very nice,' she says. 'A clever woman. I likes her.'

'She's all right. I only see her now and then. But she's all right. She's very intelligent. Her husband's a teacher. She gave me...'

'... the Rembrandt book. And the Turner etchings. So she says.'

'You had no business, there in my house, poking about my things,' I explode.

She throws the hairbrush at the mirror. There's a loud crash but the mirror refuses to break. 'Gabriel Marchant! You are as bad as Archie Todhunter. You live there in your own little world. You really need something to worry about.' She picks up a letter from the bedside table and throws that at me. It floats to my feet. I open it up. *'Liebchen!'* I can't understand a word. 'What's this?' I drop it back to the floor.

She comes across and kneels down to pick it up. I can see the shadow of her small breasts against the neck of the gown and one part of my mind registers that she is naked underneath.

Still kneeling she smoothes out the paper on the sparse carpet and, haltingly, begins to translate it. As the story of her father's persecution falls from her lips I begin to understand her despair at my truculence, my self-absorption. I've read of nasty things happening in Germany. I've heard the old men in the Raglan turn it over then turn it back to their own experience on the Somme. I've mouthed Arthur's words in the play, about land fit for heroes and injustice to the survivors of that terrible war. Maybe the Germans too needed a land fit for heroes and look what was happening to them.

But this story is about an old man being beaten in his own country for acts of simple humanity. And here is his daughter doing her bit for people here, not looking to her home country.

'My brother Boris also wrote to me. He, who had great faith in the New Germany, is faltering. He is in the army, doing well, but all this makes him doubt. I think there are plots, plans to get rid of the cause of this problem. And this too will certainly put him in danger.'

'I can see that.' How poor words are in this situation.

'I was in London to try to get help for my father. He needs papers to get out. Money. He needs a welcome in a strange land.'

'Did you manage? To get some help?' I say humbly.

'I don't know. Gabriel, I don't know.' There are tears in her ayes.

Now I am kneeling beside her, take her near naked body in my arms. I comfort her as a mother comforts her child. I think this must be how they must do it, although I have no memory of it myself. I stroke her and murmur half-words. I push her hair from her face and smooth it down.

Then she takes hold of my hand and presses it beside her throat where it swells into her shoulder. This makes me groan and before I know what I am doing I am carrying her to the bed and there we make love for what seems an eternity of time.

Afterwards she tells me more stories of her father and her mother

- very unusual types to say the least. She talks about her childhood with her brother, of the wild times with her mother and the choking, over-attendant care of her father, who seems to have tried to put her into her mother's place, to make a kind of lover of her.

Then she's raining kisses on me again and we make love for a second time, more slowly. Then we sleep awhile. My arm is stiff underneath her when I wake, so I lift it to ease it and she wakes too. Now at last I start to tell her of the gallery and my delight in seeing those great paintings as real objects. I babble on about the sheer driving power of the paint, the eternal quality of the light. 'It made me think. Seems stupid to think I can paint at all, seeing that. Here am I painting the dark. However can it compete with the light?'

'Always the dark and the light for you, Gabriel.' She puts a finger on my lips. 'You *can* paint. I saw your painting. In your house.'

'Did you?' I know she did. Wasn't that why I was so angry, feeling exposed like that?

"It is a very powerful piece of work. Such depth.'

I am silenced.

'You've learned so much, Gabriel. You have taught yourself. Learned... Tell me about the painting.'

Now I'm telling her about the woman in the Goaf and there are no secrets between us. She talks to me about the way I've referred to the Rembrandt pictures in my painting. I know about this, but I listen, wait for the criticism.

'But somehow that painting is purely your own. No one else could have painted it. None of those painters you have seen today.'

With that I have to be content.

Suddenly we're hearing voices, sharp and unpleasant in the room below us. I sit up, dragging her and half the bed clothes with me. 'What's that?'

'It's Cora and Archie. They're quarrelling a lot these days.' She paused. 'Cora's not well,' she whispers. 'Not well at all.'

'I thought she looked under the weather, like.'

'More than a bit.' She hesitates.

'What?'

'Nothing.' Then she pushes me. 'You should go home. Archie will be furious if he knows you're here.'

'Cora knows I'm here.'

'She won't have told him. She knows how to keep secrets.'

39. The Possibility of Another War

'These rehearsals are taking longer and longer. Don't they know you've got school to go to?' Mrs Pallister put a jam sandwich, neatly cut into triangles, beside Greta's cocoa.

Greta closed her eyes, savouring the smell of chocolate. 'Full-performance rehearsals now, Ma. Takes some time, with Archie's notes afterwards. I've got to get it right.'

'How many weeks to go? Three? It'll have to be right for the Prince of Wales.'

'You don't think he'll really have time to see the whole play, do you?' Dev Pallister's voice came from behind his rattling newspaper. 'There is the visit to the Club, and the Allotment project. He'll have no time to sit through a play.'

'But that's what we're doing it for,' said Greta crossly. 'For the Prince's visit.'

The newspaper crackled again as Dev crumpled it in his lap. 'I'd'a thought you were doing it for yourselves, for that swaggerer Archie Todhunter, even for the poor folks in this town. Not for some prince who dips his toe in the working class and gets his footman to polish it off.'

'You've changed your tune,' said his wife.

'Only within these four walls,' he said. 'Do you know what was being said in the meeting today? That another war would be the only thing to wipe out this misery. They'll need coal then. And steel. Uniforms. Manufacturing.' He sighed. 'And d'you know I found myself agreeing? Another war? After that last lot? And losing our Ernie and Alan? But if Moseley and htoffs like him get a hold here and still we lose all that we fought for. They're saying we've gotta fight again. Got to! '

'Why can't the countries come to an agreement?' said Greta. 'Talk instead of fighting? Seems stupid to me, fighting. Rosel Vonn - her brother and father were soldiers for Germany last time. And her cousins died, like Uncle Ernie and Uncle Alan.'

Dev shook his head. 'There are them who say let the Germans get on with their own thing and we'll get on with ours. But ugly things are happening in Germany and it'll spread like the Black Death right across Europe if we don't watch. Even self-interest says we should re-arm. I'm sure of it now. They'll leave us behind, else.'

'My teacher says if we re-arm as well there's bound to be another war.' Greta wiped a crumb from her lip. 'She says it's bound to happen. A drawn sword must strike.'

He laughed. 'Ha! How easy are the comforts of pacifism!'

His wife collected the dishes. 'Seems like the last one never really ended, somehow,' she said, shaking her head. 'Not twenty years gone and here we are at it again.'

'Now there speaks a wise woman,' said Dev, drawing up his newspaper like a fire curtain before him.

'So you're right, Dev. It is a bit trivial to worry whether or not the prince will watch the play. You're right, isn't he Greta?'

Dev grunted agreement, from behind his rustling newspaper. Greta nodded and stood up, grabbing the battered book by her plate.

'*Wuthering Heights*!' said her mother. 'Reading it again? How can you stand that Heathcliff? He's a cruel one.'

'He has passion, that's all,' said Greta. 'Passion.'

'Passion is it? Well passion or no passion, don't you read too long. The light in that bedroom's not what it should be. Your eyes are bad enough already, my lady. And there's school tomorrow.'

40. The Bogie

On Thursday Rosel catches me after the long rehearsal. She's keen for me to take the painting of the woman in the Goaf down to the Settlement, but I'm not so sure about that. For one thing I am not sure it is finished.

'You'll never be sure of that, Gabriel. Work on it down in the shed. The light's better there, than in your house. Your room is good for atmosphere. But for painting, no.'

'I don't need the light. I need the dark.'

'Don't talk nonsense. All painters need light. The point about that painting is the light with which you've imbued the figure of the woman, set off against the Goaf.'

'You're wrong. The point about the painting is the quality of the dark. The Goaf. The black behind the black.'

She stares at me a moment. 'Well … yes. It's your … But I think the real reason you don't want it there is because you're frightened.'

'Me. Frightened?'

'Frightened, perhaps, of some of the things people might

say. It always makes one afraid. I know this. A stranger's eyes on your canvas is like his eyes on your naked flesh.'

'My portraits are already there. People see them.'

'Ah, my dear.' She shrugs. 'Your portraits are exercises. Illustrations, merely. Very good. Admirable. Skilled. But how much of yourself is in them? But in that one in your parlour … you are there. You have invested so much of yourself in this one.'

I know I'll give in to her but I delay giving in. It's so easy to give in to her. I can't say I've been closer to her than any human being but between us it seems again that we must now maintain some distance. I have to take my cue from her.

I change tack. 'So what has happen about your father?' At least I can exploit this intimacy of a confidence between friends.

She shakes her head. 'I telephoned the man in London and he says he is making enquiries. That is all.'

'He was a toff, that one, wasn't he? The one you visited?'

She frowns. 'A toff?'

'A posh lad. A lord or something? Sir something or other

'Is that a toff?'

'Didn't he live in a grand house?'

'Well, no. Yes. It was rather grand rooms in a grand house.'

'Like I say. How old was he, this toff?'

'What does that matter?'

'As old as my Aunt Susannah? As old as you?'

She frowns. 'This is ridiculous. About as old as Archie, if you wish to know.'

I don't think she likes this talk of age. 'Oh, well, that's all right then.'

Her face hardens to a mask. 'It's not all right. You have no right...?

'Oh,' I say softly. 'I have a right.' I put my hand on the top of her arm and rub the ball of my thumb over her shoulder-bone.

She slaps me so hard that I reel. 'I have told you...'

I stand upright and rub my injured cheekbone. 'Rosel. There-s no need...'

She moves swiftly to the door of the echoing rehearsal room. She looks at me over her shoulder. 'You have no right, Gabriel. No right at all. You are a child. I have no more in common with you than your Aunt Susannah. Like her I am fond of you, but more than that ... no! Never, never again. It is ridiculous. It was ridiculous. We make ourselves ridiculous doing that. No more, I tell you!'

So, to make up for my gaffe with Rosel means I've had to give in about the picture. But now there's the problem of getting the big canvas down to the Settlement. It's far too big to manhandle, even if that were possible. And it's not possible because the paint is still wet. It takes weeks for this stuff to dry.

Tegger has the solution. 'We'll have to get your Dad's bogie[3] off the allotment.'

I don't let Tegger see how my heart jolts at his suggestion. I haven't been there since we cut down my father's dead body and carried him home. I occurs to me that we didn't think of using the bogie to carry his body back home. But I'm glad we didn't think of it. I'm glad that I carried my father home in my arms.

I thought the allotment would be derelict and overgrown. But it looks much as it did. The chickens still cluck away in and out of their cree and the soil has just had its winter turnover.

My father's marra Steve is backing out of the cree. In his hand he is clutching his cap, in which nestle five eggs.

'Why Gabe, son, how's it going?' he says, smiling slightly. 'I've given up thought of seeing you down here again!'

I look round. 'I thought it'd be overgrown, like.'

Steve shakes his head. 'Saw the Allotment Committee. Said I'd tek it on for the rest of this year. Called on you with eggs now and then, but you were never in. Left a note.'

'I found the eggs. And the note,' I feel guilty of not responding to his kind gestures. 'I should have come...'

'Canny eggs, them,' Tegger butted in. 'We enjoyed them, those eggs.'

'We wanted me dad's bogie,' I say. 'We need it for ... a job we're doing.'

'All in there. In the big cree. Yours by rights. Tek it back any time, Gabe. Garden too.'

'Nah. I couldn't.'

'In the cree, take a look.'

The bogie is in the cree, upended. It's a kind of long box, home made, set on pram wheels. A kind of coffin on wheels, really. Maybe that's why it was unthinkable that we'd take my dad home in it, that day. I close my eyes and there is his body, swinging on the tree.

Tegger pulls the bogie out into the daylight. 'This'll do fine. We could mebbe do with it down the Settlement anyway. Always hauling things down there, one way or another.'

We take our leave of Steve. 'Always remember, son, it's here when you want it. Your dad…'

'I won't want it,' I shake my head.

At the house we find the canvas barely fits onto the bogie. Tegger knocks up a kind of frame so we can stand it upright. I protect it with an old tablecloth from the wooden press, then a blanket off the spare bed, where Tegger and Marguerite do their courting when they're in the house. Tegger insists on wedging it in with my easel, the one her made for me. 'It'll stop it moving about. And you'll need it down there in the shed.'

'I'll need an easel here as well. I like working in the vertical now. An' I like working on my own.'

'I'll make you another one. Just a few planks and screws. Nee worries.'

We draw a few interested glances in the street, but a couple of lads dragging God-knows-what through the rainy streets on a bogie is not a new sight in Brack's Hill: potatoes, coals scrounged off the heaps, furniture, livestock, sickly relatives - homemade bogies have been used here for such tasks for many years. And before that it was probably medieval barrows and roman sledges. But never before, I think, had a bogie been used to carry a still-wet oil painting of a near-naked woman. So it's just as we are trundling it down the narrow side-street that I start to wonder for the first time what the people of Brack's Hill will make of the woman in the Goaf. There'll be a few raised eyebrows.

Todhunter's brows certainly climb towards his glossy silver-grey thatch when we unveil the picture in the big room. He caught us in the alleyway and smiled a little at our bogie. Seems like he's recovered from his paddy last week about my absence from the rehearsal. He doesn't hold a grudge. I'll say that for him.

He watches inside the long room as we put up the easel and carefully place the painting on it. I hold my breath and listen for some kind of judgement from him. I'm much more worried now than when I'm delivering my lines as Arthur. This is despite the fact that though Archie knows everything about drama, he's a less than competent painter. But he's studied pictures in those books of his, and talks knowledgeably about what painters should or shouldn't do.

He walks up to the painting and away from it, as Rosel and Susannah, Tegger and Marguerite have already done. He opens the door to the hallway to dredge more light into the room. Like others he's disturbed by the darkness in the painting.

'Extraordinary,' he says. Then he turns it so it's even more in the light. 'Extraordinary. The effect of that drape and that ... is it a flower? Decadent, somehow.'

'Extraordinary? Decadent? What does that mean? You don't like it,' I growl.

'I do. I do. It's very ... very well done. Compelling. Such depth. Incredible, the progress you've made, young man.' He does the dance again. Near and far. Near and far. 'So what inspired this ... masterpiece?'

I don't tell him of the dream. I describe it to him as an idea. Of the woman as the earth and all that.

'I see. And...' he coughs ... 'it can only have been painted from life.'

'Yes.'

'I haven't seen this person. This person in the painting. Never seen her here at the Settlement?' He coughs again.

'You would have, if you drank at the Lord Raglan. She works there. Well known for it,' says Tegger. 'Her name's Marguerite Molloy.'

'I see. She has the looks of a ... of a colonial.'

'She's my friend,' says Tegger. 'And she comes from South Shields. Her father's from Africa, like.'

'I see.' Todhunter pulls the painting back into the corner so that it's alongside the portraits which now line the walls, but still slightly in the shadow. 'It's very big.'

'It could go up on the wall, I suppose,' says Tegger. 'It'd need a bracket, like. You'd not believe how heavy it is.'

Archie shakes his head. 'It can't be in the exhibition, of

course.'

'What!' I say. 'Why?'

'Well. It wouldn't go with the others. They are all to do with the play. It would be out of place.'

'But it *is* to do with the play,' says Tegger, his voice confident. 'What's the play about except miners and their lives in peace and war? When you look at this, this one's all about a miner and his life, and what goes on inside him as well as outside him. And see the red? That's the poppy. The Flanders poppy.' I've never said that to Tegger. In fact I've never worked it out myself till now.

Archie lights another cigarette. 'That's all very well, dear biy, but then there's the problem of the woman. If it had been an ordinary underground scene, perhaps. But the woman...'

'That's what it's about,' I say. 'The woman.'

Archie stares at me then back at the picture. He draws a lungful of tobacco through his amber holder. 'People...' he says.

'What he's saying, marra, ' says Tegger, turning towards me. 'Is that he can't have a picture of a naked woman on these walls. In this town'

I scowl. 'What? We've just been to the best art gallery in the North and there's plenty of naked and half-naked women there. Statues too.'

'Ah,' says Todhunter. 'But that's...'

'Proper art? Not pitman's daubs?' I spit the words. 'Howay Tegger, get that bloody bogie and we'll have this away home.'

'You must allow Gabriel to show it Archie,' Rosel's voice comes from behind us. 'How could you not show it?' She's standing in the doorway. Cora, looking haggard as she has recently, is at her elbow.

'There'll be difficulties, Rosel. You don't know about this place. There's a reserve. They're not used to… I depend on the goodwill of the local people. A section of my money comes from the Council. They'll have it that I've led young Gabriel here astray.' He seems to have forgotten that all of Brack's Hill knows he's here in this same building living tally with his fancy-woman.

Cora takes a closer look at the picture. 'I can see what you mean Archie. That scarf on a naked body. *What* will Mrs Pallister and Mrs Stewart think?' She looks at me. Her white, tired face smiling slightly. 'You're like a mushroom, Gabriel, growing to full strength in the night. This is really very good.'

I look at them all and beyond them to the picture where the woman in the Goaf glows at me from her dark nest. 'It's my work, honestly done, saying something I want to say.' The thought is dawning in my head as the words come out of my mouth. 'If that can't be shown, then neither can the others that I painted. The ones of Greta, Cora, and of yourself. Mr Todhunter.'

'Oh dear,' said Cora. 'My moment of eternal glory vanishing before my eyes.'

'Cora, shut up!' The words are like a whiplash. Todhunter is very still now, a rock carved against the dusty air of the room. 'You can't say that, Gabriel! Those paintings don't belong to you.

They belong to the Settlement.'

'What?' The word explodes from me. 'They are not mine?'

'The paints, the materials came from here. You'd never have painted them without … the inspiration you found here. Without Fraülein Vonn's instruction.'

'And that makes it yours?' I am speaking through grinding teeth. 'It means it belongs to you?'

Archie opens his mouth to answer, but Rosel interrupts him. 'This can't be so, Archie. An artist owns his own work. He's no slave, nor Russian serf. Do you know in Russia before the revolution the Tzar owned troupes of artists as well as actors and ballet dancers? We must be beyond that, Archie.'

Archie's jaw sets hard as granite. 'Don't interfere with something which is none of your business, Fraulein.'

She goes to stand in front of him and looks him in the eye. 'It's so much my business, Archie, that if you rob that boy of his paintings, I will take mine away. And I will take an axe to the stage set which I have designed. And I will be off these premises within the hour.'

Archie stares at her.

'Archie!' says Cora.

He coughs, and then blows his nose, making a great bit of business about it. 'Very well. Of course the paintings do belong to the boy. A slip of the tongue. I wasn't thinking…' Now he looks at me and when he speaks, his tone is more conciliating. 'Don't you see Gabriel? The painting will get such attention, will cause such a scandal, that the whole point of the play, the whole message that I … that young Tegger here and I … have worked so hard to plant at the centre of the play. All that will be lost as people discuss, or rage around your painting?'

There's logic in this, and the room is silent.

Then Rosel speaks up again. 'But the painting has its own message, Archie. Why should the world be deprived of that? And if there is controversy. Has not art always caused controversy? Are not artists are fleeing my own country even now because their paintings are being called decadent and they cannot practice their art because they live in fear. My own father's books with his drawings have been burnt.

'Look,' I say finally. 'I don't want to spoil the play. Far from it. But this is still the best thing I've done and it means a lot to me. Just like the play means a lot to you, Mr Todhunter, that painting means a lot to me. It's something I've been dreaming about for a long time, without even knowing it. And somehow, though it's not perfect, there it is. Outside my head.'

Todhunter put his hand up and pulled it down his face, dragging his flesh with it, distorting his large features. It seems like he's wiping years of tiredness out of him. 'Well. It is a good thing. I acknowledge that, Gabriel.' He glances at Rosel. 'And I'm no ogre whatever you might think. Perhaps I should get Dev Pallister down here to take a look at it, alongside the other pictures? He's close to what other people think. He's a sound man.'

'Aye,' says Tegger.

'What if he says it'll cause too much of a ruckus?' I still can't let it go.

Cora breaks the silence. 'What say that we still have the painting, say in Archie's office or in the room upstairs? So anybody who likes Gabriel's paintings could be shown it.'

'No!' says Rosel sharply. 'That is like ... like...'

'... dirty pictures,' says Tegger.

It seems insoluble. One part of me is sympathetic with Todhunter's concerns. Another ... 'I tell you what,' I say. 'Why don't we wait to hear what Mr Pallister has to say? There really is no way I would spoil the painting exhibit, or the play. Let's just see. If he says no, I'll take it home. There's others that might be interested.'

So the tension fades a bit and we leave it at that. The painting stays in the corner. The bogie is tucked into the painting shed and we get on with tonight's rehearsal which focuses on the women. The spotlight's off me, thank goodness. I sit in the corner watching Todhunter put Cora through her paces like she was as young as Greta. He's a perfectionist that one, and no mistake. Greta and me play draughts in the corner and she beats me twelve games to three. Todhunter calls her up and she whispers in my ear that next time she'll bring her chessboard and thrash me. Her breath tickles my ear.

Later on, when we play the kissing scene, I remember that tickle and clutch her harder and put my hand on her face as I kiss her, a move which goes unreproved by Todhunter, despite the fact that it's not in his movement plan. He's not usually keen on us using our initiative, so this is something new.

41. A Girl Well Known in the Town

Tegger has brought me some wooden offcuts from a cabinetmaker's where he's been doing odd jobs At least the furniture factory has kept going, although the cabinetmakers are on short time. People out of work do not buy furniture.

Tegger's been leading some scrap away for them with another fellow and his van. It's 'tally work', like, done at night so no spies tell on him. It seems Marguerite knew this foreman from there. Regular friend of hers, he says.

Now Tegger and Marguerite together are not don't come so often. It's more him on his own. When I ask him about it he just shrugs his shoulders and lights another cigarette. Then one night he loosens up a bit and tells me, 'Looks like I'm getting in the way of her work.'

'They don't like you hanging round at the Raglan?'

He looks at me strangely then and shakes his shoulders in that way he has. 'Sommat like that…' he says. Seems she got him this tally job at the cabinetmaker's as some kind of compensation for him losing her constant company.

They were funny together, those two. Not inseparable, not really like a girlfriend and boyfriend. Marguerite is a very kind person. Look at her treating us to the Newcastle trip. Look at her getting Tegger this tally job. Her heart's in the right place.

So I'm the beneficiary of Tegger's new job. Some lovely bits of pitch pine and elm here. All kinds of shapes, squares, rectangles. Well seasoned. They're raw wood, so there's nothing to scrape off. I pick three big rectangles and set about sanding and sizing them. Even as I do this I have two images pricking at my brains like swords. One is the slag heap where I pick my fossils - the way it was the other night. Black against the white sky. I have some more ideas about light since I saw the Turner. I want to do this, even though the learning-by-copying gremlin still grabs at me.

Rosel would disapprove. But she had her college and her teachers didn't she? She had her father in his studio. Her uncle in his work place. Maybe when she was little, she copied. her hand guided by one of greater authority. I have no greater hand to guide me, apart from those old masters speaking to me from their canvases and prints. Maybe one day I won't be looking for techniques. But now I am. There's so much ground to make up.

The other painting in my mind has something to do with the effort of pushing tubs up an incline. I have knowledge of that in my sinews that I'd like to set out for others to see. This one will be about the depths of the tunnel. All the time when I am visualising it the petrified fireflies and wizards are staining my mind. Maybe they'll find their place in that picture.

****

I'm in the middle of priming the boards when my Aunt Susannah drops by. She's taken to doing that lately. She examines my work. 'Lots of scope here, Gabriel. Seven boards ready primed. A year's work, is it?' She glanced around the room. 'More like a workshop than anybody's home, this room.'

'It's the way I like it. Only meself to please.'

'I see that. I can't think any woman would tolerate it.' She sits down in my father's chair. 'So, Gabriel, what fetches with you?'

'As you see. I'm fine.'

'I feel guilty. You being on your own across here. No family to support you. I was saying to Jonty...'

She takes off her gloves and I am impelled to make her a cup of tea. She talks about her husband Jonty whom she has just left at the Settlement to teach his Politics class. 'The Settlement and your Fraülein have certainly brought you on, Gabriel. That Archie Todhunter is a remarkable man. The difference he's making to so many lives. It puts us all to shame.'

Working with Archie Todhunter day to day, with the play and the paintings, you don't think of him like that. You think of him as obsessed and pernickety, rather domineering and a bit of a know-it-all. You take for granted, I suppose, and that it's his sheer drive that underpins all our lives; the fact is that without him those hundreds of people would not have their classes or their library books, or their plays or their painting. Without him - and Rosel –

I'd still be scribbling sketches, cursing in my father's shadow. Without him I'd not have painted the woman in the Goaf which I count as my first real painting, as a beginning of something.

She reads my mind. 'That painting I saw in here, the day I met your art teacher. It was very good work. Individual. Dramatic.'

'Glad you think so,' I mutter.

'And the woman. Rosel, isn't it? She is your teacher?'

'Aye. An artist herself as well.'

'And your friend?'

I wish she'd lay off. 'Aye,' I say.

"She must be thirty-six, seven?'

"What's that to do with anything?'

"Nothing. You're right.' She drinks off her tea and stands up to go. She pulls on her gloves. 'It's none of my business. It's just... after what happened with your father. If you want any, well, help, I'm here. And there's Jonty. There might be something...'

'There's nothing. But thank you.' I hate how grudging that sounds. 'Thank you,' I say, more heartily this time. 'I appreciate the thought.'

'You know where we are.'

It's only when she goes that I think of a question I'd have liked to ask her. Or Jonty. It's the question about The Promise. The one about how not to get pregnant. For no reason at all Greta has been on my mind recently. I notice her more in rehearsals and I notice her noticing me.

Rosel is still there in the centre of my days, like. She is still in and on my mind. Many, many times in bed do I go over what we did together, frame by frame, like they do in a film. No one will ever be the same for me. Not like her. But she's taking one step back these days. She's genial enough, but there's a glass wall around her. To be honest, it's a bit of a relief. I have this feeling that if that thing between us had gone on and on the painting would have been a problem. Maybe it would have stopped. I don't know why I think this. She is a quiet teacher.

I know too that she's worried about her father. He's been in trouble for sticking up for his Jewish friends. Not many of them around here, mind you. Jews. There is a doctor on Back Row. And there's a new factory set up near Priorton. It was in the paper. They've built new white houses for some of the key workers, which is nicknamed Jerusalem. There's some shouts about Jews in the papers. Blackshirts are fighting Jewish types in London. But not much of that around here. No one moves into this district. They're all moving out to get work elsewhere.

No. I couldn't ask Rosel that particular question for Greta. It's funny, that. When you've seen someone virtually naked, you'd think you could ask them anything. We did nothing to stop such asking when we were together. Risky when you think about it, but that was the last thing on my mind. And I can't ask Tegger because that'd make me look like a twerp. Maybe Marguerite? She's open and knows a lot of things that would surprise you.

She's a woman. She might know. I've been trying to think of a situation where I could ask the question, but that defeats me.

Maybe I'll go down the Raglan tonight. I have the price of a half. Tegger's gone absent without leave with some dog-racing friends. He won't surface for a while.

Dev Pallister was having a problem finding Archie Todhunter. The library at the Settlement was in full swing but he wasn't there. There was a loud argument in the little classroom. He recognised the teacher, the pacifist schoolteacher from Priorton, Jonty Clelland. He was going at it hammer and tongs with Nathan Smith. Something about Russia.

Archie Todhunter wasn't in the dusty workroom or his office. Dev mounted the stairs and knocked on the living room door. On the instruction to enter he pushed open the door. Cora Miles was sitting curled into a chair clutching a large cup of something. Dev glanced round the room. 'Is Mr. Todhunter around? I had a message from him.'

She shook her head. 'He has a meeting in Durham but should be back...' she glanced at the mantel clock, 'about quarter to. Off the three-thirty bus from Durham.'

'Oh,' he said.

She unwound her long legs and stood up. 'You could wait here. I'm sure he wouldn't want to miss you.'

He smelt the not unfamiliar waft of whisky as she wove her way past him. 'I have to go. There are chores to do.'

The door clicked behind her. A fine looking woman, Cora Miles. Good shoulders. But more than a little haggard these days. Letting herself go. He hated to see that in a woman. His Pauline was a homely person but she was as trim now as the day they were married. Good ankles and fine bust. That's what had attracted him when he first met her at the chapel dance they'd held for the lads on leave from the war. 1915. He'd been more than a bit downhearted at the thought of going back to France, but Pauline with her quick ways had cheered him up. Not a bad reason for getting married, being cheerful. They got on well, him and Pauline. No fireworks. But that suited. He was so busy. She'd always been busy too, first, with the lads, then Greta to see to and everything.

He didn't have time to pursue that thought because Archie Todhunter came in, rubbing his hands against the cold, delighted to see him. Seems he wanted help with a problem. 'I want you to look at a painting.'

'Why?'

'It was done by young Gabriel Marchant.'

'Now that's not a bad lad. Turns up with our Greta sometimes.'

'Well he's painted a very good picture, but ... I want to show you something.' He led the way down to the big workroom, clicked on the overhead lights and walked with Dev along the row of paintings. Dev nodded his appreciation of each of these, standing before Greta's in special appreciation. He stood for a while before Cora's portrait. 'Our Greta says Cora Miles takes a right good part in the play. I saw her upstairs here. You know. Thought she was looking a bit tired and poorly. Has she been ill?'

'Ill?' Archie frowned. 'No. Cora's as strong as an ox. A bit on the stubborn side lately, but that's mood, not substance. Now then!' In the corner was a crude easel and a painting covered lightly in a green cloth. He whipped off the cover and carefully adjusted the painting on the easel.

Dev's mouth dropped slightly at the sight of the picture.

'Yes!' said Archie. 'It's good isn't it? Fresh. Powerful. But you can see the problem, can't you?'

Dev nodded slowly. 'Once you make it out, you can see the pit seam. It's clearly there. Well shown, in fact. Any miner would recognises it. But the scarf.there. And the figure of the woman. Is that a poppy? The problem...' said Dev.

'The youngster wants it displayed on the day of the performance like the others. Insists on it, in fact.'

'Insists?'

'You see the problem. The subject matter. The naked woman. The lad speaks very well of its symbolism. What it means and so on. The ball of red wool on the shoulder for the Flanders poppy. All very well, I say. But would the good folk of Brack's Hill understand?'

'Good folk, you say?' said Mr Pallister, brows raised. 'You think those 'good folk' might think it was a dirty picture?' His tone was very careful.

'Let's say, they might judge it as in questionable taste. They would be wrong, but it gives me a dilemma.'

'Is that why you're showing it to me?'

'Well. I thought … your judgment, Mr. Pallister. You know the people of Brack's Hill. Would they see the … well … art of it? Or would they be offended? If that was the case would they be offended by the whole exhibition, and the play, and the Settlement itself for that matter? I'm reluctant to censor anything which is a true artistic expression. But there are sensibilities.'

'I can see that.'

Archie Todhunter started to defend the painting. 'It is very tastefully done of course. And the boy is an innocent. Earnestly defending his muse, as it were.'

'I can see this.' Dev coughed. 'The model. She's a person from the town.'

'I believe so. Although we've never seen her here. She's friendly with young Gabriel and his friend Tegger. She works at the Lord Raglan.'

'It's a good picture,' said Dev slowly. 'He's got the pit. And many of our good folk would get this message you're talking about. Yet this young woman, who lives hereabout. She's well known in the town.'

'Yes?'

Dev walked up and down the line of pictures again. 'You'll know that the men have a very big objection to women in the pit? Like sailors. See it as bad luck. Many of them would see this as wild fancy, at the very least. If not dangerous.'

'But this is not a woman in that sense. She's an idea.'

'She looks more like a woman to me, like.' Pallister paused. 'Showing this picture could do two things, Mr Todhunter. It could get you a great deal of attention. Draw attention to your play, and the work here at the Settlement. That could be very good.'

'Or the opposite,' said Archie. 'It would swamp it. Perhaps even destroy it. It depends on the kind of attention it would get.'

'Could you not display it separately? In another space?'

'Where? In my office? What would that say about me then? We thought about that but Tegger MacNamara talked about 'dirty pictures', and I'm inclined to agree with him. If it were seen like that it would not be seen as a concept, would it?'

'I tell you what, Mr Todhunter. I'll talk to the lad, See if there's some give there. Then whatever the decision is it'll be part mine. So the the pall of prudishness would not sit completely on your shoulders.'

Archie recognizing the shrewdness of the man, shook him by the hand, very satisfied and relishing a degree of admiration for Dev Pallister's tact.

As he swung out of the Settlement and down the road Dev blew air from his lungs in quick relief. The fact was that Gabriel Marchant's young model was quite well known to him. She was quite well known to a few prominent citizens of Brack's Hill. It was true that she worked at the Lord Raglan. It was also true that she occasionally showed great kindness to these citizens, for a modest payment, of course. Perhaps for this reason the painting would be more than embarrassing if it were displayed here. It could be downright dangerous.

42. A Time of Risk

Since receiving the first letter from her brother Boris, Rosel Vonn had drawn and painted very little. She'd not even completed the final touches to Gabriel's triptych. She attended to the painting classes, sharpened pencils, laid out paints. She responded to requests for advice and praised good efforts. But she no longer sat beside a painter and painted with him. She no longer set up her own easel and led by example.

Gabriel had a new easel at the Settlement: a new version of Tegger's scrap-wood contraption that had held the big painting. That painting was still under wraps in the big room, until the great decision was made. Nathan Smith and the others had lifted the veil and taken a look. There were smirks and embarrassed half laughs about the subject matter.

Rosel watched with interest as Gabriel set about his current work on a primed-up rectangle of timber. It was a study of the pit heap where she first saw him, the one with the glittering pool beside it. At some points the penetrating grey light of the sky swirled into the white light of the pool and the two became indistinguishable. From a distance it might be a study of

Switzerland or the English Lake District. It was only when you got nearer that you realised that the mountainous heap consisted of an intricate jigsaw of jagged stones. Each of these was marked with a motif of petrification. There were leaves and lizards, tree barks and sea creatures. Each stone was a different shade of black or grey, thickly layered in paint. The motifs were scratched into the paint with a knife, which gave them a faintly shocking, crude quality. They were like those chalk drawings children drew on pavements. As the days went on, and Gabriel laid on more and more paint: all of the slag became covered with gouged out reflections of the flora and fauna that grew unchecked in crevasses and around the pool below.

Now here, thought Rosel, Gabriel was at last beginning to show his own hand. Only he could have painted this one. At least on the surface it owed little to the artists he admired.

Rosel did not voice her opinion. In the main she was keeping her distance. The open sensuality and directness of his painting of the woman of the Goaf had disturbed her. She found herself thinking of the girl who had modelled for him. Under her calm exterior, she still worried about any closeness between herself and this boy. He was far, far too young. She must keep her distance. There was security, and dignity in that.

In any case she was preoccupied these days with thoughts of her father. She turned over the pages of his war book in her room. She'd taken Archie's copy for Gabriel that day she met his Aunt Susanah. She took it as an excuse to see him. And she'd brought it back, when Gabriel ran away. The faces of the men on those pages leapt and surged across the pad, often disembodied, emerging from the swirly mud of the trenches. She thought of her father at the front, with his pencil in his hand, peering at them in that short-sighted way of his. When he drew and painted them he had been not much older than these young soldiers.

He had been much younger than Rosel herself was now. Through his eye you could see each soldier as an individual: a young man writing home; a bewhiskered captain standing by a staff car; a boy curled up as though asleep, blood seeping from his footless leg; a game of cards in a dugout, two men peering over the edge of a trench into no-mans-land. Each one of these was an individual. These were no ciphers, no pegs on a board, no toy-soldiers marching off to war.

You could see why the new militarists had the book banned from the university library, had even recommended the copies be burnt. Perhaps it was decadent to show the sheer vulnerability of the human frame and expose the ridiculous inhumanity of warfare; how leaders retreated into the easy delights of national pride. But such images would not encourage a young man to throw himself into unquestioning defence of his fatherland. No wonder they wanted to burn the book.

She received another letter by an English messenger from Boris, saying that their father had settled back into his apartment and had been undisturbed since the last onslaught. The police had taken some of his books - including the original war notebook -

and had not returned them.. Some of drawings were removed from a gallery which regularly sold them and had vanished without a trace.

So, dear sister, although he is physically safe, he is, with some cause, full of melancholy. So many of his friends have emigrated; some have been arrested. I had not realised so many of his friends were Jewish. One did not think like this, did one? Among some of my fellow officers my attitude is seen as wilful blindness. But there is one fellow, whom I shall not name, who has other ideas. His father was one of the Kaiser's generals and he has ideas of honour other than these tin-pot bullies who're rising like scum to the top. He thinks something should be done about it and I am not far behind him. I will join him in his endeavours, Something must be done. But first I am concerned to get our father away. He is very vulnerable here. He is still writing letters of objection to the wrong people. He is still voicing his protest to anyone who listens. But these days, those who listen to you are Janus-faced. These are few whom you can really trust. You have to be careful.

Beside such considerations Rosel's own concern about her obsession with a man young enough to be her son was, she knew, essentially trivial. After the first defence of the boy's work to Archie she could not the quandary over his painting of the woman in the Goaf..

So, as the days went on she ignored Gabriel's soulful, sometimes angry looks and avoided being on her own with him. It was the only way. She could only see his dark looks through smoky glass. She had other things on her mind.

43. Earning With Art

These days, for all the attention I'm getting off Rosel Vonn, you'd think we were strangers. You'd never believe that a little while ago, for a spark in time, we were as close as a man or a woman can be.

I wish it were otherwise but there are new things to think of. I had a letter this morning from a strange address in Newcastle. The signature, as far as I can make out, is E Crump. Tucked into the letter is a postal order for ten guineas.

Dear Mr Marchant,

Your sketches were passed to me by Sybil McNeil from The Gallery. I showed them to my colleague Mr Tennant who deals with the buying and selling. I should tell you that your sketches were displayed in our gallery a mere five days before they were bought by a Northumberland gentleman, who expressed interest in further work by you. I also had a visitor here from the Shipley Gallery, Gateshead, who evinced an interest. Alas, when he returned to purchase them the paper birds had flown. So, dear sir, should you have further examples of your work, they will certainly find space in our gallery. Next time you find yourself

in these parts we trust you will call, as we are keen to make your
acquaintance and appraise more of your work.
With respect
Yours faithfully
E. Crump

To say I was stunned by this would be an understatement. I'd almost forgotten those pictures I left in Newcastle; forgotten the apparently snobby woman at the gallery. (My mind was more on the paintings I had seen, and the sheer wonder of the Gallery itself.) Now it seems this same woman has done me a favour.

Just at present I'm almost entirely on my own, day by day. Rosel's not talking to me so there is no point in going to her. Tegger has gone on one of his trips to the moon with the dog man. I think he and Marguerite have fallen out and he's in a huff.

When this letter came in the post I did this daft thing. I held this postal order, a flimsy thing, up in the air and whirled round and round the kitchen. 'Here, Dad, here! Look at this! My bloody pay! Money for drawing. Earning from art!' But my voice rang as though the house was a hollow cave and there was no one to receive it. 'Beats slaving in the dark, don't it!' I shouted the words. I felt foolish then, so I stuffed the postal order in my pocket, put on my cap and went out of the empty house.

So this is how I find myself walking through the swing door of the Raglan, peering through the fug and the crowd to catch sight of Marguerite Molloy. And here she is, flashing smiles and pints in good order. I squeeze my way to the corner of the bar and wait for her attention to get to me. She flashes me a grin. 'I needed to see you. Be with you in a sec, Gabe.' She works through her orders and leaves me till last. Now here she is. 'That's those seen to. Pint, Gabe?'

'It'll have to be one of your tally pints, cos I've got no money.' I can be the beggar here, as I know tomorrow, once I've been to the Post Office, I can treat her royally.

She's already drawing the pint. 'Where's that rascal Tegger? I only told him he didn't own me and off he goes with a pet lip on him like a gorilla.'

'He's gone to ground with the dog-man. He does this sometimes. He'll be back soon.'

The foam from the beer slops over her slender fingers as she places it before me. Then she folds her arms, leans on the bar and looks up in my eyes and says, 'So how have you been, Gabe?'

'Well...' I take a large mouthful of that bitter velvet. 'Very well, in fact.' Like a magician producing a rabbit, I produce the postal order. She peers at it rather short-sightedly and frowns. 'What's this?' she says. 'Money, is it?'

I show her the letter from the gallery. She squeals with laughter and claps her hands. The noise in the bar dips for a second and a dozen or so men stop talking and look across at Marguerite. And me.

She turns her back on them and the hum starts up again. 'What a thing, Gabe! What a thing. And you do have more sketches don't you?'

'Oh yes. Plenty sketches. Boxes of them.'

'Well. Now it's beginning. Something is really beginning.'

A voice comes from the other end of the bar. 'Hey Marguerite! Get some beer in, will yer?' She's called away and has to pull six more pints before she gets back.

'So when are we going through there?' she says,

'We? When are *we* going?'

'Well, sweetheart, if you think you're going there without me you've got another think coming.'

I laugh at this. This girl always puts a smile on my face. 'Well this time it'll be my treat. When I've been to the Post Office, like, to cash this postal order.'

When I finally get out of the Raglan, leaving Marguerite with her last customers, the world is spinning around me as a consequence of my delight at my good luck and three pints of the Raglan's strong ale. The landlord stood me a pint. He's pleased with his picture which is now behind the car in a neat mahogany frame and has been much admired.

I really do need some fresh air to clear my head. As I turn into the High Street I bump into a lad wearing a grammar school blazer and cap. He apologises to me despite the fact that I'm the one at fault. My feet turn in the direction of the grammar school and soon the blazered and capped legions are spilling around me like a river in flood.

Greta is just making her way through the ornate iron gates

when I reach them. Her satchel is slung over one shoulder, her school hat is awry, her glasses have slipped down her nose and her head is bent over a book which she reads as she walks. I want to hug her where she stands. Instead I clap her on her shoulder. 'Hey! Bookworm!'

She drops her book and scrambles to rescue it from the wet pavement. 'Gabriel. What kind of trick is that?' She pushes her glasses back up her nose. 'You shouldn't go scaring people out of their skin.'

'Never, never!' I shake my head. 'Never would I scare you out of your skin.'

Her pert nose wrinkles. 'Gabriel. You've been drinking.'

'Not much. Not much...' I shake my head very carefully. It is still spinning.

She grins a bit at that. 'Here. Walk me home, will you? Everyone's looking.'

It's easy walking along with her. We know each other now, and are calm together. After a few minutes walking, she looks up at me. 'What is it?' she says. 'Something's happened, hasn't it?'

'Yes. Yes. So it has.' I stop and take my postal order out. 'Look. Look at this!'

She adjusts her spectacles again and looks at it. 'Ten Guineas. Where's this from?'

A gallery owner in Newcastle paying for my sketches. My drawings.'

She sets up a whoop at this, grabs my arm and kisses my

cheek. 'Hey, Gabriel. Isn't that wonderful?'

I grab her and kiss her full on the mouth and for a second every part of my body is alive to her. I can feel the cut of her glasses on my cheek, the rectangular shape of the book she holds in her hand. She struggles away.

'Sorry,' I say.

'No,' she says. 'It's nice to celebrate. You're pleased, that's all.' She starts to walk. 'Come home with me and have a cup of tea. My Mam'll have shop cakes. We'll tell her about the drawings. Dad too. They'll be pleased. Dad was on about that painting of yours. The naked woman. I wasn't supposed to be listening of course.'

When we get there Dev Pallister's in the plushy sitting room Greta pushes me in there and leaps up the stairs two at a time. He puts down his paper and looks me in the eyes. 'I took a look at that picture of yours, lad.'

'Aye.' I watch his face. This man runs the Council. Manipulates his comrades and his constituents. How do they ever know what he's thinking? I don't.

He lights a cigarette. 'True sense of a seam, lad. But the rest's a bit rich, I'd say.'

'It's what I wanted to paint.'

'I'd have thought a clever lad like you…'

'What?'

'Well, there's things to do in this town. Clever lads like you should get involved. The council. The state of the place. You could make changes. But painting this kind of thing…'

'It's what I can do. I'm good at it. Those other things are not for me.'

He stares hard at me. 'Aye. I see. It's painting that is for you. Well to tell the truth I can't see what the fuss is about that painting of yours. Old Archie Todhunter seems to think that we're out of the egg here at Brack's Hill. That we've never seen a naked woman afore'

'And we're not?' I force him to meet my gaze. 'Out of the egg?'

'Are we buggery!,' he says.

'An' the picture in the exhibition won't cause a riot?'

He frowns a bit at this. Something's on his mind. Then he shrugs his massive shoulders. 'A bit of a stir, mebbe. But we need stirring up now and then. These are sluggish, half-alive times. Can't see no harm in it myself. But mebbe it needs a bit further thought.' He puts on his cap and his muffler, puts his head round the door and shouts. 'I'll be gone two hours, Pauline, no more.' Then he looks back at me smiling slightly. 'I reckon that picture of you in my army togs does me credit. I like it. Reminds me of me before the scales fell from my eyes. And that German lass did a good job on you.'

'She's very good,' I say. I think again of those hours of intensity, with me just standing and her just looking and drawing. Then looking and painting. They were the most intimate times, before I laid a hand on her.

'And she's done a good job with you, as well, showing you how to paint as good as that.'

I wanted to protest that I could paint before I met Rosel Vonn, but I didn't.

'That picture, the one Archie's so uneasy about.'

'I have called it the *Woman in the Goaf.*"

'Aye.' He paused. 'A funny thing. All Goaf one way you look at it. Any miner would know that. And all woman the other way.'

'You see it like that?'

'I've seen the Goaf many a time. But I've never seen no woman.'

'It all depends on the way you look.'

'Aye. I see that. I was thinking about hat. Mebbe the town *is* ready for your picture.'

And he is gone and I am left in the cluttered, plushy parlour alone, thanking heaven that Dev Pallister is an intelligent man.

Greta bursts into the room. She's still in her school uniform; one of her grey socks has fallen round her ankle. Her cheek has a finger-mark smudge of navy blue ink. 'What was that about?' she says.

'About that picture I did for the exhibition.'

'The one with the woman?'

'You've seen it?'

'Everybody has. Easy enough to lift the cover.'

'Oh.'

'Are you not bothered about the woman?'

'Because she's bare?'

'Aye.'

'You can hardly see her. I had to go to one side and squint my eyes. Then I saw her. At first I thought it was all black and wondered what you were doing painting a picture all black.'

'Archie Todhunter doesn't want it put up. Says it will shock the people.'

She laughs.

'But your dad seems to think it's all right.'

'He would. He's not stupid.' She paused. 'Mr Todhunter doesn't really know the people round here, does he? Aside from the Settlement people?'

'How do you make that out?'

'I heard him talking to that vicar pal of his, the one with the dog-collar. He was saying the people here had no culture. One step from the barbarians, he said.'

'Cheeky bugger.'

'I thought so too.' She stood with her shoulders back and started to recite 'I had to learn this for English. "Only connect the prose and the passion, and both will be exalted, and human love will be seen at its height. Live in fragments no longer. Only connect, and the beast and the monk, robbed of the isolation that is life to either, will die." She smiled. 'Don't you see?'

I shake my head.

'Mr Todhunter sees us all in fragments. The Settlment people and the rest. But look at everything that happens here in Brack's Hill. The men who breed pigeons and know lineage as well as any horse owner. And the men breed new flower species. And the choral societies and the women's poetry and discussion groups. My Dad's political stuff. We are all connected, This is our culture. Mr Todhunter doesn't see this. He thinks he plucks us out and shows us culture. He sees them as beasts and monks. Don't you see?'

I see. 'Makes you feel like punching him doesn't it.'

'It does for a second. But then we all know he's a good man, Mr Todhunter. Wonderful. A magician in his own way.'

'But not as perfect as he thinks he is?'

She throws up her head and laughs. Her glasses slide down her nose. 'Poor old feller. *"He knoweth not of which he sayeth"*.'
'Is that the Bible?'
'No. It's me!'
I make for the door and those strong slim fingers grasp my forearm. 'Did you find out?' she says.
'Did I find out what?'
'That what I asked you? About stopping … you know what. Babies.'
I'm blushing of course . 'No … well.'
And then I am standing in the middle of this plushy parlour and kissing this schoolgirl with ink on her face. Her soft form is

pressed against me and her slender fingers are thrusting their way through my short hair. For a split second I want her more than I have ever wanted Rosel, or even desired Marguerite.

Her mother's voice calls in from the kitchen and I drag myself away. 'I'll find out, Greta. I will.' I throw the words over my shoulder as I flee.

44. Forms of Flight

Through her fog of worry about her father Rosel found herself watching Gabriel's increasing familiarity and intimacy with Greta Pallister. In the beginning she'd been drawn to this boy with his intensity and his bud-like sensitivity to life around him. She'd been floored by his undoubted self-taught accomplishment and flattered when she saw that her own approach to painting had influenced him. She was relieved of course that he did not imitate her as he did his beloved Rembrandt and Turner. He was making progress, though. These days he looked, he pondered, and transformed what he saw into something peculiarly his own. Modernism had not touched him and perhaps never would. He'd never fit into a trend or any school of painting. He would always, stubbornly, plough his own idiosyncratic furrow. That might very well mean that artistic success in worldly terms would pass him by. He would be his own man and that, thought Rosel, was a very good thing.

Greta had passed on to Rosel the news of Gabriel's success in selling sketches to the Newcastle dealer. This struck alarm bells in her. It was far too early for Gabriel to sell! It could easily fix him in a style and stop him making proper progress. She smiled at the possessive, maternal trend of her thinking. Quite clearly there was no way she could, or would, make love with that boy ever again. That would be little short of incest.

Her father now leapt back into her mind. Those intimate, playful rompings in the big white bed in the Berlin apartment. How she and Boris would run round and round the room to escape their father's insistent tickling. How at last they would all subside on the bed, the last exhausted bubble giggle escaping from their mouths. How she would wake in the early morning to her father stroking her face, her shoulder. How eventually it was a relief to get out of that flat away to Uncle Berti who kept his distance and loved her like you would love a dog who gave you occasional pleasure in his company.

She wondered what she would do if she were successful in getting her father away, here to England. Could she really take a house here in Brack's Hill? They were cheap enough. But this place would be too desolate for him, she was sure, after Berlin. No. It would have to be London. She closed her eyes briefly. To be together with him would be a mixed blessing.

A sound on the staircase told her Cora was on her way up. She came up most days now, sometimes to talk to Rosel, sometimes just to sit at Rosel's window looking out into the street, preoccupied by her own thoughts. She was definitely in retreat from Archie and her work in the Settlement. Sometimes Archie called for her from downstairs and she shook her head at Rosel and did not go down.

'Any news about your father, Rosel?' she said now.

'I've had another letter from Sir Peter saying they're taking steps. Still taking steps.' She paused. 'I've been wondering what I should do with him when he arrives. Perhaps rent a house here in Brack's Hill, or...'

'Not here!' said Cora sharply. 'He'd die here. Anyone from any other place would die here. So dark. So intense. The end of life. You should go to London. Bright lights. A bit of life.'

'Do you hate Brack's Hill so much Cora?'

'Not at first. It's been a bit of an adventure, to be honest. But now. I'd go like a shot. I *will* go like a shot, once the play is over. I'd go this minute if...' She glanced around the room.

'You don't want to let Archie down.'

'Not him! Not him!' The words rapped into the air. 'No. I won't get down the people who've worked so hard on the play. And the Prince is coming.'

Rosel wondered at this. When she first came here she'd admired the funny, dry, mutually respectful relationship between Cora and Archie. Now all that had vanished and Archie seemed hardly to notice the change. The baby, of course. It was about the baby. And he had never known about that.

'Where will you go?' said Rosel. 'When you leave?'

'Perhaps to London. It's a while since I've been in London. I could do with that, a few bright lights. You should take your Pa to London, Rosel. You go there with him. You stay here too long and you'll rot on the stump, believe me.'

45. A Significant Deal

Marguerite and I have decided this time to come to Newcastle on the bus. It takes longer than the train but it is cheaper. I'm treating Marguerite this time but I want to conserve my money. It'll be nice to buy my own paints instead of having to be grateful to Rosel, who has now receded even further into her shell. She is kind enough, tender even. But she is so distant.

And me? Well I'm very confused. I want Rosel, just like I did before. I need to be near to her like I did before, but I don't know how to make the moves. So I, in my turn, am kind and polite and distant with her. What goes round comes around.

And I find that I'm kissing Greta every opportunity that presents itself. We don't go out together but opportunities do arise. She wants me to kiss her and I do. It feels very nice and she's excited, grateful. It's not at all like Rosel and it's easier really.

And now here I am. I've just been sitting thigh to thigh with Marguerite Molloy on this long journey. Tegger's back from his sorties with the dog man but is a bit grumpy these days. He's cutting with Marguerite now she's finished with him and short with me over the fact that I go to see Marguerite at the Raglan. He seems to think her finishing with him is something to do with me. Now, although I protested strongly to him, in my heart of hearts I think there might be something in it. Especially after this bus journey where she has laughed into my face, clutched my arm with mirth, allowed her musky perfume to invade the air I breathe. I've had to take some very deep breaths to keep myself from grabbing her and kissing her on the spot.

Like I say, I'm confused.

As the bus wends its way through Chester-le-Street she starts on about my painting of her as the Woman in the Goaf. 'I was talking to Dev Pallister about it,' she says.

'You know Dev Pallister?'

'Everybody knows Dev. He drops into the Raglan now and then. He thinks that painting is very good. Recognised it was me straight away.'

'It's not you,' I rap this back. 'It's *her*.'

'We know that. I explained that very carefully to Dev. But all the people in Brack's Hill won't realise that,' She hesitates. 'A lot of them know me. *They* drop in at the Raglan.'

I'm about to ask her why she's suddenly so bothered about that when the bus swings into the station and we are preoccupied with getting off the bus and finding just where we are.

We find we have to get a town bus down to the Haymarket

to find this place where the man has his gallery. It's a shop downstairs, with fine art copies of paintings and statuary. On the walls there are original paintings of the Tyne Bridges, and spookily lit scenes of Northumberland high country. There is one of an old house with a cherubic child laughing out of the window, ringlets falling on either side of her face. One of the paintings is a dark, cityscape where the lights sparkle through the pall of smoke settling the city into twilight during the day. I liked this one and looked for the painter's name.

The woman behind the desk in the shop has a child-size body with an old woman's face. She knows all about me and my work. Her name is Edna Crump. The name on the postal order. She is the friend of the woman in the gallery. It seems she is my fairy Godmother. She leads us straight away up the steep stairs to a large room that is half-gallery, half-office. The walls are hung with pictures. There are three long tables with black folders on them. At one end there is a large desk, littered with papers. On a small table beside it is a smart black telephone.

Sitting at the desk is a large man with a bulky, square head. He is in his shirt sleeves and his silk tie is slightly loose at his neck. He stands up and nods at the small woman once. Her voice flutes like a blackbird. 'Here's Mr. Gabriel Marchant, Mr. Tennant. We sold his drawing to Mr. Herberts of London and Morpeth. You'll remember. Mr. Herberts was very keen? Wanted more.'

He scowls at her as she leaves the office and then takes his jacket from the back of his chair and pulls it on, with urgent, clumsy movements. 'Well…' he says, coming forward, his hands reaching forward. He is heavily built, turtle shouldered. A red silk handkerchief hangs untidily from his breast pocket. He has long cheeks and these dark eyes which are almost all pupil. This makes him hard to read. He pumps my hand up and down then turns to Marguerite. 'And this is?'

She takes his hand in hers. 'Marguerite Molloy, Mr. Tennant. I am…'

'My friend, she's my friend,' I jump in.

'I model for Gabriel too. He draws me,' she says.

'Does he now?' He frowns at her for a second, then, 'Well, sit down, sit down won't you? Have you some more for me? I may have buyers.'

I lift up my battered music case; he grabs it and takes it to an empty table by the window and spreads out twelve drawings of various sizes. Two of them are practice sketches of Marguerite. He pays special attention to these. He holds them up to his face, peers across at her, then back at the paper.

I find myself resenting his eyes on my drawings and on Marguerite. I've seen that same look on butchers' faces as they peer at plump cattle at Priorton Mart.

He comes back to his desk and wedges himself back into his seat. 'I can give you two guineas apiece for these drawings, Mr. Marchant. I'll take the chance on the buyers. My risk.'

That's such a lot of money. Twenty guineas. Twenty-one pounds. There's paint and brushes and even a new jacket in that.

There could be a pretty scarf for Rosel, another for Marguerite. A fountain pen, even, for Greta Pallister. That would be nice.

I take a breath and open my mouth. Before I can speak Marguerite jumps in. 'There's another way, though, Mr. Tennant isn't there?'

He turns towards her. 'And what way would that be?'

'A percentage. You sell it an' you get twenty per cent of what it goes for. I saw a drawing downstairs in the gallery, not a patch on Gabriel's. For sale for twenty guineas on its own. By that count, you're giving Gabriel twenty percent and keeping the rest. It should be the other way round. That's not fair. It can't be right.'

He smiles slightly. His smile has no warmth. 'Ha! Not born yesterday, Miss Molloy?'

'No. Nor the day before. '

'You've done deals before?'

'You might say that.'

'I can see you have.' He turns to me. 'I see she's not only your friend and model, she's your guard-dog.'

I've caught Marguerite's drift. 'We're only after fair pay for fair work Mr. Tennant.'

'I see.' He hauls himself to his feet and goes to the window, leaving a trail of old tobacco scent in the air. He stares into the busy Newcastle street below, humming slightly under his breath. He does this for ages. He must be quite mad, this man. Perhaps he'll tell me to go away and take my scribblings with me and I'll have lost those precious guineas. Marguerite reads my thoughts.

She presses my arm with her gloved hand. *Don't weaken; do not take the money and run.* I can feel her thoughts.

Tennant turns back to face us and comes to stand before me. He holds out a podgy hand. 'Thirty percent for me Mr. Marchant, and I'll give you twenty guineas on account against any money they make. This is not charity, mind you. My instinct is that you're a fine craftsman. You may be even better than that. I'd like to see more substantial work. Do you paint as well as draw?'

'Painting's what I mostly do.'

'So where are they? I see no paintings here.'

'Well…' nothing wrong with the truth I suppose. 'They're too big. We couldn't bring them on the bus.'

A snort emerges from that fleshy mouth which might almost be a laugh. 'Well, then, how am I to see these paintings? I can't buy them unseen.'

I don't want him to come to see me, to come to my father's house. 'There's an exhibition,' I say slowly. 'An exhibition in November. In Brack's Hill, in South Durham. At the place where I paint. Not just me, others too.'

'The prince is coming,' put in Marguerite. 'The Prince of Wales is coming to see a play and to see the paintings.'

'You yourself will have paintings in this exhibition?' he says to me. 'How many? What are they?'

'A couple of portraits,' I say. 'And … and a kind of underground landscape.'

'Me, I'm in that,' says Marguerite, eyeing him narrowly.

'That's the one I modelled for. Brrr. It was really cold. Didn't have a stitch on, of course.'

Tennant blinks very slightly at this, but keeps his gaze on me. I'm blushing. 'I'd like to see this exhibition Mr. Marchant,' he says. 'And especially the underground landscape. When? Where?' He scribbles the details on his desk. Then he asks for my address and writes that down. 'Now,' he says pulling a book towards him. 'Your cheque!'

'I can't have a cheque,' I say hurriedly.

He scowls. 'Why not?'

'Because I haven't any way of getting the money. You can't have a bank account if you've got no money.'

Muttering, he reaches into a bottom drawer, pulls out a battered black box and extracts some notes and some coins. I scoop the cash from the desk and stuff it into my top pocket without counting it. 'Thanks Mr. Tennant.'

I'm dying to be away from here now: full of delight at the deal, mixed up with distrust, even dislike for this bear-like man who is such a stranger.

He comes round the desk and shakes me by hand again. Now his tone is warm, his face not so severe. He might just be all right. 'Could be we'll be able to help each other one way or other, Mr. Marchant, you never know,' he says. He turns to Marguerite, takes her hand in both of his and looks at me across her shoulder. 'You have a fine watchdog here, Mr. Marchant. Take her advice and you'll not go wrong.'

Outside on the pavement Marguerite dances around me; she hugs and kisses me, oblivious of the disgusted looks of the passers by who part around us like waves round a rock. 'Now, Gabriel, for slap up dinner,' she says. 'We deserve that,'

'Why did you tell him about that? About being painted with 'no stitch on'?'

She laughs at me. 'You are silly, Gabe. Innocent as a babe you are.'

I leave it. 'Well, then, Marguerite Molloy. Slap up dinner. And then what? After that?' It's really dawning on me now. I have twenty guineas in my pocket. And the promise of more.

She puts an arm through mine. 'And then what? Who knows? Who knows, Gabriel Marchant?'

46. An Urbane Visitor

'There's a chap downstairs for you, Fraŭlein.' Archie had struggled up the second staircase himself: an unusual event. His heavy smoking was taking its toll on his breath and he measured his physical efforts carefully. 'I've left him in my office.'

'A chap? What chap?'

'Sir Peter Something. Tall fellow.'

She turned to the round mirror and ran a tortoiseshell comb through her hair. She straightened her collar and dabbed her nose with a powder puff. 'Is there anyone with him?' she said carefully. 'Is he alone?''

'Alone? Oh yes. Entirely. Came in a Daimler car, would you believe? From London, apparently,' he ventured.

There was a question in his voice. She realised Archie was impressed. He would never admit it but he tended to flutter a bit when those Durham professors were around. Then there was all this tension, all this fuss about the Prince.

'His name is Sir Peter Hamilton Souness,' she told him.

'He has- or has had - something to do with the Foreign Office, I think.' She put on some lipstick. 'There! That's better.'

Archie led the way. 'The Foreign Office, you say?'

'He was a friend of my father's. He offered to help me. Perhaps get my father to England.'

'He'll have news of your father? Cora tells me there's some concern. About your father?'

'I hope … well, he might have news for me.' She wanted Archie to get out of the way so she could fly past him down the stairs and rain questions on Sir Peter.

He was sitting in a wooden chair, homburg hat on his knee, his hands joined over silver-topped cane. When she entered he stood up, bowed slightly, discarded his hat and cane, removed his right glove and shook her hand, half bowing over it in the continental manner. 'Miss Von Siegendorff. It is a relief that you are at home.' He glanced round the cluttered, none-too-clean office. 'I thought, perhaps, I was mistaken.'

Archie edged into the room behind Rosel and started to fiddle with things on the desk. Rosel stared at him for a second, and then said, 'Perhaps you would like to come to the workroom, Sir Peter? We can talk…'

'Good, good,' said Archie heartily. 'Show your friend round the Settlement, Fraülein. Show him the work we do. The woodworking class is in progress and the library's open. All our work here is voluntary, Sir Peter…'

Rosel swept her visitor away, sympathetic with Archie's

desire for a convert to the cause, but eager for news of her father. She set up two of the folding chairs in the long room and they sat opposite each other. Then, 'Well, Sir Peter? What is it? It can only be bad news that brings you so far.'

He shrugged his smoothly clad. 'Well, my dear, this is where you are wrong. I was already up here, on my way to the wedding of my niece in Northumberland. I am half a day early, so the thought occurred that one might seek you out.'

Her head went down. 'So, my father? You have no news of him?'

'I did not say that, my dear. I have had a note from the Embassy. Someone called on your father and he is well, although he is ... a little distracted.'

'Distracted?'

'It seems he eats little and does little painting, although he had a lively conversation with our chap on the decline of Futurism. Our chap delivered a letter from me and he sent me his return in the diplomatic bag. I have it here.' Sir Peter dipped into an inside pocket and drew out a large envelope. The letter, addressed to him, had been opened. She scanned her father's close writing: a ramble about things he saw or thought he saw, in the flat and out of the window. There on the page were drawings in the margins of the letter: nightmarish images of the men who invaded his flat, who attacked him in cells. 'Oh!' The paper rattled as she gripped it tight.

Sir Peter's fine fingers were on her sleeve. 'Don't disturb

yourself dear Fraúlein. There are things we can do. Things we will do. The documentation is all in place now. The papers are ready.'

'But how will he deal with all this? See this garbled rubbish! He's not fit to set out. Not by himself. He will be silly and will get arrested.'

'Do not worry, dear lady. I myself have a journey planned to Germany. Semi-official visit, don't you know. I will bring him back with the baggage myself.' He smiled slightly. 'He's an old friend, after all.'

She looked at him and nodded slowly. Her father had sent her to this man. He'd trusted him. Perhaps he had loved him. 'A friend?' she said.

'We were very close – for a short time – when we were very young men. Before the Great War. I think I told you.'

She blinked. More than just a good friend, she thought. Into her mind came the image of Brownson, the young servant; and Sir Peter's kindly attitude to one who was obviously not his class: as though the two of them were playing some kind of game. This man had no problems with friendships across all kinds of barriers.

'You were intimate?' she said abruptly.

He chuckled. 'How very German, my dear! How very direct. We were very young, he and I. We thought we knew the world.' He looked round. 'What a dreary place you have wound up in, m'dear. I do admire missionary works, but to do it in the cold and wet seems to be rather an error. Why not try Africa? My brother is there. Some kind of judge, I'm told. Not missioning, of course. But at least in Africa the sun shines and the sky is clear blue.'

'I am not missioning,' she said sharply. 'These are people like us. It is the times that are dark, not the people.'

'No, my dear, the people you help in this town were never people like us,' he said softly. Then he stood up and leant on his silver-topped cane. 'Perhaps you would like to show me round your haven for the down and the desolate? Mr. Todhunter was very keen for me to see it all.'

'He's eager to gain support so his work can continue. That is all.' She flushed. Resentful of his patronage of Archie, angry with him for his contemptuous tone. She wanted to dismiss this man, to show him his place. But there was something about him that she found appealing. And he had her father's safety in his hands and this she couldn't jeopardise.

'Yes. Yes,' she said. I should show you around.'

She led him through the rooms, showed him the portraits and told him about the play and the Prince's forthcoming visit. He spoke with benign grace to some cobblers and cabinetmakers, asking quite intelligent questions about their crafts. He talked to the people borrowing library books, and placed one manicured finger on the back of a rather soiled copy of *The Mayor of Casterbridge*.

He hesitated beside the growing wall of paintings.

'Interesting but rather immature except … this.' He laid a finger on her triptych of Gabriel.

'… mine! I painted that.' She looked at the images, now more than a month old. The images of Gabriel with his long, then his short hair, showed change in him. They could almost be two different people.

'This reminds me. I spoke with your friend Vanessa at an opening for the Artists International charity. She sends you her cordial greetings and asks me to say that your artist friends wish you well in your work up here. She also told me that you were very accomplished yourself. That you had worked with this fellow Henry Moore.'

Rosel laughed, 'I cannot claim to have worked with him. He was kind enough to talk to me about some reliefs I had done. To tell you the truth he put me off the idea of being a sculptor altogether,'

'Well,' he said heartily. 'Look at this! Perhaps he is right. You are a painter, my dear, not a sculptor.'

'And these…' They had come to Gabriel's little group of paintings. 'These are more the ticket.'

'Ah, those are by one of those down and desolate people whom you mentioned. A very young man. He is a member of my class. This also is his.'

They moved on to the last painting: The Woman in the Goaf. Rosel slipped off the green cover. Like all the others who had viewed the picture he drew very close, and then drew back. Only when he drew back again did he really see the woman. 'Well I'm blessed! I see you have taught him well.'

'I have taught him hardly at all. He is naturally talented and highly observant. He uses books a great deal.'

'Ah. An autodidact! Very wearying, I find, autodidacts. Always spouting their learning in their braying voices.'

'Gabriel is not like that. He is quiet. Too quiet, I would say. Many people in this town are quiet. Reserved. Perhaps even taciturn. He is like this.'

'Ah,' his laughter pealed out. 'I sense a *protégé*, even…'

She flushed.

'Are these paintings for sale? Perhaps I should buy one.'

'No.' She was surprised at how vehemently she did not want him, or anyone, to buy Gabriel's paintings. 'They are for exhibition only. For when the play is performed and the Prince of Wales comes.'

'Well now, how old is this young genius?'

'Nineteen. Perhaps twenty.'

'Ahh. I see.'

She saw the way he saw it. Twenty years. The difference between her and Gabriel in one direction, between her and Sir Peter himself in another.

'I think you don't see, Sir Peter,' she said gruffly, stalking ahead, back towards Archie's office.

Archie stood up behind his desk and looked from one to the other. 'Well, Sir Peter,' he said heartily, 'How do you like our little kingdom here?'

'Very commendable,' said Sir Peter, reaching for the hat and gloves that he had left on Archie's desk. 'Very fine work, Todhunter. Crucial in these difficult times.' He turned to the door, and then turned back. 'Perhaps I could make a contribution?' he said abruptly. 'A small sum?' He took out an enormous flapping cheque-book from an inner pocket of his tweed coat.

'That's very kind, Sir Peter,' said Archie, his eyes glinting with satisfaction. 'Very kind.'

Peter leaned on the desk to write the cheque, and then paused. 'Do you think you could spare Fraülein Von Siegendorff this afternoon, Todhunter? It would be a good opportunity to take her to lunch. Useful for me to find out more about her work here, don't you know?'

'Archie, I…' protested Rosel.

Archie beamed. 'What a wonderful idea. And perhaps the Fraülein can tell you of our outreach programme in New Morven. You would be delighted to go, wouldn't you Fraülein?' He turned the beam of his pleasure on Roseland she could not refuse.

Later, sitting opposite Sir Peter in the rather stuffy dining room of the Royal County Hotel in Durham, Rosel wondered that she had allowed herself to be manipulated by these two older men. The one pressuring her because he could save her father, the other because he knew she would help him for the sake of his beloved Settlement.

Over lunch, however, Sir Peter transformed himself into the most entertaining companion. He told her of his travels in America and Russia. He told her tales of scandal in the British Government and certain rumours about the Prince of Wales. He referred to the changes in Germany but only in passing, as a background to some escapade of a member of the Romanian royal family.

Her reluctant smiles turned into laughter as his tales became more *risqué*. He stopped mid-sentence. 'You laugh just like your Mama, my dear. She had the most surprising, hearty laugh.'

Her laughter died. 'You know where she is now, with all her wild laughter? In an asylum. Boris tells me there are proposals… Ugh!' she shuddered.

Then his hand was on hers. 'Don't be sad, my dear. We may even be able to do something about that.' His tone was soft, reassuring.

'But … you said… my father.'

He stared at her. 'If I say all things are possible, then will you start to smile again?' he said abruptly. There was something in his tone which gave her confidence, despite herself. She managed a smile reluctantly deciding that she liked this man, really liked him.

He took his hand from hers. 'May I ask you a question?'

he said.

'Yes… yes,' she said.

'You have no husband?'

She shook her head.

'But you have had lovers?'

She lifted her chin. 'How would you know that?'

'Have you ever seen a bud that has died on a tree without ever being opened? That is like a woman in middle years who has never known fulfilment. Beauty unresolved. I have some such in my acquaintance. You are not one of these poor souls.'

She was made uncomfortable by his comfortable certainty. 'And you, Peter? You were obviously beautiful.' He was still, in fact, a very handsome man. 'Is your beauty unresolved? It is so much harder to tell, in a man.'

He blinked at her turned table, and then laughed. 'Well, I was married once. And I have had lovers.'

'And these lovers,' she persisted. 'Were they men, or women?'

That shout of laughter again. 'Ha! No English woman would have asked such an indelicate question.'

'And being an Englishman you didn't answer it.'

He stared at her. 'Well, if you want honesty, I don't feel there is a great deal of difference between the two, as far as affections are concerned. I became interested in the person. The varieties of … er … Well. We'll leave it at that.'

It was her turn to touch his hand. 'Sir Peter, when I first met you I thought you were … well … typically English. Boring. Restricted. But now…?'

His hand turned against hers and grasped it firmly. 'But now, I am just like any man. Even a young painter of the dark!'

She let her hand lie there. She felt warm and comfortable with this man. Safe in a way she had never felt with any man in her life, she glanced around the restaurant where the scattering of well upholstered guests were tucking into substantial repasts. What a world away this was, from Brack's Hill with its soup kitchens and thin children. She closed her eyes. Just let me enjoy this comfort for a little while, she prayed to anyone who was there. Let me enjoy it without feeling guilty.

'Rosel?' Peter was looking at her intently.

She blinked. 'Sorry. What was it?'

'I wondered whether you would care to stroll up to take a look at the cathedral. I believe it is very fine. Or perhaps you need to get back?'

'Yes,' she said, 'I would like to stroll to the cathedral. And no. I am not in any hurry to go back there, to be very honest.'

'Three hundred *pounds!*' Archie threw the cheque, made out in Sir Peter's sprawling hand, onto the couch beside Cora. 'Feller gave us three hundred pounds just on a walk round the Settlement by the Fraŭlein. She should give guided tours all the time.'

'I wish you wouldn't call Rosel that, Archie. The

Fraŭlein. It sounds so sarcastic.'

'Three hundred pounds, Cora! What good can we do with that? Re-equip the joiner's shop! Those tools are falling to pieces. New books! New Art books! No doubt Sir Peter would approve of that.' The couch creaked as he sat down beside her. 'Perhaps we could get the main hall painted for the Prince's visit. Yellow! Bright canary yellow. That'll make the Prince blink.' He laughed wholeheartedly, then coughed and spluttered.

She smiled slightly at him. His joy at his visitor's generosity had stripped him for a moment of his hag-ridden obsession with the place, and made him more his old self. His usually smooth hair was sticking up all over and his usually tired eyes were gleaming with pleasure.

'You should buy yourself a little car,' she said suddenly. 'Traipsing around like you do, going to meetings, carrying all that charity stuff. You're getting worn out. With a little car you could do so much more.'

She watched as he considered the suggestion, then rejected it. He hugged her absently. As though she were a cat. 'No, no,' he said. 'I couldn't justify that. I can spread it out to so much more benefit. Yellow paint!' He stood up. 'I'll pull together some volunteers and we'll paint the main hall.' He made for the door and she called him back.

'What is it?' His gaze was absent. In his mind he was already distributing brushes and yellow paint into willing hands.

She held the cheque towards him. 'You need this,' she said. 'You'll have to put it in the bank.' She threw it. He caught it, and vanished. A second later his head came back round the door. 'Cora?'

She looked up from her book.

'Are you all right>'

'Why?'

'It just seems that you've been a little *hors de combat* lately. Lost your *joie de vivre*.' His tone was hearty. She knew his sudden caring was some kind of a residue from his recent goodwill about the cheque.

I've lost more than that, she thought. 'It's nothing, Archie' she said. 'Nothing at all.'

'Good. I'm pleased about that.' His head vanished and Cora, as she very well knew, had vanished completely from his thoughts in that very instant.

47. Nights Away

Marguerite and me ended up spending the night in Newcastle in this little hotel she knew. It was not far from the station and you could hear the trains steaming in and steaming out, rattling on the rails. Sometimes the passing trains made the room shake. I think it was the trains. It could have been something else.

I asked Marguerite how she knew of this hotel and she told me she used to come here once, with a friend from London whom she'd met on a trip down there. Seemed he travelled selling fine goods from India and such places. He sold them to the big department stores in Newcastle. 'A bit artistic, he was,' she said. 'He was the one who first took me to the big Gallery.'

I suppose that this man was the reason why she knew more than the average Brack's Hill person about pictures and things like that.

The wizened old women who sat by a table in the hotel vestibule was not troubled by our lack of luggage and did not blink when we signed ourselves as Mr. and Mrs. Smith. Above us were Mr. and Mrs. Jones, with Mr. and Mrs. Thompson before that.

We'd spent the afternoon raging round Newcastle. With its high buildings, broad thoroughfares and teeming side streets it vibrated with our own need to celebrate. Marguerite dragged me in and out of noisy pubs. We would have one drink then glower at the people there who glowered at us, (resenting our jollity I think) and leave. We went to one cinema where we saw Charlie Chaplin in a very heart-rending love story.

Then we went and bought me a new tweed jacket and cap. I put them on, leaving my old tattered things to be discarded by the delicate assistant. Then we went to another cinema and saw Claude Rains in *The Invisible Man*. We talked for quite a time about how on earth they got the effect of the man being invisible. After that we had high tea in a place where the women wore frilly aprons and pursed looks.

I was just dragging Marguerite through the majestic portals of the Central Station when she stopped.

'What is it?' I said.

'I think we've missed the last train.' She looked into my eyes. Deep. I started to pull her again. She pulled back. 'We don't know that we have,' I said. 'Missed the last train.'

'Believe me!' she said. 'We'll have to stay overnight and get the first train back.' Again she looked hard into my eyes.

'How can we do that?'

'I do know a decent place,' she said. 'Not far from the station.'

So here we are, having spent the night here at the hotel, pretending to be Mr. and Mrs. Smith. The trains have woken me up and I have opened the window to let some air into the stuffy, overfilled room. The air that the window gap sucks which has salt in it from the tidal river and soot from the city fog. The buildings outside our window, still looming and dark, are edged with the butter light of the winter dawn and are full of promise of a very fine day.

I turn back to the room. Marguerite is lying, long legs half out of the stifling blanket, one hand under her cheek like a child, her massy black hair spread on the pillow like moss.

Greta Pallister should be pleased with me now. I finally know how to stop yourself from having babies. Marguerite showed me how to do it tenderly and with great laughter. Having a baby is not, she said, a risk that she'd ever take. Bbies and poverty went hand in hand and she was having nothing of that.

I can't remember how many times we made love. We seemed to be waking and waking and doing it, languorously, again and again. Sometimes I might have just dreamt that we did it. One time I mentioned Tegger and she put a finger on my lips. 'We belong to ourselves, Gabriel. Remember that. Or we imprison each other and we start to shrink.' She gurgled with laughter. 'In more ways than one.'

Rosel is on my mind too. I know now that I love her. I am sure of that. But the way she has been with me makes me think, well, what's the use? Now you might say that's very convenient, in the light of what happened last night. But mybe that's not the case.

This wonderful event has been characterized by ease and the freedom. Here there has been no-hole-in-the-corner lurking, no agonising about how old one person is, or how young is another. Here there has been a whole bed for a whole night. True luxury.

Now in the grey gold of the morning Marguerite's eyes snap open and stare into mine. 'What is it, Gabe? Never seen a sleeping woman before?'

'Well, now you ask it, no.'

'But you have done the...'

'Yes.'

She swings her legs onto the floor, stands up and stretches like a cat, unashamedly naked. My eyes, my mind are filled again with the woman in the Goaf.

She clips on a small corset and pulls on her stockings. 'Come on, Gabe. The early train. That was what we stayed over for, wasn't it? The early train?'

It was nine thirty in the morning when Rosel Vonn returned to the Settlement from her trip with Sir Peter. He dropped her at the end of the road and speeded North in his Daimler. In the sitting room Cora looked at Rosel over her newspaper. 'What was that about, Rosel? A night away? Very thoughtful of you to send a telegramme. Otherwise we would have worried.' She rattled the paper. 'So this must be quite fellow, this Sir Whatsit? Archie was telling me about his generous cheque.'

'Peter Hamilton Souness is his name, Cora. Do you know I believe he will save my father? I think he may even save my mother who is in an asylum.'

'Do you like him?'

Rosel shrugged. 'At first I wasn't sure. I thought he would just be useful. But then, now, he has such kindness. And he is entertaining,'

'And, I bet, not bad *you-know-where*.' Cora's tired eyes sparked with their old humour.

Rosel blushed, 'Cora!'

'Don't worry, darling. You're among friends here, darling.' She winked. 'You must like him quite a bit, if you ask me.'

Rosel sat down beside Cora, slipped off her shoes and stretched her slender feet in front of her. 'I must like him. I do like him very much. How could one sleep, Cora, with someone one does not like?'

Cora put a hand on hers. 'Happens all the time, dear girl. Believe me.'

48. Yellow Light

Archie Todhunter has had his way over the colour of the walls. He bought the paint and we did the painting. Even Baffer Bray joined it. Our joint efforts have made a great impact on the long room at the Settlement. It has taken five of us two days to put two coats of yellow paint on everything that does not move. The place is blazing with a yellow light that hurts my eyes.

In the end just Greta Pallister and me are left to do the final touches. The very last task is the second coat on the cupboard in the corner.

'This must have been a bit of a comedown for you,' she says.

'How d'you make that out?' I'm squinting at the narrow cupboard door-return. I've been given everything to do which demands a small brush and any degree of accuracy.

'More used to painting masterpieces, you are.'

'Get on!' I'm unmoved by her sarcasm. She's been good to work with: neat and able to concentrate. I don't have to say much. She's been talking as usual about school and her ambitions, about books she's been reading and how her normally imperturbable father is in a bit of a flap about the Prince's visit. 'It's really funny, this, as he's no time for royalty or what he calls all 'them up there'. But here he is, getting carried away.'

'He's not on his own. I think people like to put on a good front, whoever's gawping at them.'

With only two days to go the place has been humming with a sense of suppressed anticipation. Archie Todhunter has been very tight-lipped, complaining at how long the painting was taking. He only has tomorrow now to get the pictures rehung and the display tables laid out for the crafts and the quilting, the joinery, and the samples of shoe mending.

As well as this there's the Church Hall, where the play will actually be performed. Even at this moment Archie Todhunter is across there in workman's overalls wielding a brush. I'll say one thing for him, he will get stuck in when needs be.

'So, where's your naked lady?' says Greta. 'Why has Mr Todhunter banished her to the outer darkness?' Yesterday, in the dark of early morning Tegger and I took her back to my house.

Greta has finished her bit. She starts to dip her brush in a bucket of turpentine and rub it with a rag. He slender fingers are freckled with yellow paint.

'Nah. We took her home. She didn't fit with the rest, see?' I stop talking to concentrate on the last tricky corner. 'It was me. I realised she would take the attention off the business of the day.'

'Poor thing. I really liked her, even under her veil. Mind you I did hear my Dad say to my mother she'd cause a bit of havoc in the town. Here, give us that brush if you're finished.'

She takes it from me and I sit back, watching her as she makes a very efficient job of the cleaning.

I dip my hand in the turpentine bucket and rub them together. 'Well I didn't withdraw my Woman in the Goaf for that. I withdrew her for personal reasons of my own.'

I'm still not certain it was the right thing to do; to keep her on display or take her home to allow a few men in Brack's Hill to sleep more comfortably in their beds. I suppose it was really for Marguerite, so she would not be the centre of critical attention.

I also suppose that because of making the sales in Newcastle I am now more confident: that the Woman in the Goaf will get proper attention when it is her time.

Archie Todhunter was very pleased, of course, when I told him of my decision to take the painting home. He did say that of course he didn't believe in any kind of artistic censorship but there was so much about this 'day with the Prince' that could go wrong. He had to admit to some relief in not having to ride the storm which the picture would inevitably have raised.

Greta wipes her hands with the rag and comes to sit beside me. 'Personal reasons?'

'Yes.'

'It's a shame though.'

'Not really. She … well, she'll be hung in a gallery in Newcastle. More people will see her there than would ever here. And that'll be more people that know something about proper painting and art.' I have to cross my fingers at this. There's no saying Mr Tenant will really agree to Marguerite's plan.

'So, that should do you some good? For her to be in the gallery?' Her head is on one side. There is a smut on her nose.

'I hope so.' I've been through all this with Marguerite and it seems right. As she said to Tennant that day at the gallery, she knew how to strike a bargain. As he said, I could do worse than having her keep an eye out for me. But there's more to Marguerite than just that. There's lessons to learn from her about how to belong to yourself. How not to look to the past or the future; just to be, and belong to yourself, in the present. There's intoxication in that.

'Here. D'you want one?' Greta is nudging me with a battered bag of toffees.

'Don't mind if I do.'

'I'm pleased I've got you here. I wanted to talk to you about something.'

'About what?'

'Our bargain. The promise. You remember?'

'Greta, I…' I was just about to tell her that at least I've discovered how not to make babies when she puts up her hand like a policeman on traffic duty. 'Stop!' she says. 'I said I wanted to say something. Me, not you.'

Very humbly I concentrate on chewing my toffee.

'Now Gabriel, I know we had a bargain for after the performance. That you were going to show me…'

'Greta, I…'

That hand again. 'Shush! Now I don't want to hurth your feelings, but I have to tell you I've changed my mind.'

'Why's that?' I say, trying to keep my voice neutral.

'Well, to be very honest I didn't know the bargain I was taking on. I didn't know you that well, then. It was easy to strike the bargain, when I didn't really know you.'

'Now…?'

'Now I know you better. Now we're … well, kind of friends. And doing that – although it might be very useful to me – doing that thing would spoil everything. I can see that. If we did that thing. There'd be no future. For you and me I mean. It's too important to spoil.' Her dark eyes are sharp as a hawk behind her spectacles.

'D'you think so?'

'Yes. My mother always says there's a time and a place for everything. The problem with clichés is that they're usually true.' Now she leans across, puts a hand on either side of my face and kisses me. I think it must be the toffees because the kiss is very sweet indeed. Then she jumps up and dashes off and I'm left not knowing whether I'm relieved or disappointed by her decision to let me off the promise.

Rosel Vonn moved to one side to avoid the hurrying girl. She'd seen the two young heads close together and witnessed the fleeting kiss. She stood still for a second until all was quiet in the room and then the knocked on the door and bustled in, pushing her makeshift trolley that had held all the paintings, except the Woman in the Goaf, while the hall was being painted.

I make my way across the room towards with the turpentine bucket in one hand, cleaned brushes in the other.

'Well!' she says carefully, 'so the long room is transformed into our new gallery?'

'Looks like it. Archie Todhunter insisted on the yellow.'

'It's very cheerful,'

'The painting's'll look like decorations on a birthday cake.'

'But not your Lady in the Dark?'

I nod. 'Not my Woman in the Goaf.'

'Do you really think it will be better this way, Gabriel? Archie shouldn't have insisted. You have a right to hang it, you know.' There is a thread of anger in her voice.

'It's better this way. I know it.' I look down so she cannot see what I'm really thinking. 'No one pressured me. It would hve taken attention off the portraits. They're more important just at this time. I have other things in mind for the Woman in the Goaf.'

Rosel puts her hand on the trolley. 'I have all the other paintings here. I will lay them in place on the floor now. The paint on the walls should be dry enough by tonight for Tegger and Mr

Conroy to come and put in the picture hooks. Perhaps you would like to help me to lay them out?'

I shake my head. 'Sorry, Rosel, I promised Mr Todhunter I'd go across and help them finish the church hall. He's in a flap because we're all behind.'

'Very well. That is fine, Gabriel. Cora said she would come down to give me some help. She will only be a moment.'

Rosel watched Gabriel walk down the length of the long room and out of the door. Out of the door with him, she suddenly thought, went the final shreds of her own youth. Now all they would ever be was a fragment, a spark of memory in each other's life. Perhaps there was a certain comfort in that.

The door clattered and she shook off the sentiment as Cora came through the door looking very grim. 'There's two fellows in long coats in the office and Dev Pallister and a vanload of men at the gate, talking about cameras and boxes and ladders. Looking for Archie. 'Where is that man? He's impossible. Never anywhere when you want him.'

'Archie?' asked Rosel. 'He's across at the Church Hall, according to Gabriel Marchant.'

'Church Hall?' said Cora wearily, looking around in despair at the bright yellow room. 'D'you think your friend would have made his donation, Rosel, if he realised his generosity would contribute to *this* monstrous yellow light?'

Rosel got a folding chair from a stack in the corner and set it by the window. 'Sit here, Cora. I will go and tell Archie of his visitors.'

Cora was still sitting there when Rosel returned. She was staring at her hands and her eyes were full of tears. Rosel put a hand on her shoulder. 'What is it? What is it, Cora?'

'I don't know.'

'You are bound to feel bad, Cora, after…'

Cora pushed her hand away and sniffed. 'I thought we were here to place the pictures Rosel. Although whether it's worth bothering I don't know. I don't know anything about painting but my guess is this yellow willl drown the portraits out of sight.'

Rosel shook her head. 'You sit there, Cora. I'll spread these paintings out and you can give your advice. Which beside which? The problem is, balancing out the work coming from the class with the portraits, the ones to do with the play, and the other odd paintings the class has done.'

Cora sparked up a bit. 'I see that Gabriel's naughty picture's not to be included.'

'It seems not. I would prefer now that is were here. It is a better painting than anything here.' She frowned. 'I fear that pressure was put on him.'

'Yes I reckon Archie must have leaned hard on him. Drat the man.'

Rosel came to Archie's defence. 'I do not think so. He was reluctant, but it was Gabriel himself who withdrew it. He told me.'

'Kind of him, I'm sure.'

'Cora! This is not like you...'

'Shall we get on placing these pictures? We can't give Archie something else to go frantic about.' Cora's tone was not just weary, but cold. Rosel knew there would be no more conversation about Cora, or Archie for that matter.

49 The Man with the Long Shadow

Archie stopped in his tracks when he saw the Daimler. 'Visitors, visitors, the Fraŭlein said! It's Lord Chase, for goodness sake,' he said to Gabriel. 'And goodness knows who else. And Cora playing silly beggars yet again.' He glanced down at his overall and his hands, still covered with the dust from the Church Hall. 'You go and talk to them, Gabriel, while I scrub up.'

'Me?' said Gabriel. 'I'm covered with paint as well as dust.'

'Well, it doesn't … it doesn't…'

'Matter about me? Well, thank you very much.'

'I don't mean that. I don't mean you to think that at all,' said Archie as they reached the door.

'I don't like talking to strangers,' said Gabriel flatly.

'Do it! It's good for you! Something you have to learn!' Archie pushed past him and hurried up the stairs to restore himself to the state of a man who could face such visitors on something like equal terms.

****

I don't want to do this for Archie but I have to admit a certain curiosity about Lord Chase. Owning the mines in Brack's Hill, he casts a long dark shadow in these parts. My father and I worked in his mines. It was on his direct order after the big Strike that activists like my father should find no work in the mines and would be condemned to live without work for the rest of their lives.

I thought he would be very tall but when I look him in the eye I look downwards. He's wearing a country cap, rounder and softer than any pitman's, and a long tweed coat. He looks at me with a blank look which takes me in but doesn't see me. The man beside him is taller than he is and is wearing a military uniform of some kind.

'Mr Todhunter says he'll be here in a minute.' I say. 'He's just gone to change. He has been working to get the hall ready for the performance.'

His Lordship nods but fails to ask me who I am. He glances at his companion. 'I hear this Todhunter fellow's done great work among the poor in the district. Old-fashioned sort: a man of principle. Needed around here.' The man in uniform makes sounds in his throat that sound like agreement and appreciation.

I might just as well not be there. These men have forgotten me. I should rage at them, I should tell them of my father driven by Lord Chase's decision to hang himself from a tree. But these men strike me dumb with their easy assurance and the way they fill the space around you so that you almost suffocate. They ignore me but I can't find a way to get out of the room without backing out like some servant maid.

Now at last Archie Todhunter comes breezing in, scrubbed immaculate, with his film star hair just so. He's wearing a very dark suit I've never seen and his round spectacles gleam with recent polishing. 'Ah! Lord Chase!' He moves into the room and takes possession of it. He shakes his Lordship heartily by the hand and turns to the other visitor.

His Lordship makes the introductions. 'This is Colonel Black, who will oversee arrangements for Thursday.'

'Good, good,' says Archie. He turns towards me. 'And you will have met the wonderful Gabriel Marchant here.'

Lord Chase turns to me. 'Mr Marchant!'

'Gabriel is a coming man, your Lordship. A credit to the Settlement. A painter of great talent. A coming man!'

'Is this so?' My hand is grasped now in a wiry, close grip. 'And are you a painter of great talent, Mr Marchant?'

'I wouldn't say that.' I rescue my hand, only to have it pumped by that of the Colonel, who says. 'So you are one of the unemployed?' he says breezily.

Archie interrupts. 'Gabriel's very much employed these days, Colonel. Apart from his remarkable painting he's been working very hard rehearsing the play and getting ready for the visit, as have all our Settlement people. We don't define people here by their unemployment Colonel.'

I delight in the way Archie Todhunter has reproved the pair of them, put them in their place. I gather courage. 'I *was* a pitman,' I say. 'In fact I worked in Lord Chase's pits. My father too, until 1926. Then he was blacklisted.'

Lord Chase's jaw hardens. 'It is all very unfortunate. These are hard times for us all.'

An image of the glossy Daimler rises before my eyes and I open my mouth but Archie Todhunter gets in before me. 'Now, then, your Lordship, Colonel! I will show you around the Settlement, just as I will show the Prince. But first, here is Church Hall where the play will be performed.'

'Play?' rapped out the Colonel. 'There was no mention of a play.'

'This is the whole point,' said Archie. 'the play *is* the Settlement. It shows the best of what we have to offer here. Talented writers, artists, performers, people of ideas...'

'How long is this play?' The military voice raps out.

'Not long, colonel. Just over the hour...'

Chase and the Colonel exchange glances. 'Impossible,' says the colonel. 'We have a schedule...'

'Just the first act,' Todhunter goes into bargaining mode. 'These are scenes on the Front in the Great War, Colonel. I know that His Royal Highness served at the front in the war. Perhaps he would be interested?'

The other two men look at him blankly.

'And it tells of there's the state of the mines in the middle of the war, in the middle of their war effort....' I say urgently. They all look round at me. It's as though a duck has spoken.

'Yes, yes,' says Todhunter, 'and that. Their war effort.'

'The schedule is very tight,' says the Colonel. He glances down at a small notebook in his leather gloved hand. 'Mr Pallister wants His Royal Highness to meet old soldiers at the Working Men's Club, and there is a poultry project and this Allotment Project...'

Lord Chase claps his hands together in this peculiar way and we know that this bit of the discussion is over. 'Well, Todhunter? Lead the way. Walk us through it. The Colonel can get out his stopwatch and we can see if His Royal Highness can fit in some scenes from your play.'

'I'm gonna wear my cap for the Visit,' Dev announced. 'Not the bowler.'

They were sitting round having their tea.

'Well,' said his wife grimly. 'That was a waste of money we couldn't afford.'

Greta looked up from her copy of Brave New World which she had propped against the teapot to make it easier to read. 'You didn't suit the bowler anyway, Dad. Made you look like a grocer.'

'You should wear it, now we've got it,' said Pauline firmly.

Dev shook his head. 'Do I want to stand out like a pea on a drum? I was talking to these film lads today. Seems the Prince wears a soft cap when he visits the natives, so the other toffs do that as well. No top hats, even bowlers. Wouldn't do to stand out. Bad taste.' He scooped a spoonful of rice pudding and looked at Greta. 'And you can say goodbye to any thoughts of him seeing that play of yours. According to these film lads he's through in ten minutes, fifteen at the most.'

'Well!' said Greta. 'Mr Todhunter'll be really upset.'

'That one! He was enjoying himself today hobnobbing with Lord Chase and the Colonel. Glowing with it, he was.'

Greta frowned. 'You don't like him, do you? Mr Todhunter?'

Dev put down his spoon. 'I wouldn't say that. I do and I wouldn't say thatI don't. The feller means well. You can see that. It's just that Todhunter's' an unusual type. Can't place him, somehow. I can place Lord Chase and his colonel. I can place young Gabriel Marchant. But Todhunter … his heart's in the right place I think … but he's all things to all men, so who the hell – sorry Pauline … who is he? Does he know himself who he is?'

'That's very clever, Dad,' said Greta approvingly. 'Issues of identity and characterisation. We've done that at school with the novels of Charlotte Bronte.'

'Well, thank you very much, Miss Knowall,' said Dev. 'I'm honoured to know that I can do issues of Identity and Characterisation. Now, Pauline, is it out of order to take a second helping of the rice pudding?'

****

All this cleaning and painting has me wacked. I must be getting soft. I wonder how I ever lasted a shift pushing and hauling tubs up and down inclines in the pit.

Tired as I am, when I get home I see Tegger sprawled in my father's chair reading a sporting paper. He has the fire stacked with filched coal. He grins. 'What cheer, marra! You look paggered.'

'So I am. Where were you today, man, when all this work was being done?'

'I've been down at Wetherill's printers all day. Took the play down for them to bind it. A gift for our Great Visitor. You know!' He nods to a slim volume on the table. I pick it up and flick through it. I look back across to his grinning face. 'But this ... this is...'

'Aye. *Properly* printed. I took my typescript down to get it bound and the old man there asked about it. When I told him who it was for he said it should be properly done. Put his jobs on hold and set the thing up himself.'

'I flicked to the title page

Brack's Hill Settlement

BLOOD and COAL

A Play in Three Acts By
Archibald Todhunter
& Edgar MacNamara

'Edgar! Sunday name, eh?'

'Archie Todhunter said I'd gotta put my name on.'

'Only right, that. It looks very good, Tegger.'

'Doesn't it? The old man printed me twenty copies at a go. Beats typewriting any day. Bound three of them very fine, like that one: one each for me and Archie, and one for the Prince of course. And the rest. More ordinary bound, for the Settlement folks for if they do it again.' My friend is still grinning ear to ear.

I wink at him. 'Proud of you, marra!' And we laugh together like mad things.

He splutters to a stop. 'Now then, marra, what say we go and have a pint to celebrate?'

'Yeah. Yeah!'

'Raglan's no good like,' he says looking at me closely. 'Not these days. With Marguerite and that.'

I return the look. 'Mebbe not.'

'We'll go to the Club. Build the fire up afore we go. Plenty coal.' He grins amd winks. 'I made a little visit to the coal dump with me sack.'

It's a very long time since I've been to the Club. The last time was on the morning of the Durham Big Meeting in 1932. my father and his friend Steve bought me a beer in a half pint glass. Steve clapped my on the shoulder and said. 'Half a pint for a half-pint!'

Tonight the place hums with the usual routines of talk and the playing of games of draughts, chess and shove-ha'penny. The old men sit as usual by the roaring fire at the far end. A few men are buried behind well-thumbed newspapers. It still smells of hops and old sweat but someone has given the place a lick of paint and the floor is unusually clean.

We stand at the end of the bar watching the buzz around us and having our own quiet celebration. Then Dev Pallister comes up behind us and nods at the barman, who silently fills us another pint.

'Strangers here these days, lads?' he says, leaning easily against the bar between us. 'I thought the Raglan was your usual haunt.'

'Not tonight,' I say, too conscious of Tegger who is suddenly tense beside me. 'We fancied a change.'

'Aye. A change is often a good thing.' He looks very directly at me. 'I hear that the big painting of yours won't be in the display.'

'No it won't. I already have three paintings in that show. I decided there were better places for this one.'

'Did you? Our Greta went on about it not being there. She talked about censorship.'

'Did she?'

'Said it was like censors cutting a piece out of a newspaper. A dangerous thing.'

'She has a way with words, has your Greta.'

'She's on her way up and out of this place and that's no bad thing.' Then Dev does an unusual thing, especially in such a place. He puts a hand on my arm. 'You too, lad, are going up and out if

I'm not mistaken. Just one thing though. Be careful not to leave the best of this place behind you.'

Then Dev leaves us with our pints and rejoins the man he was talking to, who doesn't look like any pitman. He's wearing a coloured shirt and tie. And a tweed jacket with leather patches. It's that critic who watched the rehearsal. Herbert Grossmith. Dev Pallister hangs about with all sorts.

But we're here to celebrate. I take a sip of the strong ale and suppress my wincing reaction. Tegger tells me of a sure thing that's racing at York on Saturday and can I lend him the wherewithal to get there on the train? If I can see my way to that, he says, he'll go halves with me with the winnings he'll inevitably make. 'Honest, kidder,' he says.

Dev Pallister took an appreciative sip of his frothing pint and eyed his companion. 'I forgot that you were not much of a drinker yourself Mr Grossmith.'

'I've said in a hundred times if I've said it once. It's not the drink, Mr Pallister.' Herbert Grossmith patted his creased waistcoat. 'Dicky stomach. I'm a martyr to dyspepsia. Beer is poison. A single glass of port in a week is all I can take. The rest of the time I stick to plain water. Adam's Ale, if you like.'

'I'd have thought that a bit of a disadvantage, myself. There's a lot of information in public bars.'

Grossmith shook his head. 'It causes me no problems, Mr Pallister. No problems at all.' He took a delicate sip of his water. 'So! You were saying? Everything ticketty boo for tomorrow? '

'Everything in place. The committee has covered all eventualities.'

'So!' Grossmith's slightly bulging eyes dropped casually to the notebook, which stood guard on his glass of Adam's Ale. 'His Royal Highness will be here at the Club, seeing the war veterans at the Cenotaph, and will look in on the poultry project, the new Allotment project and … er… the Settlement.'

'That's right. Colonel Black, who's being checking things out for the Lord Lieutenant, says the arrangements are fine.'

Grossmith scribbled something on the page. 'And the Settlement? Will the Prince see their play? I saw a rehearsal. OI hate to say it but it wasn't half bad.'

'Well we're still not clear whether the Prince will have time to see it. But the actors'll be there in costume and the Prince will receive a copy of the play. And there'll be an exhibition of the work, painting, woodwork and such.'

'Paintings?' Grossmith turned back a page in his notebook. 'I was talking to Nathan Smith. He was saying that one painting, by a lad who's shown great promise, had to be removed. Questionable subject matter. Offensive.'

'Did he say offensive?'

'Not in so many words, but…'

'I know nothing about any painting,' Dev flicked out a hand, rejecting the question as you would swat a fly.

'So. How do you find Archie Todhunter, Mr Pallister?'

'Fine man. A visionary. Idealist. His heart's in the right place.'

'I've heard him called big-headed … pretentious…patronising.'

'You must have been talking to some narrow ignorant people, Herbert. There are a few around.'

'Well, I…'

Again the dismissive gesture. 'If you want to know about Archie Todhunter you go and talk to him, son.'

Grossmith stood up. 'Perhaps I can get you another drink, Mr Pallister?'

Pallister smiled slightly and stood up himself. 'No thank you son, I always buy my own beer, thank you. I make it a rule.'

Grossmith shook hands with him. 'Perhaps I will see you tomorrow, then? We'll have our photographer there. I hear the newsreels will be there too, How d'you feel like going to the pictures and seeing yourself on Pathe News? Now that would be something!'

'To be honest Mr Grossmith I don't like it at all.' Dev's gaze strayed over Grossmith's shoulder. 'Oh, there's Herbie Masterton. I need a word with him about the football team. If you'll just excuse me.'

Herbert Grossmith watched his retreating back. Cagey number, Dev Pallister. Buzzing round like a bee, finger in every pie. But there was no pinning him down. Never mind. Herbert thought he would have a go at this young painter. Bound to be a bit of resentment there. Worth a stir.

50. At the White Leas Pool

I am in a bad state. It must have been the strong beer at the Club, followed by a very late session in my kitchen poring inch-by-inch over the pit-heap picture. I spent at least half an hour scraping off the part by the edge of the pool, where the single lime tree sticks up at its funny angle. That is the third time I've cleared that square of board and still I can't get it right. Even with four heady pints of strong ale inside me I could see the problem more clearly but was nowhere near a solution.

Now my head thumps with a steady rhythm and I try lifting it off the pillow. The thumping doesn't stop. I stagger to my feet and shake my head. Even the violent shaking will not get rid of the thumping.

Knocking! Someone's knocking at the door. I have to lift my father's tin clock to the window to peer at it in the grey November light. Eight o'clock.

It must be Tegger. Some kind of trouble, I suppose. I leap down the narrow stairs three at a time and scramble to open the door. My bleary eyes make out Rosel Vonn in the dark light of morning. 'Come in, come in! You should've some straight in. The door's not locked. It's never locked.'

'I did not wish to surprise you, Gabriel.' Her glance takes me in, head to toe. I am wearing the old shirt of my father's in which I usually sleep. 'Come in! Sit down!' I say and bolt back upstairs.

When I get back down, decently covered, she's there in the kitchen peering at the new picture. I turn up the gas and the room is bathed in pallid light. 'What is it?' I say. 'What's the matter?'

'It's Cora. Archie came to get me half an hour ago. When he went to sleep last night Cora was there beside him. When he woke up she was gone. We've walked the streets around the Settlement and there is no sign of her. He kept saying *Today of all days. Today of all days.* At last I fear I lost my temper with him and told him to go to the police. He said he couldn't. It would cause an uproar. *Today of all days!* The police will be busy enough. He said that we should find her ourselves. That she would not be far. That when we find her there should be no fuss. He is a very obsessive man.' She shudders inside her heavy coat. 'I do not know where to look, so I came for you. He went for Tegger.'

Already I'm tying a muffler round my neck and reaching for my cap. 'Where have you looked?'

'Everywhere within five streets of The Settlement. Then I came for you and Archie went for Tegger.'

'Why us?'

'Because Archie thinks that you know the town, that you will find her and will keep silent. You have no wives or…'

'Yes, let's go. Come on!'

We meet Tegger and Archie two streets from the Settlement. Tegger and I divide the town between us and then, street by street, back-street by back-street, we set out on our search.

'Why has she gone?' Why has she run off?' I ask Rosel as we hurry along. 'What's happened?'

'She has been ill lately. So very unhappy.'

'I thought she looked, well … ragged. But we're all ragged these days, trying to put on this show. And I don't just mean the play.'

'But Cora is different. She has a real reason to feel this way.'

'What's that then?'

'What is it? It is something about which I cannot tell you.'

We're in the alley behind the Lord Raglan. Looking up, I can see the light in Marguerite's curtained window with her shadow moving behind it. It's early for her. Perhaps the excitement of the day has even got to her. She has her invitation to the play.

Rosel's hand is on my arm. 'Come on, Gabriel! Cora is not down here.'

In twenty minutes we're at the edge of the town. We've scoured every street, every doorway, and every back alley. 'Not here,' said Rosel sadly. 'Poor Cora. What has she done?'

'The colliery buildings!' I pull her by the hand and start to run. 'She could have holed up there.'

We make our way through the warren of buildings, thankful that the thread of dawn light which is now illuminating our search.

We rattle rusty padlocks, peer through dusty windows, call and call. But Cora is not here.

'Not here. Not anywhere,' says Rosel. 'We must tell Archie, perhaps he and Tegger... The police.'

My eye sweeps across the dark buildings past the White Leas pit heap, to the empty horizon that is shimmering now with white light as the day really begins its journey. Then my gaze comes back to the heap. 'There's places here. She might have wandered onto the heap.' I walk on quickly.

'Gabriel!' she calls desperately. 'No. Not here!'

'Yes!' I say. 'Come on.'

We skirt around the heap, scanning the heights where the spoil has curled into ridges in a tide of shale and then where the persistent whinny bushes have started to grow again. This is where the children make dens to play. I did this myself.   Here are the play-trenches here where the children play Germans-and-English. Here are innocent stretches of slag where treacherous holes open up to steal lives.

We follow the path round and blink now at the pool, which glitters in the morning light as bright as any Swiss lake. I've tried and probably failed to catch all of this in my new painting. My eye automatically seeks the spot with the lime tree: the spot that has given me so much trouble with the painting.

And there she is. Not on the edge by the crooked lime tree, but in the water up to her knees and walking, arms held out carefully for balance.

'Cora-a-a!' screams Rosel. And she starts to run. I run beside her, shouting and whistling the crudest playground whistles; anything to take Cora from her deadly intent. In my mind's eye as I run I see my father walking steadily, steadily from his allotment, the old chair in one hand, the strong rope over his shoulder. He too has his tree, like this one beside White Leas Pool. 'Cora-a-a!' My voice is screaming now, enveloping Rosel's bird-like cries.

At last Cora looks up from the water and sees us. She freezes there, arms still held like a crucifix. We slow down, walk gently towards her, breathing hard. 'Cora,' calls Rosel softly. 'Wait there, *liebchen*, we are coming.'

'Stand still, flower,' I gasp. 'Just stay there and we'll come and get you.' *Flower*! My grandmother called me this when I was a child. A term of endearment.

'Rosel! Where've you been?' Cora's mumbling now, through frozen lips. 'I went for a walk. Clear the head...' She's wearing Atchie's mackintosh over her nightdress.

'Shsh,' says Rosel. 'We come for you now, dear Cora,'

We wade out and stand beside her. We each take an arm and half-pull, half-lead her out of the icy water. She has nothing on her feet. I take off my muffler and wind it around her head, then her neck. Rosel takes off her coat and puts it round her, peels off her warm gloves and puts them on Cora's chilled hands. 'Come on! We must get you back. Quickly. The Settlement.'

Cora puts a gloved hand on her arm. 'Not the Settlement,' she says. 'Not Archie...'

'My house,' I say. 'You can come to my house.'

I hoist her into my arms and thank God for the thousand tubs I've hauled through the years that have given me the strength for this task. Cora is much heavier to carry than my father was and I welcome the extra strain on my back, the pull on my muscles. She clutches her arm around my neck. This body is alive. There is the difference.

There are quite a few people about as we make the journey back to my house. We get a few curious looks but, as we're not asking for help, no one interferes with us. At the house my muscles scream with gratitude as I put Cora into my father's chair. Then I rake out and build up the fire while Rosel starts to rub her hands and feet.

Cora's teeth start to chatter. Rosel stands up. 'Clothes! I need to get her out of these wet things.' She looks round the paint-strewn kitchen despairing. 'Blankets.'

I have the fire blazing now. 'I'll get you the blankets off my bed. And in the front room, there's a press. A big cupboard. In the bottom drawer are clothes off my grandmother. My father never touched the press. My grandmother's clothes are all in there.'

When I get back down with the blankets Rosel has already starting to get Cora out of her clothes. 'Run, Gabriel! Go and tell Archie,' she says over her shoulder. 'He will be very relieved. Tell him she's here. And she's safe.'

'No Archie,' mumbled Cora. 'Not Archie.'

'Tell him to leave her here. Tell him to get on with his day. We will take care of her here.'

When I get to the Settlement Archie and Tegger are in the office. Archie has his head in his hands. His normally immaculate hair is awry. He looks up at me, then straightens his back and stands up. 'You've found her. How …where...?'

'Sit down Mr Todhunter. We found her by the pit pool. She's a bit wet but she is all right. Rosel's taking care of her in my house. Getting her warmed up.'

'Your house? Go back and bring her here. Your house is no place...'

'She wouldn't come, Mr Todhunter.'

'Then I'll come...'

'She doesn't want to see you.'

There are bright red patches on his cheeks. 'What are you saying?'

Tegger shuffles his feet and scowls at me. 'Steady, marra.'

'She says to get on with what there is to do. This is the big day. She doesn't want to be in the way.'

His brow clears at this, and he runs his hands through his hair to tidy it a bit. 'Well … well. Did she say why, why she has done this? She knows how inconvenient...'

I can't believe him. 'I just saved her from drowning, Mr Todhunter, I don't think...'

'Gabriel!' warns Tegger.

'Will she be better this afternoon, for the … Will she be here?' He persists.

'I'll get back,' I say. 'I have to see to the fire.'

'Gabriel!' his tone is odd: reprimanding and pleading all at once. 'I know it sounds hard, uncaring. But I need to know about her. First I need to know that she is safe. Then I need to know if she'll be here this afternoon to play Maggie Olliphant. If not, well…' he coughs. 'It's all for nought, that's all.'

Across Archie Todhunter's head, Tegger throws me a powerful glance.

I rein in my feeling. 'Look Mr Todhunter. I'll go now and see what I can do. See if she can raise herself for Maggie Olliphant.Rosel will come and talk to you later.'

'Just assume she'll be here, Mr Todhunter,' said Tegger. 'That's all you can do for now.'

I call for bread and milk and jam at the corner shop, using some shillings from my sales to Mr Tennant. When I get back I have to blink. Cora is sitting there in my father's chair dressed from head to foot in my grandmother's clothes: closed necked blouse and long red skirt; a yellow knitted shawl around her shoulders.

Rosel is kneeling at her feet making a bit of a job of pulling on my grandmother's home-knitted green socks.

I throw the bread and jam on the table. 'Well, Cora. I could'a sworn it was my old grandma sitting there!'

She manages a weak smile. 'Cheeky boy!' she whispers.

'Is that milk?' says Rosel. 'Then perhaps we can make some tea. For the English, tea is medicine. Is that not so?'

Half way down her second cup of medicine, Cora shouts. 'Ophelia!'

I blink. Rosel puts a hand on Cora's. 'What is it?'

'Who d'I think I was? Ophelia? Played her before, but never for real.'

'I saw Hamlet in Berlin. In 1929,' offered Rosel. She's smiling slightly but her eyes are watchful.

'That would be in German, I suppose.'

'Of course.'

'What d'you think of Ophelia, Rosel?'

'Well, I…'

'Miserable as a drink of watered milk on a cold morning. If ever there was miscasting, it was me in that role. In that play.'

'That's not so.,' I say. 'Greta Pallister says you can be anyone you want. That you have a gift.'

Cora's eyes spark at this. 'Did she, now?' The light fades a bit. 'Well then, what does she know? She's just a kid.'

'Did you think you were Ophelia, out there at the pool?' asks Rosel.

Cora frowns. 'I can remember putting on Archie's coat and having to get away. I can remember running out of house. The next thing I remember is standing up to my arse in that freezing water and you two shouting like a pair of hoydens.'

'So you didn't want to…?' I have to ask her this. 'Did you want to finish it all?'

'Not when I heard you shout, I didn't.'

'When I was young I cut my wrists, three times,' says Rosel suddenly. 'At the point when I cut them, I wanted to do away with myself. And then when the blood flowed that was sufficient. I no longer wished to die."

'You?' I say.

'Now that's a surprise.' Cora smiles. 'Seems like she's impregnable, Gabriel, doesn't she? But she's not. No one is.'

I try to say something, but Rosel is preoccupied, putting my paints in rainbow order on the table.

Two whole pots of 'medicine' later Cora is looking much brighter and Rosel decides she should go and tell Archie that things are all right.

'Tell Archie I'll be there this afternoon,' says Cora. 'For the show. I won't spoil his show.'

Rosel frowns at her. 'Surely, Cora…'

'I'll be there for this shindig, and I'll be there to be Maggie Olliphant.' Cora's tone is now firm, resolved. 'Between you and me, I'm not going back to him. But I'll do all that for him. You tell him I'll be there. But afterwards I'll be away.'

Herbert Grossmith stood astride his motorbike, pulled it back onto its stand and watched as the elegant woman let herself out of the back yard gate, closed it with a click and made her way down the back lane.

'That a Triumph mister?' Two lads of eight or nine were sitting on the next door wall. Their mother – at least he assumed it was their mother, although she looked quite old - was leaning against her gate, smoking. She had long creases in her cheeks.

'So it is. Called a *Silent Scout.*' Herbert leapt off the bike with a flourish and hung his goggles over the handlebar.

'Why's it called a Silent Scout?' asked the older lad.

'Because it doesn't make much noise.' Herbert nodded at the gate whence the elegant woman had just emerged, 'Was that Mrs Marchant?'

'That?' The woman sniffed. 'There hasn't been a Mrs. Marchant in years.'

'Just a visitor?' Must be. The woman had been a bit up-market for this street. Compare her with this one leaning on the gate.

'Plenty visitors to that house. All sorts. You wouldn't believe it.'

'Is that so?' Herbert made his way down the yard. Experience told him that going in the back way in these streets put you on a much better footing when you tried to talk to folks inside. Front door was for telegrammes, death and the landlord. No good for a newspaper reporter.

The tall good-looking youth who came to the door proved to be the Gabriel Marchant he sought. He remembered him from

Archie's big rehearsal. Apparently neither troubled nor impressed by the fact that this was Herbert Grossmith of the Priorton Chronicle, the boy led through to a kitchen which smelled of linseed oil and turpentine mixed with fire smoke. Paintings and drawings were slung on the walls in no particular order and a half-completed painting was leaning on an easel which stood at right angles to the window. By the roaring fire sat an old woman in a shawl.

'This is … 'Gabriel paused.

'I'm his Grandmother,' the quavering voice came from the depths of the shawl. The old woman didn't seem to notice the hand Herbert held out to shake hers.

'What can I do for you, Mr Grossmith?'

'Well, son, I'm just making the rounds of people involved in the Prince's visit. Getting some opinions. Colourful background. You know the kind of thing. Six pages to fill.' He glanced around the room and sat down, unasked at the kitchen table. 'This'd make a fine photo. The artist at work. I could get the photographer down.'

'No you couldn't,' said Gabriel pulling out the chair opposite him and sitting down. The boy certainly had a very direct look, thought Herbert. Wouldn't like to cross *him* on a dark night.

Herbert took the small notebook from his inside pocket. He was surprised he hadn't been offered a cup of tea. He was offered endless cups of tea in these forays into the streets. It wreaked havoc with his poor stomach. But you couldn't turn it down. Not when you wanted people to talk to you. 'Now, then, Gabriel,' he said genially. 'Seems like you're very involved in this business this afternoon. With the Prince.'

'How d'yer make that out, like?'

'Well, I was down there with Nathan Smith this morning. He says you act in the play, helped to build the set. Oh, yes! Saw your paintings. Characters. One triple thing, all of you in the play. Very clever.'

'I didn't paint that. It was painted by Rosel Vonn. She's the art teacher.'

A penny dropped with Herbert. 'Ah! Was she the lady who was leaving as I arrived? Very attractive lady.'

Here the 'grandmother' had a coughing attack, covering her embarrassment with the edge of her shawl.

'That would be her,' said Gabriel.

'Nathan said she'd had a great deal of influence on all the painters.'

'Aye. She has.'

Herbert glanced round the walls and back at the easel by the window. 'He mentioned a painting that was in the exhibition and had to be withdrawn.'

'Did he now?'

'Bit of a naughty picture, by all accounts.'

The boy stood up and took up a big book from the sewing machine which was standing in the corner. With a clattering sweep of his hand he cleared half the table of its paint tubes and brushes.

He opened the book and turned the pages almost too swiftly for Herbert to make them out. 'Look at this one, this, this and this! Is this lewd?   Is this offensive? Well, Mr Grossmith, in case you didn't know, this is the work of the great painter Rembrandt.' The boy shut the book with a slap, returned it to its perch, and then crouched down on the floor to retrieve his paints.

Herbert watched while the boy reassembled his table into what Herbert now saw was a very formal order.   The rackety appearance of the room was deceptive. Then he said. 'So your painting was banned?'

'He didn't say that.' A squeaky voice came from behind the Grandmother's shawl.

'I just decided,' said Gabriel wearily, 'that it didn't go with the other pictures, that it would draw attention away from them. Nobody banned it.'

'Can I see it?' Herbert looked around.

'No. You can't.'

'Fair enough.' Herbert scribbled in his book. Then he looked up, pencil poised. 'And what would you say The Settlement has done for you, Gabriel?'

The table was now back in proper order. The boy sat down again. 'Well.' He said slowly. 'Do you know The Pilgrim's Progress?'

'Yes. Yes. Of course I do. Read it in Standard Three.

'Well, it's like I plodging about in the Slough of Despond and suddenly I came upon The Settlement which was the House Beautiful.'

Herbert's pencil was still poised. He frowned. 'But what do you think, feel about your experiences there? About Archie Todhunter and the German woman?'

'Archie Todhunter is a magician. Turns base metal, the most ordinary ingredients, into gold. He converts a difficulty to a possibility. People going there have had chances, experiences, that'll live with them all their days.'

Herbert was writing furiously. 'And the German woman?'

'Miss Rosel Vonn is the other side of an equally bright coin.' Gabriel frowned, thinking hard. 'She freed in me what I could do and has made me realise how little I know and how much there is to learn. She's given me self respect and a life challenge at the same time. And I think it's the same for the others.'

'Good stuff!' said Herbert scribbling quickly. He glanced round. 'And what do you think you'll do with all this work, when it's done?'

The boy eyed him narrowly. 'What'll you do with that piece when you write it? Show it and sell it? Well that's what I'll do. I'm no fancy-pants doing this for fun any more than are the cobblers working at the Settlement. I'm a workman. An artisan. I'll sell the fruits of my labour.'

Herbert scribbled a few words and glanced around again. 'You think you'll sell them?'

'I've already sold some. And I have someone waiting for others.'

'Now who would that be?'

The grandmother was taken again with a fit of coughing and the boy went over to help her. When he had patted her on the back and adjusted her shawl the boy looked up at him. 'Don't think I should talk about that just now Mr Grossmith. Do you?'

He went to the door and opened it. 'Now then, we must have finished here. I need to get my Grandma onto the bed.'

Outside, the woman and boys were still there. 'Manage all right?' she said. 'Did you meet the lad?'

He pulled on his goggles. 'Yes. The grandmother too.'

'Grandma?' she chortled. 'They're having you on. There hasn't been no Grandma there for twelve, fifteen years.'

Herbert looked at Gabriel Marchant's door, now firmly shut. Then he shrugged. Whatever had gone on in there he had some good stuff for the paper. He stood hard down on the motorbike pedal, the engine roared and he made his way back down the back street, throwing up the packed earth as he did so. Behind him the two boys had jumped off the wall and were miming the pedal action and making *bru-u-mming* noises, ready to set off on their own motorbike race. The older boy put his hands on his hips. 'Not much noise be buggered!' he said. '*Silent Scout?* I don't think so.'

51. 'Cora is a Trouper...'

When Rosel got back to the Settlement Archie Todhunter was in the long room surrounded by a buzzing cloud of quilters, carpenters and cobblers who were setting up their displays on the long tables. On the wall behind them someone had hung the painting in Rosel's designated places. The blazing yellow of the walls had dimmed a little under this onslaught of colour and texture. The effect was bright and positive. It worked very well, despite Gabriel Marchant's misgivings.

Rosel reflected that Archie had an instinct for things that worked; like toiling on with the play as though the Prince were really going to see it, when Dev Pallister and the others had said there was no question of this. Ten minutes, they'd heard. That was it.

Archie hurried towards her. She held up her hand. 'Don't worry, Archie. Cora is well. She is a very resolute lady. She is most definite that she will be here. She is resting at this moment.'

'Good, good,' he said almost absently. 'Cora is a trouper, and this is so whatever kind of brainstorm has assailed her.' He led her to one of the seats that were now lining the walls under the picture. 'Sit down, Rosel.' He sat down beside her, and took hold of her hand. She had never before felt his touch. His hand was very dry. 'Now dear girl, prepare yourself. Your friend Sir Peter is here.'

She looked round.

'Not here,' he said. 'Here in Brack's Hill. He came an hour ago, took one look at this chaos and insisted on leaving. He has perfect manners, that man.'

'Left?' she said.

'He asked where they could get tea and I directed them to The Gaunt Valley Café.'

She stood up. 'Them?'

'There was someone ... he introduced me to your father, Rosel. We talked of his war drawings... wait wait...'

Rosel wrenched her hand away, ran out of the hall and hurried along the pavements into the café which, perhaps because of The Visit, was unusually crowded with people who weren't from Brack's Hill.

She scanned the crowd. Her eye passed over them twice before she recognised them. Peter's tall frame was almost hidden under the shadow of an overhanging staircase. At the table with him sat a little old couple: the woman's face was almost hidden by the large fur collar of her cape and the wide brim of an old fashioned hat. Rosel squeezed and pushed her way through the tables to them.

Peter stood up, cracking his head on the underside of the staircase. He smiled as he rubbed his head. She felt a flush of affection for him, returning his smile.

Her father, when he stood up, seemed half Peter's size. 'Rosel,' he said. '*Meine* Rosel.' He took her hand and kissed it, then drew her to him and kissed her, first on one cheek then the other. She stood away from him. There were dark rings under his eyes and he looked twenty years older than Peter, who must be almost his contemporary.

Her father turned to the old woman who sat beside him. '*Lilah! Hier ist Rosel.*'

Rosel looked down at her mother, who looked back at her blankly from a wrecked face. Rosel bent down to kiss her cheek. 'How are you, my dear mother??" Her mother struggled away from her and looked at Sir Peter. 'The cakes are dreadful here,' she said in German. 'Such dreadful cakes. I wish to go home. At home the cakes are so good.' She looked back at Rosel. 'Who is this woman?' she said.

Peter turned Rosel towards him and kissed her on both cheeks. The familiarity was comforting. 'Sit down my dear. I fear your Mama is somewhat *hors de combat* after her journey.'

She looked him in the eyes for many seconds. 'Peter! How on earth did you do this? Never will I be able to thank you properly.' She sat down, then leaned over, took her father's hand in hers and held onto it.

'Well,' Peter signalled for the waitress who came scurrying across. 'Another cup, some more tea and some more of those delightful cakes, if you please.' He turned to Rosel. 'Your brother was enormously helpful. He broke into the asylum and stole your mother from under their noses, don't you know. Brave young man. Risky, I would say.'

'Is Boris all right?'

Peter paused a split second too long before he said heartily, 'Of course he is all right my dear. A resourceful man in adverse circumstances. And in your country I find there are many adverse circumstances. He has friends who… '

Her father squeezed his daughter's hand. 'You look well, *liebchen.*'

She gazed at him. 'I am well. I am well. I am painting again. Not very much, but more than for a long time.'

'Good, good.' His gaze wandered to his wife who was cutting the cake on her plate to ever-smaller pieces, her eyes vacant. 'Your dear mother has been through some bad times. But we will make her well, you and I, is this not true?'

'Yes, Papa. We'll make her well.' She was desperately thinking of her cramped quarters at the Settlement.

Peter read her mind. When the waitress came back with a laden tray he said. 'Is there an Hotel where one could stay in this unfortunate place?'

'Where *one* might stay?' The waitress looked at him. '*An* hotel?' (Rosel, now accustomed to the ironies of Bracks Hill talk, heard the sarcasm in the voice that went over the heads of the others.) 'An hotel? Well there's public houses that take people in, but ... Mebbe the Grosvenor?' (She said Gros-*ven*-or)' ... at the top of the town's your best bet. They do commercial travellers. I worked there once.'

'Gros*ven*or!' said Peter genially. 'That sounds very grand.'

The waitress replaced the empty cake plate with a full one. 'Oh no,' she said. 'You couldn't never call it grand. You can't miss it though. Up the length of the High Street, under the railway bridge past a row of big posh houses and it's on your left. If you get to the Co-op you've gone too far.'

'The Gros*ven*or will do for tonight, Rosel,' said Peter. 'Then you must decide what you all want to do.'

'I was thinking I might rent a little house here, for us all' said Rosel. 'Then I can continue my work and...'

'Here?' He raised his brows. 'Do you think so Rosel? Don't you think perhaps your work here is done?'

The scrape of Lilah's knife on her plate, as she decimated another cake, impaled the hum of talk in the café.

Herr von Stiegendorff was looking at his daughter with shining eyes. He spoke almost timidly. 'We need some special help for your Mama, *liebchen*. Doctors. A hospital for a while. I thought perhaps London?'

Peter coughed. 'I have a pair of small houses in Chelsea, my dear. One of them is empty at the moment. Quite small. But the second floor has a top light. It has been used more than once as a studio.'

She put both her hands over her face. 'I can't think about this now, Peter. My father and mother are just now here and … there is the play, the Prince...'

'So Todhunter tells me.' Peter poured out a cup of tea and handed it to her. 'Just relax, my dear girl. Relax, won't you? Nothing is insoluble. We will see. London seems the obvious choice, but we will see!'

Lilah von Siegendorff's knife clattered to the ground as she leaned across and grabbed her daughter's hand. 'You must help my son, Fraülein. He is in great danger. They will kill him.'

Rosel put her hand on her mother's. 'Boris?' she said.

Lilah shook her hand hard. 'They will kill him, Fraülein. Such a handsome boy and they will kill him. They think he is naughty. Do you know Fraülein? I saw them kill people in that place where I was? They killed the naughty ones.' A cunning light came into her eyes. 'Those were the days when you had to be very, very good. You had to be very good, on those days.'

52. Moving On

My Aunt Susanah, who turned up at the house ten minutes after Rosel left, is getting on like a house on fire with Cora. The first thing she did was explode with laughter at the sight of Cora in my Grandmother's clothes. 'I thought for a second it was your old grandma sitting there.'

My Aunt is concerned about how Cora got herself into this state. But soon they are talking in the safer areas of their mutual experience: the Settlement; Cora's acting and all the work Aunt Susanah's husband Jonty has been doing there. 'He's there now, seeing what he may do to help Mr Todhunter.'

'I should be there,' says Cora, pushing her shawl to one side.

'Don't let her do that,' I warn my aunt Susanah. 'She's had a shock. Nearly drowned this morning. In White Leas pool.' It's only as I say this that I recall a tale told me once by my Grandmother about Susanah's own mother drowning in those same waters. My Aunt sees the memory in my eyes and shakes her head slightly.

'Why don't you go off and do something, Gabriel?' she says. 'I'm sure Mr Todhunter can use a fit young man today. I'll stay here with Miss Miles. We'll talk. I'll make her tea. She'll be fine.'

Cora nods her head in agreement. 'And you'll tell Archie that I'll be there by the three o'clock cast call, Gabriel. Do that for me, will you?'

'I'll bring her at that time myself,' said my aunt. 'Don't trouble yourself Gabriel. I'll take care of Miss Miles like she was my sister.'

As I tie my muffler around my neck my eye falls the painting with the scraped out place by the pit pool, the place on the board that has always been wrong. Now I know what I must do. What it needs is a figure in the water, holding her arms out like a crucifix. Cora. My fingers itch for my brushes, my paints. I want to throw these irritating women out of my house and paint. I can't do this, so as I walk I start to paint tht part of the picture in my head.

I am nearly onto the High Street before I remember that I've left Cora Miles to get across to the Settlement with only my Grandmother's clothes for her back. Well. They're two resourceful women. They'll come up with something, I'm sure.

When I call in at The Lord Raglan the clientèle is in its best bib and tucker: white silk scarves rather than mufflers; here and there a bowler hat. The place buzzes with an air of unusual celebration, optimism. I suppose this is what the Prince's visits are about. To cheer people up a bit. To make them feel seen.

Marguerite is wearing a pale mauve, shiny frock I've never seen before. It has artificial violets at the shoulder. Her hair is pinned up on her head but there are tiny curls falling on her fine-boned cheeks.

I watch her for a while before she sees me. She talks to one man then to another, making them smile and stand straighter in their battered boots. In a way her presence here is like a Prince's visit every day. Into these poor lives a little light must fall.

She grins when she sees me and then brings me my tally pint. 'Now, then. How's my golden-haired genius?'

'Shut up, Marguerite.'

'Everything tickety boo at the Settlement? I've arranged with my boss to get off at four o'clock to come and join in the merriment.'

'There've been dramas already.'

'Dramas? I thought that was what would happen later.'

Her green eyes widen as I tell her the tale of my morning. 'Well! It's a relief that Cora's all right. D'you think she meant to...'

I shrug my shoulders. 'I don't know. Rosel says...'

'Rosel!' Her eyes narrow. 'I think that teacher has a soft spot for you, Gabe.'

'Come on, Marguerite. She's...' I was going to say that Rosel was just my teacher but she interrupted me.

'Yeah, I know. Old enough to be your mother I suppose. But you wouldn't believe how many times I've been proposed evil things by men old enough to be my father.... Yes! Yes!' She's called across to the other end of the bar and I stand there a while, watching talking and laughing with her customers.

As I sip my way down to the bottom of the glass I consider the miracle of Marguerite. I'd thought that loving somebody is wanting them to belong to you alone. I do know this is not on the cards with me and Marguerite. But still what I feel for her is something like love.

I come out of the Raglan to a the sharp cut of the November wind and a driving drizzle. I push my hands deep into my jacket pockets, dip my nose into my muffler and head off for the Settlement at a run. I turn the corner into Cheapside and get tangled up with a tall man in a fur-collared coat who smells of cologne. He holds me away from him smiling slightly with his large teeth. Now I'm in the middle of a crowd of well-dressed strangers. One of them addresses me. 'Gabriel! You are in a great hurry!' says Rosel Vann.

I pull myself away from the man.

'Peter,' says Rosel. 'This is the young man I told you about. The one whose painting you wished to buy.' The man called Peter shakes me heartily by the hand and Rosel introduces me to her father and her mother, whose hand drops listlessly from mine. I am all bones and elbows in this company, in a rage with Rosel that I can't explain.

'Dreadful weather, what?' says the tall man.

'We're just taking my parents to an hotel,' says Rosel. 'They have just arrived.

Now I notice the Daimler that's purring on the road beside the pavement. At the wheel is a lad no older than I am. He winks at me and I watch as the man called Peter ushers the two old people into the car. Then he turns to me and shakes me again by the hand. 'Good to meet Fraülein von Stiegendorff's protégé. You have great talent, young man.' And he vanishes into the car's plush interior. He sits in the seat by the driver.

I turn to Rosel. 'Well then, the posh fellow got your father out of Germany for you!' I say. Stating the obvious seems the safest thing.

She puts both her hands in mine. 'And my mother,' she says. 'They got her out of an asylum. Can you believe that? The government have plans to kill people in the asylums.' She shudders. 'Can you believe that?'

'And your brother?'

She frowns. 'He is still there. My mother babbles that they will kill him too.'

'But at least she's here. And your father. ' I forget about my wet jacket and hold her close. A woman walking by clicks her tongue. 'That's something.'

'Yes. Yes. Of course it is. But my brother. Perhaps I must also do something about my brother.' She pulls away and her hands loosen from mine. 'You must be going to the Settlement?'

I nod.

'Will you tell Archie that I will be there for the cast call at three? And could he mark chairs for Sir Peter and my parents as they will attend for the performance?'

'Right.' I clunk the door shut after her and watch the car as it purrs away along Cheapside onto the High Street. One thing's sure. That car carries Rosel Vonn back to her world and her life: a life that's nothing to do with Brack's Hill.

The rain is thinning and the white light behind the clouds hints at the sun. I set off for the Settlement, arms swinging and heels down, as though I really am young Arthur setting off for war in 1915.

52. Curtain Up

Dev Pallister, designated one of three council marshals, had a busy time after leaving the house, and his excited Pauline, that morning.

He and his two colleagues had walked the length of the town on the Prince's route. All was in order. Of course, there were depressing sights here and there but that, after all, was what His Royal Highness was here to see.

They talked to the men in the Pathe News van and the BBC motor car. They were parked outside the Club, ready for the first sighting. They all agreed it was a pity about this cold drizzle. The poor newsmen had had quite a wetting. But the sun was coming out now and they agreed that things looked better for the afternoon.

They went to the police station to talk to the inspector and checked out the allotments. The allotment men were already there, clustered into the new 'goods-exchange' hut, smoking like fury.

They called on Archie Todhunter at the Settlement. He was marching around looking a bit white about the gills, smoking like fury. Even so, everything looked remarkably well organised. The display was particularly good. Dev lingered with some pride before Gabriel Marchant's fine portrait of his daughter and stopped again at the sight of the lad himself portrayed in Dev's own uniform, decked out with his medals.

Then they went to Archie's little office and Archie poure a glass of single malt so they could all toast the Prince. Archie showed them the leather-bound edition of the play, which young Greta would present to the Prince.

He talked about the timing of the performance. 'Of course we're expecting to put on the play for His Royal Highness. We need to get our message to him. And to the gathered dignitaries. We'll start at approximately four thirty. I imagine he'll be just about at the end of his tour by then?'

Dev shook his head. 'I think I said to you that it couldn't be on the schedule, Mr Todhunter. It is impossible. The Prince will be moving through. Moving through and moving on.'

'He's a busy man,' put in the other councillor. 'He is a very busy man.'

'Well, in that case' said Archie flatly. 'I can't for the life of me think why we've been doing all this work all these months.'

'He'll see the exhibition, the paintings. He'll get a copy of your play,' said Dev.

'It's not the same, Mr Pallister. The living play, that's the best of what happens here. The people at their finest.' Archie was grim. 'He'll be seeing them at their most desolate, won't he? Is that the way to send him away? He needs also to see these good people at their best. There's balance in this.'

There was no way to counter Archie's optimism. The trio drank off the last of their whisky and began to move out of the room. Dev Pallister turned impulsively and shook Archie by the hand. 'By rights His Royal Highness *should* see you play, Mr Todhunter. I see that. But I can't think that he will. I'm sorry. I really am.'

By three o'clock there was a full turnout in the Church Hall for the last cast call. Even Baffer Bray got the time right. Cora came hobbling in on Susanah Clelland's arm at three minutes to three. Archie blinked when he saw her, dressed in old woman's clothing. 'Changed your costume for Maggie Olliphant, Cora? I thought you already had that backstage…'

Cora hugged the shawl around her. 'I found these. Much more suitable. It'll freshen up the part. But I just need to find poor Maggie's boots.' They looked down at her dirty bare feet.

'What have you been up to, Cora? On today of all days! Walking through the town with no shoes on.'

She had Archie's full attention at last. 'I was at Gabriel Marchant's house with his auntie here, gathering my wits.' She nodded at Susanah 'She very kindly ran to the corner to get Mr Soulsby's taxi. So I didn't walk barefoot all the way.'

Archie shook his head. 'You're making my mind spin, Cora. I will not ask you to explain further.' He turned away. 'At least you're back and I thank heavens for that.'

She put a hand on his arm. 'I'm back for this show, Archie. That's all. Not back to The Settlement. Not to you. Afterwards I am going to Priorton to stay with Mrs Clelland. Seems she has a spare room. Then, who knows? Somewhere.'

Archie frowned at her, and then shook her hand off his arm. 'We'll talk about it later Cora. Later.' Then he strode off, making for Rosel Vonn, who had just come through the doors.

Susanah Clelland touched her shoulder. 'Don't worry, Cora. He has things on his mind, poor chap. Are you really sure you will want to do this? To come back with me?'

Cora sniffed. 'Course I do. I don't know what it is about the cold water that I nearly drowned myself in, Mrs Clelland, but it doesn't half give you a clear head.'

Of course Archie Todhunter gets to Rosel before I do, so I hang around while they talk, impervious to the old boy's sour looks. Rosel's hair is shining and she's wearing a smart black dress I've never seen before. At the neck, just near the collarbone she's wearing the Roman brooch we found near the river. I want to say something about it to her but Archie is between us.

He's close to her, speaks in her ear. 'I need a favour from you, Rosel. Perhaps your friend Sir Peter could help?'

'What is it, Archie?' She's flushed from running I think, but she looks so bright, so full of life. I want to touch her. But something is happening to her, taking her right away from me. I can tell.

'Anything, Archie,' she says.

'I wonder. Is your friend on terms with him? His Royal Highness? Does he know him?'

'I do not know this. Perhaps.' She sounds more foreign than ever she has before, somehow. She'll have been talking to her mother and father in their own language. 'Some things he says …'

'What about you?'

'I do not know the Prince.' She hesitates, frowning. 'I think my father, he has known the Prince. Once a very, very long time ago. Before the War.'

'Right!' Archie beams. 'Perhaps he will talk with him? You will talk with him. In German. Anything to take his attention away from the fact that this is just another routine Royal visit.'

She shrugs. 'Why? What will this do?'

He draws nearer to her. 'Rosel. I want you to persuade him to stay to watch the play. Do anything. Dev and the councillors say no, it's impossible. Out of the question! But it will be his final thing here at Brack's Hill. He *must* see the play. Why else have these people - young Gabriel here, and his friend Tegger; Cora and Greta - worked so hard? Have they worked so hard for so long to have their endeavour valued no more than a bit of quilting or a cobbled shoe?'

'Mr Todhunter!' A voice calls him from across the room and Rosel and I almost fall into each other's arms in laughter.

'Poor Archie!' says Rosel.

'I've never seen a man so frustrated,' I say.

'Or so very determined,' she says. 'This is his great quality.'

'So what will you do?' I say. 'If the councillors say it's impossible it must be impossible.'

She frowns. 'Archie's right you know. He's determined, how do you say it? Pig-headed. But he is right. What better way of showing the truth about the people in Brack's Hill than the play?'

'So…?'

'So I will do it. Or try. See if my father will recall… see what Sir Peter can do. Perhaps, perhaps…'

'Gabe!' Tegger is bellowing from the other end of the hall. 'Come and get thee clothes on or thee'll never fight a war.'

So I have to leave Rosel, with so much unsaid.

Tegger has taken on the role of chief harasser and director and is bustling everybody into their togs backstage, checking the set, checking the prompter's copy, checking that the pianist has her music.

Tegger for one certainly thinks the prince will see the play.

I'm busy pulling on Dev Pallister's army boots when Tegger comes to sit beside me. 'Still on with Marguerite, marra?'

'Is anybody ever *on* with Marguerite?' I say.

'You gotta point there. You realised finally, did you?'

I bend down to tie the long bootlaces: round the back then back round the front to tie in a double bow. 'What about us, Tegger. Am I off your friend's list, then?'

He knocks me on the shoulder and I only just save myself from falling off the stool. 'Dinna be daft man. Like I say, it'd take more than any woman...'

Greta comes bowling across the room, looking the complete pit-lass in her canvas apron and clogs. 'Hey, you two! You're to come across to the Settlement. The Prince is nearly there and you've gotta be beside the portraits, to talk to him.'

'Who says?'

'Archie.'

Greta takes me by the hand and leads me along the streets and through the house door into the long front room of the Settlement. There's this flurry of activity at the other end of the room as His Royal Highness comes in and makes his way down the room. He has a very highly decorated soldier by his side and a man behind him whose long tweed coat and round tweed hat match his own.   He flashes his smile everywhere, paying close attention to the quilters and the cobblers. He looks people directly in the eye and listens attentively to Archie who is murmuring in his ear.

I can hear his clear, slightly high voice. 'The paintings are done by people here, you say? Amazing!'

He reaches Greta, who curtseys deeply to him. He is quite a short man. Just about reaches my shoulder. 'A fine portrait of you, my dear,' he says to Greta.

'It's not *me*, sir,' her grammar school voice flutes on the air in contrast with her ragamuffin appearance. 'It is me in the role of Dorothy, who's an historical character from 1915 and is important in the play.'

'A jolly good likeness even so.'

She points to me. 'Gabriel here painted it.'

He moves to me, and, not being able to curtsey, I duck my head forward as I've seen the other men so.

'This is Gabriel Marchant, sir,' says Greta, not fazed at all by the prince. 'He has painted three of these portraits and, as you see is the subject of this triptych in his role of Arthur in the play. That was painted by Fraŭlein Vonn who is the painting teacher. In the play Arthur's both a soldier and a miner, as many Durham men were. As you will know, sir, having been on the war yourself.' Greta's doing Archie proud.

The Prince casts an eye back at Archie Todhunter. 'And the German teacher painted this young man in this magnificent uniform?'

Greta leans sideways to keep his gaze on her. 'That's my father's uniform sir,' she says. 'From the Great War.'

One elegant brow is raised. He glances back to the man in the long tweed coat behind him. 'Curiouser and curiouser, Robbie!' he says. Like in some private joke. I decide his face is far too brown for real life. And his cheeks are pink. Rouge. For God's sake, he must be wearing make up! For the Pathe News very likely.

Archie leads him on. 'And this is Fraülein Rosel von Stiegendorff, our art tutor,' he says. 'Fraulein von Stiegendorff has exhibited her work in London, alongside that of Vanessa Bell and Duncan Grant. She has consulted Mr Henry Moore, the sculptor. We're lucky and very proud to have her here in Brack's Hill.'

Now Rosel, elegant in her black dress is curtseying deeply to the prince. And then the two of them speak together in rapid German and I've no idea at all what they are talking about. Now she has made him laugh and he shakes her hand again.

He turns back to speak to the man behind him again. 'Amazing coincidence Robbie. Fraülein von Stiegendorff is the daughter of a chap I learned to ski with. Before the Great War.' He turns back to say something to Rosel.

'Sir! In English!' his companion says urgently. He looks very uncomfortable. 'We must move on.'

The prince turns back with a flourish and kisses Rosel on the hand. 'And your father, Fraülein?' he says. 'How is he?'

'We have just got him away from Germany. He was in difficulties there, sir. He will be present in the hall where they will perform the play for you.'

The prince frowns. 'This play. No one mentioned a play, did they Robbie?'

The soldier beside him is muttering under his breath.

Archie coughs. 'We have been rehearsing it for months, sir. It's about the War. I understand you were a serving officer, sir.'

'So I was, Mr Todhunter. So I was!' The prince turns to his companion, shutting everyone out of his eye-line. 'Where do we go next, Robbie?'

'The train, sir. Back…'

'Well then, the train can wait for us. Perhaps we should see something of this …er…play. It would do us all good to see this play. Don't you think so, Fraülein?'

She smiles and nods vigorously.

The soldier standing beside the prince splutters. 'Sir, you can't…' but the Prince cuts him short, repeating, 'Don't you think so, Fraulein?'

Rosel nods so vigorously that her head is nearly drops off. Archie Todhunter whispers in my ear. 'You get straight back across there, Gabriel. Tell Tegger to get everyone in their places.'

Across the road, Tegger sets everyone in their starting place and reminds Maggie, as if she needed it, that hers is the first speech. 'But where's Archie?' she says. 'He has to get over here yet.'

Archie comes in on cue, fastening his braces and buttoning his coat up for his role of the pit manager. 'Listen everyone,' his voice barks out. 'She did it! The Fraülein did it! She has persuaded the Prince to watch the play.'

Everyone cheers him to the roof and Tegger has a bit of a job to settle us down again. Everyone in their places. Defying

Tegger's cross looks I climb out of my trench and peep through the side of the curtains. There are five empty rows at the front. In the sixth are Rosel's posh friend and her parents. Behind them the rows are filled by town dignitaries with chains, soldiers in uniform, men in caps, women in their best hats. The senior councillors are there with their wives. I can see Dev Pallister and his wife. Mr Conroy the joiner and his wife. Teachers from the grammar school. Jonty Clelland and my Aunt Susanah are sitting half way back. Squashed on the seat beside my Aunt is the reporter fellow, Herbert Grossmith: the one with leather patches on his elbows. The doctors and the clergymen take a row to themselves. Marguerite, wearing a purple hat with a veil, sits beside a man. I focus more closely on him and realise it's Mr Tenant, the man from the gallery. They look very cosy.

So. All these people are here for a sight of the dashing Prince. This might be second in their head but the most important thing they're really here to do is to see the first performance of Archie Todhunter's – and Tegger's - play.

A kind of humming quiet settles on the hall as the Prince, (with Rosel on his left and his fretful friend 'Robbie' on his right), comes through the double doors, followed by a gaggle of people who are part of the tour party. Behind them the much-decorated soldier who's obviously in charge, then the insignificant figure of Lord Chase and two senior policemen all stay by the door. They look very glum. Perhaps they thought they would be getting away soon to some fine dinner. But here they were, having to watch some pitman's poxy play.

Rosel takes the Prince and introduces him to her friend Peter and the old man who is her father. There is all this standing and bowing and shaking of hands. Then the prince leads them all to sit with him in the centre of the front row. Now the whole following group of people, whether they want to or not, have to sit on the rows behind them. Uniformed policemen stand at the end of the front row where the Prince sits. Is this to protect him from us? What do they think we'll do to him?

I return to my starting position and find my hand grasped very tightly in Greta Pallister's slender fingers. 'Good luck to us all, Gabriel!' she whispers.

Archie stands behind the centre curtain perfectly still for a second, then he puts his shoulders back and steps through them.

The room melts into total silence. His voice, slightly muffled by the curtain comes back to us. 'Your Royal Highness, my Lord, ladies and gentlemen. In these hard days our suffering is greater because we feel the cruel wheel of our lives grinds away unseen by anyone. Yet the presence of his Royal Highness here in Brack's Hill reassures us that our sufferings are visible. But I ask you, Ladies and Gentlemen, is it just about suffering? Here in Brack's Hill, especially at the Settlement, we have people of spirit and courage, culture and dignity. It is by their endeavour in the arts and in the crafts that they express their relationship with, and significance, in the whole of our society.'

Archie's voice rolls on. Tegger's harsh whisper spits from the wings. Get on with it will yer?

'The play we have written, called *Blood and Coal*, shows that it has always been so. It is our privilege today that you, sir, and the wider community will witness for the people of Brack's Hill.'

He steps back. Closes the curtain tight, and takes his position. The pianist plays her few mournful chords and as the curtains open Cora swallows a small smile, becomes Maggie Olliphant, and begins her first, powerful speech in *Blood and Coal*.

54. Forward to November 1963: Only Connect

In the high space of the chapel I stumble through my eulogy for Archie Todhunter, conscious that my oratory is not a patch on that of the Presbyterian clergyman, a plainly dressed man with whom Archie had hooked up in his own retirement years in this southern seaside town.

The clergyman talked of the heritage of Scottish Mission into which Archie had been born. How Archie had suspended his faith and sublimated it in the fine lay missionary work in the Dark Areas of Britain during the Depression. And how, after the war, his work was gradually superseded by the changed society for which he had fought. And then how, after all his labours, he had rediscovered his faith and found rest here by the Atlantic Ocean.

Rediscovered his faith? This made Archie sound really pious, so I was pleased that I could begin to talk about his inspired atheism in Brack's Hill. Otherwise the people who packed this tall seaside chapel might have gone off with quite the wrong idea about Archie Todhunter and alongside him we anonymous creatures from the Dark Areas of Britain. Perhaps Archie knew this when he wrote in his last will and testament that if anyone were to speak for him, it would be me.

As I say my piece about knowing and working with Archie in those years I relish the nods and ripples of recognition that sweep the packed benches.

As I speak I scan the long aisles of the chapel for familiar faces. First and foremost, in the front row, wearing her Kaftan and her sheepskin coat, her fashionably swept-back glasses slipping, as always, down her nose. She still has those brilliant dark eyes. And she's still called Greta Pallister of course. She never took my name, although we have been well and truly married for many years now.

And I can see Tegger at the back of the chapel. He's bulkier than ever with his grey-white beard. Thank goodness he made it here. We timed the funeral for four o'clock so that he could make his journey down from the North.

Tegger's the only one of us who has kept the faith and stayed up there in Brack's Hill. We talk regularly on the phone and the sound of his voice takes my back to that Brack's Hill seam. Of course he no longer lives in a van but has a tall house near the Grosvenor Hotel where he lives with his third wife and two elderly greyhounds, once good runners.

He's doing all right, is Tegger. His first broadcast play went out just after the war: a wireless version of *Blood and Coal*, with him named as writer. Archie had insisted on this. They performed it with Yorkshire voices, not Durham. But still it worked very well. This year Tegger's has had three plays on the BBC and his recently published collection of short stories has been praised to the heights in what is called the quality press. Shades of our younger selves live on in these stories and I have tears in my eyes as I read and re-read them.

Archie should really have told Tegger to do this eulogy. He is truly the one for words. He wrote a fine extended obituary for the Guardian: an appreciation of Archie's life-work, far better than this Presbyterian's milk and vinegar tribute. It was Tegger who telephoned me to tell me that Archie had asked me to speak the eulogy. 'He said it was time you used words as well as images to say your piece.' Tegger said. 'Always the silent witness, Gabe. Archie says to me, "Such a silent boy, he was. Get him to say something, for God's sake." '

I had a twinge of guilt then. In the busy years between Archie had rather faded from my mind. In the end had I left Brack's Hill altogether. First there was Art College, courtesy of a mysterious scholarship that I later discovered was from Rosel Vonn's friend Sir Peter, who liked and had bought my paintings. After that, of course, there was the war where I survived the frightening rigours of the North African campaign by drawing in my tent at night. For me the vast blackness of the desert sky was a kind of cosmic Goaf. After that I experiences paler skies of Italy. This is how, like the father of Rosel Vonn, I now have my own volume of images of war.

When I came back I was submerged in the bouncing tide of exhibitions and work and a modest degree of acclaim, ending up with a cosy post as head of Department in a Lancashire College. And with all this I kind of lost touch with Archie when he retired after the war. But I know that Tegger has kept in touch with him in these last years. As I said Tegger has kept the faith.

As Greta suggested this morning I did finish today's eulogy with reference to the cruel assassination of President Kennedy and some words about people who have an impact on the lives of others. Greta smiles her great smile and nods at me. Then, with Archie in his coffin, centre-stage, she stands up, turns round towards the congregation, and reads Maggie Olliphant's fine speech from *Coal and Blood*. Today we keep the faith with Brack's Hill and with our own personal magician, Archie Todhunter.

When she ends there is a short pause, then a patter of applause emanates from Tegger at the back that crackles through the chapel. Suddenly everyone is clapping and smiling. They nod at each other. Some of them even shake hands. Strange at a funeral you might think. The plain Presbyterian looks bewildered.

The funeral over, we make our way to the hall beside the church for an alcohol-free wake. I smile at the thought of Archie's ever present single malt in his Settlement office. In the hall are tables and chairs and a long buffet with the now familiar *vol-au-vents* and *quiches*. The room has been painted bright yellow and hanging on the walls are art works: some representational, some earnest pastiches of Mattisse and Braque. There are even some collages, very fashionable now. Those of us from the Settlement recognise Archie's hand everywhere.

Standing behind the crowd, holding a cup of tea I watch Tegger and Greta working the room like professionals. A voice punctures my silence. 'She is such a person now, our little Greta! Is that not so? Remarkable, all those books and articles of hers. She is a very fine academic.'

The accent is much thicker than before but the voice is recogniseable. I turn around and we almost bump faces. 'Rosel!' The body I hold to me is slender to the point of brittleness; the cheek I kiss is still very soft but lined now. Her putty coloured hair is white, and swept into a pile on top of her head. She is wearing a dark green jacket with frogged fastening. I smiled as I recognised the small round brooch in blackened metal that she wore on her collar.

'Rosel! Rosel! I say her name over and over again like some daft lad. She pulls back to stare up at me. 'It was a very fine eulogy, Gabriel. But Archie was a very fine man. He touched so many lives.' She pauses. 'So how are you, Gabriel?'

The morning after the performance of the play Rosel called on me at my house. She heaped praise on my White Leas Pool painting, now graced by a vestigial cruciform figure of Cora by the water. Later we walked out of town and along by the same pit pool. She told me how important to her had been the time she had spent in Brack's Hill. But now she had to take her parents to London and help them to settle there. 'Peter says he will keep an eye on them.

Then I must go to Germany to seek out my brother Boris. He is at even greater risk than my father. I am sure of this.'

'Sir Peter Whatsit,' I said. 'Is he ... are you ...?' I couldn't bring myself to say the words.

She shrugged in her infinitely foreign fashion. 'As I say I must go now to help Boris. My father understands this. Peter understands this.'

After that, before and during the war I wrote to Rosel, via Peter Watsit. No reply. So I gave up, thinking she must have married him. It was Tegger – back working in the mines as a Bevin boy - who wrote to me in Italy during the last stages of the war and told me otherwise. Rosel had returned to Germany and got mixed up with her brother and some of his friends. Then, in 1943 Boris was involved in the plot to assassinate Hitler and was executed on the direct order of Hitler: the hardest way, with violin wire/

Rosel stayed on to carry on his resistance work. She featured in post war articles about the plot and was said to be living in West Berlin. It seemed that she had stopped painting. She was helping displaced persons, the distressed flotsam and jetsam of the post war years. I suppose I could have contacted her then. But I didn't.

'Yes,' she says now. 'These days I live in Berlin. In my father's old apartment. Is that not strange?'

'So, you must have been in Berlin during the Blockade?'

'Yes,' she shivered. 'The Russians are now our great enemy. That was not good, the Blockade.'

'Rosel!' At last I put my arms around her and hold her close. Then I stand clear, take her arm and lead her to a table. 'Come on. Sit here. I'll grab you a cup of tea.' I need to get away from her for a minute to put the past in its place.

I stand in the long queue and watch as Greta and Tegger join Rosel at the table. Then a dark-haired girl sits beside them, followed by an old woman with pinkish hair.

As soon as I get back to the table the hum of the room is silenced and lights flicker onto a temporary screen at the back of the room. And now there in front of us, flickering on the screen in black and white, is the road outside the Settlement in 1935. Crowds of people are held back by three policemen. Everyone is wearing caps and hats. And there in the middle of a flurry of obvious gentlemen is the neat figure of the Prince of Wales, as glamorous as any film star. Beside him in a ludicrous soft cap is the man who was so worried about the Prince speaking German with Rosel. The sound track is quacking and neighing away but I can't hear the words.

And now *we* are standing there, shockingly young and smooth faced. The Prince is shaking us by the hand, looking us in the eye. I remember seeing newsreel of Adolf Hitler doing this same thing with his young Scouts. Then I remember the rouge on the Prince's cheek.

Now here at last is Archie talking to camera about his ideals, about the Settlement and the work he is trying to do there: he speaks on the crackling sound track about dignity, honesty and social justice. And here now is the magnificent Cora, as Maggie Olliphant, delivering her great speech, very comfortable before the whirring cameras.

Cora continued to be comfortable before cameras. She never stopped working after that day. Corinthian Small, her new agent, got her into films, radio, even into the new television dramas. She's performed in two of Tegger's plays on radio. How far this has been from standing like a crucifix 'up to your arse in water'! That painting of her by the White Leas pool last changed hands for twenty five thousand pounds. We borrowed it back for my Retrospective in 1960. Sir Peter Whatsit came to that exhibition. That's where he let slip about my scholarship.

Now the lights go up and the hall is filled with a gale of sustained applause. The old woman at our table stands up and bows, acknowledging the applause, a mischievous grin on her face. I laugh out loud, 'Cora!' I lean towards her and she gives me a very theatrical kiss on both cheeks, her white-pink hair rising and falling in the air. 'You said the right things in there about dear old Archie, Gabriel,' she tells me. Her voice still rounded and deep-timbred.

'I meant every one of those words, Cora.'

She nods. 'That part where you said he was a driven, ambiguous person, that was true, too,'

Now Tegger is prodding me in the back. 'Aren't you gonna say hello to Pearl, marra?' he says, nodding to the girl beside him. She's in her mid-twenties perhaps. Her hair is short and sharply cut in an asymmetrical style. I stare at her and then realise who she is. 'Marguerite!' I say, looking around the room.

'My mother,' she says, grinning.

'Where is she?' I am still looking around.

'She's on the West Coast of America living with my second step-father. She wrote me about the death of Archie Todhunter and told me to get on touch with Mr Tegger MacNamara, which I did and here I am.' Her American drawl adds to this girl's glamour. 'She says to tell you she'd had a very good war and that even so she still belongs to herself.'

'Pearl's a singer,' said Tegger. 'In cabaret over here.'

'Your mother was a great free spirit.' I say. 'I liked her very much.'

'Free spirit! Don't I know that?' she says with feeling. She pauses. 'She got me to go to your retrospective in 1960. I saw your painting of her as *The Woman in the Goaf*. It was so spooky to see her there like that.'

I smile. In silence I think about how I have turned down very high offers for that painting. I will never part with it.

Greta, clever as ever, fills the gap. 'That painting is still on our wall,' she says and puts her hand on mine. 'We would never part with it.' She smiles at Pearl, 'Our own children are in America just now. They're both studying International Law in Boston. Our young Archie has just finished a stint with Kennedy's Peace Corps in South America. He adored Jack Kennedy.' She frowns. 'Like many of us he's floored by yesterday's news about the President.'

My hand tightens on hers. Last night when I was mulling over Archie's eulogy she finally allowed me read her diaries of those years. A last piece of the jigsaw fell into place for me.

It wasn't all straightforward. I didn't pin Greta down until I came back after the war when she was nearly twenty six. But I see now it was always meant to be. Me with Rosel, then me with Marguerite, then me for all time with Greta Pallister. As Greta would say: *only connect.*

'Well!' The chair creaked asTegger leaned back in it and looked around him with satisfaction. 'Just look at this constellation of talent! If Archie were here he'd be bullying us to put on a ply about *The Berlin Blockade* or *The Death of a President.* 'What d'ya think, marra?'

I put an arm around his shoulders. 'What I think is I became a painter is because of Archie Todhunter and because of all the people sitting around here this table. That's what I think, marra.'

Ends

The Players

Gabriel Marchant (19) (Ex-miner. Aspiring painter, He plays 'Arthur' in the play)

Rosel von Siegendorff (38) (Called Rosel Vonn by the people of Brack's Hill.) An accomplished artist and sculptor.

Greta Pallister (16) Brilliant schoolgirl. She plays 'Dorothy' in the play - Daughter of Dev Pallister)

Marguerite Molloy (26) A barmaid. Always a free spirit. - Daughter of the late Janey Molloy of Bracks Hill and the late John Carbonius of Mauritius.

Tegger MacNamara (19) Gabriel's best friend. Ex-miner and joiner. Writer and poet.

Archie Todhunter (Aged 48) Director of The Settlement. Ex-medical student, actor, producer and idealist.

Cora Miles (aged 45) Plays 'Maggie Olliphant' in the play. Actress and teacher. Very close to Archie Todhunter.

Dev Pallister (aged 43) Local politician. Union man. Father of Greta, husband of Pauline

Susanah and Jonty Clelland: Gabriel's aunt and uncle who also appear in *the novels Riches of the Earth* and *Dark Light Shining)*

Lilah, Max, Berti & Boris von Siegendorff: Rosel's mother father, uncle and brother

Also Nathan Smith, Jake McVay, Mr. Conroy (Joiner) Sir Peter Hamilton Souness, Brownson (his servant) etc. etc.

About The Author

Wendy Robertson has published more than twenty best selling novels, two short story collections and she continues to write occasional articles on issues close to her heart. For two years she had her own community radio programme called The Writing Game.

She lives in historic South Durham, in a Victorian house that has played a role in more than one of her novels. She spends her time writing, painting and working with other writers,

'My novels are mostly set in some crosspiece of time and place. The unique, sometimes quirky lives of my characters reflect the wide range of people I've come to know very well in my life.'

She writes about her life and her books at:

www.lifetwicetasted.blogspot.com.uk

Also By Wendy Robertson ....

Journey to Moscow: The Adventures of Olivia Ozanne

Reader Review 'Olivia Ozanne is the writer abroad, the stranger alone, a woman who can see the surface of things and beyond. Well rid of her ex Kendrick and his leather sofa fetish, she comes to stay with her daughter Caitlin.

This is post-glasnost Moscow with its fallen statues, burgeoning mafia, newly restored churches, its phones tapped but no longer listened in to, a city that demands hard currency. Through Olivia's eyes we see into the heart of this city and its people. We peer inside their tiny flats into their constricted interior lives, where we meet the mysterious Aunties whose surprising histories, stretching back to the revolution, are slowly uncovered by Olivia.

This is a richly painted canvas of an iconic city, in many ways relevant to our understanding of the Russia of today. It is a story about a woman in search of a new self and it's hard not to fall in love with Olivia with her enormous appetite for life or for that matter her lover Volodya who she meets at the flower stall.

Gorgeous."

The Romancer: A Practical Guide to Writing Fiction

'Dreamers, optimists, visionaries, enthusiasts, escapists.' Wendy Robertson declares that all writers are 'Romancers
'

'This book) *gives a rare glimpse of what it's like to be inside the process of writing - the exact moment when the events of a writer's life become the fabric of fiction.*' Kathleen Jones

'*A moving and compelling exploration of the links between a writer's life and her work. The Romancer should appeal to readers and writers alike.*' 'Pat Barker

'*More than just a memoir, this is a master class on the writing process.*' Sharon Griffiths..............................

This book explores the way memory and dreaming - alongside conscious and unconscious memory - have flourished at the roots of Wendy Robertson's fiction. In these pages aspiring and experienced writers will find writing processes and practical approaches – including Wendy's *Forty Day Plan* for writing a novel – to re-imagine their own lives, inspire their fiction and develop their writing to the point of success.

Paulie's Web

Inspired by Wendy Robertson's experience in prison, *Paulie's Web* distils the tragedies, comedies and ironies of women's lives not just behind bars but out in society. The charismatic Paulie Smith - rebel, ex-teacher and emerging writer - comes out of prison after serving six years. . In the next few days she relished her freedom but struggles to readjust to the scary realities of life 'on the out'.

Important for her readjustment are Paulie's reflections on her life in prison. Her mind goes back to her first few weeks inside when she lived alongside the four very different women whom she first met in the white van on their way to their first prison.

Paulie's thoughts move from Queenie, the old bag- lady who sees giants and angels, to Maritza who has disguised her pain with an ultra-conventional life, to Lilah, the spoiled apple of her mother's eye, to the tragedy of Christine - the one with the real scars out and inside.

And then there is Paulie herself, serving the longest sentence despite having done no more wrong than being her own woman.

The unique stories of these women, past and present, mingle as Paulie - free now after six years - goes looking for Queenie, Maritza, Lilah and Christine, who have now been 'on the out' for some years and are - Paulie hopes - remaking their lives.

Cruelty Games

Rachel, an idealistic young teacher, tries to make changes in the lives of her tough pupils. The school - tough as it is - is a haven for Rachel's pupil Ian Sobell, whose mother neglects him and whose grandmother abuses him.

One of Rachel's adventurous projects leads her class to a place where, hundreds of years before, a boy hung for days in a gibbet until he died in agony: a punishment for the murder of his employer's children.

Events on this day have a disastrous impact on the lives of both Rachel and Ian: a shock which lasts nearly two decades before they both move on to some kind of resolution, triggered by Rachel meeting Ian again after sixteen years.

This novel was inspired by my experience teaching in schools where I worked with pupils like Ian who soldiered on under great difficulty, walking the line between violence and normalcy every day. I also know that their desperation and stress is often mirrored in the plight of good, sensitive teachers who have to deal with the ambiguity of children who may be seen as evil.

Gabriel Marchant

Forms of Flight:
Twenty Seven Short Stories

A young burglar shatters a glass roof and drops in on a vicars wife; a man who loves tin soldiers has a near miss with a knife killer; a woman plans to take flight in a Dormobile; an old woman on the streets sees visions of giants; a woman breaks free from a long and confining marriage; boy learns his craft deep in the bowels of the earth.

Wendy Robertson: 'I admire the short story form. It sits neatly between the novel and the poem. It combines the broad narrative significance of the novel with the precision, economy and illumination of the poem. The novel, the poem and the short story demand of the writer the precise and focused use of language and insight into the processing of unique human experience. The novella – fashionable nowadays - shares a mixture of all these qualities

Gabriel Marchant

Gabriel Marchant